581

ALSO BY *James M. Cain*

THE BUTTERFLY

PAST ALL DISHONOR

THREE OF A KIND
Career in C Major
The Embezzler
Double Indemnity

LOVE'S LOVELY COUNTERFEIT

MILDRED PIERCE

SERENADE

THE POSTMAN ALWAYS RINGS
TWICE

THESE ARE *Borzoi Books* PUBLISHED IN NEW YORK BY
Alfred A. Knopf

THE MOTH

❉   ❉

The
M O T H

❉

B Y

James M. Cain

ALFRED A. KNOPF: NEW YORK

1 9 4 8

THIS IS A BORZOI BOOK,
PUBLISHED BY ALFRED A. KNOPF, INC.

FIRST EDITION

THE MOTH

✳ *THE MOTH* ✳

✳ 1 ✳

THE first thing I remember was a big luna moth. I saw it in Druid Hill Park, which is up the street from our house, in Baltimore, on Mt. Royal Terrace. On cloudy days it's a little dark out there, and things like fireflies and bats and swallows get their signals crossed up and come out. Well, one day when the sky was about the color of a wet slate shingle, I was over there with Jane, my colored nurse, and this thing began flying around. I followed it quite a while, to a wall and a hedge and a bush, and then I ran off to find Jane so she could see it too. When I got back, there was a boy, I guess ten or twelve years old, but to me then bigger than any Yale guard was, later. He had a stick, and he was whacking at the moth to kill it. Never in my whole life, in a dream or on a battlefield or anywhere, have I felt such horror as I did then. I screamed my head off. When Jane got there she told the boy to stop, but he kept right on whacking. She jerked the stick out of his hands. He kicked at her, and she let him have it on the shins. Then he spit, but I didn't pay any attention. All I saw

3

was that beautiful green thing, all filled with light, fluttering off through the trees, alive and free. It was a feeling I imagine other people have when they think about God in church. It makes no sense, does it, to say that a few times in my life, when something was happening inside of me, I could tell what it meant by the pale, blue-green, all-filled-with-light color the feeling had?

There's no law it has to.

The next thing I remember was a Bartlett pear. It was given me by my aunts the first week of school, to take to my teacher, Miss Jonas. A tree was in the backyard, and they got the idea Miss Jonas should have a pear, so my Aunt Sheila went out and picked a big yellow one with a pink cheek on it, and sent me off with it. The school was three blocks away. The second block I smelled the pear. The third block I ate it. When I got to the school I didn't have it, and began to worry. It was the day we were given cards with our names on them, and I found out I was John, not Jack. That was quite a piece of news, but I didn't have my mind on it. When I got home there was Aunt Nancy, in a gingham apron and one of my father's felt hats on, out in the yard raking leaves. She brought me in and sat me down and gave me milk, and then here it came: Had I remembered to tell Miss Jonas I hoped she *enjoyed* the pear, instead of just handing it to her? And I heard my mouth take over and hand out the damndest line of chatter you could imagine—all about how Miss Jonas had been tickled blue, had said she certainly *would* enjoy the pear, and especially because there was no tree in *her* backyard, so it would be a special *treat* to her, and it sure was swell to be *remembered*. It got by and it never bounced. And yet under it all was a sense of guilt, maybe the first time I ever felt it, that's been down under some things I've pulled, quite a few of them, a pink, hot-faced sensation as much the color of that pear as my high spots have been the color of the moth.

*

My aunts had no brogue in their speech, though they were older than my father was, because they grew up in this country, while he stayed in Ireland till he was twenty-four. His father, Francis Dillon, was a stationary engineer, and an uncle in New York had got him a job on a new project just then starting up, a powerhouse to run electric lights on Broadway. So he came across, in 1881, and the two girls came with him. But my grandmother stayed in Derry, where they all came from, as my father wasn't born yet, and the idea was she'd come later. But that wasn't how it worked out. Why I don't know, and my father didn't. A little interfamily friction may have had something to do with it, or it may have been my grandmother was doing pretty well for herself, and hated to uphook and start over again. Or it may have been there weren't enough kisses on the end of the letters she got from my grandfather. Anyhow, soon after my grandfather and his daughters moved to Baltimore, she moved from Derry to Dublin, where she opened first a little shop, then later a rooming house off Merriam Square. Of course, the old home was really Londonderry, but in the family it's always been Derry, as it was in olden times, before the city of London adopted it for some kind of stepchild. The old lady must have done all right, because she put my father through Trinity College, and had just got him started at law when she died. He took that hard, and while her affairs were being settled, the doctors said he should take a sea trip for his health. So he joined some Irish players on their way to the St. Louis Fair. He didn't turn out to be much of an actor, and left, but on his way back he stopped at Baltimore, and at last the Dillon family met Patrick, whom they had never seen. I guess they went a little nuts and he did. Anyway, he stayed, and it wasn't long before he was practicing law, with all of them pretty proud of him for being so high-toned. By that time my grandfather had charge of a West Baltimore powerhouse, and as a matter of fact, he lived two or three years after my father got there. Then he died, and my father and his sisters kept house in Walbrook, a suburb, some distance from the house we're in now. They worshipped him, he did them.

I didn't worship them, because they didn't have my respect, but I loved them the way you can only love something you pity. Why they didn't have my respect was that they were such fools. I guess the pear, and forty-seven hundred other things like it, had something to do with it. They were born gulls, and would fall for anything, so it was romantic and silly and impossible. They were nuts about music, all three of them, but the Old Man didn't kid himself he was a musician the way they did. Of course, being from the north of Ireland, they were Episcopalians, and Nancy sang in the church choir, up to the time they put the boys in, and closed her eyes and put expression in it. She was small and dumpy and dark, so when she sang *We Praise Thee, O God* she looked exactly like Slicker, our black cat, when he began yawning around ten o'clock. She always said I had inherited her voice, though how this came about she never explained. I had quite some voice for a little angel between nine and thirteen, and quite some left hook for a little rat of the same age. But what voice she had I couldn't tell you, because in spite of all the faces she made, I never heard one sound come out of her you could hear above the organ.

Sheila was tall and had brown hair and played the piano, with the stool raised just so and her dresses spread out all around her and the music corners bent to little ears and one hand crossing over the other. But if she ever played a piece through and played it right, I don't know when it was, and fact of the matter, when I came along as the boy wonder of North Baltimore and had to have somebody to play for me, it speedily became clear, kind of crystal clear, that Sheila wouldn't do, and it led to quite a few things. At that time she put on an act about not being able to play accompaniments, as though accompaniments were just an unimportant sideline to a big-time pianist, and in her own imagination I think she really thought she was one. But just when and where and how she had done all that important work she never bothered to explain. There was plenty of music in Baltimore as the Peabody Conservatory is there, but she and Nancy and my father were always going up to New York to hear some special brand, and one time, just three or four years after he came over, they got a surprise. The attraction was Mme Luisa Tetrazzini in *Lucia,* and right after the curtain went up who should come out in a plumed hat but the boy who led the olio in St. Louis. His name was John McCormack.

The first I remember of my father was when he took me down to North Avenue one day and held my hand while we walked along, and I chirped it was easy to tell how tall I was, as I was exactly half as tall as he was. He said it was easy now, but the question was: Would I stay that way? I think it was my first encounter with the idea I was growing and next year might not be the same size as I was then. We were on our way to his garage. He hadn't started out to be a garage man but became one by accident. Around 1908 he bought a car. He was driving it along, and pulled out for a traction engine and wound up in the ditch. He swore, though he's never convinced me, that the steering gear was defective, and sued. So the company made propositions, but as they didn't have much, he settled for an agency, selling the car. Later, he said he wanted something on paper, a commitment he could put a price on when they'd be in shape to buy him out, and never expected to peddle the things because it was a cross between enlarging pictures and insurance. But when I came along in 1910 he was making more money from cars then five lawyers were making from clients, because the car became a very celebrated one, even though it was cheap, that you'd know if I chose to name it.

So a lawyer that was doing fair turned into a mechanic that was doing terrific. If you asked me, it made his life bitter. To an American, a business is a life. To an Irishman, especially one with a university education, it's not, because there's no such intellectual snob. I've heard him prove it a thousand times, that the automobile has done more for man than anything since Moses. Law, he said, makes property, steam makes power, but petroleum makes light, and the great light lit up when they put the stuff on wheels, so the lowliest "wight" could drive out of his village and see what the wide world looked like. I've seen him take a ball bearing from his pocket and orate on its being the finest jewel ever made. And yet, in their shelves around his study, I think those books, row on row of them in leather bindings, looked down to mock him. When he closed them something went out of his life, and money didn't take its place. And there may have been a family angle too. His mother, as I piece it together, never liked that title, "stationary engineer," that was worn by my grandfather. The automobile agency was not quite the same as superintendent of a powerhouse, but it was like it, and I imagine he wondered what she would have thought of it.

My mother I saw once, to know it. She was born in Baltimore, but she and my father didn't meet for some years after he got here. Then at a Christmas party, when she was home from school, they danced together, and before New Year's got married, in Elkton, after running away. She was sixteen, he twenty-eight. You'd think they were the right age to be happy, and that they'd got started the right way. But his hair had started to gray, and from things I've heard from Nancy and Sheila and others, he got the idea the difference in their ages was an Irish Sea between them. And then he began figuring she moved in a world of kids that thought he was funny. Three years after I was born in 1910, a rich boy came down from Philly. It was over him they had the bust-up, and it was on account of him, or what the Old Man got in his head about him, that it was put in the settlement he should keep me. But I'll go to my grave believing it was all his imagination, and I've got my reasons for thinking he went to his grave believing so too. The bust-up knocked him galley-west, and he never remarried. He and she had set up shop in Roland Park, with Nancy and Sheila staying in the Walbrook house. But after she left he sold both houses, and he and his sisters moved to the house on Mt. Royal Terrace, and they even started going to a different church, which I'll call St. Anne's. So far as they were concerned there had never been a Louise Thorne, and I was a boy that had really been brought by a stork, and had a father and aunts but no mother.

All that, though, was before I was four years old, and I had no memory of what she looked like, and no pictures of her were around. All I knew about her was from a little trunk I found in the attic, that I doubt if the Old Man or my aunts even knew about. It had in it some of her clothes, especially a dark-blue velvet dress I loved to touch, and a black leather case with a nail file in it, a buffer, an orange stick, a powder box, a fluffy puff, and a little bottle of perfume with a glass stopper. By the time I was ten I must have smelled that perfume a thousand times, and when something had gone wrong, I'd go up there in the attic, open the trunk, touch the velvet dress, and smell the perfume. Well, came the time when I was the wonder child of Baltimore, the sweet singer of Mt. Royal Terrace, the minstrel boy of Maryland, with the church full whenever I sang, pieces about me in the papers all the time, and money rolling in, specially those twenties for *Abide with Me* at funerals, very joyous occasions in the life of a cute boy singer. And one morning we hadn't even finished the first hymn, when I noticed this number on the aisle in the second pew, that was alone, and seemed most interested in me. By that time, though I was only thirteen, I'd had plenty of admiration from the female sex, partly from how I sounded, but partly from how I looked, with my big blue eyes and bright gold hair, in my little white surplice. But if you think I had got bored with it in any way, you've formed a false impression of my character. And if she looked older than I was, I had already found out even if they were older, the pretty ones could be awful sweet. She was plenty pretty. Her hair was gold, but the light from the Resurrection, streaming in through the stained glass window behind her, turned it red. Her eyes, though, were blue, and they stared straight at me.

So when we got to the offertory and I started the Schubert *Ave Maria,* I gave out with plenty, and beamed it right at her. After about three bars of it she looked away quick, and then back at me again, and I knew she'd got it, I was singing to her. When I finished and sat down, our eyes crossed and she nodded and this beautiful smile crept over her face, and for the first time I began to wonder if there was something about her that was more than a pretty girl that had liked how I sang. I was still crossed up when we started out, and she put out her hand as I went by, and gave me a little pat. We robed in the basement, not because there wasn't plenty of room in the vestry, but so we could file out through the church, singing a recessional *a cappella,* and our voices would die away in the distance as we went down the stairs.

I had already passed her when it hit me, the perfume she had on, and I knew who she was. I wanted to turn around and speak to her, but I was afraid. I was afraid I'd cry. So I kept on, one step at a time, just like the rest, and hoped nobody would notice that I wasn't singing any more. We got back to the basement at last, and I tore off the robes and ran back upstairs. People were all over the place, in the vestibule and outside, just leaving, some of them talking with Dr. Grant, the rector. She wasn't there. It was part of the deal, I know now, that she would never visit me, and the way I dope it out, somebody had tipped her that my aunts and the Old Man were on one of their trips to New York, with me left behind with some friends, so she could see me without anybody knowing who she was, and hear me. But I hadn't doped out anything then. All I knew was she was beautiful, and my mother, and I wanted to touch her, the way she had touched me. And when I couldn't find her I went down to the basement again and cracked up, but good. The organist was a young guy named Anderson, that could play all right but thought he was a wonderful cut-up. He winked at the other boys, and began to whistle *A Furtive Tear,* from *The Elixir of Love,* or *Una Furtiva Lagrima,* as I sang it, in Italian. I almost killed that organist. I beat him up so bad even the boys got scared, and the men, the basses and tenors, called a cop. But when he got there I was gone.

MY first friend was a boy named Glendenning Deets, and I met him in the park. He was a little older than I was, so instead of a tricycle, like I was riding, he was on a bike. We stopped, and he passed some remarks about the gocart, as he called it, then said that for five cents he'd let me ride the bike. I said all right. But when he got off the bike, I grabbed it and tried to run off with it without paying the five cents. He mauled me up pretty bad. But then something happened that gave me the bulge on him from there on in. I went down, from the hook he hung on my jaw, and as I got up I stumbled into the tricycle and went down again. That hit him funny, and he began making a speech about it to the nursemaids that were looking on. That made me sore, though until then I had felt like a few uppercuts were coming to me for what I had done. So I piled into him. But all he did was wrestle me off and back away and duck. And I smelled it that knocking me down and making a speech about it was all the fight he had in him that day, and he was my potato if I wanted him. I let him have it. Somebody pulled me off him and made us shake hands. I took the bike over to some grass, but when I tried to ride I couldn't.

When I got tired of trying he said we ought to get ourselves some peaches. "Where?"

"From the orchard."

"What orchard?"

". . . On Park Avenue."

"Just steal them, hey?"

"What do you mean steal them? They're prematures."

They were a few trees in a backyard, what was left of an orchard, and like all old trees they produced prematures, fruit that ripens ahead of the regular crop. It was the first I knew about that, but he got it off with quite an air, like it was inside stuff you had to get wise to before you had it straight what was stealing and what was not. He said the prematures were no good to sell, "and they'll thank you for taking them away." But by the time we had eaten four or five white clings, something in overalls came through the fence and we got out of there quick. He was pretty sore. "The dumb buzzard, with not even enough sense to know we're doing him a favor."

People with not enough sense to know you were doing them a favor by taking whatever they had seemed to be quite numerous whenever he was around.

Denny lived in Frederick, but he spent his summer in town with an aunt, Miss Eunice Deets, who lived on Linden

Avenue, while his father and mother went to Europe. The summer after we hooked the peaches he said we should have a job, to make some money. That was all right with me, but what job I had no idea. One night, though, he was over after dinner, and got to talking with my father about the garage, and how he'd been noticing things there, specially the time the men took going for wrenches, jacks, and stuff, so why couldn't he and I be hired on to do that running, and save a lot of time? What he was doing at the garage, which was half a mile from his house, he didn't bother to say. But he made my father laugh. When he was asked how much we wanted, he said ten cents an hour apiece. So my father said a buck a week, for five hours' work on Saturday, wouldn't break him, and we could consider ourselves hired. It was still only eight o'clock, so he drove us to an Army-Navy store near Richmond Market, and got us a jumper suit apiece, visor hats, brogan shoes, lunch buckets, and cotton gloves. I don't say we didn't earn our money, because the men ran us ragged, though if it was for the time it saved or the fun of seeing us trot I wouldn't like to say. But one day, around twelve thirty, when everybody was out back sitting against the fence eating lunch, a guy came in with his car boiling. We took him back to Ed Kratzer, the foreman, who said leave it and he'd see what he could do. The guy got loud about how he had to get to Germantown, Pa., by six o'clock that night. "Then in that case take it somewhere else. If you want us to fix it, leave it and we'll see what we can do. Just now we're eating, and if you ask me that's what you could be doing, and you'll get there just as quick."

". . . Where do I eat?"

"There's a drugstore across the street."

So after he swallowed three times that's where he went. But of course, when he was gone I had to look big, so I lifted the hood of the car, which was standing in the middle of the garage floor, with nobody around it but us. But when I opened

the door I noticed the hand brake was on, hard. It should
have been, of course, but it came to me I hadn't noticed him
set it, and you generally did notice it in those days because
the ratchet sounded like somebody winding an alarm clock.
Then something else came to me. It was a Ford and I don't
know if you remember the old Model T. It had low and high
gear on the left, reverse gear center, foot brake on the right,
and hand brake straight up the middle. You set the hand
brake when you stopped, but in low gear, the car could still
go, and I had a hunch. As soon as I cranked it I got in and
let off the brake. Sure enough, when I pushed in low gear the
car went, and when I dropped the pedal back into high it
still went. I stopped and tried reverse and it was all right. I
cut my motor and got out. "Well, now, there's a dumbbell
for you."

"How do you mean, Jack?"

"Driving with his brake on. You can't do it."

"And that's all that was wrong with it?"

"That's all."

I got a can, put some water in, and that helped with the
temp. He kept studying me. "What we going to charge him,
Jack?"

"We got nothing to do with that."

"Why not?"

"The men attend to charges."

"When they do the work, they do. But for crying out loud,
we did the work. *We* made it run. We—"

"I thought that was *me*."

"Oh, pardon me."

"We, my eye."

"Then it's all yours—for whatever *you* get."

What I would get was nothing, as I very well knew. Pretty
soon I said: "What do you think we ought to charge him?"

"*Who* ought to charge him, Jack?"

"*We* ought to."

"That's better. That's a whole lot better. Gee, that's a pain in the neck for you, a guy too dumb even to see chances to make dough, and then when somebody *else* kicks in with a little brains—"

"What do you think we ought to—"

"Two dollars."

"For just taking off his brake?"

"I thought you put in a new bearing."

"I don't like to crook anybody."

"Who you crooking? Not your old man, that's a cinch, because we haven't even used a handful of his waste. And not Kratzer, because *he* was too lazy even to get in here and see what was wrong. And not the guy. He'll *thank* you for getting him out of here on time. He'll *want* to pay you. He'll—"

But my face must have told him, because he shut up and slid over to the back door to check on the situation out back. Then he had me roll the car out front. Then he raced across to the drugstore.

I drove the car up the street, took a U-turn, and had hardly run back before there the guy was, so excited he could hardly talk. I played it just like Denny said, with a whole lot of stuff about how I didn't want to see him wait while the men finished their lunch, and some more about how he should be careful to let the brake off, "as that's generally the answer when you burn out a bearing." He hardly heard me. It turned out he had had the car two days, and probably didn't know what the hand brake was until somebody set it for him the night before in the garage where he stored it in Washington. He paid the two dollars without a whimper, and even gave me a half dollar extra for helping him out. Soon as he drove off that was divided, in the drug store. Denny saw to that. "All you need is a little brains, Jack. In the garage business it's like everything else. It's initiative that counts, every time."

It was Denny, that summer or maybe the next, that got me started on my singing career, though all it amounted to, at first, was some more of the Deets initiative. They had had a mixed choir at St. Anne's with four paid soloists and I guess maybe fifteen to twenty volunteers like Nancy. But when Dr. Grant came in, after Dr. Struthers died, he was very High-Church, and pretty soon there was a fight, but he had his way. The soloists were out and the mixed choir was out. The men stayed, to sing the tenor and bass parts, but the sopranos and altos were to be boys. I'd hate to tell you what Denny and I did to them. We chased them up alleys and yelled at them and beat them up. One night a couple called, the man with a buggy whip. He wanted to dust me off for something that had happened, and my father had to get tough.

But then one day Denny found out that the cutie pies got eighty cents a Sunday for doing it. He almost set Nancy, Sheila, my father, and his aunt, Miss Eunice, crazy, that he and I should get a shot at the sugar. Finally it turned out two places had become vacant, and we would be given a trial after rehearsal one afternoon. We waited quite a while, sitting in the rear of the church, while they went through *Te Deums* and anthems and Gregorian chants, or plain songs as they're called. They seemed to be the main reason Dr. Grant wanted boys, as it was dry, gray music, some of it sung without accompaniment, and women would have ruined it. But the director was a woman, Miss Eleanor Grant, Dr. Grant's cousin. She had sung with the Century Opera, but after we got in the war married a French officer, and when he got killed she didn't go back on the stage right away, but stayed on in Baltimore and taught. She was small and dark and pretty, and even watching her from the back of the church, where I was sitting with Nancy and Sheila and Denny and Miss Eunice, I fell for her hard.

We had been told, when our turn came, not to sing anything religious, but whatever we happened to know and like, so

Denny sang *A Perfect Day,* with Anderson playing for him,
and I sang *The Rosary,* with Sheila. Denny got as far as "when
you sit alone with your thoughts," when Miss Eleanor stopped
him and said it was very nice of him to sing for her, but he
needn't bother to finish it, and later, maybe when he was
older, she hoped he'd come back. The cutie pies, who were
hanging around, all began to laugh, and for once I didn't
blame them. Because Denny sang it in the same gashouse
bark he used on *Over There,* which was his favorite tune at
the time, and maybe it sounded funny but it didn't sound
good. Me, I only got as far as "The hours I spend with thee,
dear heart." Because Sheila, as soon as she got spread out on
the organ bench, and got the stops pulled open, and got a
heel-and-toe grip on the pedals, unfortunately let her music
go sliding to the floor. However, she started anyhow, and that
was how I came to be thrown out at first base. Because of
course her fingers would start it in the key she knew it in,
which was two flats, but when Anderson put the music back,
her eyes would read it in the key they saw it in, which was
six flats. That was how it happened that the first chord and I
were in one key, and the second chord and Sheila were in
another key, and it sounded like a lunatic asylum.

Next thing I knew, there was Sheila, as usual, giving out
with the gushy alibi, like she was a real virtuoso or something,
and small chores like this were quite beneath her, and Miss
Eleanor was smiling and nodding and patting me. By that
time I had somehow swallowed that string of pearls and
maybe a couple of tonsils, but I got the surprise of my life.
Miss Eleanor put her arm around me, and said there wouldn't
really be any need to go on, as she thought I was a boy they
wanted, and would I report next Wednesday to rehearse?

Walking home I never heard three women have so much
to say about another woman in all my life. Miss Eunice was

burned up at the way Denny had been cut off, though how much he had sounded like a crow with the croup she didn't mention. Sheila said no wonder I was flustered, the highhanded way things were done around there, and as for that *draft,* that practically blew the *hair* off your head, to say nothing of the *music* in front of you, well! Nancy, who was still sore about being fired, criticized Miss Eleanor's "method." Denny had nothing to say, until he and I were alone together, out in his front yard. Then he hauled off and hit me. Then he hit me again. By that time I had got to know him fairly well, so I just waited. Pretty soon he began to blow and backed off, and I stepped up and let him have it, but with the flat of my hand, a slap on the cheeks that sounded like a seal clapping for himself in the circus. "Now do I beat you up or do you cut this out?"

He burst out crying and plumped down on the bench beside the front walk. I sat down beside him and let him bawl. Until then he'd been the smart guy, but when I got the job and he didn't, he hated me for it. Not that he let it interfere with our beautiful friendship, or kept him from figuring what we would do with the money, once I began collecting my eighty cents. Or, as we could truthfully say, our eighty cents.

BUT the one really to blame for my singing career was Miss Eleanor, and she got interested in me, as you might expect, on account of my trying to get away with something, though up to then she hadn't tried to hide it that she liked me. She rehearsed us, as I said, on *Te Deums* and anthems and chants, but on hymns there was no rehearsal, only home work. It was her test for character. Because if a boy, once he got his book to take home, and was given next Sunday's numbers, wouldn't go to his mother's piano and beat out his part and learn it, there wasn't much to do about him. If he would, maybe he had something and she would work on him. If he wouldn't, he was out. Well, she gave me a hymn book, and also another book, that explained how to tell one key from another, major from minor, treble from bass, and 3/4 from 4/4. So I wanted the eighty cents, and made Sheila play the stuff for me, so I could learn it, which wasn't hard, as my voice was high, and I always got the soprano part, which was melody.

But pretty soon I thought: Why all that work? The notes, once I got straight how they worked, seemed to tell all you had to know, like when to go up and when to go down, how much, and how long to hang on. So of course, by my system then, I used initiative instead of work. Sheila would be all ready to brief me, and I'd say I'd already got the parts up. She wouldn't believe me, and would shove the book at me and I'd read the part off and there'd be nothing she could say. It cut her out of a chance to act important, but if I knew it I knew it. Quantum quantum, as the Old Man would put it. But one Sunday something happened. By that time I was already a bit of a feature, but more on account of my angelic looks, I imagine, than my heaven-sent golden voice, which hadn't developed a lot yet. I was put on the end, with a lectern in front of me, and a big leather-bound hymn book on it, that Dr. Grant found in his library, with a ribbon marker that had a golden fringe, so I made kind of a picture. And this morning we were singing a thing called *Parting Hymn,* with me on the melody, the cutie pies and the men on the parts, and the congregation doing whatever it felt like, mostly nothing. The organ wasn't in it, except to play it through once before we started, because with just the voices and nothing instrumental there was that ethereal angelic effect Dr. Grant seemed to be so stuck on. And we were going fine until all of a sudden it sounded like eight cats in a barrel and everybody stopped, except that after a split second Miss Eleanor motioned at me and I went on. Then the rest came in, and we were moving again. To pull things together, Anderson brought the organ in. But on every verse, even with the organ, there was the same mess, and on every verse Miss Eleanor motioned me on. At last, though, it came to an end, and pretty soon after that we filed out singing our chant, and when she came down to the basement everything was straightened out, or so she said anyway, when she showed Anderson the misprint in the books, which of course had made things a little sour.

Next thing I remember, I was at her house on Eutaw Place for Sunday lunch, and she fixed it herself. It was a little house in a yard with lilacs all around it, mainly studio, two stories high, with a grand piano in it, but not much else except a bedroom, bathroom, and kitchen with a sunporch at one side, where we ate. After lunch we went in the studio and sat on the couch, and she read the Sunday paper and let me play with her Airedale dog Muggsy. Then all of a sudden she put up the paper and said: "Now Jack, what happened?"

"When?"

"This morning. On the hymn."

"Why—it was a misprint. Isn't that what you said?"

"Yes, but why did you sing it correctly?"

"Well, I had a different book."

"Are you sure?"

"Dr. Grant's big book, that you gave me."

"Is that the book you have home?"

"No, Miss Eleanor, but—"

"But what?"

"I don't *know* what happened."

"Did you study the parts?"

"Of course, Miss Eleanor."

"Jack!"

"I study them, always."

"Come here, Jack."

I went to her, and she motioned me to sit there beside her, and I did, and she put her arm around me and pulled my head on her shoulder. Neither Nancy nor Sheila ever did anything like that, so I guess it was the first time any woman had touched me, and I can remember now how soft she was and how much I liked her arm around me with her face close and her eyes looking down into mine. At that time I was ten and she must have been a little under thirty. To most kids, from what I've heard them say, that would be a great-great-grand-mother, but not to me. I never notice much how old a woman is. She seemed like a pretty girl I knew, and we were having a little talk. "Now Jack, if you studied the part on that hymn, how does it happen you sang it in the right key, and didn't make the misprint mistake, the way the others did?"

"Too much for me, Miss Eleanor."

We sat there, and her arm was around me, but she wasn't looking at me, and all of a sudden she wasn't friendly any more. Then she winked away a tear and gave me a little shake. "Jack, why do you lie to me?"

"Why, Miss Eleanor, I wouldn't lie to you."

"You have lied to me. Now there's no use your trying to deceive me about what you've been doing. I've been suspecting it all along. You don't study these parts up at all. You stand there with a cheeky look on your face and read them off at sight and only pretend you got them up. And this morning, when you sang it right and everybody else sang it wrong, it was because you were reading it off Dr. Grant's book, which is a very beautifully printed collection of celebrated hymns with no misprints in it at all, where all the others had the cheap edition that belongs to the church, and that you have at home to study from. So I know, of course. Now why do you still look me in the eye and say you don't know how it happened?"

"I don't even know what you're talking about."

She stared at the piano a few minutes, then got up and went out. When she came back she had a bunch of lilacs she said I was to take to my aunts. I knew I was to go.

I don't know why, but when I got halfway home I turned around and marched right back again. I wish I could say I woke up to the wrong of lying, but I can't. All I can remember is that I kept thinking how soft she felt, and it was like when you touch a baby and you feel like Christmas Eve and never want to do wrong any more. I knew I had to go back and do something about it. She looked surprised when she saw me again, but I started right in: "Miss Eleanor, I did what you said."

". . . Come in."

She took me over to the couch again, sat me back on the cushion, and ran her fingers through my hair. "Did Miss Sheila teach you how?"

"How to what?"

"Read at sight."

". . . What's reading at sight?"

"Well, most people, unless they're professionals, have to read on some instrument, usually piano, for pitch and to make sure they're getting it right. But—Jack, do you mean you just stumbled on it by accident? That you looked at the notes, and after a little practice there in the choir you knew how they went? That *nobody* had to tell you?"

"Is it supposed to be hard or something?"

"Jack, I just love it."

She took me in her arms, and hugged me, and gave me little pats, and then went to the icebox and got out some sherbet she had stashed there. She explained to me about sight reading, and how unusual it was for somebody to be able to do it without particularly knowing how they did it. What excited her was that she thought she had some kind of a musical genius wrapped up in the same package as a pretty good boy soprano. In that she was wrong. But we didn't know anything for sure then, except that I was a kid that wasn't getting anywhere at a rapid rate of speed, and that she was a pretty girl widowed by the war and somehow out of step with her trade. It seemed exciting that we should cook up a secret between us, that I was to say nothing to anyone about it, that she would give me lessons and make a famous singer out of me, and I would make her laugh. "The way you've been standing up there, with a pious look on your face, and pretending to have your parts down pat, and not doing a thing but reading it off stone cold—*that's* what enchants me."

"If you like it, then—"

"Oh dear."

"What's the matter, Miss Eleanor?"

"It's wrong, isn't it, to encourage deception in the young? Then, I guess we start all over again. Well, I won't do it. How do you like that?"

"I like anything you say."

"Sometimes you have to kid them, don't you?"

"You mean—use initiative?"

"Use *what?*"

I told her about Denny, and the car, and how I took the brake off, and she whooped. "You're simply precious."

"Can I stay to supper?"

"I'll see."

She called up my aunts, and they said I could stay, and she explained to me why she had to be so formal. "Your aunt, Miss Nancy Dillon, has certain reservations about my method, I believe she calls it—"

"Oh boy, you ought to hear *her* method!"

So of course, we had some more laughing over that, but then she went on: "It'll be simpler, in the beginning anyway, if we keep our schemes to ourselves. You drop by, on your way home from school, and I'll work you over, step by step, and we'll see what we'll see. That is, unless there's something you'd rather do."

"Nothing *I* know of."

"You're a sweet baby."

That night, after she made some omelet and we had that with some ice cream I got at a drug store, she played for me and told me about grand opera and how she sang in the Washington and Baltimore Aborn seasons of 1912, 1913, and 1914, and the Century Opera in New York the year after that, and it was my first taste of romance. Because I went nuts about her, and she went a little nuts about me, but I sometimes wonder if that didn't have something to do with the baby she lost, not long after she married the Frenchman. The nicest part was how funny it was, the great trick we were playing on everybody. It seemed wonderful to hook a tone up, see her eyes light, have her pull me into her arms for little kisses, and then feel her burst out laughing. Pretty soon I'd kiss her on the cheek and not feel ashamed about it.

THE trouble with boys, it turned out, is that they've got breath trouble, but they've got so little time to be boys that nobody does anything about it. So everybody pretends the "reedy" quality is pretty terrific and makes them sound like little angels. She, though, she didn't buy it. "All they sound like to me is brats that can't sing. But *you* might be the one now to show what a boy might sound like if he sang instead of wheezed. Of course, it may not turn out like that. You may sound like some pip-squeak imitation of an operatic tenor. There's such a thing as letting a wild Irish rose be a wild Irish rose, and not trying to make an American beauty out of it. Still, I'd like to try. At least you have a voice. It has every fault there is, from escapement to tremolo to four or five other things. It's like a stream of warm honey that shatters in mid-air. But we may be able to coax it to flow, clear down to the waffle, and if we do, I'll eat it with a little silver spoon. . . . Kiss me now, and we'll start."

How we started was to take a streetcar down to a five-and-ten and come back with a red balloon. We worked on it quite a while. She'd have me blow it up and squeeze the neck with one hand and press the air out with the other, then wet the neck and hold it tighter or looser, while I pressed the air out harder or easier. Then she'd make me notice how the higher the pressure the higher the whine of the air going out the neck. After a while I got it through my head that pitch is a matter of tension and pressure. Then we had to go over the way it worked in my throat and my lungs, and she drew a lot of pictures of how I was put together inside, with vocal cords and windpipe and lungs and diaphragm and abdominal muscles, all with exact shape and names, so I can remember them yet. Then I had to get it through my head that pressure from the abdominal muscles, exerted on the relaxing diaphragm, is transmitted to the cords, which are under tension, and that pressure and tension had to balance. If there was too much pressure on the diaphragm and too little tension in the cords, there was escapement, and if it was the other way around there was clutch, or hard throat. In the beginning it surprised me how little she let me sing. Pretty soon, though, there was some of that, and I had to learn to forget what it *sounded* like, to me inside my head, "as you didn't buy a ticket, alas," and get my mind on what it *felt* like, "as that's what'll determine what it sounds like to the customers, who after all are the ones we're trying to please." The only one I was trying to please was her, and to me it felt thin, but she seemed satisfied. And then one day I didn't know if it sounded thin or thick, but only that it felt solid in my belly and like bubbles in my throat, and her eyes began to shine. "Felt good, didn't it?"

"Yeah, felt easy."

"Rest, and we'll work it higher."

The first song I got was the Mozart *Alleluja*. Now you'll hear that Mozart is the delicate tracery that Jack Frost puts on the window pane, that every picture is different and the number of them infinite, that even the crystals have their own design and that it's never once repeated, that it's the greatest musical talent we ever had, that it's genius. Just the same, it's ice. And yet, the first time I sang that number in church, I could feel the congregation catch its breath, and see women all over the church take out their handkerchiefs and hold them to their eyes. When I got through, Miss Eleanor had found what she'd been looking for. A boy, if he's taught, has something that a tenor hasn't got and a soprano hasn't got and that all of them haven't got. I guess it's what a bud has, before it's a flower.

From then on, I showed speed. Before I knew it I had four or five operatic arias, some songs and ballads, enough to put on a show with whenever I got booked. That was all the time, at the Masonic Temple, at the Rotary Club, at the reception to the Bishop, at anything you could think of. It caused kind of a situation at home. By now, of course, I had to come out with it that Miss Eleanor had given me a little help, so of course nothing would suit Nancy but that I had to switch to a good teacher, like a friend of hers, Mrs. Pyle, and of course Sheila took it for granted she would play for me. That didn't sit so well with Miss Eleanor, because I think I've told you about Sheila's ideas on how to ruin a number at one fell swoop. It was the Old Man that knocked it all in the head, and for the right reason: "The two of you will keep hands off, for it's my considered opinion that you don't know enough music between you to shake out a Tipperary clog, and why you'd be cluthering into it I don't know. The little lady, the rector's niece, seems to have things well in hand. Lad, do you knew *The Minstrel Boy?*"

"No, I don't."

"Ah well, it makes no difference."

But he didn't know his son's slick ways. In the house was an album with *The Minstrel Boy* in it, so of course in ten seconds I was in the hallway, singing it for him, reading at sight. That clinched everything.

Who Miss Eleanor finally picked to play for me was a girl named Margaret Legg, whose family owned one of the big hotels in town, the Cartaret, over on Charles Street. She was about my age, and played a lot better than Sheila. We made a nice pair, specially after we got booked into a New York vaudeville house, she in kind of an Alice in Wonderland outfit Miss Eleanor got her, me with a Little Lord Fauntleroy suit, all in blue velvet with Buster Brown collar. We were always spic and span, as her mother was always there, in New York and the other places we went, and she shined us both till we gave off sparks.

Margaret pulled one thing I didn't understand. She went to a private school, Kenneth Hall, where most of the girls boarded, but some came from Baltimore as day scholars. One Friday she asked me to take her to the german, as she called it, that the school gave now and then, and that the girls could invite their friends to. I was all crossed up. The big news with me was I had my first long-pants suit, and as I had grown exactly as tall as Miss Eleanor, I had invited her to go to a movie that was coming to town, called *Little Old New York,*

with a girl in it named Marion Davies, and some old-time
fire engines. I sulked, but she kept saying we could see the
movie some other time, and I had better take Margaret to the
german. So I did and we led some kind of a march they
started with, and I felt like I had been sent off to the tots'
wading pool. But what got me, after I took her home, was that
she started bawling, right there in the lobby of the hotel, with
her mother and father and a dozen people looking on. After
that I took her around quite a lot, on Miss Eleanor's say-so,
though what it had to do with our appearing together I
couldn't see. There was only one thing about her I liked, at
least at that time, and that was her baby sister Helen. She was
just able to walk when I first ran into her, and was the cutest
thing I had ever seen. I used to bring her apples and ice cream
and lollipops and gocarts, and play with her by the hour, and
a new word she learned was bigger stuff to me than knocking
off an E flat above C, which finally became my record for the
event.

The row with Anderson came just as Miss Eleanor was
packing for St. Louis, where she was to sing some summer
opera, so she had hurried home after service, and wasn't there
for the grand finale. The phone kept ringing, and I didn't
answer, as by that time the cook had gone and I was alone in
the house. About five my father and Nancy and Sheila
drove up in a cab, and about five thirty the phone rang again.
Nancy answered, and it was the mother of one of the cutie
pies. So now they had it, here in the house. I went on the
carpet, before Nancy and Sheila, with my father listening,
his face dark. What I told them was nothing, as I was afraid
they'd get it out of me about my mother. The doorbell rang
and it was the cop, with a warrant for my arrest. My father
rolled his r's and refused to let him in or say where I was or

help him out in any way. We were all three in the front room
to listen, and pretty soon the cop went. Then my father
went to the phone, and there was some pretty sharp talk, but
from the way Sheila and Nancy began looking at each other,
I knew it had been fixed up, somehow, and I wouldn't be
arrested. Then my father brought me back to his den and
had a look at my chin, that had a mark on it. Then we went
into it. "What started this thing?"

". . . I don't want to talk about it."

"What started it?"

"He laughed at me."

"What for?"

"Making a fool of myself. Crying."

"What were you crying about?"

"I didn't feel good."

"Were you sick?"

"I don't know."

"Are you sick now?"

"No."

"If you were sick, you could hardly thresh him."

"Then I wasn't sick."

"You did thresh him?"

"So the cop said."

"So the complaint said, with many affecting particulars,
and so several affidavits said, with a startling unanimity."

"Then I beat him up."

"What are you concealing?"

"I don't want to talk about it."

"You may go to your room."

For the next hour or so there was a lot more telephoning,
all of them trying to find out what it was about, and a fat
chance I'd tell them. But then the phone rang, and I could
tell from the way Sheila began to talk that it was Miss Eleanor,
and I knew I had to see her no matter what they did to me
for it. I took off my shoes and stepped out the window to the

roof of the back porch. There was an arbor at one side with
Virginia creeper on it, and I climbed down on that. As I
started for the back gate Sheila called. I didn't stop, and it
wasn't till I got to North Avenue that I sat on the curb and
put on my shoes.

"What happened?"

"Miss Eleanor, I saw my mother."

"Where?"

"In church."

"Ah—the one in green?"

"I didn't notice her clothes."

"She sat on the aisle? One or two pews back?"

"Yes, that was her."

"And you recognized her?"

I told how I had felt those eyes looking at me, and about
the pat, and the perfume. I broke down two or three times
telling about the perfume in the attic, because it seemed so
silly, but she held me close and said it wasn't silly at all, and
after I got a little bit under control I let her ask me questions,
and answered them, and finally she had it. "I'm sure it was
she."

"I know it, Miss Eleanor."

"I saw her, and do you know what I noticed?"

"What was it, Miss Eleanor?"

"How much she looked like you."

"Like—*me?*"

I had a light, happy feeling, because she'd been so beautiful.
"You're very beautiful, Jack. Now tell me the rest of it."

"In the basement, when I got the surplice off, I waited a
minute, so I wouldn't make a holy show of myself, and then
I came back upstairs in the church, looking for her. And I
looked everywhere, in the vestry room, in the vestibule, in

the library, in the chapel, all over. Everybody else was there, saying goodbye to Dr. Grant, but not her. Then I went down in the basement again, and then it hit me and I tried to keep from crying and couldn't. And then that son of a —"

"Yes, Mr. Anderson."

"Started to whistle *Una Furtiva Lagrima.*"

"Mr. Anderson has beautiful hands and an ugly mind."

"And I hit him, that's all."

"There'll be some who won't exactly weep."

"You mean it was all right?"

"Jack, hitting Mr. Anderson, just because he made himself objectionable in some way, wasn't so very important, one way or the other, except to let him have it good, if you were going to let him have it at all. Hitting him because it got mixed up with your mother and how you felt about her was beautiful. Silly and utterly divine. My little Jack, that's no longer a boy, but has become a man. I've thought about her, Jack, and I've tried, in a way—"

"To take her place?"

"Well?"

"I think you're wonderful."

"And it was with her in mind, anyway quite a little with her in mind, that I made the arrangements for the records we're going to do tomorrow. So she could hear them, and keep them. So, if you want really to do something for her, sing as well as you know how, and then when they're made I'll see that she gets them."

"You're coming with me?"

"Of course. I don't leave for St. Louis until night."

The first number I was to record was *The Glow Worm,* which was to be done with the cutie pies. The studio was in Camden, New Jersey, and they went by train, with a man from the company. But Miss Eleanor drove me in her little green coupé, after quite some argument about it when she took me home. The Old Man was all for having a showdown about me running out of the house, but she had to get it through his head that a boy who has to stand up in front of a symphony orchestra and do a performance can't be put through a workout the night before with a hair brush. But on the chorus, where I was to do an obbligato with the others singing under me, I had hardly started when I broke. They put in a new master and we got going again. I broke again. Miss Eleanor said something to the conductor about my having had a trying time the day before and took me outside in the hall. She made me take a drink from the water bubbler, then squeezed my hand and brought me back. "All right, sir, I think I'm all right now."

But even as I was talking to him my voice popped. And one of the bull fiddlers said: "That boy's got the goslins."

It was the cutie pies' turn, and from the way they yelped I knew what was the matter with me, and that that ended my days as a soprano. Miss Eleanor didn't take me home right away. She took me to her house, and phoned my aunts about it, and made me some supper, and had me ride with her in the cab to the train she was taking for St. Louis. It wasn't till we were in Union Station, sitting on one of the benches in the waiting room, that she really said anything about it. "Now nothing has happened. You're going to forget it."

"It's all right. I don't care."

"But you *must* care!"

"For that bunch of—"

"For yourself! And singing and music and beauty and doing things well and everything we've been so excited about! Hasn't it meant anything to you?"

"Why, sure. But if I've got the pip—"

"Don't you know why? *You're a man!*"

She put her arm around me and looked at me a long time

and smiled. "You're growing up so fast, and I'm so proud of you! And soon it won't be a boy's voice any more, but a man's, much more beautiful, and then we'll go on, and—"

She kept on talking like that, but pretty soon came the rumble of her train, and I went down to the platform with her to see her aboard. She wouldn't let me take her to her berth, but said goodbye on the step, after the redcap went aboard with her things. We shook hands, and she pushed her cheek against my face, and I remembered to wish her well with the engagement. She turned to go, then came running down the steps again, pulled me to her, and kissed me warm on the mouth, the only time she did, ever. Then she ran into the car.

* **5** *

BUT we never went on with my voice, because in the first place when it got through turning it was nothing but a beer-barrel bass, just good enough, with what was left of the belly support she had given me, to fool somebody that didn't know anything about music, and just bad enough, from the wood that had got into it, to set crazy somebody that did. And in the second place she never came back, except once, when she dropped by the house at the end of the summer to say hello, after she got home from the opera. I was plenty glad to see her, and proud of the two inches I had grown, and of the blue spot on my lip, where I had begun to shave. But she seemed anxious to get away, and I thought it funny she said nothing about coming over to make peach ice cream, which she had cooked and I had cranked. Next day I found out she had met another lady, and was going to open a studio with her in New York. She wrote me for years and I wrote her, and she didn't drop out of my life. But she wasn't in it either, and it would come over me all the time, the loneliness I had felt the day I beat up Anderson. I didn't mope off by myself, it was nothing like that. I went around with guys and played on the high-school basketball team and got moved from forward to center on account of the way I was shooting up all the time, and studied a little. Anyhow, I got A in math and physics and mechanics, and C in English and French and Sociology. But I got D in deportment on account of the fights I got into, which was the tip-off on how I was enjoying life.

It didn't help any, the Old Man's idea of how to get me interested in the serious side of life, on the basis of what we were going to do with the music money. I hadn't paid much attention to it, that I remember now, except to do what Miss Eleanor had said do, which was to put most of it, around $4,500, in a savings account, and try to spend as little of the rest as possible. But when the end of the summer came around, and all the stores advertised sales on suits, it seemed a good idea I should buy one. There was nothing very new about it, as I'd already bought one, the one I wore to Margaret's german, my first with long pants, back in the spring, so it wasn't as though I was starting a one-guy revolution. But when I found a number I liked pretty well, a pin-striped, double-breasted blue in the window at the Hub, with fedora hat, malacca stick, and two-toned, suede-topped shoes to go with it, all exactly like the signed picture of Antonio Scotti that Miss Eleanor had had on the piano, you'd have thought I had set the garage on fire or something. Sheila wept and tore her hair and said I looked like "lower Broadway," whatever that was. Nancy said I certainly had fallen under "peculiar influences." And it was all the worse, from the standpoint of crossing me up, because the suit had had one effect of a most desirable kind, before they even saw it. I wore it home, of course, but took the car that ran near Miss Deets's house to check with Denny on what we were doing that night, or anyhow that's what I made out I was stopping by for. Mainly it was to let him get a load of the dazzola-dizzola, and it certainly worked. Since the flop at Camden he had been getting familiar again, marching right beside me, catching in step. But the suit did it. I didn't advertise it, didn't even remember it. I just asked if he could make it the late show that night, instead of the first, as there were things I had to do after dinner. He nodded and didn't say anything. He didn't have to. I could tell by the look in his eye.

So when I ran into this bawling out on Mt. Royal Terrace I felt like a typographical error. But so far as my father was concerned, nothing came of it that night, or the next, or for a month or two. It wasn't till the cold weather hit, and Miss Eleanor had left for New York, and Denny for Frederick, that I was invited in the den one Saturday afternoon, just after lunch, and just before I was due to shove off for a football game. "Jack, I think you need a new coat."

"I'm going to get one."

"I'll get it. I—had intended to."

"I can get it. I've got money."

"I think it my duty to clothe you yet, whether you've been fortunate about money or not. And, as to attire, you might be guided by older persons' advice. On taste, suitability, such things. I—can't say the latest acquisition impresses me a great deal."

"You mean my suit?"

"Aye—and accessories."

"What's the matter with them?"

"A bit romantic, I would say."

"I don't get it."

" 'Romantic' means associated with the Mediterranean Sea."

"I got it at the Hub."

"I talked with Mr. Spicer down there, and he was good enough to inquire of the salesman who served you, and learn the circumstances. It seems you mentioned certain singers."

"Mr. Scotti's a dresser."

"Perhaps that's why I take exception."

He started talking about clothes, and why a dresser's not generally a guide on how to dress, all pretty good stuff, as I know now. He said taste is always acquired, and invariably relative, and that the main thing to be remembered was that appropriateness was its basic element. Wine fit for fish, he said, is not necessarily fit for beef, and clothes fit for the Metropolitan Opera weren't necessarily the right things for Mt. Royal Terrace, Baltimore, Md. But I was still pining for Miss Eleanor, and all I could make out of it was some kind of a crack at her. "If there was something wrong with singers it's funny Dr. Grant would put one in charge of us."

"Did I say something against singers?"

"Sounded like it."

"Why, I've been a singer. Mr. McCormack and I—"

"Yeah, I know about that."

"As for Miss Grant, I've nothing but admiration for her. I was perfectly content, you may remember, that you study with her. I may say that the first suit you got yourself, at a time when you were seeing so much of her, and as I suppose accepting her guidance, did you credit—so much so that I refrained from raising the issue of parental authority, and forbade my sisters to do so."

"I had no guidance."

"Then you did very well. However, we'll do better, for the next few years anyway, if you accept some sort of supervision. Tomorrow we'll both go over to the Hub, I'll resume my duties as a father, and I imagine come out of it with something creditable in the way of a coat."

But who went to the Hub was all four of us, Nancy, Sheila,

he, and I. And for some reason I don't understand, even now as I write about it, I just wouldn't try anything on. I just sat there, and when we came home it was pretty thick and each of them went upstairs.

But the weather kept getting colder, and I kept thinking of a coat I had seen a guy try on that day, a blue, with a belt, and long loose lines that would just go with the double-breasted suit. So one day I went down there, and it was still unsold, and I tried it on. It fit like it had been poured on me. I paraded up and down in front of all the mirrors, and tried it with the stick and without the stick, and the more I tried it the better I liked it. So I took it and sat down and wrote a check. I wanted to wear it out of there, but they said something about pressing it and lengthening the sleeves a bit, which of course I know now had to do with the check, which wasn't something a fourteen-year-old boy came in there with every day. But then I paid no attention, and went home, and began watching for delivery trucks. But instead of a truck, one day came a letter from them. They said no doubt there had been some mistake; but would I kindly straighten the matter out so they could send me my coat? And enclosed was my check. On it was a stamp that said payment had been refused, but the reason it had been refused was written in ink, and I couldn't make it out. So at lunch hour that day I went around to the bank and talked to Mr. Parrot. "Yes, Jack, it was the only thing we could do, and in fact I handled it myself. But there's the court order, and it's binding on us."

"*Court* order?"

". . . The one obtained by your father."

He rummaged in his desk and came up with a paper with brass staples and a blue cover and handed it over to me. It had my father's name on it and the bank officers' names on it and the bank itself, and said something about John Dillon, a minor. "You see, Jack, sometimes a situation arises, as a rule in connection with some child actor or athlete or in your case a singer, where considerable money has been earned and the parent is right smack up against it to know what he should do. Because if he lets the child keep it, the chances are it'll be dissipated, where if he takes over himself he's assuming a responsibility, but at least the money's safe. So that's what your father has done with you. All very friendly, and for your own good. He went to court, had himself appointed guardian, took possession of your accounts, and got an injunction, this thing I just showed you, that prohibits us from honoring your checks or paying out money to any order but his own. Now my suggestion would be you go home and talk it over with him, because it so happens I'm pretty familiar with the plans he's made for you, and I think you're going to be pretty happy about it, and on his part, he'll be relieved."

But I didn't go home, anyway right away. But at last, if I was going to get anything to eat, I had to meander around to Mt. Royal. And it was in front of my aunts, at the dinner table, that my father opened up: "Mr. Parrot rang me to say you'd been in."

"Yeah, I saw him."

"I—took over your funds."

"So he told me."

"Purely as a precautionary measure."

"Precautionary against what?"

"Further indulgences in extravagance."

"Which indulgences are you talking about?"

"That suit you have on."

"I like it."

"I regard it as a waste of money."

"I didn't ask you how you regarded it."

"If I'm responsible I'll not wait to be asked."

"And how did you get responsibility, is what I—"

But I never finished it, whatever bright remark I was about

to make. Because Nancy jumped up and slammed out, saying she wouldn't listen to such insolence, and Sheila burst out at me, wanting to know how I could dare talk like that. To her I said nothing. I didn't regard her as bright anyhow, or think it was any of her business, so what I would be saying to her I didn't quite know. But there was another reason too. My head was pounding by then, with a steady stab that's always been a warning to me I'm going to blow my top. So when she stopped, for fear I might say something mean, I sat there a few seconds just looking at my plate. Then the Old Man rasped at me: "Answer her!"

"You answer her."

"You ungrateful whelp, here I've embarrassed myself, gone against my inclination, all to save you from your own silly weaknesses, and—"

On the end of the table, where Nancy had been sitting, was the silver tray with the coffee service. I got up, hauled off with the foot that was to score so many football points later, and whammed that tray against the kitchen door with a crash you could hear a mile. My father jumped up and came at me. But I hadn't forgotten what I did to Anderson. When he grabbed me by the coat collar I knocked his hand away. He ran out of the room, and when he came back he had my stick that I had parked in the umbrella stand in the hall. He began cutting at me with it, trying to beat me across the rump, while Sheila began to scream. I took a couple of whacks, to catch his cadence, and on the third I grabbed it and wheeled so I had both hands on it and twisted. He was pretty strong, a medium-size guy, but heavy-chested, with a ruddy, sunburned face. To me, even at that time, he seemed weak as a child. The stick came away in my hands. I handed it back. "Will you put it where you got it, please? I don't like things to get mislaid."

He set it in the corner, his face the color of firebrick, and sat down to the table again. Sheila got up sobbing and left the room. Arabella, the colored cook, came in the room and began to clean up the mess. I sat down and told her: "Arabella, would you make a little more coffee, please? I think I'd like some hot."

That settled it, whether anyone around there could lick me or not, but it didn't get me my money back, and it didn't help much with the feeling I was having all the time, that I was on my own, with everyone pretty much against me. It was a long time before I came to the table. I ate in the kitchen, and used the back door to go in and out. I had no trouble, by that time, getting work. I've got kleptomaniac fingers, that can untie jammed shoelaces in the dark without turning on the light, and can pretty well tell, from the feel of the motor, whether it's the distributor, pump, plugs, or what, and by that time there was hardly a garage that wouldn't take me on whenever I wanted a job. So for a while that's how I got my money, because my father wasn't the kind to go soft and arbitrate.

"Will you help trim the tree, Jack?"

". . . All right, Nancy, I don't mind."

"Is Denny in town yet?"

"Not yet he isn't."

"Is he spending Christmas with Miss Deets?"

"I think he is, yes."

"Then would you and he like to go out and get a tree from Mr. Olson's place? For us *and* Miss Deets?"

"I imagine that's all right."

It was in the kitchen, on a cold morning in December, right after Arabella had finished giving me scrapple and buckwheat cakes. So when Denny got to town, which was a couple of days later, we drifted over to the garage and Kratzer gave me the light truck and we went on out to Olson's place for trees. Olson had a chicken farm out toward Relay, but there was a woods on it, and in return for us taking eggs off him the year round we had a standing invitation to come over and help ourselves to Christmas stuff. So pretty soon we found trees, a bunch of scrub pine on a hillock. Denny was for chopping them down, but I hate sloppy work, so we sawed them, one for Miss Deets and one for us. Then we found some holly and sawed it out. Mistletoe took us quite a while, and as nothing had been said about getting any, I was for coming home with what we had. But Denny got to laughing so hard at the idea of anybody kissing Nancy or Sheila or Miss Eunice that we had to find some, just for the hell of it. So at last, on a black walnut, we found three or four bunches. The limb it was attached to took some sawing, but when we finally got it, it looked like something. That night I stayed at Miss Deets's for supper, but as usual he went too far, and got to imagining just what it would be like if any one of the three got a chance at what mistletoe was for, and I had to shut him up.

On Mt. Royal, when we lit the tree Christmas Eve, I had candy and handkerchiefs and stuff under it for Nancy and Sheila, and a scarf for the Old Man, so by the time the carolers got there, things were easier. Then I found a little box marked for me, with a key in it. Something inside me gave a jump, and I went to the door and looked. There at the curb was the snappiest little gray Chevvie you ever saw, and when I went out there and tried it, the key fitted and the car went. I drove it around the block and came back and went inside. Well, what do you do in a case like that? I took the Old Man's hand and held it, and his eyes filmed over, and I had to run up to my room. I bawled until I thought the house must be shaking, and pretty soon I could feel it, he was there in the room with me. Then he wiped my eyes and we went down. I'd be a liar if I didn't say I wasn't so glad it hurt.

Not long after that, two or three days I guess, anyway during the holidays, he brought me in the study again, and for the first time opened up, in a fair and square way so we could talk, on the subject of my money. "To begin with, I want to explain what I did, to tell you the reason I had for doing it, of going to court without telling you, and plastering papers all over your accounts."

"Well, what *was* the reason?"

"I was afraid to tell you what I intended doing."

"I don't know why."

"You were under a certain influence."

"I hadn't seen Miss Eleanor in weeks."

"Be that as it may, my risk, if I dallied with it, was that it would be out of my hands before a court could act at all. All you had to do was withdraw the cash, as you had a perfect right to do, and once you handed it over to somebody else, or hid it, or got it out of the state, that would end any chance I might have of taking it over for you."

"I never even thought of anything like that."

"So I now realize."

"But why have *you* got to take it over?"

"It's my responsibility."

"I made the money."

". . . I've been over that, in my mind, a thousand times. However, the fact that by some freak chance you briefly had a singing voice, an overwhelming thing to me, I may say, if I never said it before, does not change the basic fact: It is my duty to see that you get the full benefit of this money, to make sure it is not dissipated by some youthful impulse, or extravagance, or at the suggestion of well-intending friends. I can't evade that, and I'll have you know, at the outset, I haven't evaded it, regardless of how you feel about it, and I won't. In a friendly, wholly affectionate way, it that clear?"

"I get it, if that's what you mean."

"But you don't accept it?"

"It's gone and done."

"I want you to understand the right of it."

"If you're satisfied, then O.K."

"It's for your sake, not my own, that I did what I did. Don't you understand that at your age you face a temptation to squander this money?"

"Sure."

"I'm protecting you from that."

"But if it's my money?"

"You nevertheless should have the benefit of my guardianship, to save you from something which is not for your own good."

"Everybody squanders money. You do."

"That is true."

"Why not me?"

"You assume no responsibility. . . . As you say, the whole world squanders money, and indeed whole industries rest on the assumption that mankind will indulge any luxury it can pay for. But mankind assumes its own responsibility. You, as a minor, are unable to assume such responsibility. Who sees that you eat is not you, but I. And so long as I have responsibility, I demand authority."

"Well, you've got it."

"I want you to think this thing over."

"Don't worry, I have."

"It's all in the bank, Jack, I'd like you to know that, with every cent of interest, as compounded."

"Well, I never thought you'd steal it."

"Now what shall I do with it?"

"It's your responsibility. Suppose you say."

"Do you know what an investment is?"

"We had it in school. Six per cent? Like that?"

"Something like that."

He went over it, one thing at a time, one word at a time, and explained the different kinds of investments. Then he showed me how he'd worked the thing out: We'd buy so and so much stock, so I'd get regular dividends; so and so much bonds, so I'd cut coupons the months I didn't get checks from stock, and so and so much savings, so I'd always have cash. All in all, it meant I'd have about twenty dollars a month coming in, which seemed to make sense, I had to admit. "Well, Dad, I guess that's all right."

"Then it's agreeable to you I go ahead?"

"Just what do you do?"

"First, I'll see Sam Shreve, who handles my brokerage account, and have him buy in this list, at favorable times. For some time there's been a bull market, but it goes off now and then, and you'll have to give him time to buy on off days. Then, we'll put the stock away, in my box. The dividend checks will come to you direct, and I'll take off the court orders from your account so you can spend your income as you please. On a boy's current expenditures I don't believe parents should be too inquisitive. Your clothes, subsistence, school expenses, and so on, will be paid for by myself—a light burden, and I welcome it. Your dividends will be yours as spending money."

"That sounds all right."

"It's the best I could work out—"

"I've got the idea, and from now on I'll shut up."

"Now I think we're progressing."

ONE of the main things in my life, from then on, was the new car I had. Up to then I'd been a guy, fourteen going on fifteen, overgrown maybe, with now and then a pal that I went around with like Denny, or a friend that really meant something like Miss Eleanor. But as soon as I got this thing I was the most popular guy on earth. Girls in school that I'd never paid any attention to, to say nothing of their brothers, all acted like they were my long-lost relations, and like I wanted nothing better than to haul them wherever they were going, and then turn around and haul them back. And they had the funniest idea it was their car too. They just took it for granted if they wanted to use it, maybe overnight, I'd just hand the key right over. I give you one guess how I fell for that. Then Nancy and Sheila, that had never taken any interest in where I was going, all of a sudden found a million things I ought to be doing with the car, and people I ought to be taking somewhere, specially them. On that, I've got to say for him, the Old Man put his foot down. He said if they wanted a taxi they could call one. And then, right there beside me so often I didn't know how it happened, was Margaret.

I guess she was fairly good-looking, though her looks never did anything to me. She was dark-haired, with white skin, pink cheeks, and a stocky little shape, that got better as she got older and taller and slimmer. She had shiny black eyes that hardly ever looked right at you, though that wasn't because she was shifty-eyed or anything like that. It was because she was always looking at something imaginary, like some new sofa she'd be telling you about, with a little set smile on her face, like she'd be nice about it till you got in a suitably admiring frame of mind. I guess that maybe was the key to her, and why I died around her so easy. Her people, I think I said, had the Cartaret Hotel, and it wasn't enough for them they'd sign in a guest, quote him four dollars for a room with bath, and tell him the main dining room opened at six, until then tea in the Peggy Stewart Room. They had to let him know they were doing him up pretty nice to let him stay there at all, because Washington and Hamilton and Burr and God knows who-all had stayed there, and if he was good they'd let him look in the Dolly Madison Room, where all the old furniture was, and the Cartaret Gallery, with the portraits, and the Colonial Hearth, with its copper. And Margaret, she had that in her, too. She'd *let* you hear her play. I don't think, up to the time she was booked out with me, that it had ever occurred to her that letting somebody hear her play wasn't the biggest favor in the world she could do them, or that letting people look at the sofas and the paintings and the pots wasn't the biggest favor the family could do. They were all born smug, her father, with the cutaway coat he always wore, and her mother, who was more of a manager type, awful cold. That is, all except little Helen. She was the cutest thing I had ever seen, and at Margaret's parties, that seemed to come oftener than tests in school, I'd get off with her, and feed her ice cream.

Then, after Margaret started playing for me, an awful thing happened to her. Until then, as I've said, it hadn't occurred to her that her playing wasn't the most wonderful thing in the world. But then she'd look in the paper, and there I'd be with a picture of me in the Little Lord Fauntleroy suit, and two thirds of the notice given to me, and there she'd be, down with the acrobats and the trained seals, with two lines about being "promising," and no picture. From then on, I think she just had to show me. After my voice broke, of course that got my picture out of the paper, but it didn't get hers in. She played, just the same. About every week and a half Sheila would tell me Margaret was "appearing" somewhere, and I really should go. So I'd take her. One time it would be a woman's club in Towson, another time some Peabody thing, and each of those, so far as the papers went, would be let out with three lines. But the little smile was there. What we talked about, going and coming from those places, I don't know, and I've racked my brains to remember, because after what happened it seemed to me I should. I can't.

Her parties in the wintertime were given in what was called

the Walnut Room, which was just off the lobby, and had been the bar before 1920. In the summer they were given out on the lawn, at the side of the hotel, under the maples. I've got to admit, whether it was the afternoon things they gave when we were younger, or the night parties they put on later, they were pretty nice. At first the Rocco Trio, then later the Woodberry Jazzbabies, made the music, and we all had a good time, even when Margaret consented to play. While she was banging out Hungarian Rhapsody No. 2, I was feeding America's Sweetheart No. 1.

But a gray car is a gray cat, and at night I went places that had nothing to do with school kids or Margaret. I'd clean up my algebra around eight or eight thirty, begin to yawn and say I'd just as well take in the picture show. But once out of the house, where I went was an uncertain proposition. Sometimes I'd go to a bowling alley, or maybe I'd slip over to Washington. It wasn't new to me, as my father had taken me there, to sit in the gallery and look at Congress, or go to the top of the Monument, so I knew my way around. But sliding in Rhode Island Avenue, finding a place to park near the Treasury, maybe taking in a Washington movie, all that was a kick, even if it didn't mean much. At the same time I was getting a feeling I'd never had before, and it meant business. I began to notice girls. I didn't notice them the way I noticed Margaret, *if* I noticed her, like she was a friend in a girl's dress, but nothing to have ideas about. I had ideas about them, plenty. How to get them, I didn't know. But getting them was the idea. When Denny hit town that summer, it turned out he'd been thinking along the same line, but he'd learned more tricks than I could have dreamed up in a lifetime.

Not that I'd call him original, or in any way refined. If he could pull some gag and get started with them in a soda fountain, he'd do that, and we'd all four walk out together. Outside, if the best he could think of was to fall in step behind them and fire some crack past their ears, he'd do that. But if he had to, he'd whistle at them, right from the car, and get me to slow down, so we were rolling right beside them. I didn't enjoy that much, but I'd do it. Whatever we did, a half hour later it was always the same. One of them would be on the front seat with me, and the other back in the rumble with him. He was always trying to sell me the rumble, on account of the "stuff you can get away with back there," but I figured if it was all that chummy he wouldn't be so hot to come up front. Nothing ever came of it. We'd go to some picture show, or to some dump on the edge of town, where Denny thought he could get beer but couldn't, or past East Baltimore, to the beach. The beach, somehow, always seemed as though it was going to work, because at least there were the bay and the sand and the moon. With some of those girls we picked up and another pair of guys I think it might have. Our trouble was we were fifteen years old—or I was, and Denny, though he was nearly sixteen, looked younger.

But Labor Day we got ambitious, and ran down to Annapolis to see what we could see. We kept on over Spa Creek to Eastport, and there we decided to get some gas. And across the street was this pair arguing with a guy in blue jeans. One of them, the one that was doing most of the talking, was dark, I suppose eighteen or nineteen, with a pretty snappy shape, and dressed in pink sweater, white skirt, and red shoes. The other was a fat girl, maybe seventeen, with frizzled blond hair, a striped blue-and-white jumper, and a blue skirt. By then, Denny took a gander at them all, but I don't think we'd have paid much attention to them if the dark one hadn't ripped out a cussword: "That's a hell of a note. I'll say it is. One hell of a *hell* of a note."

The fat girl kind of looked at us and made a face. Denny

went over and helped himself to some of her gum, and we stood around while the argument went on. It was about the delivery of ice. "I'm sorry, Miss, but I've got no way to deliver to the bay. It's like I told you: my truck's in the shop. Right around the neighborhood, where I deliver by barrow, I can accommodate you. But the shore is out of the question."

She turned away and started up the street, the fat girl after her, but of course Denny got in it: "Hey, hey, hey! Wait a minute! What is this?"

They stopped then, and Denny said: "*We* haul ice. Naturally we do. We love to haul ice. But we don't haul it unless people act friendly and say please and work on us."

The fat girl came over and stuck another piece of chewing gum in his mouth. He put his arm around her and didn't exactly stop at the fifth rib. The other one came over and shot her eyes first at them and then at me. "What's he talking about?"

"Hauling ice. For friendly people."

"*How* would he haul it?"

"How would you?"

". . . I'd need a car."

"So might we."

"You mean he's got one?"

"I mean *I* have."

"Say, that's different."

She took the last piece of gum Fats had, stuck it in my mouth, and patted my cheek. "Is that friendly?"

"For a start, that's fine."

I put my arm around her, and I didn't stop at the fifth rib either. She said I had a nerve, but didn't pull away, and I could feel the blood pound in my mouth. Denny said pull the car over, he'll get the ice. So next thing, she and I were crossing the street. She hooked little fingers with me. "Now look, big boy, *you* act friendly."

"Me? I *am* acting friendly."
"How old are you?"
". . . Nineteen."

The guy loaded the ice, a fifty-pound cake, on the floor in
front, so she had to sit close beside me. It turned out her name
was Lina, but Fat's I never found out. I gave my real name.
Denny said his was Randall, Randy Thomas, he said. "I
thought you was Calvin Coolidge," said Lina. But Fats did
plenty of squealing as he helped her in the rumble, so it looked
like she didn't much care. It was a hot day, and going through
the scrub woods toward the bay it seemed to get hotter, not
cooler. Lina began flapping her dress to give herself air. Then
she got the cutes and asked if that was allowed. I raised one
foot and kicked open the hood vent, so her dress blew up, clear
to her waist. She kept looking at me as she pulled it down.
"You're over nineteen, my handsome young friend. Considerably. What's the big idea, telling me lies?"

It turned out she was from Glen Burnie, and her family had
some kind of hot-dog stand up there, but her brother had
taken over this place beyond Eastport, not because it was much
of a place, but because it had a big icebox, and they could use
it for storage. And today, with the brother away and a lot of
dogs, butter, ground meat, pop and stuff on hand, there was
plenty to spoil if we didn't get the ice there quick. So when
we pulled up outside I piled that ice in the box, and she made
sure everything was all right. Then she began to clown and
ask if we'd have something cold. So while she and Fats were
getting bottles Denny and I had a look around. It was just a
soft-drink joint, with a front room that had a counter in it,

and two back rooms, one a bedroom, the other a combination kitchen and pantry. Pretty soon Lina came out with soft drinks and sandwiches, and Fats passed them out. Denny suddenly seemed awful hot. After he got down some ham and ginger ale, he said: "You know what I'd like to do?"

"What's that, Mr. Coolidge?"

"Go swimming."

"And ruin all those clothes?"

"Oh, we got suits."

"You have?"

"In the car. Right in the dashboard."

"But we girls, we're to swim in our birthday clothes?"

"Well, we could take turns on the suits—"

"How you know *we* haven't got suits?"

So they dug in a closet and came up with Lina's brother's suit, which was blue flannel shorts and a white woolen shirt, and her sister-in-law's suit, which was a one-piece job with the little short skirt they wore at that time. Then Denny and I got our suits from the car. Then an argument started as to where we'd put them on. Denny said one locker room for the four of us, and Fats acted like she had no objection. But Lina took her in the bedroom, and he and I put on our suits by the counter. Pretty soon both girls ran by outside, on the catwalk that ran around the place, and skipped on down to the water, giggling.

Lina had a hard, trashy face, but in the brother's outfit, with the blue pants flapping and the white shirt hugging her, she had something. In the water she didn't squeal and splash like Fats did, but really liked to swim, and could. When I got out there she was in deep water, headed for a float, so I went out there too. Pretty soon we had it to ourselves, letting the swells rock us, with Denny and Fats and their whoopdedo where we

could hardly hear them. She watched me, then: "You do a
nice crawl, Jack, all except your arms. You're forcing them
out, and it's all right for a pool, maybe. But on long stretches
it sure will wear you down.

"How do *you* get them out?"

"Roll 'em out."

She swam for me, and showed me. "Roll out your elbow
first and leave it lift your hand out. And relax your hand, so
it goes limp. And sling it forward, don't push it. Sling it easy.
Let your middle finger riffle the water as it goes along. And
don't reach. Don't stretch for distance and grab. And don't
dig your hand in. Roll it in. Roll it in, blade your hand, and
let your weight push you ahead. It's all in rolling your hips to
get foot action and your shoulders for arm drive. Do it right
you can keep it up all day. Do it wrong you poop out in fifty
feet."

It was play the way I liked to play, quiet, friendly, close.

But there was no getting around it, the air might be hot but
the water was cold, and pretty soon we had to come in. So of
course Denny and Fats came too. She was all out of breath
from laughing and he from making her laugh. In the shack
it was so hot you could smell oilcloth, suits, ham, mustard,
pop, and girls. Lina opened Cokes and we drank them. I took
mine to a table by the window, where there was air coming
in. Lina turned on a fan and let it blow her hair around.
Denny moved to get some of it, but just shifted from one
counter stool to the other. Fats was at the end of the counter,
and all of a sudden there was a spitting sound and something
popped Denny in the eye and she began chasing a cat. Denny
wiped off his face, and went back in the kitchen to look, and
Fats kept on talking about how that darned cat kept spitting
at people. Lina looked at me and winked. Denny came back

and took another swig at his pop. Then here came the spitting sound again and Fats chased the cat again and Denny went out to look again and Lina winked at me again. Then I saw what had happened. Lina had opened two or three spares, and Fats had one, out of sight from Denny under the counter, and she'd shake it up, keep her thumb over it, and then when the pressure was good, she'd ease her thumb and a little pip of foam would spit out and hit Denny in the eye. Then right away she'd kick at the cat, chase it, and hide the bottle. If you ask me Denny was fooled, but maybe he wanted to be. Then he caught her at it, and that was all it needed. In just about ten seconds the whole afternoon we'd been piling up for ourselves exploded.

He grabbed her, shook his own Coke, held his thumb over it, and began popping it in her face as fast as he could get the pressure up. She squealed and pulled away and Lina whooped and held her. Then he tore her suit open and slopped Coke all over her and she did the same for him. Then her suit slipped off and she had nothing on but fat, that shook all over her. Still he kept throwing Coke. Then she got loose and dodged all around. Then she ran in the bedroom and he ran in after her and slammed the door. Lina beckoned me, tiptoed over, opened the door on a crack, and peeped. You could hear them in there, but what made me sick was the look on Lina's face as she watched them, her mouth wet, her eyes shining, and her breath coming in little short gasps.

"What's the matter, don't he like me?"

"Listen, Lina, take it easy. He's not a horse, see? In the first place you kept him swimming around out there, right on top of all that stuff he put in his stomach, and—"

"What stuff?"

"Sandwiches. Pickles. Ginger ale."

"What was wrong with that?"

"It was swell. But in the second place, it's hot—"

"It is, Coolidge, but he's not. What ails him?"

"Hell, he's just a kid—"

"Oh, I am, am I?"

When the other two showed, it was our turn in the bedroom, Lina's and mine, that seemed to be the idea, and Denny's and Fats's turn at the keyhole, no doubt. But my imagination didn't run on that track. Nice made as Lina was, much as I'd liked the swimming, I could no more have gone through with it the way it was being done that afternoon than I could have flown. And the sorer she got the greener I turned, as I could see by the mirror back of the counter, but I couldn't want her, to save my neck. When Denny made his crack about my being a kid I meant to take a poke at him, but I never got that far. Two steps from my table and I had to dive out the door. There by the car everything came up, ham, bread, pop, and girl. When I got back I knew she'd been told, my real age, I mean, because she stared at me with tears shaking in her eyes, partly from rage at me, partly from pity for herself, that she'd been kidded and didn't know it. In a minute she picked up my clothes and threw them out. "Get that sick pup out of here!"

Now, as I tell it, it all seems simple enough, and if I couldn't take it, the wild afternoon the other three had got started on, I guess I don't mind, looking back at it. I wouldn't like it, if I *had* chased her around, torn off her suit, and dragged her in the bedroom, with Denny and Fats at the door. But at that time nothing was simple. Here all summer we'd done nothing but chase girls, not knowing how very well, but hoping. And here at last we'd bumped into exactly what we were looking for: a pair of trollops pretty enough for what we wanted, and trampy enough that they wouldn't get big ideas in their heads of what they had coming to them afterwards. And they had the time and the place, which were slightly more important than we had any idea of. And then I whiffed out like a wet match. Doing it in front of Denny was bad enough. But that crack of hers, about the sick pup, was the worst of all. *Something* seemed wrong with me, and not knowing what it was, feeling like some part of a man was left out of me, bothered me, and bothered me plenty. After that I didn't go out much. Fact of the matter I didn't go out at all. I found the Old Man's library, that had been there all the time, and started reading. I read Thackeray and Dickens and Bennett and Wells and Conrad and Hergesheimer and Lewis. There was a lot in their books about what was worrying me, and for a while I wasn't too proud to get educated second-hand.

∗ 7 ∗

THE football was an accident, and as you might expect, came from some ideas Denny got. The day after the big afternoon on the bay he was due to leave for Frederick, but didn't. Baltimore Polytechnic, where I had entered the year before, opened, and you'd think Frederick High School would have opened too, but he didn't start for it, and every time I'd see him there'd be a lot of mysterious talk about something he was cooking up. Then one Sunday his parents were in town, and they came over to the house. Then I was called in to answer questions about my teachers. Denny's mother was a tiny little woman, that smiled and listened to what everybody said, but his father was a big, two-fisted customer, that wanted attention whenever he talked, and what he wanted to know about was physics. So it turned out that Denny was so serious about engineering, and the course so limited at Frederick, that it was practically a necessity that he check in at good old Poly, where I was, and where everything of that kind was wonderful. Now this holy consecration that had come over him was news to me. I think I've mentioned I've a mechanical gift myself, and I was hep, even if they weren't, that his lech for cam shafts and turbines and belts was about as hot as last night's potato, and what he didn't know about them would fill a public library, and what he did would go on one side of a rubber washer, with plenty of room for his autograph. So when it was all fixed up about Poly, I took him out into the garage, and threw on the squeeze. "What is it, smart guy?"

"Weren't you listening? As *prerequisite,* for all *engineering,* every one of these *technical* schools put physics *first* on the list, because—"

"I'm asking you, what is it?"

". . . Well look, I could show you about this mechanical stuff, but—"

"All right, show me."

I threw open the tool chest of my car, which at that time I carried under the seat, and he looked at it. I pointed at a Stillson wrench and said: "What is it?" He looked uncomfortable and said: "So all right. What difference does it make?"

"Listen, this is not *them*. It's me. Talk."

"It could be football."

"Football?"

"It's a game. Or feetball, maybe you call it."

"And?"

"Maybe I'm going out for it."

"Why here?"

"Why not?"

"Why not Frederick?"

"Does anybody pay attention to Frederick?"

"Who pays attention to Poly?"

"Everybody. . . . Listen, dope, you think I'm passing up all that moola? It's amateur, sure it's amateur. Just the same, they slip you. Don't tell me they don't."

He was awful sure that he was on the trail of something big. "To cut in, you've got to have a rep, and the only one place to get that rep is in some high school that gets in the papers. For Frederick you could play till you dropped and not one scout from anywhere would come to see you. Poly, though, that's different. So—engineering, physics, what's the dif? You got to tell 'em something."

Of course that made sense. That you could tell your father the truth and not fool him wouldn't occur to you at that age. Well, can you? If Denny had come out with that stuff about football, what would his father have said? That he was crazy, as of course he was. Just the same a crazy guy came for a good time too, and now and then, not too often but sometimes, a crazy horse wins.

Denny didn't have his growth yet, but he wasn't far from it, and at least he looked like something that ought to be playing football. He was about medium height, five feet eight or nine, but stocky, specially in the chest and upper legs. His waist was small, but his torso bulged out above it, and from his hips to his knees he was thick, specially in back, so his hindside stuck out like a girl's. But you had to see it to believe how fast he could pump his legs along, and after he went out for practice and I stood around watching him, I suddenly got it through my head that maybe he was right, he could be going places. The coach must have thought so too, because pretty soon he had Denny standing by the first team to learn formations. And then sure enough, on Friday, when we played our first game, with an outfit I'll call Calvert, there was Denny in the opening line-up, at right halfback. But on running, blocking, passing, and kicking, everything except tackling, he was as bad as he could get and still have on a suit. Toward the end of the second quarter he got yanked, and Gus Schoenfeld, who had had the job in the first place, was put in, and Denny wasn't put back. That ended his career, for the time being anyway, in spite of his big talk, his limp, and his alibi, which was that he had turned his ankle on the kick-off. He kept going out for practice, but was shoved over to the third team, or the ninth maybe, some outfit that the coach never even saw.

But I kept wondering why. In the first place, I'd tangled with him a lot, and he could take it, I knew that. Maybe he folded after round one, but for that long he was a tornado. And in the second place, there were those tackles he made. Football's rough, every part of it, but the tackle can't be faked. A guy that'll come up fast, slip past the interference, line out his runner, then cut him down and really cut him down, so he's on the grass and the ball is dead, that guy has something. Mind, I don't say he's much good to his team yet. Tackling's defensive, and you can't win games with a 0–0 score. For that you need touchdowns, but if they take more than the guts that tackling takes, they don't take any less either, and that's what crossed me up. Because that much Denny had. And yet, even in Scrubville where he was now, he couldn't make two yards before he was thrown. Then after a while I saw what the trouble was, and as usual it came from a slight case of looky-looky-looky. On defense that was all right, because on busting up plays he could show off fine and nobody did it better. But on offense, advertising how fast he could run, shooting past his interference until he was away out front, that may have been a fine way to lead a parade but it was a poor way to hit a line. Because then the line hit *him* and it was the same old story: second down, ten to go. I argued with him about it, and he got hot and said he knew what he was doing and what counted was speed and he had it and he meant to use it and soon he'd get the recognition that was coming to him. I said he should follow his interference, and I even put on a suit and went out there, got myself put in the squad that he was in, and because I could run a little too, made the backfield. When I was part of his interference I'd try to keep him near me, but it was no soap. And then one time when he was out in the open, with no protection, some kid piled into him head-on, and it was an hour before they could get him quiet, from the hysteria the shock brought on, and he was so ashamed of the way he had blubbered that he came over that night and at last asked me to lay it out for him, what he had to do.

So I drew him some pictures of the plays and what he ought to be doing, and he studied them and tried to reform his character. Then at night we'd slip over to the park and try a few things. I'd trot and he'd follow, and no matter how I'd duck or turn or twist, he'd stay with me. Then we'd step up the speed, until we looked like a lunatic and his shadow zipping around under the trees. Then we'd reverse it and I'd follow him. Then we thought we better try a little blocking, and right there, trying to figure things out by electric light, was where I learned what was to make me famous a second time. There's more bunk going around about blocking than anything else in football, and it's seldom done right, and I came to the conclusion, fooling around out there with Denny, that the trouble was that guys tried to do too much. I mean, from what's said to them in practice, they get an imaginary idea they're to aim for some spot about three feet ahead of the tackler, so when the lines cross they'll catch him in the middle and spill him cold so the runner can go on for a touchdown. And occasionally that's how it happens. But mostly what they hit is fresh air first and green grass second, and the runner gets smeared. So I thought: Why not aim for the tackler? Why not just bump him? If you bump him hard enough it takes him out of the play but not necessarily you, if you hold your feet.

So that's how we did, and from the speed we both had, and the weight we got into it after we caught the hang of it, it looked like we were going to be bad news for somebody, sooner or later.

The day we began pulling our stuff with the third team Denny went down for so many touchdowns everybody kind of lost count. But the word must have been sent over, because pretty soon the coach was there and next day Denny was back with the first squad, and I was right at his side. So our next game was with an outfit I'll call Chesapeake, and we went over to the stadium with paper streamers on our cars and making quite a little noise. What they did to us was murder, for about a quarter and half the next quarter. In our stands was nothing but gloom, because they ran up three touchdowns on us before we could turn around, and kicked two goals. Denny and I sat with the other subs on the bench, and it wasn't till the third touchdown had been made that we got sent out, both of us together. "Don't forget to report to the referee." A fat chance we'd forget. They called an off-tackle slice, which was what they'd been doing so well with before, and Denny busted it up before it got to the line of scrimmage. Second down, twelve to go frontwards, but only thirteen backwards, to be sitting on their own goal line. They tried it again and Denny smashed it again, a little quicker that time. Third down, fifteen to go frontwards, ten to the rear. The fullback dropped back. So did we, me and Denny, he to take the kick, I to cover. But when he caught it he did just what I'd told him to do. He let me lead him, headed for the sideline, for maybe ten or fifteen yards, with the whole Chesapeake team coming over at us, and our guys splitting up to block them.

When they were nearly on top of us I cut right, hit it up, and let them see, for the first time, how fast Denny could run. They all cut over, but of course losing speed as they went. As soon as I saw they were going to pass to our rear I let them go. They'd never catch Denny that day. I ran on, headed for the kicker, who was laying back as safety man. I aimed and caught him. He staggered and I did. It jarred me so bad I thought I'd never get my breath. But that was all Denny needed. He hooked it up, and before I even got the ring out of my ears there he was over the goal line. We did it three more times.

The street was jammed with girls after we dressed, and I don't think Denny even thought about me, or knew I was there, or even considered thanking me. He was gone before I was even through the mob, and I drove home alone. But by accident, I put it over on him anyhow, anyway in the papers. They had pictures of him, that had been taken earlier in the season, when he went up with the first squad. But they had none of me, except the other stuff, with the Little Boy Blue suit and the Come Blow Your Horn collar. So that hit them funny, and there was I, smeared all over the Saturday-morning sport pages. My aunts called people up on the telephone, and I could listen and feel a little proud. My father kind of passed a few remarks at breakfast, and seemed pleased. Myself, I began to get that tingly feeling again, that I hadn't had in a long time. I went out and bought an extra *Sun* and clipped the story out and went upstairs and wrote Miss Eleanor and put the clipping in with the letter.

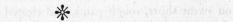

College, after three years at Poly, taking Denny over goal lines, catching his passes, and protecting his kicks, was just a matter of calling our shots. Just like he said he would, we got bids from all over, especially from Alabama, Southern California, and Georgia, with U.S.C. indicated, if football was what we wanted, but none of them indicated, if we were thinking about something else. I didn't mind glory, but it wasn't getting me anywhere either, as I wanted to go on with the mechanical stuff I'd had at Poly, and the football schools weren't right for it. Denny was all hot for U.S.C., as Howard Jones was alive then, and he was plenty big. But then things settled themselves, in a way that was all right for me and terrific for Denny. At that time, Maryland was doing a little better at football than it does now, as Curley Byrd wasn't president yet, but just coach, and he didn't turn out many flops. Then after a game we played in 1927, we were brought down to the Belvedere Hotel to meet him, and Denny fell for him hard. Maryland didn't hit me at first, but after I went to College Park and found out they were pretty good in mechanical engineering, I decided for the deal. So in 1928, after we graduated from Poly, we entered, shared a room in a dormitory that looked out on the Washington Road, and checked in for the freshman squad.

At that time Byrd was in his late thirties, but I think he still could have held a job on most teams himself, college or professional. He was a little heavier than he had been when he played, but he was something to look at, tall, straight, with high color and a mane of curly hair that had been black, but was getting gray, and now, of course, is completely white. He gave us plenty of time, even if we were only freshmen, and taught us stuff we'd never had before. So we weren't too proud to get on the field early, boot a few, and do a little passing. And as soon as the snow melted in the spring, we put on sweat shirts, rough pants, and cleated shoes, and got out there for a little more of it. I had my growth then, the same six feet I am now, and weighed 170, though I got a little heavier later.

So, early in October of our sophomore year, when at last we could play on the varsity, all of a sudden Denny was an A.P. dispatch, on practically everything he did. But I was a special article, with pictures and inside dope. I mean, they fell for me, and specially the coaches did. I was that player they prayed for, that did everything right, and was even better helping somebody else than at doing stuff himself. I was a big shot once more, and would get clippings and postcards and boxes of fruit from Miss Eleanor, and felt pretty good.

One day in early November we had played Yale and tied, 13–13, by something I'd done as it happened, when I hooked a pass and made a forty-yard run. We were given our tickets from New Haven back to College Park, but separate instead of club, so we could stay in New York if we wanted to, take in a show or something, and be back Monday. So Denny and I took our bags to the McAlpin, but we couldn't get in and went to another place a block or two away. We went upstairs, brushed and came down, and then sure enough, there by the newsstand, he picked up a couple of girls. On that stuff, by now, he counted me out, so he went off with them and I took a walk. On Broadway, around Fortieth Street somewhere, I saw a place I liked and went in and had dinner, then went down to Loew's State where I had sung years before. But I didn't like it, so I came out and called Miss Eleanor. There was no answer. I started to go back in, but was restless and went out on the street. Then I caught a cab to the hotel. I still had a paper, and I thought I'd drop her a note and enclose the picture of myself being a hero.

The desks in the writing room were in pairs, facing each other over kind of a low partition, and opposite me was a blonde girl in a black suit and hat, writing letters too. Her pen wasn't working so I handed her one from my side and she wrote two letters and stuck a dollar bill in each. "Aren't I the big-hearted, generous thing, passing out money like that? Oh well, easy come, easy go. I put over a fast one on a whole-

sale house today, and then won ten bucks on a football game,
so—"

"Which game did you see?"

"Yale-Maryland. Felt like a ride and went up there."

"You go to college?"

"I—? Well now, that *is* sweet of you. But you'd better take
another look. I'm an old widow with two children—that's
where the money goes." She held up the letters, one addressed
"Master," the other "Mlle." The last name on each letter was
Lucas. "Then you're Mrs. Lucas?"

"That is correct."

"My mistake."

"But I'm not in the least offended. Is it really possible, even
under these soft lights, that I look like somebody going to
college?"

"I took you for a co-ed."

"But you—*you* go to college?"

"Yes."

"Don't you have a name?"

"Don't you know it?"

"Why—I never saw you before. Or have I?"

I picked up the picture that I'd cut out for Miss Eleanor,
and handed it over. She gave a gasp, put it down, stared at
me. "But of course! . . . The wallop you gave me today—I'm
still not over it! And you're just a baby."

"Well—thanks."

"Don't you like being a baby?"

"Would you?"

"I did."

"That's right, I—sort of said the same, didn't I?"

"And I loved it."

"Then thanks again. This time, real thanks."

"I think I owe you something."

"You certainly do."

"I'm not talking about the ten dollars you helped win for

me—I bet Maryland would score—though that I can use. Something else. What I felt looking at you out there, with that taffy hair shining in the sun, and the heavy determined look on your face. Did anybody ever tell you how your head cocks to one side?"

"Hadn't heard of it."

"And when the other team is up to something you stand there for all the world like a cat watching a mouse hole. Then your shoulders go forward. Then something happens to your jaw. Then you spring. Then the cat's no longer a cat. He's a tiger. . . . Let's go to some club."

"All right, but I'm taking you."

"It's *I* who owe *you*. And besides, I'm a very successful widow, as I'll probably tell you all evening, now we've discussed you a little bit. Quite a high-pressure girl, and today I put something over, as I think I said."

"I'm not exactly a failure, myself."

"Well, listen to him!"

"I too can pick up a check."

"Can't we match for it?"

She was standing beside me and we both laughed. Then her eyes crinkled up in a way that made me like her even better than I had liked her, and we both got out quarters and cupped our hands and rattled them around. "You're matching me, Mrs. Lucas, and if you win the drinks are on me." So she won, and I got up and bowed, and she picked up her letters and I put the clipping in mine and stamped it and sealed it. Then we went out and across the lobby to the mail chute. Then she headed for the elevators. "I'll have to put something on."

"I have no evening clothes with me."

"All right, but I can't go in a suit."

"Then I'll wait here."

"Why? Come on up."

It was my first contact with a suite, because while my father

always took one, it was on account of the gang he always
had with him, his sisters, me, and like as not some friends,
and I hadn't known that one person, if they just take that
sitting room extra, can have anybody up there they please.
She was on the ninth or tenth deck, her windows overlooking
the Hudson, and as soon as she turned on the radio she ex-
cused herself and went in the bedroom. I sat and listened and
looked out at the lights, but it seemed to me my heart was a
little high in my throat, and why I didn't exactly know.
Everything was straight down the middle, exactly according
to Hoyle. And yet here we were, the two of us alone together
in a strange city, and I was excited. The buzzer rang and the
bedroom door opened a little bit. "Will you see if that's the
boy? I thought we could have something before we started.
Just let him in and ask him to wait."

I opened the door, and a bellboy was there with a pitcher of
ice, some fizz water, and two glasses. She came out in a kimono
and paid him and he went. Then she went into the bedroom
and came out with a pint of rye. "It's prescription stuff, so it's
all right. You like it plain or highball?"

"Highball."

I'm glad, looking back on it now, that I said nothing about
training. For all I knew, this was about nothing whatever, but
if it was about anything at all, it was a lot more important
than football. She made the drinks, then sat across from me
with the cocktail table between, and talked about herself. Her
husband had been in the hard-coal business, the mining end,
but died on a trip to Cuba. They had lived in Easton, Pennsyl-
vania. She had to do something, and got a job in their big
department store. Soon she was children's buyer, and had come
piling to town yesterday to stop shipment of stuff ordered for
Christmas. She seemed pretty stuck on herself that she'd
found a clause in the contract to let her off the hook, on account of some delay in deliveries. That there was any connection between those toys and my stock never entered my

mind, and fact of the matter, I'd been too busy running, kicking, and passing to pay any attention to finance. They tell me now it was all over the front pages, but if so, it must have been on days when I was looking for my picture inside.

So I just listened, sipped my drink, and once or twice, for no reason I could see, my heart would give a little bump. After a while she said she'd better get her things on, then drank out and went in the bedroom. I tried not to see it but my heart kept reminding me: she hadn't closed the door. Pretty soon, sounding like a homesick foghorn, I heard myself say: "You need any help?"

"No, thanks. . . . Of course now, wanting a little help, that might be different."

Somehow, my legs took me in there. She was in a little pair of filmy pants, bra, shoes, stockings, and nothing else, standing in front of the mirror looking at herself. She had a round, perky little figure, and it did things to me. She stood first on one foot, then on the other foot, with her hand on her hip and one little finger sticking out. Then: "For an old woman of twenty-five, I *do* look young."

"You look young, beautiful and—kissable."

"What are you trembling about, Jack?"

"Am I?"

"The bubbles in that glass are making a regular razzle-dazzle. If it shakes any worse the ice will be clinking."

"Reaction, maybe. Hard game today."

"Why don't you ask why I'm trembling?"

"All right, why?"

"Reaction—or something. . . . I knew we weren't going out, Jack. That we were just pretending. So I could blow smoke at you and muss up your hair—will you *ever* stop pasting it down like that? It would have a nice wave if you'd *let* it wave. I knew all that, but I never *did* anything like this."

"Did you say children?"

"That's different. And *you* never did, either. All right, I suppose it's the worst insult you can offer a man, to insinuate, or even hint that he could be anything but an expert on the subject. Just the same, I know what I know. And I want it like this. It's a lot sweeter that you come to me—as a little child might. As a little taffy-haired boy entering a new and beautiful garden, a little forbidden, and utterly mysterious. . . ."

"Mrs. Lucas, what is your other name?"

"June."

"June, come here. . . . It's all true, what you know."

"Does it hurt, to admit it?"

"No."

I told her about the car, the way Denny and I had chased girls, and the afternoon on the bay. She listened, then went to the window and stood looking up at the stars. Then: "Jack, I'm so glad it made you sick! . . . I guess I understand it, how those girls felt, how your friend felt—I wasn't born yesterday. They want to be exalted but all they're capable of is to be excited. What was it Wilde said? 'Each man kills the thing he loves'—? Except that such people don't kill it, they merely befoul it. I'm proud of you that you didn't and couldn't. Tonight is a night you can never have twice, and it's wonderful you saved it—for me. I'm happy it's me. And that it's silly, romantic, and cockeyed. Can I give you one little ideal, I'd like you to keep? . . . Let it always be beautiful. Don't *ever* befoul it."

She kissed me then, and through the night spread the color of the moth.

* 8 *

THE rest of that fall, I guess we played some football, but who we played and how it came out I wouldn't know. I wrote her or wired her or sent her something every day, and then after the Hopkins game, which was played in Baltimore, I called up Doc Henry, that had tended me ever since I could remember, and got him to certify by wire to the college that I needed a little toe-nail-ectomy, something like that. Then without any more than calling up the house, I beat it for the station and took the train for Easton. I saw her a little sooner than I expected. I got in late at night, and next morning went down in the dining room and had breakfast, wondering if I could ever make the clock go around until it would be time to ring her telephone. But I had sent her a wire I was coming, and when I looked up, who should be there, following the waiter over to my table, but her, even younger-looking than she had been, with a little brown hat over her blonde hair, a fur coat, and a flower for my buttonhole. I was so glad to see her I could hardly eat my eggs. "Well, June, what would you like to do? I put a few lies on the wire and had a doctor send some, so I'm free till this time next week, if you are. I mean, we played our last game yesterday, and I've fixed it so I'm not due back to the kiddy-pen until after the Thanksgiving holidays."

"Who won, by the way?"

"We did. . . . And I have a suite. Would you like to see it?"

". . . Jack, I'm afraid I can't."

"Why not?"

"For the same reason I'm here so early to head you off from coming to see me. So I won't have to have you at my house. . . . Jack, it happened. If it just took us by surprise so we had a lovely night—oh, all right, two lovely nights and a long, dreamy day—and I'm not ashamed. Life is like that, and it has little lyric poems in it, as well as other things. But a lyric is one refrain, and there's no second verse. I loved you, for one week end, as beautifully as I'm capable of loving. But I couldn't go on with it. And not here. I forgot to tell you, I guess. I'm prominent. I belong to clubs and things. I have friends, who wouldn't understand. And you'd be most difficult to explain."

"Why?"

"Well—who are you?"

"A guy in love."

"Yes, but—they'd expect to know more."

"All right, tell them more."

"What, for instance?"

"A guy in love that you're engaged to."

"That wouldn't do."

"People get engaged, you know."

"Grown women, with children, don't get engaged to babies going to college—or if they do, they don't expect anybody to believe it. What they get taken for is what they are, somebody's sweetie. And that I won't have."

"All right, a guy in love, that you're married to."

"*What?*"

"They get married, too."

"When?"

"Today."

"The bureau's not open on Sunday."

"Then tomorrow."

"Jack, please be serious."

"I am."

I began to lean on it, then, to get it through her head that I meant business. I told her about myself, the money I'd made singing, the way I was going ahead at the mechanical engineering, and all the rest of it. I said we'd sell my stock, if that was what we'd have to do, and she could come with her kids and live at College Park, or I'd come to Easton and make a deal with Lafayette to play football. Or, I said, I'd quit school and we'd start over, here in Easton or wherever. She looked at me sharp when I spoke of the stock, asked me some questions, and said I'd better check on it, as things had happened. Then: "Jack, I see I'll have to tell you the truth. Let's go up to your suite."

So we went up there and she called her home and told the maid she wouldn't be in until supper. Then she was in my arms and it was late afternoon before we did any talking. But when she started she hit it on the nose: "Jack, I think I'm going to get married."

"To me?"

"No."

"Well—that's making it plain, so a guy can understand it. When did all this happen, or do you mind my asking?"

"It hasn't happened."

"You're just considering?"

"Not even that. But—it's being considered."

"I see."

"A woman knows, I suppose, when something of that sort is in the wind, and I'm quite sure at the proper time, in the proper way, I'll be asked. I've done nothing with you I'm not free to do, nothing I'll feel bound to mention, as it concerns nobody but ourselves. Just the same, it makes sense, and you don't."

"Why not?"

"You're a baby, for one thing."

"Just an infant. But why does 'it' make sense?"

" 'It' was a friend of my husband's, and he's known me since I was married, and he's fond of the kids, and they're insane about him, and—I hate to bring this up, but it's important: He's very rich, and—"

"I got it now."

"I don't think you have."

"Do you love him?"

"Not as I love you, here and now."

"But, he's rich—"

"Jack."

"What?"

"Stop being offensive."

"Am I?"

"Yes. . . . If I were myself alone, and you asked me to do this mad thing, I don't say I wouldn't. I might. It's mad enough, to be with you, like this. But I'm not myself alone. I have children, family, friends, position, all sorts of things to think of, that I will not give up. To have you I must give them up, for as you've said, it will involve a complete new start. With him, I do nothing much about it, and life goes on, pleasantly, sensibly, satisfactorily. And one other thing: When did riches become so loathsome?"

"All right."

"They're the foundation, at least moderate wealth is, of practically everything people want out of life, and this idea they're so horrible, that a woman should never consider them, is just plain silly. Of course, that's a man's idea. No woman ever had it."

She put her arms around me and came close. After a long time she said: "It's not so terrible now, is it?"

"I just hate it."

"You won't."

"Time the great healer, I suppose?"

"Partly. Partly that after you've thought it over, and the romance has palled, you'll be turning handsprings I did marry somebody else. Because you're not ready yet, for a wife and two children that aren't even yours. You'd have to quit school, and I'd have to keep on with this job I've got, and—a lot of things. But, Jack."

"Yes?"

"Send me one red rose a year."

"All right."

"You love me?"

"Yes."

I guess trains run between Baltimore and Easton, because if they had one to take me there it looks like there'd be one to take me back. But I don't remember any train, any change at Philly, or anything of that kind. All I remember is wandering around that night, on a bridge over some river, on a street with picture shows on it, and up and down a hill near Lafayette College, trying to get through my head what was going to happen, so I could kill what I felt for her and get used to it she was going to marry somebody else. As to what it meant, from where he sat, if he ever heard of it, that she'd go around with him and then spend a week end with me, I tried not to think and I can't even make sense of it now. I guess, when you come down to it, if it was cockeyed enough, it could be what she said, a lyric, to be sung once and then forgotten. Then next day, Monday, I was home, in my room, going through the whole thing again. I thought it was funny my aunts had so little to say, specially about running off after the football game. But they just said hello and asked me no questions, and the house was so still you could hear the kids playing outside. Then along toward dark I heard my father's voice downstairs, and Nancy called that he wanted to see me.

He was in the study, and didn't look at me when we shook hands. He had nothing to say about the football game, or anything, until I had sat there some little time. Then: "Jack, I've bad news for you."

"Yeah? What about?"

"Your securities."

". . . Oh. I've been hearing about them."

"Then you know of the crash?"

"What crash?"

"Of Black Tuesday, as they're calling it."

"I've been—playing football."

"Yes—I should have congratulated you."

"It's not important."

He began, then, telling me about the stock-market drop, twisting his face with his hand, or untwisting it, maybe. He told me about this stock and that I'd had, how some of them had been sold and replaced with others, how he'd watched the dates so I'd always have dividend checks coming in, some due one month, some another. It seemed to give him quite a lot of satisfaction I'd had some profit on some of the deals, and that for four or five years now I'd been cashing dividend checks at the rate of twenty or thirty dollars a month. "But—I'm broke, Dad, is that it?"

"I don't know yet. I didn't do what many did, throw everything overboard for salvage value. I thought it over, I even resorted to prayer, I'm not ashamed to confess. And I decided if I held on, at least the stock was the stock. If, as, and when, the market recovers, it'll be there, it'll have a value, and it'll pay dividends, or so we hope. Except, of course—"

"Come on, let's have it."

"Some I carried for you on margin."

"And—?"

"It's gone."

"Well, what does the totalizer say?"

"I have the list here. . . . It says, at the prices I paid for it, there's three thousand dollars odd of stock in the clear, and two small government bonds. What any of that is worth now I'd hate to say. It could be sold, I guess. Whether dividends will continue, that we don't know. But, disregarding the future, considering only now—it's gone."

"Everything?"

"Practically."

"Well, that's that."

"Jack, it tortures me, it humiliates me, it—stultifies me, that I have to tell you this, after the issue I made of it. I'd give my right hand not to, for I think you'll believe me when I say if I could draw the money from the bank and hand over what I lost for you, I'd do it. I can't. I haven't told you everything. There's more. I myself am heavily hit. I said nothing to you, but I've expanded. With your friend Denny's father, I leased a lot, on Mt. Royal near the Automobile Club, and started a big garage, with general service, pit for car wash, pumps, tanks, jacks—an installation in six figures. We were unequal to it alone, naturally, and went to a bank. And since this they're pressing us hard. And while we've raised something—how I simply *won't* tell you—we're still in frightful shape. The big service station is completely gone as a possibility at this time. The agency, the North Avenue place, I keep, but it's—involved. Heavily. All I can say is, when I can, if I ever can, I shall regard your funds as a debt, and you shall—"

"Look, everybody makes mistakes."

"—be paid. Now, as to college—"

"I have a deal. If I want it, there'll be a job."

"What kind of a job?"

"I don't know. They've got ethics now, though, whatever they are, and I can't just play football."

"But you can finish?"

"Oh, sure."

"Thank God for that."

"Don't worry about me."

"Sam Shreve shot himself, if that helps."

"I'm sorry to hear it."

"He—gave us the benefit of his best judgment, but it wasn't good enough, let us say."

"That often happens."

I went back to my room, lay down again, and thought of what she had said, about checking up on my stock. That seemed about all it amounted to: one more thing to remind me of her. As to being broke, that didn't seem to mean anything, and as for his losing my money for me, I didn't hold it against him. But it seemed funny to me, from the brush-off I gave it, that he wouldn't know there was something on my mind, and at least ask me what it was. Well, why couldn't I *tell* him what it was? If I knew that, I wouldn't be writing all this up.

Almost at once, from a house where things were done in a freehanded way, it turned into a house that needed money, where everybody drew deep breaths, let them out trembly, and went whole days without looking at each other. It was the same up and down the street, all you heard at the drugstore on North Avenue, or anywhere. Denny felt it, and it was the first time I found out what his father did, besides going to Europe all the time. He was an investor. He had inherited property from his father, a cement works somewhere near Catoctin Mountain, where Lee and McClellan tangled just before Antietam, and then branched out into contracting, road-building, bridge-building, and stuff like that. But he let the superintendent attend to construction, and concentrated on backing businesses, or buying into them, or foreclosing on them, as some said, and taking his profit on those that panned out. So that was how he and the Old Man came to be mixed up in the Mt. Royal Avenue thing. Mt. Royal Avenue, in Baltimore, is a continuation of Mt. Royal Terrace and the same street they've got in every big city, the center of the automobile trade. The Old Man was a little ahead of his day, but he saw the need for what is now called super-service, with every kind of work done on the spot and none of it sent out, and troubleshooting on a twenty-four-hour schedule. That kind of location cost money, the equipment cost money, and the stock cost money. But Mr. Deets got hit too, because he was one hundred per cent in the market, with no sidelines for a cushion if something went wrong. One day he was rich, the next day he was a bum, or as near it as a guy like that, with forty-seven connections, ever really gets. Denny took it hard, and that I could have stood, but he also took it big. I mean, he'd drop around, and we'd take a ride, because at least I had the Buick that followed the Chevvie. Then he'd talk about what we were going to do about it. I didn't know, and I was still mooning about what happened in Easton. And then one day, just after Thanksgiving, when we'd gone back to college, he came in the room and closed the door in his same old hush-hush way. "Jack, I've been in town."

"Baltimore?"

"Washington. The Willard. And I ran into the gang from Fall River."

He didn't say Fall River. He said a city not far from Fall River, but I've got my reasons for not naming it. ". . . What do you mean, Denny, you ran into them?"

"Maybe on purpose."

"But not any *good* purpose, naturally."

"Listen, Jack, they need players."

"Why?"

"They had a row. Over a bonus that was supposed to be paid, or that some of them *said* was supposed to be paid, after their last game. And it wasn't paid. And the backfield quit."

"Sounds like a nice outfit."

"I said they need men."

"Stop feinting and jabbing around—"

"We could change our names, Jack."

"And our faces?"

"That's not so hard. . . . O.K., I talked to the manager and tonight I'm to call. They're due in New York, the Polo

Grounds, Sunday, and I think it's ours if we want it, fifty bucks and our fare apiece, and me, I'm in. I need fifty bucks."

"I'm listening, stupid."

So from then on, on Sundays, I played as a pro. Denny called himself Rex Atlas, but I settled for Jake Healy. We gave out that we were Washington "sand lotters," whatever that meant, but it seemed to get by. Denny worked on my brows with some kind of dye he got, so they'd be brown, instead of yellow. For the pictures, whenever they were taken, he made little pinches of cotton, that we carried up the sleeve of our jerseys, and would stick in our mouths, between the gum and the lip, upper and lower, and it certainly gave us a queer, buck-toothed look all right. Looking back at it now it seems funny. It didn't then. I felt ashamed, and if we were caught I didn't know what I'd say to Byrd. From then on I was doing all kinds of things I couldn't look myself in the eye over. I wasn't a cocky, tingle-fingered kid any more. I was a guy with muscles for rent, that took no pride in what he did with them, and wanted to talk about something else whenever the subject came up.

IT was in the Christmas holidays that Margaret called, and asked me to a party at the hotel New Year's Eve. I said I'd come if I could, as it was still heavy on my mind about Easton, and I wasn't much in the humor. But then, the morning of the party, it came out in the *Sun*, under an Easton date line, about the marriage, and it turned out she was even more prominent than she had said, because it was on the society page, and got some space. So I thought to myself: My young friend, you're going to the party. So I put on the black tie the Old Man had given me the previous Christmas, and went. I was surprised at the change in her, as I hadn't seen her in some months. She had slimmed quite a lot, so she wasn't so corn-fed and had a figure. And her face had lost the blobbiness it had had, so it was reasonably good-looking. She had on a pink dress that went nice with her dark hair, so I shook hands and admired the new shape, and she didn't seem to mind that kind of talk at all. When the music started I asked her to dance. Denny was there, and he'd got a load of the reconditioned shape, so while the fiddlers were tuning he whispered that by God, he was going to do something about that. But who she danced off with was me.

Then I asked her again, and after that again, and if there was anyone else she danced with I don't know who it was. Supper was served in the main dining room, where the hotel celebration was going on, and the party orchestra moved in there, hitting it up at one end of the room with the main orchestra at the other, so of course that meant I danced with her all the time. When the bugle blew and then both orchestras started *Auld Lang Syne,* I danced her out in the hall and around a corner, and as the clock struck twelve I kissed her. Her lips were hot and wet and soft. They said one thing and one thing only, and I let them say it. Then somebody ran by with a horn and we broke. "Jack, I'll have to go back."

"This hallway is no good."

"My studio might be better."

"Hey, what's this?"

"If you had come around, I'd have showed it to you."

"I've been away. What kind of a studio?"

"Music."

"Where?"

"Here. In the hotel. Just a suite, but they fixed it up for me. The piano is a Christmas present. It's a Steinway."

"Yeah, that we'd expect."

"Well, it's the best make there is."

"Of course. When do *I* see this studio?"

". . . You *want* to see it?"

"Sure."

"When?"

"Why—whenever."

"Tonight?"

"Why not—this morning?"

She looked at me and I danced her back in the dining room and pulled her up against me so hard I wonder she could breathe. She began to whisper. I was to say good night when the rest did, and get my things from the check room, and go out, and on up the street toward my car. But then in the basement of the hotel, on the Charles Street side, I was to find a door, with steps leading down to it. Over the sill was a key, and I was to let myself in and take a turn to the right and keep on to the freight elevator in the rear, and wait. So I followed instructions. The party began breaking up pretty soon, and I shook hands with her father and mother and asked for little Helen, who was spending the holidays with cousins in Trenton, relatives of the Cartaret the hotel was named after. Mr. Legg, as I've said, is a bit on the stuffy side, a slim little man with a white mustache that looked like something in an oil painting, but he patted me on the shoulder and acted friendly. Mrs. Legg was a gray-haired woman, kind of heavy-set, with light china-blue eyes that have the same trick Margaret's have, of never quite looking at you with a little set smile. She's a cold dame, but she kept me there five minutes at least, asking me questions about myself, especially whether I sang any more, and seemed to think it was a good idea I had quit. Then she told me all about Margaret's playing, and how "splendid" it had become, but how, nevertheless, she wanted my "opinion." What that was worth I couldn't quite see, but I was to find out. Then I shook hands with Margaret, and made a little speech that everybody could hear, about the wonderful time I'd had, and how I wished her the best for the coming year.

It seemed a year before there was nobody on Charles Street and I could slip down the steps and find the key and let myself in. It was dark down there, but I could see that on my left was a door leading into the barber shop, and on my right a concrete passage that went past furnaces, pumps, and electrical stuff. I turned right, like she said, and came to a cross passage, at the rear of the hotel, that led to the freight elevator, off in a corner. I went over to it, and I could see the car through the glass but she had said wait and I did. I don't know how long I waited, but it seemed that hell must at least be frozen over and thawed out again before I heard something. There'd be a click, then steps, then another click. All of a sudden I knew it was a watchman with his clock, and that he was down there, in the basement, where I was. I had a panicky two seconds, but then, as easy as I could, I opened the car door, stepped in, and coaxed it shut again. Then I stooped down, below the glass. The steps came on and stopped, then after a click went away. Then the car moved and I was going up.

At the eighth floor I could see her, through the glass. When I got out she began more whispering. I was to give her a head start, then slide around to 819 and go in without buzzing or knocking. When I had that straight she took a long look around and ducked around a corner, with a tiptoe, guilty look. I counted twenty, then followed along, watching the numbers. The door to 819 was open a crack, and I stepped in and closed it after me. Then arms were around me and lips were against mine and she was pressing up against me and trembling. It was dark, but by the light from the street I could see a grand

piano, some chairs, and at the far end of the room, a sofa. I
carried her to it, held her close, and kissed her some more.
She locked her arms around me and kept kissing me and
catching her breath in little short gasps. ". . . You surprised,
Jack?"

"At you?"

"That I can be so—demonstrative."

"Not with the it that you carried around."

"Really, Jack?"

"You always did get me."

"You never said anything."

"*Did* anything, you really mean."

"Well, you never did."

"With pigtails hanging down your back?"

"I'm as old as you."

"You're still pretty young."

"You really liked me?"

"Why, I used to stand in the wings while you were playing
Rachmaninoff Prelude and think how I'd like to put my arms
around you, from behind, while your hands were there on the
keyboard, and—"

"Yes, Jack? And—?"

"Like this."

With that I made my first grab at something that meant
business. She pushed my hand away, but I found a zipper and
slid it and it slid pretty easy. Then she stiffened. ". . . Somebody's outside."

She pulled up the zipper and I snapped on a light. She
wiped my face with her handkerchief. There came a knock
on the door. "Who's there?"

"Your milk, darling."

It was Mrs. Legg's voice and Margaret let her in. When
she saw me she acted surprised, but no more than surprised.
"Well, of all *things!*"

"Had to see the studio, you know."

"But of *course!*"

"Pretty."

"Lovely! . . . Pet, you *mustn't* forget this any more! She's started skimmed milk, Jack, and it's done such wonders for her, slendered her down so her figure is *divine*. One wouldn't believe it's one and the same *girl!*"

"It's taken weight off her all right."

"Well, Mother, do sit down."

"No, it's getting late—well, just for a minute."

She talked of the party, and how nicely the boys had knocked off the music, and quite a few things, and you'd have thought that a guy and a girl and a studio at three thirty in the morning were just one of those things that happened. But her eyes were cold, and they meant go, so after a couple of minutes I looked at my watch and gave an imitation of a whistle. Then we were in the hall and then in the elevator, going down.

"Jack, how *did* she—"

"Don't blame me. I laid low, even when—"

"I know you did! How *could* she know we were there? I told the board no calls until noon, then hung the don't-disturb card on the door, and I know *nobody* saw me go up—"

"I even ducked the watchman."

Margaret never paid much attention to what went on in the hotel, but later on, I found out if she had painted a green line from her bedroom to 819 she couldn't have left a plainer trail than by the don't-disturb card and the call block through the exchange, two smoke screens the old lady always kept an eye on. And when she pulled the freight car up to the eighth floor, which was reserved for women alone, and left it there, that made it simple. But we didn't know about any of that then, and all we did was stand there in the lobby and whisper, have a quick kiss good night, and make a date.

So I began going with her. It all turned out bad, and I've said mean things about her, and maybe will say more. It seemed to me, and still does, that she was a spoiled, self-centered girl, but of course what I really held against her, and what she held against me, was that while I liked her a little bit I didn't like her much, and not enough, after that one time, to pull her zippers, though of course I mumbled a lot about how wonderful it would be if we didn't have to do our courting in the Goldfish Bowl, as we called the studio from then on. If I could have lived my life as I wanted to live it, I don't think I'd have showed up at the Cartaret once a year. But I had no life to live. My money was gone, so those twenty dollars and thirty dollars every month didn't come any more. And I couldn't get any work. I was still an A-1 mechanic, and getting better from what I was getting in college, but there *was* no work. Even my father had none. In the house was nothing but gloom, whispers, and nerves. The Cartaret was a place to go, where there was something to do, and she was somebody to do it with. When summer came and Mr. Legg offered me a place on the desk I took it and tried learning to be a room clerk. I guess I did, somehow. Anyhow, I got so I could put up the mail in less than an hour, the worst chore a room clerk does. I figured out one thing: alphabetize everything, so all D. P. Jones's stuff comes together before you start putting it in his box. Then you don't have to look him up eight different times.

"Jack."

"Yes, Mr. Legg?"

"Let's talk about your future."

"Time somebody did."

"Have a cigar?"

"Thanks, I don't smoke."

"How many summers have you worked for us now?"

"Two."

"I thought it was more."

"No, my sophomore summer and last summer."

"You graduate this year, Margaret tells me."

"In June."

"What had you thought to do?"

"Well, I'm taking my B.S. in mechanical engineering, and I had thought of going to Detroit and trying to get started there, but the way I hear it, things are pretty shot in the automobile factories, with labor being laid off all the time, and no technical people being taken on, on account of their own men, the ones already laid off, having first call. Of course, until the last couple of months, that hadn't worried me, because I could have fallen back on football until things get better, but the cracked kneecap I got in the Georgetown game isn't improving. I don't limp, it's nothing that'll bother me, but it's taken about two seconds off my speed. I mean it's stiff. I—"

"That doesn't upset me at all."

"Yeah, but I played some pro, if you have to know."

"I suspected it."

"And—now that's out."

"I'm relieved. I think very little of sport."

"To me, it was a means to an end."

"May I stress that word 'end'?"

"It's ended, all right."

"Then we'll pay no more attention to it. Jack, you've impressed me most favorably, the short time you've been with me. How would you like the hotel business?"

"Well, what do you think?"

"I think you'd make a go of it."

"Is this an offer?"

". . . It could be. It could very well be. I'll go so far as to say I'd like it to be. But—you created the situation. It's you that's here morning, noon, and night, and it's you who would continue to create a situation if you came in here permanently. Jack, before we discuss offers, I'd have to know your intentions toward Margaret."

"Your feelings are inside, and I think you know about them. Your intentions are what you're going to do about them, and frankly, Mr. Legg, it wouldn't be fair to Margaret or you or anybody to put on an act that I wanted to do something about them when there's nothing I can do. My father's in a bad way. I've got no work, and I don't know of any work. So far as my intentions go, suppose you tell me."

"But if you had work?"

"Watch me."

"Then let's fix things up."

"O.K., I'd like a chance to get a little money together, say three or four or five months to pay off a few things that have come up in my senior year and bulge the bank balance up a little bit, and then, say around October or November—"

"Fine, Jack. I like your attitude. Ah, before you go, I'd like you to know her mother will be—shall we say?—relieved. Not only pleased, but *eased,* in her mind. To be perfectly frank, with Margaret having notions of going to New York and concertizing, we've been concerned."

"I don't think you need be."

"Why not, Jack?"

"I doubt if she's got it."

". . . So do we."

We were in his private office, a small paneled room with pictures of Charles Carroll of Carrollton and Francis Scott Key and some Cartarets in it, and he came over from behind the desk and leaned close to me and let me have it out of the side of the mouth in a way you wouldn't think a member of the Maryland Club would ever talk. ". . . We think she's kidding herself, and badly. Frankly, when Harold Randolph was alive and the piano seemed something for a young lady and one

could be proud of her but not alarmed about her, I was all for
it. But then when that vaudeville business started, and Randolph died and this new crowd came in at the Peabody—we've
been growing uneasy, uneasy, uneasy. Jack, am I making myself clear?"

Randolph was an F.F.V. that had run the Peabody Conservatory as long as anybody could remember. But somewhere
around the time I entered college he had died, and Margaret
had gone with some bozo from Texas that had pumped her
full of stuff about temperament, and I knew what Mr. Legg
meant. I just winked and he winked back. "Jack, suppose she
did have it? It's no life for a woman. I want her married. She's
crazy about you, so take it over. And Jack, I like that idea
of getting a little stake, so you're your own man. But don't
overdo. I mean, don't worry about money. Soon as you're
married, get a baby started, so she—you get it, boy, get it?"

He cackled and laughed and shook hands and opened the
door on a crack and peeped out and then opened a panel and
in there were bottles and glasses and fizz water. So we had a
drink and he laughed and clapped me on the back some more.
It sounds like one nice guy talking to another nice guy about
what had to be settled before they could do something nice for
a pretty nice girl, and I wish I could tell it that way. But what
I said, which was what I meant, makes no sense unless you
know what had happened, over at the college, the week before, on a Friday afternoon that Denny and I had to spend
there, on account of a test we both had coming up the next
morning. Denny had long since forgotten about engineering,
and switched over to psychology and business practice and
advertising and some more courses like that, that he could piece
together for a degree, but we were in the same calculus class
and they were throwing a test at us. We were both good at
math, and there was no need to bone the test, so it was just an
afternoon to kill. About three o'clock he came in our room
carrying a big carton, with a colored fellow behind him carry-

ing another, and he acted pretty mysterious about it. Come to find out it was beer, and where it came from I don't know, but if you ask me his father had given an order and then asked the bootlegger to stop by, on his way into the District, with a little for Denny. But of course, in a case like that, Denny would have to talk big about his "connections." That didn't bother me any. It was a hot day in April and I took the bottles out, then took one of the cartons to the drug store and filled it with cracked ice and came back and put the stopper in the basin and loaded some bottles in and put ice around them and pretty soon we were set.

So of course, nothing draws like beer, so it wasn't long before we had company. We didn't have many, not over four or five or six, because on a Friday afternoon nobody sticks around there that doesn't have to. But we had that many, drinking out of the bottlenecks after Denny used the opener, and getting kind of sociable, that is, all except Morton. Morton was known simply as Salt, and when it rained he poured and at all other times he poured, a thin, do-gooder line that got on everybody's nerves and of course only got worse with beer. However, nobody got sore at all, until after Cannon began his toasting. Who Cannon started to toast I don't know, maybe the college or Governor Ritchie or General Pershing, it doesn't make much difference and one guess is as good as another up to and including the Queen of Sheba. But where Salt began to look thick was on the toast to the class of 1931, that had graduated the year before. Cannon took a little trouble with it and it went something like this:

"To that noble aggregation, which beat us by one year down life's broad highway, the class of '31—may they always be right, but right or left, '31. Where, my friends, does one find such distinction, such achievement, as in the class of '31? I pause for a reply, not knowing where to look. Is highway construction our test of solid accomplishment? This outfit has pressed more bricks than Coxey's Army. Is it architecture?

Think of the buildings that are being held up by the class of
'31. Is it philanthropy? This outfit has panhandled more dimes
than John D. Rockefeller would be able to give away the
whole coming year. Is it agriculture? Think of the apples '31
has peddled in the streets, and only a year out of school yet.
Is it tonsoriology? A blind man could shave himself by the
shine on the seat of these bastards' pants. Is it—"

"I don't care for that."

"Salt, what have I said to offend you?"

"It's not what you say. It's how you say it."

"You mean my deep, mellifluous voice?"

"I mean your scoffing tone."

"Are you by any chance taking up for these sons of bitches
that showed not the least fraction of a human soul when we
got here four years ago, that razzed us and taunted us and
hazed us, that—"

"I don't take up for '31 at all. To hell with them! But if
they want work, there's still work to do—"

"Oh, yeah? Pray tell us."

Then Cannon asked Salt what he was going to do when he
got his dip. He said he was going with the Consolidated
Engineering Company, but it was quite well known that
Consol was owned by his uncle, and had contracts all over,
specially wherever the government needed dredges. That got
him the raspberry, and Cannon went on: "Here's to Admiral
Byrd!"

"Ray!"

"Babe Ruth!"

"Ray!"

"Jean Harlow!"

"Oh, boy!"

"President Hoover!"

"Hip, hip—"

"*Morituri, te salutamus!*"

But Salt had stood up when Mr. Hoover's name was mentioned, and that was when Denny swung. There was quite a roughhouse, and I guess it was five or six o'clock when I got it quieted down and all of them thrown out. But along around ten, when the beer had worn off and we'd had something to eat, I lay down and kept thinking about it. "Denny, what was that he said? That sounded like Latin."

"May be in the dictionary."

I thought I remembered the first word of it, and sure enough after a while I found it. "Denny, you know what i‧ means?"

"Not noticeably."

" 'We who are about to die salute you.' "

"Well?"

"Is that how he feels?"

"Why not? He's on the end of the plank."

"Is that how you feel, Denny?"

". . . I don't know."

"What are you going to do when we graduate, Denny?"

"Point of Rocks."

Point of Rocks is a place on the Potomac, thirty or forty miles up from the District on the Maryland side, where Mr. Deets had a little farm, but he used it mainly when he felt like fishing. That Denny would hole up there just gave you an idea how far things had gone in the way of jobs. Of course there hadn't been much out of him about pro football since I cracked my knee. It turned out in a professional game if he didn't have me to take him through the line he wasn't going through the line, so after getting the liver, lights, and gizzard knocked out of him a couple of times he didn't get called any more. "You *really* going to Point of Rocks?"

"Well, where the hell would I go?"

If it was the beer wearing off, or he'd been worrying, I don't know, but he was disagreeable and sounded bitter. That was when I got it through my head at last: if it could take the starch out of Denny, it was bad. So that's why I talked like

I did to Mr. Legg. That wasn't a nice kid talking to a nice father about a nice girl. It was a guy that was losing his nerve making the best of things he could.

✳ **10** ✳

ALL that time, not only after the New Year's party but before it, when I'd be booked to appear with Margaret or tagged for one of her parties or seeing her for one reason or another, little Helen was growing up. When Margaret and I first began doing shows together she was around two and couldn't talk yet. Just the same she knew me whenever I came, and I'd have to stand there and listen to her tell me all about it or anyway think she was telling me, and a little later, at the parties, I'd stuff her full of ice cream and the more I saw of her the more wonderful she thought I was and the more wonderful I thought she was. She was just a little tyke, with blue eyes and yellow hair, but I had never run into anything like her, for prettiness and friendliness and the smile that lit her up like a Christmas tree. When she was a little older we'd go out together, to the drugstore for a soda or wherever it would be, and we didn't exactly walk, but we did a pretty good sashay: her in front, dancing along backwards, me coming along behind, with a doll in my arms or one of the puppies on a leash or the stroller, so I could push her if she got tired. A little later we'd go to the picture show. Then a little after that, when I was in college and she was in the Sarah Read School around the corner, she'd see my picture in the paper and call me up after the games and want to know why I hadn't sent her tickets. I'd say she was a little young yet. It wasn't until after the New Year's party that I began coaching her in arithmetic. She was just naturally dumb at it, and there was some talk about it at dinner one night. Her father kept saying, "It's all right, we'll get a tutor," but Mrs. Legg was pretty disagreeable about it that Helen didn't *study* the subject, as she said. Then she got off a lot about the honors she had taken when she was a young girl at school, and you kind of got the idea she was sore because Helen wasn't a credit to her. I kept thinking how easy everything, the music at least, had been for me at that age when Miss Eleanor made a game out of it, and then I heard myself say: "Mrs. Legg, why can't *I* be her tutor?"

"*You,* Jack?"

"At least I know my math."

"Whoo!"

Margaret exploded like it was the funniest thing she ever heard in her life, and Mrs. Legg was crossed up because she wasn't in favor of a tutor. But Mr. Legg jumped at it. I don't know why, but my guess is that even at that time he had his eye on me, on account of Margaret's career bug, and this was just one more knot he could tie in my tether. The upshot was she was to come up to the house Saturday mornings, and I was even to get paid for it. I squawked at that, said I'd be glad to do it for nothing, but he was set that I had to get something, so we made it five dollars for two hours, ten to twelve.

"Well, of all the cheap, chiseling *suh-lugs,* my overgrown friend, you certainly take the hand-whittled *potato* masher!"

"Sit down and speak when I speak to you."

"Even gypping little chee-*yildren!*"

"Little hoodlums, more like."

"And for a *measly* five *bucks!*"

Hanging under some prints was a riding crop my father had had when he had chased the deer around Tara Hill, and I took it down and whacked her with it. Then we had some light scrimmaging around the study until Sheila came in with some cookies for the new pupil, when Helen turned from a brat into an angel, which was something she could do at the drop of a hat. "Oh, you darling! Cookies! I just love them!" She ran over and kissed Sheila, who didn't quite know what her cue was, so I took over: "Nothing to get alarmed at, Sheila. Just inculcating a little discipline around the classroom. but she's got a hide like a rhinoceros, so it's a little noisy."

"But, Jack! You could *injure* her!"

"Any change would be an improvement."

When we were alone again, she draped herself over my chair and told me what she thought of me for a while and I did the same for her and then I got out my big inspiration. It was an abacus, that I had got at a bazaar, as they call it in Baltimore, out on East Baltimore Street. They're a Chinese adding machine, with little red and green and blue and yellow and purple and black balls that slide on wires in a frame. I figured that with her eyes telling her how to add and subtract and multiply and divide it would be easier. "What is it, Mr. Loathsome?"

"You use it to count."

"You think I'm weak in the mind?"

"Yes, only more so."

"Well, I'll be—"

"So far, I figure the trouble has been that nobody, anyway nobody on the arithmetic assignment, has any idea how dumb you are. But I have. By dint of this hard application your mother keeps talking about, I have finally worked down to it, that alongside of you, a backward tree toad would look like a glee club of Einsteins, so—"

"Cookie?"

"O.K."

She stuck a cake in my mouth, picked up the abacus, shook it, smelled it, and tried it sidewise. "Cute."

"Listen, stupid, I have an idea."

"Then let's have it."

"That teacher of yours—"

"Lamson? She's a dope."

"However—"

"I owe it to her to do something with the subject. But *why?* Tell me that."

"You could harpoon her."

". . . I don't get this at all."

"I don't say, Miss Legg, that she's not a dope. If you ask me, they're all dopes. If they weren't dopes they wouldn't be teachers in the Sarah Read School. If you ask me the arithmetic's no good to you and you'll never have any use for it that a third assistant bank clerk couldn't straighten out for you in five minutes and no charge for the service. Just the same, there it is. The rule book says you've got to learn it. And if, all at the same time you could learn it and give this Lamson a nice kick in the teeth—"

"You mean, with this thing, I could learn?"

"Well, you could try."

Her face lit up the way it had when she was a little thing and you'd stuff lemon ice cream into her. She wasn't that little any more, but she certainly wasn't big. She was about medium, on height, but awful slim, even in the plaid skirt and red sweater she wore to make herself look thicker, and with the yellow curls hanging down her back in thick snakes. They had a little gold in them, and were soft and glossy and silky. Her eyes were blue, and right now they were dancing. Pretty soon she was cackling out loud, and I was. Putting one over on Miss Lamson seemed to be the funniest thing we could think of. I knew that if she, I, and the abacus could do it, Miss Lamson was due to have a surprise.

That, as well as I remember, was early in 1930, the end of my sophomore year, when I was twenty and she was ten. I held her on the abacus three or four weeks, to make sure she had things straight, but then she began doing it with a pencil. And then one day, as she was starting on the stuff I had waiting for her, she half closed her eyes, stared at the pencil, and said: ". . . Wait a minute."

"Take your time."

"Jack."

"Yes?"

". . . I can see that abacus."

"And?"

"I believe—I can do it in my head."

She read off the first problem, looked out the window for a few seconds, and gave me the answer. I figured it up. It was right. She zipped through the next problem and the next and the next after that, and had the answer before I could work it out on paper. Then we both said it at the same time: "Miss Lamson!"

Because she hadn't pulled any of her stuff for Miss Lamson yet, being regarded as kind of a hopeless member of the awkward squad, so she didn't get called on any more. We both had a sudden idea of what it was going to be like if she could do the stuff quicker than Miss Lamson could.

And then we had a perfectly hellish idea. At that time, on WFBR, there was an awful kid named Willie Saunders they found in the Roland Park School, that could do stuff in his

head for some kind of a cereal program they had Friday
evenings. So our idea was that Helen would challenge him.
The station was pretty leery of it, for fear she'd flop, and
wouldn't give it any build-up at all, but after we thought it
over that suited us fine, because that way we could spring it
as a surprise. So the night she was to go on, it wasn't much
trouble to get myself invited to the hotel for dinner. She got
permission to go to a movie, and around five forty-five I slid
by in the car and picked her up and hauled her to the station,
which was only a few blocks away. So around six fifteen I
showed up for dinner and put on a big act that I didn't want
to miss Willie Saunders. None of them had ever heard of
Willie, but they brought me in the Colonial Room where there
was a radio and all of them kind of kept me company, Margaret, and Mr. Legg, and Mrs. Legg, none of them quite
knowing what it was for, but taking my word for it Willie
was pretty terrific. So it wasn't long before the announcer gave
one of those jolly statements, and asked Willie if he minded
a little competition, and Willie, who had a wind-up so slow
it took him a minute to say anything at all, said: "If if if if
anybody thinks they can figure faster than I I I I I can they're
perfectly welcome to to to to to to try." So then the announcer
introduced Helen.

What she said I can't tell you because Mrs. Legg jumped up
like she'd been hit by a thousand-volt wire, and then Margaret
did and Mr. Legg did, and then they all turned to me. I
shrugged and spread out my hands, like I was just as buffaloed
as they were. Then we all closed in on the machine.

"Now, Willie and Helen, the government reports that coal
production for last week, final week of the month just closed,
was up one and one tenth per cent above production for the
preceding week, which in turn was up one and two tenths per

cent for the week before that, which in turn was up one per cent for the week before *that*. If production last week was eight million, eighty thousand, six hundred and forty tons, what was production the first week of the month?"

Willie began to sing it back at him: "The government reports that coal coal coal coal production for last week, final final final final final final—" She said nothing, but I could feel her eyes close and her mind focus on that abacus, while her finger tips played little tunes on her thumbs. Then, before Willie had even finished his song, she cut in with a bunch of figures.

"Right!"

The announcer fairly yelled it and from then on she mowed Willie down like a field of hay. By the end of the third question, he couldn't even talk, but sat there blubbering so bad you heard somebody mutter: "Better take him out," and that was the end of him. Then, when the announcer got chummy and said: "Well—well—*well*—Helen, you *are* a surprise. *Quite* a surprise! And where did you learn all this higher mathematics?" she shot it just like we had rehearsed it up: "All that I have learned or achieved I owe to my beloved teacher Miss Josephine Lamson of the Sarah Read School, East Read Street." But I could hear the shake in her voice that said she would explode if they would all kindly step out of the way so she wouldn't injure anybody.

I give you one guess how that set with the family, especially with Mrs. Legg, who never let you forget those "honors" she had taken in school, and was all hot, a little too hot if you ask me, for the girls to be a "credit" to her. We all went down to WFBR with Sandy, and got Helen, and brought her back, and when we got to the hotel who should be there, all excited and waiting for us, but Miss Lamson herself, and it knocked me over, that such a small slice of nothing could have been the cause of all the fuss. She was a tiny, dowdy little woman, in a rusty black coat and felt hat, maybe sixty years old, who giggled and laughed and took it all on herself that Helen had done what she had, and never even suspected that maybe there were a couple of other angles to it. To her, it was a surprise that Helen had saved up for her, nothing more. The rest of them, I'll say that for them, knew some pretty good coaching had been pulled, and Mr. Legg was plenty grateful. Margaret, at the picture show that night, kept whispering I was a "swell guy," and patting my hand, and in the studio, as long as her mother left us alone together, she was awful affectionate.

But the real celebration came next day, when Helen came up to the house as usual, and as soon as Nancy and Sheila and the Old Man had had their say, and we had the door closed she did a standing broad jump into my arms and I swung her around and we had the light scrimmage we generally led off with, meaning a general roughhouse. But it didn't last as long as usual, and pretty soon she pushed me over on the sofa and sat down beside me and began stretching her hand over mine like it was a piano keyboard and she was trying to touch octaves. She had small, slim hands, but she was always trying to measure them against mine. "Thanks, Jack."

"For what?"

"Everything. Un-dumbbelling me."

"That's impossible."

"But you did it."

"All we did was get back at Lamson. And did we—"

I started to cackle, but she wasn't laughing. She was looking at me in a bashful, self-conscious, ashamed kind of way, and I asked her what the trouble was. "Nothing's the trouble. But I want you to know I get it. That I know what it was you did for me—and it's been a lot. That's not so nice, to be a stumble-bum. Specially to that simpleton Lamson. Isn't she a dilly, now? Isn't she?"

"Well—how does it feel to be famous?"

"I'm not."

"Oh yes. Locally anyway. And rich, I imagine."

"No. Not on radio, if that's what you mean."

"But they pay! Big!"

"If you click."

"Well, what do you call clicking?"

"Willie clicks."

"You've ruined him."

"Maybe, but I'll never fill his shoes . . . I noticed something. I mean, last night I found out why he clicks. Jack, it's *because* he's so slow and poky and silly. When somebody *that* mopey can turn up with the right answers, it *is* amazing, not to say amusing and highly laughable. But me, I'll just be a smart brat—that is, if they try to promote me."

That's how it turned out. She got the right answers, but they didn't tune in. But somebody like that, of course she didn't need a tutor any more, so a little before my first summer working in the hotel I got fired. I missed her the worst way. I had got to look forward to those roughhouses.

The summer I graduated, right after I started working regular at the hotel, Mr. Legg took a place at Gibson Island, which is on the bay not far from Annapolis. The whole family stayed down there, though of course Margaret was driving into town all the time to buy this, that, and the other for the wedding. Every week end, naturally, I'd be invited. But it turned out that Helen, once more, needed help. Because, what with having a rep as a mathematical whiz, and actually being a mathematical punk, things had got crossed up at the school, and she'd been promoted too fast, and was in trouble again, this time with algebra. I'd hate to tell you how glad I was, that they'd send her up to me, at the hotel, by Sandy every day, so I could explain to her why $(a + b) (a - b) = a^2 - b^2$, and how upset I was, one of my first week ends at the island, at what Mr. Legg had to say about the people that had taken the cottage next door: "The Finleys, one of the best families in the state, Lee Finley's in the Fidelity and Deposit, she's a Dawson, from Prince Georges County, the boy, Dick, goes to Gilman—I was delighted when I heard who the place had been leased to. . . . But, Jack, that boy runs liquor. He's in and out with that boat he's got at all hours of the night, he has a pistol, and he's thick with Zeke Torrance."

"Who's he?"

"He runs the Log Cabin."

"Oh—that place near Glen Burnie?"

"That's the man. If Dick's car is parked outside of there, it might be a wild boy stopping for a drink. But when Zeke is down here, it's business, and Zeke has only one business. I complained about the pistol, but Finley only got disagreeable. It seems it's owned under permit, and the boy uses it only for target shooting as he's permitted to do. But—he wears it. It's on him all the time, and he goes around with a silly grin on his face, giving a fifth-rate imitation of some character in a ninth-rate movie, and I don't like it. And—he keeps tagging after Helen."

"*What?*"

"'Let's go get a soda,' 'Let's got to the picture show,' 'How about a swim'—"

"Does she *go?*"

"No. She thinks he's funny. But—I don't know anything in years that has made me so nervous. He keeps following her around, and *looking at her.*"

The next morning was Sunday, and Margaret wanted to fish from an outboard boat they had, so I was on the porch fixing hand lines, knives, and bait, and the rest of them were out front on canvas recliners, reading the papers. I had just checked my snoods when I saw this wild-looking boy cross over from next door, in dungaree pants and rough shoes and checked shirt. He was around seventeen I would say, fairly big, and heavy sunburned, with shaggy hair and a hangdog grin. He sat down, though I didn't notice anybody ask him to, and then Mr. Legg said something and Helen looked surprised and came inside the screened-in porch, where I was. "Well, Jack, what's the big idea?"

"Whose?"

"Dad's. 'Go put on your beach robe.'—?"

"The young visitor, maybe."

"Dick? He's a child."

"Little children got big eyes."

"And all this talk whenever Dick wants a date. 'We don't *want* her taken out yet, she's much too *young* to be going around.' What am I? Little Eva or something?"

"Going around with *him,* maybe your father means."

"Well, who would?"

"He's got to be told *something.*"

"But—"

She looked down at herself, where she was, just a sliver of brown in a wisp of blue bathing suit, and then went inside and I could see her looking at herself in a mirror. Then she came out with the robe and began putting it on. "I don't know my own strength, apparently."

I swear it happened that quick. What went in was a child, that you'd look at because she was pretty and graceful and friendly, but not for any other reason. What came out was a woman, only twelve years old yet, but one you couldn't take your eyes off of, for all the reasons there are. She wrapped the robe around her and knotted the belt, then rolled her eyes in a resigned kind of way and went switching out there.

By that time darling Dickie was gone, but when I got out there with my gear he was back, and had his gun on him, in a holster, over his right hip. He started to talk, but Helen kept snickering like he must be crazy, and Margaret and Mr. Legg and Mrs. Legg kept looking at each other in a nervous kind of way while he talked: "Honest, folks, I don't think you've thought this thing through. I'm not taking out Helen in any *formal* way, you understand. I'm only asking her to the *picture* show tonight. It's not like she was making her *debut* or something. And frankly I think it would be good for her. If you ask me, Mr. Legg, she doesn't go out enough."

"I wasn't asking you, Dick."

"Oh? Oh? Oh?"

The little grin kept coming and going, and Mr. Legg kept licking his lips and looking at the gun. I don't smoke, but there was a package of cigarettes in the sand and I picked it up and stuck a cigarette in my mouth and began slapping myself like I wanted a match. Then I stepped over toward Mr. Legg, like I would borrow one from him. Dickie paid no attention. I caught him on the chin with everything I had and he went down soft, which meant he was out. I unbuckled the holster, pulled it clear, then gave him some toe under the ribs. He rolled over. "Get up."

"What are you doing to me, you big—"

"I said get up."

I yanked him to his feet and he staggered around a little but pretty soon he could stand. Out of the tail of my eye I could see another boy, about his age but quite a lot bigger, come out of the Finley house and stand there watching. I gave Dickie a cuff on the jaw and said: "Now you cheeky little louse, suppose you get out and stay out or there'll be more of the same, only a lot more. And leave Helen alone. Don't speak to her or look at her or think about her, or it's going to be most unfortunate. And don't bring any more guns. What do you say?"

"So O.K., you hit me when I wasn't looking, you—"

I clipped him again and he went down and when he got up

I impressed on his mind he was to call me sir and he did it. Then he went stumbling through the sand to his house and the pal began looking at the marks on his face. Mr. Legg said: "Thanks, Jack."

"Sometimes it's the only way."

"I'll take that gun. I'm making an issue with Finley about it. This thing has gone far enough."

"I'll save you the trouble."

I swung the holster and gave it a heave and it and the gun went flapping through the air about a hundred feet out into Chesapeake Bay. That was the one dumb thing I did. Because I was no sooner unarmed than the pal said something and here the two of them come, one piling in on one side, one on the other. They hit me and I went down but jumped up and backed away. Mr. Legg said something about phoning the state police and Margaret and Mrs. Legg ran into the house. A shell clipped Dickie on the head and he ripped out some cussword and turned. My heart jumped when I saw it was Helen that had thrown it. Mr. Legg began shooing her into the house.

All that took maybe one second, maybe two or three. After I went down, Dickie did, and his pal did, and nobody moved fast, because in the sand you slid and lurched and tripped yourself. I backed, though, some kind of way, and they plowed along after me. I felt damp sand under me and then I was in the water, and they were, but getting closer, as they could see where they were going and I couldn't. Then I did something I'd seen linemen do on many a football field. I grabbed for their heads, but instead of headgears, I caught hair. I jerked them off their feet, and when their faces went in the water I held. They began to wriggle and kick and I held and kept on holding. Bubbles came up and the kicks got slower. By now, in addition to Mr. Legg and Helen, quite a few people, maybe seven or eight, were there, most of them yelling at me to let them have it, it served them right. Then a guy that seemed to be Dickie's father splashed in and began shaking me and screaming I was murdering his boy. I let them up and dragged them out. They had water in their lungs and I put Pappy to working it out, with artificial respiration. When they could get up I let them have a couple of kicks and chased them out of there. Next thing, I was on the porch and Mr. Legg was pouring me a drink and people were arguing about it and it was pretty unanimous I had done a good thing for the island. Mr. Legg kept saying it was "magnificent," and apologizing for not doing more to help me out. Then he told Helen to tell Margaret there was no need for the police, and to stop calling them, and she went inside. But before she did she gave me a funny, sidelong look, like she was seeing me for the first time. Mr. Legg kept on talking: "Jack, I can't tell you what it did to me. I wouldn't be capable of it in a million years, I may as well admit it."

"It's mostly muscle."

"More than that."

"And practice. I've spilled a few guys."

"It's more than muscle and more than practice. It's—what they used to call courage and now they call guts."

"Well—who am I to—"

I tilted the drink and he went on. He was, as I've said, a small, pink man with a little white mustache, and I don't know how he ever expected to be much good in a fight. People began going home, and in a few minutes it was all awful quiet. Mr. Legg was worried about what Finley might be up to, and he kept watching. Then after a while he said: "Just the same, I think I'll send her back. At the hotel Mrs. Brems will look out for her perfectly well, and if she's not here the main source of trouble will be out of the way."

"You mean—Helen?"

"Yes. I see it now. He's showing off for her."

"And the rest of you will stay here?"

"It's not fair to ruin everybody's summer."

So I sat right in the boat, watched it drift out from the bank, turn in the current, and head for Niagara Falls, without lifting a finger to stop it or steer it or sink it. What was I thinking of, to do a thing like that? Who says I was thinking? Maybe I'd lost the capacity to think. For three years I'd been living in a dead house in a dead city in a dead state, going to a dead school studying the dead history of a dead country. Maybe you've forgotten 1930, 1931, and 1932, but I haven't. All the things I'd been taught, about life and love and what it was all about, those lights I was to steer by, had turned into fish scales on me until they were just stuff for guys in college to gag about when they were half shot with beer. If I'd had the money I'd earned, that might have helped, anyway until I could figure out where I was at. But it was gone, because the things my father had learned had turned to fish scales on *him*, and it didn't help much that the broker had been gentleman enough to knock himself off with a gun. So I'd let myself in for this marriage I didn't want to a girl I didn't want and a job I didn't want, because I had as much use for the hotel business as a fish has for grass. All the thinking I was doing, I'd say, was thinking how not to think. If that meant drifting down the stream with this child, who was almost as unhappy as I was, it later turned out, picking flowers off the bank, listening to the bees, and watching the moon come up, then I was a sap all right, no argument about that. But all it meant at the time, so far as either one of us knew, was that it took two minds of what was weighing down two hearts, and wasn't due to last any longer than the landing we were headed for, that would put an end to the trip. That we might shoot past

it, that anything lay beyond it, never once entered my mind,
and I'm sure it didn't enter hers.

Not that I told her anything about it, or touched her or
kissed her or did anything out of line, or even wanted to, that
I remember. It was just that I was with her all the time, when
I lived in a misty gold dream, and when I wasn't with her I
wasn't even living. By now, she was growing to a woman so
fast it made you catch your breath. Her hair had lost that
ratty, kid look it had sometimes had, and was soft and glossy
over its red-gold color. There were dark circles under her
eyes and she had an expression like you see in the paintings of
Madonnas. Her movements, that had been quick, all slowed
down, so she was the most graceful thing in skirts I think I
ever saw. Every motion she made was controlled, it began the
right way and ended the right way, it wasn't too fast and it
wasn't too slow.

I lived in the hotel now, but for the tutoring we used
Margaret's studio. Whichever shift I worked, we'd get the
lessons in, and the rest of the time we'd swim in Clifton
Park, where there's a big lake they use for a pool, or go somewhere and dance, or see a picture. Mrs. Brems, the house-
keeper, thought it was wonderful we should be such pals, and
often put up little lunches, especially when we went swimming, so we could loaf at the pool and really enjoy ourselves.
But what we did mostly, if I was free at night, was drive. We
drove all over, down into southern Maryland, up into Penn-
sylvania, over into Virginia. But if we only had a little time
we'd drive out to Lake Roland, where there was a place we
could park and sit, or get out and walk around. One of those
nights she touched my arm. "Jack . . . up there . . . in the
trees."

"Watch where you're walking."

"But look at it, Jack! It's beautiful!"

I looked, but I knew what it was going to be before I looked.

It was a big luna moth, fluttering above us, full of moonlight. When it was gone her hand was in mine.

The algebra didn't go so well. We'd work at it, she on one side of the card table we set up, me on the other, and the book in the middle, but we didn't seem to get anywhere. It wasn't long before I saw, or thought I saw, what the trouble was. What had made the arithmetic go so well was that I'd really go into it, what she didn't understand, but of course the way to start that off right was with some stuff about how dumb she was, and then we'd have the roughhouse, but when we got done with it we had our finger on the trouble. Now there was nothing like that at all. I treated her like a lady, instead of a hoodlum, and she tried to act like one, and where we got was nowhere. And then one day, toward the end of August, it seemed to me the time was getting short and we better get fundamental if she was ever going to learn anything, so I let go with it. I mean, I hauled out the same old line, that alongside of her a parade of snails would look like graduates of the Johns Hopkins University, or something like that. But that's as far as I got with it. She burst out crying and sat there with tears squirting out of her eyes and running down on her dress. I jumped up and put my arm around her but she ran over to the sofa and threw herself down on it, face in the pillow, and shook with sobs. "Helen, Helen, what's the trouble? Don't you know it was just a joke? The same joke we used to have, so we could get to the bottom of it, what it is you don't understand?"

"Go on, let me alone."

"Come on, we'll take a drive and—"

"Please, please!"

"Here, let me wipe your eyes!"

"No! No! Go on, go, go, go!"

I walked around the room, hoped it would pass and that she'd let me talk to her, went over and patted her, but it was no soap. I left, and the next two or three days I didn't see her.

"Jack, where's Helen?"

". . . I don't know, Mrs. Legg. Why?"

"Mrs. Brems hasn't seen her since lunchtime. I've had them ring her room and she doesn't answer, I've had her paged—maybe she's just gone downtown somewhere without leaving word. But—I have a queer feeling something's wrong."

"I'll look into it and call you back."

I was in my room when they told me the island was calling, in pajamas from the heat, but I dressed quick, went down to the desk, picked up the master key, went to her room, and knocked. There was no answer. I went in and she wasn't there. I was worried twice as bad as Mrs. Legg was, because I knew there could be an answer I hated to think about. I began looking for a note or something, but didn't find anything. Her things were all in order, dresses in the closet, panties in the bureau, algebra book on her night table. Under that, when I picked it up to make sure nothing had been slipped in with it, was my picture, one I didn't know she had, that she must have swiped from Margaret, taken in the Little Lord Fauntleroy suit when I was about her age. It was face down.

I checked with Tolan, the house detective, for what little he knew, and rang Mrs. Legg. She and Mr. Legg were up there in about an hour, and put police and private detectives and God knows who-all to work on it. Around seven, when I was trying to stuff something to eat in me, in the dining room, Margaret came in. "I couldn't face a night on that island alone, so I took the bus."

"Be pretty rugged at that."

"Aren't you glad to see me?"

"Yeah, sure."

"But what's all the fuss about that brat? Can't she even go to a picture show or take a car ride or whatever she's done without practically putting bloodhounds on her trail?"

"They're kind of worried."

"Well, *are* you glad to see me?"

"Can't I be worried too?"

"What about?"

"I don't know."

I wasn't on duty that night, and around nine I went to my room. By that time the whole place was going crazy, and even Margaret was getting mildly interested. I sat there, looking at a sign go on and off down on Centre Street, and kept trying to think what I'd do if I was a young girl and had woke up to the fact I was in love with a guy that I supposed was in love with my sister. And all of a sudden I had a horrible hunch. I rang information for the Finley number on the island, and called. If Dickie was there I was going to give a phony name and say how about doing a job for me with his boat. But I never got that far. The mother answered, and said he wasn't there. "Do you know where he is, Mrs. Finley? I mean, I'd like to know when he'll be back."

"He didn't say."

"Is he out in his boat?"

"No, the car."

Anne Arundel County is the beginning of Dixie, which is just one scrub woods, and Zeke's place was right on the edge of it, forty or fifty feet off the road, in the middle of a clearing, with scraggly pine and oak and chinquapin all around it. It was one of those log-cabin jobs, known then as a roadhouse, and what went on inside I didn't know, as I'd never been to one, but according to Denny it was considerably more than the law allowed, whether it was women, wine, *or* song. I got there around ten, and the first thing I had to do, after parking, was see if the Finley car was there. There were quite a few cars out front, but there'd be no trouble spotting it, because of certain dents. It wasn't long before I found it, and from its position it had been there some time. I went over and rang the bell and pretty soon the slot opened and a piece of face showed. "Haya? Can a hungry guy get something to eat?"

"We know you?"

"Sure, I've been in."

"Just a minute."

He went and when he came back another guy was with him that I took to be Zeke. I handed him some chatter, and I'd probably have got away with it, but when I began spending some big Baltimore names I overplayed it. He shook his head. "Sorry, it's just a little family place I run here, and we're kind of crowded. And anyway, I'd have to know you. Some other time, maybe."

The slot closed and there I was. I went back to my car and tried to think. I had no proof, had nothing, except this pounding in my head, that told me to get in there, and get in quick. But I hated to go off half-cocked, hated to have this kid that I'd beaten up, that I *knew* was in there, see me looking silly over a twelve-year-old girl that maybe wasn't with him at all. Then I happened to remember something. She loved gum, and it was just as regular as clockwork, when she went in any place, that she'd take out her wad and drop it over the side of the car on the ground. I went over to the Ford. I couldn't see any gum but when I dropped to my hands and knees I could smell it. Then after I lit some matches I saw it.

I went back and rang again and asked for Zeke and he came. When he saw me he acted sore and came out, the other guy right behind him. "Listen, you, I told you once and I'm telling you again—"

"Just a minute, just a minute."

"Make it quick."

"I didn't come here for a drink and I didn't come for trouble. But you've got a girl in there, twelve years old, and—"

"You're sure of that?"

"Zeke, in a polite way, I'm asking you."

"If I had, would I be telling you?"

"You'll be telling it to a judge in just about ten minutes if you don't let me in there, so I can get her out. Watch your step, baby. Liquor's one thing, and as we all know, it's drunk in the spirit of good clean fun. But children, minor children, daughters of important people, are something else. My suggestion to you is, you ask me in, or you may be piling up more trouble for yourself than anybody you know can get you out of."

"Who are you?"

"Just a friend."

What the rest of it would have been I don't know, because just then, from somewhere inside, was a scream, a girl's scream, and then another. I dived for the door, but the two of them were there ahead of me. I got my foot inside, grabbed for Zeke, got his head out, and hooked a couple on his jaw, but then the other one came out and hit me with something, I don't know what. I must have gone out for a second, because next thing I knew I was on the ground, the door closing in front of my face, the screaming still going on. But then the screaming stopped and a door opened somewhere and I could hear a scuffle going on. I jumped up and ran off to the side, where I could see her wrestling with somebody, maybe Dickie. She broke clear, and somebody pulled Dickie inside. Then she was in my arms and I carried her to the car. "God, what have they done to you?"

"Nothing, nothing! . . . Nothing, except try to keep me

from going. I knew that was you out there. Oh, Jack, I knew it, I knew it."

Next thing I knew we were going down the hill to the Severn. I pulled off to one side and parked on the shore, and we sat there, looking at the Naval Academy across the river. We didn't talk, that I remember. What did we have to say?

* 11 *

NEXT morning, when I was supposed to check in at the Cartaret desk, I was somewhere on the road from Gettysburg to York, watching the sun come up over the hills, with no more idea what I was going to do next than a grasshopper. I'd been driving since midnight, when I set her down at the hotel, but where I went I don't know, though I remember sliding around Washington, from Rhode Island Avenue to Wisconsin, so it looks as though I must have gone up through Rockville and Frederick. There had been no gay so-long-see-you-tomorrow when she got out. After an hour, maybe, sitting there looking at the Severn, we started back and she had another crying spell like she had had in the studio. I didn't ask her what the trouble was, didn't tell her what we were going to do about it, didn't try to hide it that I was doing a little crying myself. We both knew what the trouble was, and we both knew there was nothing to do about it. A man of twenty-two can't go around with a girl of twelve, or marry her, or have anything to do with her, once he begins to notice what she looks like in a bathing suit, or she does. As we drove up

Charles Street she asked me to let her out before we got to the hotel, and by that I knew she was going to cook up some kind of an alibi and not mention me at all. When I stopped she jumped out, slammed the door, and ran on without looking back. I sat staring at her, partly to see that nobody bothered her, partly for one last look, as I felt I'd never see her again. When she turned into the hotel I kept on up Charles Street and turned west on North Avenue. But when I came to Mt. Royal Terrace I kept on going.

When I got home, some time in the morning, my father and Sheila were out but Nancy was home and called down to me as soon as I stepped in the house that the hotel had been calling and that I should ring them right away. I said thanks, went upstairs to my room, and locked the door. Then I took off my clothes, put on pajamas, and lay down. After a while I heard the phone ring and then Nancy was at the door. "It's the hotel again, Jack."

"I'll call them."

"But they're on the line."

"I'll call, later."

She went and then she was back. "They say you're due to work and won't you please get down there as quick as you can because they're short-handed already on account of people away on vacation, and—"

"Can't you understand English?"

She stood out there five minutes arguing about it before at last she went. I must have slept then because next thing I knew it was three or four o'clock in the afternoon and I had to have something to eat. I put on a robe and went down and while I was frying myself some eggs Nancy came in the kitchen. "Well, my goodness, Jack, it certainly seems you're acting very peculiarly. You could at least *call* them. They're entitled to *some* explanation."

"I'll get around to it."

"Is something *wrong?*"

"Just taking a little rest."

"From what, may I ask?"

"That desk—answering questions."

She flounced out of there, but in a minute, when I was at the table, tucking away the first food I'd had since the night before, she was back. "Well, what do you suppose that child did yesterday?"

"What child?"

"The one you tutored. Helen."

". . . She been up to something?"

"She just up and ran herself away!"

"You don't say."

"Mrs. Brems was just telling me—she got on a train yesterday, went over to Washington, took in all sorts of picture shows and the good Lord only knows what else—and didn't get back till twelve o'clock last night."

"I'll be doggoned."

That meant Helen had put over a story, so she wouldn't have to answer questions about me, and neither one of us would be mixed up in it, together anyway. I listened to Nancy, all about how the police had been called in, and cracked dumb. After a while she went out, shaking her head over what young people were coming to, and I went up and dressed. Then I slipped out, before my father and Sheila would get home. That night, at least, I remember where I ate. It was in the Princess Anne Hotel at Fredericksburg, Virginia.

It kept up three or four days. I'd come in late, slip upstairs, and be in bed with the light out and the door locked before anybody could say anything to me. In the morning, I'd wait till the Old Man went out, and then I'd get up, shave, dress, and go downstairs. If Nancy or Sheila had anything to say, I'd get interested in the paper, or stall somehow, and then I'd roll out my car and shove off. By the second day Margaret was calling every half hour and then she didn't call and then nobody called. It seemed to me, as I'd told Nancy, that I meant to call her "later," or some time, but later never seemed to come. Then her letters began coming in. She had a clammy way of writing, about three cap I's to the line, with every other word in quotes and all sorts of stuff about how ideally we were suited to each other on account of both being so artistic. But clammy or no clammy it was easy to see she was suffering from the same old yen, that the family had the heat on, and that she was going through hell.

One night, when I got in around two, my father was waiting for me. He called me in his study, where he was stretched out on the couch, and there was a highball beside him and a tray on the table. He made me a drink before he started. "Jack, there are one or two things I'd like to ask you about."

"Such as?"

"What's happened at the hotel?"

"Just felt like a little rest, that's all."

"Have you quit your job down there?"

". . . Yes, I guess so."

"What about Margaret?"

"I haven't seen her."

"Is the engagement still on?"

"I'd say it was off."

"May I ask why?"

"I changed my mind."

"In other words, it's none of my business?"

"The way I hear it, a marriage concerns two people."

"That may be true or it may not be true."

"Since when?"

"It involves two people provided he's his own man and she's her own woman. If not, it concerns, or can concern, quite a few more. And in this case, as Legg is responsible for his daughter and I'm responsible for you, the degree of your independence may not be quite as great as you think."

"I'm free, white, and twenty-two."

"You're also broke, or nearly so."

"I wouldn't bring that up if I were you. But since you do bring it up, we can go into this question of your responsibility. You had quite a lot to say about that once before and you may remember I had quite a lot to say about it too, all opposite to your idea about it. And the way you discharged your responsibility was to lose me every cent I had, that I'd earned with no help from you, and that I'd pleaded with you to let me keep. Now, since there's nothing you can do about your responsibility, no job that you can give me, no restitution of any kind you can make me for what your previous decision cost me, I'd say minding your own business for once in your life would be a very good idea."

I wasn't looking for trouble, and didn't go in there with anything all learned up to shoot at him. But I guess it was in me and had to come out. It surprised me, the amount of pressure there was back of it, but nothing like as much as it surprised me, the way he took it. He held up his hand to stop me, but in a patient, calm way, as though he'd been all over that a good many times in his mind, and had maybe got a little further, figuring on it, than I had. "Jack, you're wholly right, but you've got things backwards. You're hacking at the general, that's in the past, that nobody can do anything about, and overlooking the particular, that lies in the future, or could at least, and that might be of help, in your case. . . . Of course it's unconscionable, what we've done to you. But don't get the idea you're an exception."

"Who is 'we'?"

"This generation. My generation. I'm not the only one. We're all in it. We thought the laws of sense had been repealed, back there in the 1920's, and we went hog-wild. We squandered your heritage and there's nothing left, nothing, but what you and millions of other boys like you can salvage out of it, and perhaps rebuild, when things get going again. In your case, you hold it especially against me that you earned the money I lost on Sam Shreve's advice. Is that five thousand dollars any better, would it have bought you any more, than the five thousand dollars I could portion you with, in view of your impending marriage—"

"My cancelled marriage."

"I'll not admit it! I still have hopes for it!"

"Go on."

"Of my own money, which would be partly yours now, and all yours when I'm gone, I lost much more than I lost for you. I'd hate to tell you what I lost. But am I an exception? I tell you, we're a legion, a host. We live on every block of every city and every town and every village of this country. And you live on every block. You're one of a million, ten million, boys who must be cheated, now, because their fathers were fools. But there's nothing to do about them. Do you hear me, Jack? Some day they'll have it, some day they'll rebuild what was lost for them, but until then why stew up a corpse for the glue that isn't in it? Let's talk about you."

"All right, then, talk."

"What's gone wrong with your marriage?"

"That I can't discuss with you."

"Is it what I think?"

"I don't know what you think."

"Have you picked up some disease?"

"I have not."

"Don't lie to me."

"I have no disease."

"Does the hotel irk you?"

"Possibly, but that wasn't the reason."

"Have you rowed with Legg?"

"No."

"Mrs. Legg?"

"No."

"Margaret?"

"No."

"Then there can be but one reason."

"Which is?"

"Another woman."

I said: "There doesn't have to be another woman. It could be such a thing as waking up to the fact you've made a mistake, and don't want to get married, and especially don't want to get married to this particular woman and this particular job, and then bringing the ax down before it's too late."

"And there's such a thing as grand, tragic folly."

"How would a fool know?"

That stopped him, but it sounded so mean and his face got so white I apologized, and he said it was all right and made two more drinks. But as I watched him it kept talking to me, a hunch that there was something more to it than he had said, something personal to him, and pretty soon I said: "What's the rest of it?"

"Nothing, I guess, that concerns you."

"I think there's something."

"I—had a deal."

"With Mr. Legg?"

"About the hotel basement. He—approached me. About the possibility of converting it into a garage. I went into it pretty thoroughly, figured what I could pay for a lease, made him my offer, and it was agreeable to him. I think he's concerned, over that girl, to head her away from this career he thinks pretty silly, and wants to sew her up, and you up, and me up, as many ways as he can. However, it would be an excellent arrangement. I could put Kratzer in charge, and have a back-log, as they call it, that would carry my own overhead, and Legg, on his side, would do well too."

"And?"

"He's suddenly cool to it."

"Since—I took my powder on him?"

"After dinner, when I called him."

I felt sorry to be the cause of one more thing gone wrong, but to make a human sacrifice out of myself and go through with it anyway, knowing what would be facing me and the way it would have to come out, was more than I could do. I mumbled something about being sorry, and didn't go any further with it. All of a sudden he wheeled on me and said: "Jack, love is not all of marriage."

"It's a big part of it."

"All right, but in every country except this one they give it a chance. They help love, with dots and dowries and portions and whatever each family can do in the way of the connections that make life easy to live and love worth having. In that way they at least escape the crazy divorce rate that prevails only in this land of the free—especially the recently free grass widow. I've rarely seen such promising auspices for a marriage: a lovely girl, easy work, comfortable pay, beautiful quarters, fine connections, and the certainty that eventually you'll come into a property as valuable as most men dare to hope for."

"I don't want it."

"I hope you know what you're doing."

"Anyway, it's me that's doing it."

"What *are* you doing, by the way?"

". . . ."

"I supposed it was something like that."

One afternoon, a week or two later, I started down to Ocean City. It was a couple hundred miles, but the spot I was in, the further the better. But around Elkton it started to rain, and a few miles down the Shore I started back. I ate dinner in Havre de Grace and got back to town around nine o'clock. But on Mt. Royal Terrace I noticed a big Packard that looked like the Legg's. Then I noticed the house all lit up, or anyway, lights on in the living room, which hadn't been used that hour of night for a couple of years. I kept right on, and when I got to the park I took a turn around the lake to think it over. When I came back, instead of going down the street I went down the alley, pulled to one side, and parked. The garage was open. I went through to the yard and slipped around the house to the living-room windows. It was coming down pretty hard by now, but at least that meant there was no chance of my being heard. When I made sure the nearest window was open, I leaned my head so close I could smell the wet screen and peeped. Mr. and Mrs. Legg were there, and Margaret and Sheila and Nancy, but I couldn't see any sign of Helen or my father. Nancy was crying, and right while I was looking at her Sheila pulled a sofa pillow up to her face, stretched out and began to bawl triple forte. Then Margaret began blotting at her eyes with her handkerchief, and Mrs. Legg began patting her. Mr. Legg kept staring straight in front of him, shaking his head. After a long while my father came in from the hall, and from the way he wandered around, looking at pictures and stuff, I knew he'd been taking a little stroll through the back of the house to think things over. Pretty soon he said: "Legg, I simply can't believe it."

"Neither can I, but there it is."

"But Jack wouldn't—"

"Oh!" Margaret screamed it, and when her face snapped around, with tears glittering in her eyes, she wasn't very pretty to see. "Dicky *saw* them, I tell you. He followed them! From that place he took her to, after she showed up down at the island with all sorts of wild talk about jumping in the bay! Any idiot would know it's been going on all summer."

"I'm afraid so, Dillon."

"I see."

So that showed how Dicky had taken care of his end of it, but not what I was going to do about mine. Mrs. Legg began talking about how peculiarly she'd been acting all week, "ever since the Washington trip, or what she said at the time was the Washington trip. I knew there was something back of it, and I couldn't get it out of my mind it was connected with Jack, and the peculiar way *he* was acting." About that time Sheila recovered the power of speech and wailed that it was horrible, just horrible. Then the Old Man said: "What does the child herself say about it, Legg?"

"Say? She can't even talk!"

"Well, she must have told you *something!*"

"Why must she? After Finley came over, and that boy told his tale, she went into hysterics. Not even her own mother could talk to her—could you, dear?"

"We took her up from the island, to the doctor, and he took one look at her and ordered her to bed. I don't know what she'll say. The condition she's in, unfortunately, pretty well speaks for itself."

"And if she admits it, what then?"

"I don't quite know yet."

"Do you mean you're—considering the law?"

"I have to consider it."

Once more I was slipping in the side door of the hotel, and along past the furnaces, and up in the freight elevator. Their suite was on the second floor, and her room first on the left of the little side hallway they had. I tapped on her door and right away heard her voice, and then she was there, in a little silk bathrobe, her hair tumbling all over her shoulders, and in my arms. "Jack, Jack, I knew you'd come."

"Put on something and get down there. To the basement."

"Where have they gone? To your house?"

"They're up there now. Waiting for me. But how long they'll wait God knows, and we have to talk. So be quick. Use the freight car and don't be seen."

I went down and waited and after a couple of years the car gave a clank and went up. Then it came down, and at last she was there, and we went over to a baggage truck and sat down. "First, let me look at you. What makes you so pale?"

"The dark dress, maybe. And I've had—a bad time."

"Yes, now tell me."

"Well, the day after that night, when I'd played hooky by going to a picture show, and then had the bright idea of traipsing me down to the island, and found them all gone, and then thought I'd play a trick on you and went up to that place with Dickie—"

"After deciding to jump in the bay."

"Well? What would you have done?"

"Go on."

"After you came and got me and took me home, I had to have a story, something to throw them off the track. So I said I had gone—"

"To Washington. I know. What then?"

"Then it was decided that it was being alone so much that had slightly unbalanced my mind."

"And they brought you back to the island?"

"Yes, things having suddenly quieted down."

"Why?"

"I think Dickie got scared."

"He talked, though."

"Yes. Today, just after lunch, it was threatening rain, and we gave up an idea we had, to go crabbing. Then Margaret went to her room for a nap, and Mother went back and began checking linen. Then Mr. Finley came over and I could hear them talking, from where I was, reading a magazine in my room, for some time. Then Margaret got up and went out there. Then I began to wonder what was going on and went out there, and from the way they kept looking at me I knew that whatever it was, Mr. Finley and Father were talking about me. Then Mr. Finley called Dick and he came over."

"And what then?"

"Mr. Finley had been telling what Dick had told him."

"Which was?"

". . . That you had done something to me."

"Do you understand what that was? I mean, what it was I'm supposed to have done to you?"

"Yes, Jack."

"What did Dickie have to say?"

"He followed us, Jack. He must have, from what he said, because he knew exactly where we parked, there across from the Naval Academy, near the bridge. I think he sneaked out to his car, before we left Zeke's, and pulled out when we did, without putting on his lights. And, in his own imagination, anyhow, he saw something. And when they began asking me about it, and Margaret began weeping all over the place, I—went to pieces a little."

"Then they brought you to town?"

"And called a doctor. He put me to bed."

"The worst is yet to come."

"How?"

"Your father means to have me arrested."

"For what?"

"Contributing to the delinquency of a minor."

"But you haven't!"

"No, but Dickie says so."

"Will they believe him, instead of me?"

"I don't know what they'll believe."

It was ten minutes before I got her quiet enough even to talk. Then we heard the watchman, ducked into the car, stooped down, and held our breaths. When he was gone we went out and sat down on the truck again and her hand crept into mine. It was cold as ice. "Jack, why did you come here? Tonight."

". . . To tip you. What's going on."

"That's not all."

"No."

"You're going away?"

"Yes."

"You're taking me with you?"

"No."

"Jack, please."

"It's utterly unthinkable."

"Jack, I love you."

"I've loved you since you were two years old."

"But not only that way. You love me more."

"If I did, it wouldn't be more, it would be less."

"Jack, I've loved you since I was two years old, too. I've worshipped you. But not this way, as I feel now, until you undumbbelled me. That's not so nice, to be the family simp, that can't do algebra factors like Mother or beat the piano like Margaret. Then you came along, and believed in me, and made me happy. Then life began. Then I loved you this way, so I can't even breathe when I look at you. Jack, you'll have to take me! I'll put my hair up! I'll use lipstick and make-up, so I'll look older! Jack, I'll die without you! I love you, I tell you! And you love me!"

"Not that way."

"Yes! It's why you've left Margaret!"

"Listen, you. You're to cut this idea out, get rid of it, anything that even looks like it. You're to go back to school, study your lessons, do what they—"

But she turned from me, curled up on the truck like some kitten, and started to cry, terrible little sobs that she'd fight back and then couldn't fight back. I got up, stumbled past the furnaces, somehow found my way out to the street.

At the house, the Packard was gone and the windows were dark, so I put the car away and went in. From the study my father called. There was no light in there, but his voice had a rip to it and I about knew the thick cut he'd have to his jaw when I turned on one of the lamps. But I wasn't quite ready for the wild, maniac look he had in his eye. He was on the couch, and rose up off it like some corpse sitting up in its coffin, and stared at me, and began to talk. "You low, perverted scut, to do a thing like that!"

"Like what, for instance."

"Are you going to stand there and say you didn't?"

"I don't know what you're talking about."

"I've defended you—successfully, God help me. I've made threats that at last have had their effect, and at least the police won't be called. But if you think I for one second think you're innocent, you're badly mistaken. I should have known it would be something like this. With the rotten, depraved blood that's in you, to which something young is only a new excitement—"

Don't ask me how I got through the rest of that horrible night. I stood there, and pumps began driving in my head, like they had the day I beat up the organist, like they do still, at no more than a look in somebody's eye, if I happen to think that look means my mother. I held on to the door jamb, for control, and he talked on and on, and every other sentence he'd tell me to get out of there. I tried to tell him what the truth was, but it was like talking to something insane, and after a while I went upstairs. Then while I was packing, Sheila came in, looking thin and old in some kind of a Chinese kimono, and I told her I was taking clothes and underwear only, and might have to write for the other stuff. She said she'd send anything I wanted. Then she began to cry and I went over to kiss her but she turned away. At that I felt my face get hot, picked up my bags, and went downstairs. In the living room something moved and then Nancy was there with a thermos bottle and a basket full of sandwiches. She whispered the thermos had coffee in it. I thanked her and wanted to kiss her but hated the idea of somebody else turning away. I put the stuff under my arm and went out. Then I was in the car, driving through the night, with the rain coming down, the black road shining ahead, with no more idea where I was going than the Flying Dutchman, and just as much chance of getting there.

✳ 12 ✳

"THE future of football, of pro football, is right here in the South. With outdoor night sports the coming thing, a whole new field has opened up and pro football will claim it. I mean to take advantage of what the South offers. I mean to co-operate with baseball. I mean to begin where baseball leaves off, beginning the week after the World Series this October, and by using the ball parks, put on night games, not once a week, but seven nights a week, with doubleheaders if we skip any. But that's the beauty of football: there'll be no need to skip. Football is the one sport that never called a game on account of weather, that never gave a rain check, hail check, or snow check. Whatever it's doing topside, the game goes on. If the customers don't mind, the players don't care. But why would the customers mind? Here in the South it's always warm enough, and in a covered stand it's dry enough. Once more, the South will find out it's got something."

"You running the whole league?"

"I'm running one team, here in Atlanta."

"But, Mr. Dillon, who'll you play?"

"Chattanooga, Memphis, Houston, San Antonio, New Orleans, Jacksonville, and Miami."

"You'll go into the Southwest, too?"

"Why not? This is a pure matter of weather. Sure I'll cross the river."

"Are those teams ready?"

"They soon will be. While I'm promoting them and lining up backing—which is all in sight, my friends, I'm not out to sell stock—we'll challenge existing teams, and the way I hear it, the boys on the big Eastern clubs have quite a little time on their hands, and for a nice guarantee, maybe they won't be too proud to come down here and do their stuff for Georgia. And I'll tell you something else. I'm offering dates to colleges. For a nice cut of the gate and the fastest practice they'll ever get, you may find those campus coaches will take a liberal view of ethics, if, as, and when they've got any."

It was maybe a week later, in the lobby of the Atlanta Biltmore. I had called the sporting editors, and they'd sent three or four reporters and some photographers over. And in hardly more than an hour there I was, all over the front pages, with big pictures of me, and big banner headlines telling how Atlanta was to have a team. Seeing it in print made it seem like in a week you'd hear the referee's whistle. How much of it was real and how much was phony, just a stall to hide the spot I was in, I don't know. I had driven on to Richmond and gone to bed in some little hotel there, then after I caught up on my sleep, gone on to Raleigh and Durham and I don't know what other places. All that time I was trying to forget Helen, cut out the bitter way I was raging at the Old Man, and figure out where I was at and what I was going to do. In Durham, I guess it was, I snapped out of it enough to cruise around to get a little work. I went to garages, because at least I could talk car language and make the things go. Some of the owners just laughed at me, some of them got sore for taking up their time with an idea like that, and some of them gave me a serious talking to. They told me to go home, if I had one, because *there was no work to do*. It wasn't news, but it showed what I was up against. I toted my money, what I had with me and what was in bank, and I had about two hundred dollars, which was what I had saved during the summer, after paying a couple of bills. And I had the car. I did a little more asking around, and then it came to me I better pull something, but quick. That was when I hit on this idea of organizing a pro league in the South, and as I write it up now, I don't see such a whole lot wrong with it. I've done plenty of promoting since then, and it doesn't look even a little bit silly. I might have got away with it, at that, if it hadn't been for one of the reporters, a little guy named Harmon. The day after the press conference I was reading papers in the lobby when he crossed over and sat down. "I rang your room but you didn't answer, then I saw you buy the papers. Thought I'd give you a chance to look 'em over before I came up with my proposition."

"Which is?"

"Who's back of this?"

"Why—me, among other people."

"Just asking, shut my mouth if I'm out of order. If you've got all the backing you want, that lets me out. But—if it's an open game—I might have a friend, Mr. Dillon, and—we're all out to make a dollar, aren't we?—I might have an angle."

"No harm hearing it."

His angle was to handle press stuff, public relations he called it, for my Atlanta club, and maybe later for the league. But his friend was what interested me. Because I give you one guess how much backing I had. I had put on a tall front, but beyond that I didn't have any backing, and it was just this kind of break I had hoped to get. Looking back at it now I'm amazed I didn't go with it straight to the baseball people, on the basis of winter shows for their park, and let them put up the jack while I worked on plays. But I was doing it all off the cuff, and with this bird caught it looked like I hadn't done so bad. And when he began talking about his days on the *Wash-*

ington Star, and remembered stuff I'd pulled in the Georgetown games, and reminded me how two or three writers had
picked me for all-American, I was plenty glad to listen to him,
and let him take his time getting around to his friend. When
he did he got mysterious. "You know a cretain soft drink that's
manufactured here, Mr. Dillon?"

"Why not Jack?"

"And my name's Harry—to my friends, Hank."

"Yeah, Hank, I know the beverage."

"My friend's close to that pause that refreshes. About as
close as you can get without glue. That gives you an idea the
circles he moves in. But there's a difference. That soft-drink
dough, I'd never want it for a sporting proposition."

"Dough is dough."

"There's certain things that soft-drink dough knows about,
certain things that show dough knows about, and certain things
that sporting dough knows about—things you got to do, stuff
you've got to pay for, that looks plain crazy to other kinds of
dough. Sporting dough knows, for instance, that you can't
promote football with some guy sent out by the chamber of
commerce that's a shark on debentures, futures, escrows, and
stocks, but nothing else. For football, you need a guy that
knows football, and right there, Jack, if you don't mind my
being a little personal, is where you've got inside position on
anybody in this town that I know of. That's why this dough
I'm talking about is going to be impressed."

"Who is this dough, if you don't mind my asking?"

"If I told you all I know, where'd I be at with my angle?
I love you, Jack, but this is business. In due time you'll know
everything there is to know, but until then leave it to me."

"What time is due time?"

"That dough, right now, is on the yacht."

"It got a yacht?"

"As I told you, it's sporting dough. The yacht's off Nassau
now, sailfishing, but on a radio from me they'll break in on

it. Relax, that's all. See our city. In a couple of days you'll be hearing something. But I've got to know one thing."

"I'll tell you, if I can."

"Are you playing on this team yourself?"

"I cracked a knee cap last fall."

"You mean it's out? Your playing days are over?"

"I mean if I could run a hundred yards in fifteen seconds now it would be a miracle. You're not much good out there, you know, unless you can do it at least in eleven."

"Shake, Jack. That makes me feel better than anything you've said yet. Because a player-manager is just a headache, as every sporting man knows. It's O.K. to play, but if you're playing, play. But if you're going to run it, run it. Don't be causing jealousy and friction and distrust just because you've got some idea you're the only man that can score a point. Now I know it's a natural. Now I can put in that radiogram what it'll take to get action. You feel it yourself, don't you?"

"If I didn't I wouldn't be here."

"Right."

That week, if I ever had any respect for newspapers I lost it. Once more, I can't tell you how much I meant any of this, of whether I thought something would come of it, or if it was just one last shot in the arm before I'd have to wake up and come face to face with my life. But it seemed real, at the time, and of course by then I knew that on something of that kind, where promotion was it, you had to tear in with all you had, and put it in lights, with bugles blowing. I put out stuff so raw you wouldn't think anybody would go for it. Capone was hot then. I put out stuff denying he was back of me, and saying I'd sue anybody that said he was, and they printed it. I put out stuff saying I meant to build a team that could play even with the best there was, I didn't care if it was the Green Bay Packers or the Providence Steam Roller, and they printed it. I wired Red Baughman, that had played tackle with me in college, if he was free to work for me, and when he wired he was, I put out stuff saying the first player had been selected for Atlanta, and they printed it. I sent a dozen more wires, and when enough players had accepted, or anyway said they were free, I announced the "first eleven," and they printed it. I put out stuff that the team would be the Remuda, and they printed it. Soon I decided to put out drinks for the reporters, and that meant a suite, as they wouldn't serve it downstairs. The bellboy took nine dollars a bottle for the liquor, with fifty cents tip. Almost before I knew it the cash in my pocket was down to silver, and I had to eat chili till my check cleared for a hundred dollars.

All sorts of people were calling me by then: real-estate men, trying to sell me anything from a farm, to make a park out of, to a house to live in; insurance men, to write coverage for the team, on some kind of group plan; sporting-goods salesmen, to quote prices on uniforms; concession men, to talk about soft drinks, hot dogs, and programs; and forty guys wanting jobs, anything from usher to cutting grass. I stalled them all off, but soon I made use of them, anyway to look big. I'd sit around the lobby, on purpose not near a phone, and of course when the girl couldn't get me she'd have me paged. It got so that "Mr. Jack Dillon, of the Atlanta Remuda," was going off every minute and a half. It cost a dime a throw for the bell-boys, but I figured it was worth it. Hank called me three, four, and five times a day, and when he wasn't calling me he was dropping around. Then one night the phone rang, and he was on the line. "Well, Jack, what did I tell you? Boy, are you going to feel good. O.K., here goes, word for word—it's addressed to me here at the paper and it says:

DON'T TELL ME ABOUT DILLON I SAW HIM TWO YEARS AGO IN THE GAME WITH NAVY THREE YEARS AGO AT NEW HAVEN AND LAST YEAR AT GEORGETOWN HE'S TERRIFIC AND ONE OF THE CLEANEST GUYS IN THE GAME HOLD HIM THERE FOR ME AND AS SOON AS MY ENGINE TROUBLE IS FIXED I'LL BE IN STOP TELL YOURSELF HELLO.

Is that saying it, Jack? Ain't that one swell guy and don't it make you feel good?"

"It's just great."

"I told you, hold everything."

"I'm playing it just like you say."

Within the next three days there were four more wires, each one better than the last. But when I found out the engine was a tug job into Nassau, I began to get worried, because my money was going fast. One night when he called I said: "Hank, I got an idea that makes sense."

"Boy, let's hear it."

"While he's getting his boat in shape, why don't I jump in the car and take a swing around to Memphis and New Orleans and as many places as I can before he gets back? Then when he comes in I've got something to tell him. I'll keep in touch, and—"

"That's it! That's it!"

"I'll line it up, and then—"

"It's ready."

I don't think I said one thing to Hank the whole time that was going on that he didn't say it was great, and I guess I was beginning to notice it, that he was what you might call unusually optimistic. But, as I'm telling you, I'm not sure any of it was more than a jumbo stall. Nothing about it seemed real, from all those zanies trying to sell me stuff, and kidding themselves as much as I was kidding them, to those players wiring they were free and would be proud and happy to play under me as manager, and kidding themselves there'd be something on the fire pretty soon. But the main thing now was, I had to get out of that hotel, and at the same time I had to make it look like I was only temporarily gone, and would be back as soon as I got other stuff out of the way that was important. I packed what I'd need in one bag, left the other at the check room, and checked out. I went to a little dump on the north end of town, with some name like the Rosemary Cottage, that charged a dollar a night and wanted it in advance, and took a room. Then I began cruising around Georgia, going to every town there was: Augusta, Athens, Rome, Milledgeville, Decatur, just to name a few, looking for work. I went to every garage there was, and everywhere was the same answer: if they could, they would, and glad to do it; but every one of them had laid men off, and if there was any hiring to be done, the laid-off men had to come back. Then I began going to hotels. I don't like the hotel business, and I hated anything that might mean a query to the Cartaret. But anything for a job. It got me nowhere. One man, at the Dixie Hunt in Gainesville, it could have been, explained to me: "Brother, I hear what you say, that you'll do whatever I've got for room and meals and space for your car. The trouble is, there's been just about three hundred guys ahead of you with exactly that proposition, and some of them are friends. I mean it's personal. You don't know what this thing is, or you wouldn't even be in here. It's just about the worst that ever hit the country, and if you're up against it, don't let it worry you. Everybody else is, bad."

This, as well as I remember, was toward the end of September, maybe early in October. I was wearing my overcoat, which surprised me, as I thought in Dixie you wore shirt sleeves all the time. Anyhow, whenever it was, a political campaign was going on, or it seems it must have been. It says in the history

books that in 1932 we elected a president, but if we did I don't
remember anything about it. That's something I'd like to get
straight. Later, when relief came in and all that kind of stuff,
politics got to be everybody's business. But in 1932 there was
such a thing as being so jammed up with your own grief it
didn't mean a thing to you. The band played and the band
stopped, and we elected Mr. Franklin D. Roosevelt instead of
Mr. Herbert Hoover, but down where I lived, what we heard
about it was nothing whatever.

"Oh it's you, Jack."

"Hank, what do you know?"

"Got news at last, some of it good, some—not so hot."

"Let's hear it anyway."

"Another radiogram, sent me here at the paper, same as
usual:

BOAT IN SHAPE AT LAST BUT OF ALL COCKEYED THINGS GWEN-
DOLYN COMMANDED APPEAR PRESENTATION AT COURT JUST RE-
CEIVED WORD FROM EMBASSY TODAY SO THAT MEANS LONDON
UNTIL LATE NOVEMBER EARLY DECEMBER BUT TELL DILLON IF
HE CAN HOLD EVERYTHING TILL FIRST OF YEAR AM DEFINITELY
INTERESTED.

Don't that beat all hell, Jack?"

"Kind of louses it up."

"Gwendolyn's his daughter. Spoiled, bull-headed kid, all she
thinks about is riding horses and getting her picture taken with
some kind of a duke. What could he do?"

"Then—better luck next time."

"Knocks it in the head for this season all right. But for next
year, maybe it's even better, as it gives us more time. You know
what I mean, Jack? This way, we'll have our feet on the
ground and can do it right."

"Right."

"You'll buzz me on it? First of the year."

"Right."

"I'll be looking for you."

"Right."

Around November 1 I sold the car. It was a 1928 Buick, with only 80,000 miles on it. But the book said $170, and that's what I had to take. I moved out of the Rosemary into a place out on Marietta Street that didn't have any name. It was run by a Mrs. Pickens, and I took a back room, third floor, bath on the second floor, at $3.50 a week. Meals I ate in a drugstore. Ham on white, with mustard, mostly, and coffee. I got expenses down to $1.50 a day, and figured that with the $160 or so I had left from the sale of the car I might last till spring, with a little luck, and by then things might be different. But before Christmas it was gone.

"Two fifty."

"My God, the suit cost forty bucks!"

"Two fifty."

"Look, stop being funny. The suit cost forty, like I told you, less than six months ago, it's hardly been worn at all—now make me an offer."

"Two fifty."

I handed it over and he gave me my ticket. It had been wrapped in paper because at Mrs. Pickens's I was a week behind in my rent and both my suitcases had disappeared. So one by one I had taken both suits, the good suits I mean, the ones I could hock, and carried them out as bundles. The first one I took to a second-hand place, and they gave me $2.25. It made me sore, but I had to eat. The next one, two days later, I took to this hockshop and did two bits better. And still I looked for work, and still there was nothing to do. Then one day, when another week's rent was due, I let myself in with my key, late, so I wouldn't run into anybody, and tiptoed upstairs. The door to my room was locked.

"Mister, can you direct me to Terminal Station?"

"Keep right on down this street here till you come to the taxis all bunched at the curb, and that's it. You can't miss it."

"Thank you, sir. . . . And could you give me a lift on a ticket to Meriwether? You see, I come from there, and I've got the offer of a job, if I can only—"

Some of them cussed me out for playing them a trick, asking my way to the station when I really meant to mooch, some of them gave me a dime, one gave me a nickel, and one gave me a quarter. This last guy looked pretty sore, and as he felt around in his pocket I wondered what I was going to do if he changed his mind and gave me a poke in the jaw. But all of a sudden, as he kept glaring at me, a bus stopped a few feet away, and who should get off it but Hank. I felt my blood turn to water. After all the big talk I had handed out to him, to be caught here on the street, with my hand out like a beggar, was more than I could stand. He didn't see me. I turned and ran. I never wanted a touchdown as bad as I wanted a good, big, deep hole in the ground that day.

I didn't decide to leave town, or have some reason that made sense, or figure an angle that would take me to some other place—I mean, if you've wondered why guys on the road move from one place to some other place, or why they think being hungry in Jacksonville is better than being hungry in Atlanta. I lammed out of Atlanta for the same reason I lammed out of a thousand places: I was just washed up there, that's all. Harmon was one guy. There were two hundred and fifty others, guys I'd try to fool, guys it would make my face turn red to meet face to face, guys that had told me to scram, bum, scram, guys that had something on me, so I couldn't take it any more, and had to have a fresh slate that might be bad, but not this bad. So instead of deciding anything I just kept on going. I couldn't run very far, because by now I was getting a little weak. I had spent my last buck for a flop the night before and something to eat at a joint. Then, with everything I owned on my back or in my pockets, I had started out to bum a feed. That phony opening I didn't think up particularly. At first I just put it on the line: "Mister, I hate to bother you, but could you—" And that was all. By then they'd be gone. I had to get them to stop, somehow. I thought asking my way to the station would do it. I kept at it all day, downtown and on side streets, but not on any good street. I don't know why you hate it, that a guy with good clothes on might give you a snooty look, but you do.

I guess I was heading for New Orleans, and every time I'd hear something back of me I'd throw up my thumb. Nothing stopped. Then I saw some guys standing across the Southern yards like they were waiting for something. Then a string of gonds went past them, and banged into some flats. Then the engine would unhook and go down the yards, and I tumbled to what was going on. A freight was making up and these guys were waiting for it. I thought, me too. If that's how you go, that's how you go, and I should be here on the highway wasting my time on cars. It was, I would say, about five o'clock in the afternoon, just coming on dark with lights showing everywhere and fog hanging over. I went down in the ditch and up the other side and began crossing tracks. The guys looked up, and it was too far off to see them well, but the way they stared said there was something funny about it.

From down the yard I could see a light moving, and I guess I knew it was an engine, but as I said it was foggy, and you couldn't see anything clear. Anyway it was over on the other side of the yards and didn't seem to have anything to do with me. Then came a clanking, like a bunch of steel rods dumped down on concrete all at once. I mean it went *clank-clank-clank-clank-clank*. Then something hit me in the eyes, a glare that blinded me so I couldn't tell where I was. I knew then I'd heard switches clanking from an electric control, so the cross-overs made a diagonal line across the yards, and that the engine was coming right at me. I staggered back the way I had come, but it went through my mind I might as well stay put. There was no way to tell which track the thing had been switched to, and I could be racing right into it. I crouched down between tracks and waited. It got bigger and bigger in the fog, until it was right on top of me. Then it went by on the next track, a mile high, its firebox breathing hot on me.

* ## 13 *

WHETHER it was six months after that or longer I couldn't be sure, but it might have been a year, because I was catching one out of Chattanooga for the South, and that looks like winter coming on. A guy on the road, he goes plenty of places most of the time, but when the leaves begin to fall he heads for the Gulf. Anyway, there they were, about two hundred dirty buzzards squatting on the ties, spaced out along the Atlanta Division of the Southern, just outside the yards, waiting to hop on. Hardly anything was moving then, so it was the first through freight in a week, and they meant to get out of there. Nowadays they'd thumb the highways, and if a few ride the trains the crews hardly bother them at all, so they can hop one in the yards. But then the country was crawling with hobos, and nobody would give them a lift, let them on a train, or give them a break of any kind. If they wanted out, they hopped a moving train, so that's why they were there, waiting. Not much was said. Hobos don't mix, they don't look at each other, and they don't talk, something I didn't understand at first, but was to get a clear idea of, later.

Pretty soon, from the yards, came the cough of an engine, then three more, spaced out slow, then a string of quick barks that meant she was spinning her wheels, starting a heavy train. The coughs and the barks kept on, and then there she was, pulling hard, showing the two green flags of a through train, the one we wanted. Everybody got up. She began going by and they began going aboard, on tanks, gonds, or whatever they could grab. Some refrigerators went by, or reefers, as the hobos call them, and six or eight guys made a dive, because the ice compartment is a pretty good place to ride. But then they began dropping off again, on other guys' feet, and it was like cats fell on monkeys. A hobo, he grabs the front end of the car, because if he gets slammed, it's against the side and there's no great harm done. But on the rear if he get slammed it's against the thin air between cars, and he's almost certain to pitch down under the wheels, which isn't so good. It was just dark enough that these guys hadn't noticed the reefers were coupled with the ladder at rear, so they had no way to get topside to go down the hatch. So they had to pile on all over again, somewhere else. Me, I generally picked a flat, and that's what I did now. It's easy to board and easy to leave, and if it's a little open to the breeze you can help that a little with newspapers, and at least nobody's penning you in. I hated it, that I would have a system for such a miserable thing as life on the road, with a canteen on my hip, papers under my arm, and blue jeans over what was left of my clothes, but if you get cold enough, you'll do what you have to do to get warm, whether you hate it or you don't hate it.

I took the front end, where there was a little quiet air, and spread my papers out, two or three on top of each other so they were thick, and lay down on one edge. Then I rolled a little, so they were around me, and then I was warmer. Then, on my head, I felt something cold. Then I felt it again. Then I knew it was rain, and cussed myself out for not grabbing a reefer too. There wasn't but one thing to do. Ahead was a tank car, so I rolled my papers up, stepped over, slipped under the tank, and lay there trying to keep as dry as I could.

Then, after some little time, the train checked speed. Then, away up front some place, I heard somebody yell. Then there was more yelling. Then it got closer, and I could tell it was guys on the right of way. Then we began to go by them, while they stood there and yelled curses, out there in the rain, the worst you could ever think of, at the train crew, at the railroad, at the country, even at God. And then I knew what the reason was: They had taken it up, here in the East, what they were already doing on Western roads, letting the mob hop on, as they pretty well had to, unless they were going to hire a private army to keep it off, but then, after they'd run a little way, cutting the speed of the train, so it was slow enough for guys to drop off, but too fast for them to climb back on. Then the bull would start at the tender, and come back doing his stuff. Maybe you don't believe it, that they'd drop two or three hundred men off in the rain, with no place to go and no way to get there. Well, they did it just the same. It made your blood run cold, the things that were said, and your stomach turn sick, to realize why they were said, but however it made you feel, it was no great help when it came your turn to drop. I lay low, but the bull flashed his light, and when I didn't answer his "hey" he got tough: "It's O.K., Bud, if you want to lie there, but I'm telling you to get up and get off, because it would be just too bad if I decided you *were* some kind of a critter and began popping at you with this gun. . . ."

When my feet quit stinging from hitting the dirt, I stood there and cursed too. By now, I guess you know I'm not the yelling type, and in fact it might be better for me if I didn't keep things bottled in me so tight. But there come times when you've taken all you can take. By the water that was running off my nose, by the hunger that was gnawing at my belly, by cold that was creeping into me, I knew I couldn't get lower than I was that night. I was a human coffee ground, washing down the sink.

Pretty soon the yelling died down, and guys began pushing past me, slogging back to Chattanooga, some of them sobbing as they went. I started back with them, but then after a few steps I began to dope things out, and turned around. As well as I could figure, we were nearer Dalton by several miles than we were to Chattanooga, and I was taking a chance on it. It was just a small place, but it looked like, if I kept my mouth shut so I didn't bring any gang with me, I might do as well, at least for something to eat and a place to flop, as in a bigger place.

The train, I guess, rolled nearly a mile while the bull was throwing the guys off to where he came to me, so the bos and

I were passing each other for at least twenty minutes. Sometimes we'd bump, and they'd cuss, and maybe sock. But they generally had so little on the punch I didn't sock back. After a while I passed what seemed to be the last of them, and then the rain began coming down to mean it, and I jammed the papers under my jeans, so if I needed them again they wouldn't be so wet. Then I heard two guys talking, off to one side: "Come on, fellow! You can't lay there like that! You got to get up and—"

"God damn it, I said let me alone!"

"But that's no way to talk."

"Then beat it."

"If your foot hurts, then—"

"It's shot. And I'm shot, and—"

"But there on the ground, on a night like this, you'll die! You don't know how cold it's going to be! You—"

I made myself not hear it and went on. Off to the right there was rising ground, and I veered toward it to get out of the water in the path. I ran wham into something that sent me sprawling to the ground. I sobbed at how my toe shot fire up my leg, and jumped up and kicked at the thing. Then I went on. Then I almost ran into another one. Then it soaked into my head what I had run into. It was a couple of tool chests, six or eight feet long, with slanting lids on them. I thought of the guy back there, and how if he could get into one of these things he'd at least be out of the wet. I began telling myself to get on, or I'd be shot too. But before I got to the path again my foot hit something and I almost died at the pain in my toe that time. But my ear kept giving it to me, the clank I had heard, and then I went back. I felt around and found it was an open box of spikes. I kept mumbling to hell with the guy, to get on before I died too, but I took a spike and felt my way back to the first box and slipped it in under the hasp of the lid and pried. The staple flew out and

off on the ground. I lifted the lid and felt around in the chest.
It was empty.

"All right, grab his feet, get between them, and hold them
so he can't kick. I'll take care of the rest."

"I got 'em, big boy. Say when."

"What are you getting ready to do to me?"

"Up with him!"

"Let's go!"

I lifted him under the arms from behind, the other guy by
locking fingers under his knees, and we swung him along, me
shambling backward. When we got to the chest we set him
down and I opened the lid again and spread out my papers,
that I had dropped inside, so he could keep warm. Then I
climbed in, reached over, got my grip under his arms again,
and lifted. At last, then, we eased him down on something dry.
So he'd be out of the wet I climbed out and we dropped the
lid on him. He screamed and yelled like some kind of he-
devil inside a bass drum, and called us every name there was.
At last we tumbled to it that he thought we were going off
and leave him there to die. I said: "Well, what do we do
now?"

"Search me. I run into him this afternoon in the jungle
there by the water tank and he was pretty far gone then, what
with that raw place he had on his foot, but I talked to him and
finally got it through his head that no real hobo would let a
thing like that get him down, and at last I pumped enough
guts in him to get him aboard the train. Then on the coal
gond he got off a lot of wild talk about how his folks have a
store in Sandusky and he graduated from high school and run
a power shovel on a road job in Denver and then got laid off
last winter and never was tooken on again, until I got sick of

it. I said: 'Well, for the love of Pete, you and who else? You think you got it all to yourself? You think so, eh?'"

But when I heard some bumping in there, and then the lid was shoved up and he stuck his head out, I was a little on his side, because if there was one thing I wouldn't accept it was the idea of being a professional hobo. So I thought a minute, and then I said: "I got an idea."

"Yeah? What is it?"

"Feel the end of this box."

"O.K., I got it."

"The way *I* figure it, the lid and front and back and bottom of this thing are nailed to the ends, not the ends to them. That means, if we got inside there, and braced ourselves against the back, with our feet against the front—"

"Right!"

So that's how we did it, this guy that had helped me at one end, me at the other. We kicked with our heels hard against the boards in front, and in between we shoved. Pretty soon they began to give, slammed down in the mud, so at last, even with one guy lying against the back, there'd still be room for the other two to sit facing each other at each end, out of the wet, but at the same time with fresh air, so it wouldn't be like any coffin, which I suppose it was, more or less, if you were shoved in there all alone. I sung out to watch the nails that were sticking up, and then I raised up beside Mr. Grievous, where he was still standing in the middle. "Now, my young friend, I've had about all out of you I'm going to take. There's some kind of a bed for you here, and if you keep still and do what you're told you can keep warm and even get yourself a little sleep. After that, when we get some light on the subject, we'll see what can be done about your foot, and maybe get you to Dalton. Until then, if you don't want a bunch of fives in the kisser suppose you lie down and shut up and give other people some peace. And while you're making up your mind—"

I let him have it, not hard but hard enough, high on the chest. He went down and started crying. "Stop that."

We eased down the lid, the other guy and I, put our backs to the ends, and sat there. It was a God-awful place to spend the night, but at least we could stretch our legs and pull papers over them, and we were out of the wet. "What's your name, fellow?"

"Hosey."

It's only now, writing it, that I've tumbled his name was really Hosea. At the time, it seemed like Hosey, so I'll let it stand. "Mine's Jack. What's his?"

"He said call him Buck."

"Pleasant dreams, guys."

"Same, Jack."

"Go to hell, you bastards!"

But the cold was knifing in and my back ached, and I thought if I couldn't stretch out I'd crack up too and maybe not last. "You asleep, Hosey?"

"What do you think?"

"There's another tool chest up there."

"Why didn't you say so?"

We went out, shivering where the rain beat down on us, and I took my spike, and we pried the staple out of the other box pretty quick. But when we lifted the lid it was all full of shovels. "Shall we throw them out, Jack?"

"We and who else?"

"One hell of a job."

"Let's go back."

We dropped the lid again but something fell over inside

with a clatter. "Raise her up again, Hosey. We better have a look." What it was, was a couple of buckets that had been used for cement, and then stacked one inside of each other. We went back to the other box and sat some more, but then something in my head began talking to me about those buckets. So I got busy. I went out, stumbled along, and pretty soon came to my box of spikes. I grabbed three or four in each hand and came back. Then, keeping out of the wet as well as I could, I felt for the end of the nearest board we had kicked off the front, held a spike there. I beat on it to drive it in. I drove more thumb than spike, and my hand was all cut and bruised next day from the mislicks, but I got it in an inch or two, until with my finger tips I could feel a crack. I left that first spike sticking up, took another spike and drove it in the same way, along the line of the crack. I used spikes like a rail-splitter uses wedges, and when I started in with the third spike the board cracked like a shot two or three times. Then I jumped out there in the rain, grabbed the two-inch strip that was splitting away, and pulled. It came clear. I started in on the next two-inch strip. "What you doing, Jack?"

"Breaking wood for a fire."

"In this rain?"

"In those buckets it'll burn."

"That's right. By punching holes in them—"

"We got a brazier."

He helped, then, splitting up one board while I worked on another, until we had six or eight two-inch strips drying under the lid. We took them over to the track. Then one at a time we put them under the rail, heaved up till they broke, then did it over again, until we had three or four armfuls of wood in pieces maybe a foot long. Then we punched holes in the buckets the same way we had split the boards, using one spike for a punch and the other for a hammer. Then we stuffed one with paper and wood, put the other one on top, and lit it. Then we had the one pretty thing we had seen that night:

orange light through the holes. Then there was the sound of wood steaming, then a loud crack, then another and another. Hosey looked at me, then took off some kind of a thing that was supposed to be a hat. He was a tall, thin guy, maybe thirty, maybe forty, maybe fifty, with those queer, bright eyes old hobos have, that at first look friendly, till you see it's the friendliness of a scavenger dog. But I took off my hat too and we warmed our hands.

". . . There's a snake under this goddam box! It's crawling through that knothole!"

"Buck! After all Jack's done for you I'd—"

"Hosey, he's right. There *is* a snake down there, and the main purpose of the fire, of course, is to tempt and entice and decoy the snake, so he'll raise up through the knothole, and then Buck can bite off his head, accomplishing the double objective of getting something to eat and obtaining snake oil to put on his foot and—"

I was making it up as I went along, but Hosey kind of grinned, and I might have run on quite a while, I don't know. But just to give it some routine, I put my finger down the knothole. And when something touched it that was cold and soft and wet, I yelled. "Well, ain't you the funny son of a bitch. Get yourself a kazoo, why don't you, and play tunes at it, and then when he sticks his head up *you* bite his head off and squeeze his ribs for oil—come on, Jack, why don't you laugh?"

"Starting up again, are you?"

"Oh, I ain't dead yet."

With him jawing at me and Hosey looking first at me and then at the hole, I had to do something. I picked up a spike and went around behind. Of course, pitch dark as it was and wet as it was what you could see was nothing at all. But I lit a match, and it spluttered out but the flash was enough to give me the lay of the land. The chest had been set on top of a little rise, but behind it the ground fell away into bushes and grass, and it was a little gully, just a crease in the dirt, maybe a foot wide and six or eight inches deep. It looked like something must have crawled in there to get out of the rain, but what to do about it I didn't quite know, and fact of the matter, if it hadn't been for the razz I'd just taken, I probably wouldn't have done anything. But I kneeled down and lit another match. Then the ground gave way, and before I could get up I felt it coming toward me, whatever it was. I heard a squeal, grabbed, stood up with him, and then went running around with him to the fire. Sure enough, he was just what my ears had told me he'd be: a little piney woods rooter, as they call the wild pigs in the South, maybe three or four weeks old, kicking and squealing and biting. "Hosey!"

"Yes, Jack."

"Reach in my right-hand pants pocket, get the shiv in there, take it out, and open it."

"O.K."

"Hand it to me."

"Here it is."

"Stand clear. I'm going to stick him."

I'd never stuck a pig in my life, but there's plenty of things you can do if you get hungry enough. I jabbed the knife into his throat, then held him by one hind foot and went over to the track with him, so we wouldn't have the blood so near. I had no more feeling about it then than if I was emptying a bottle. When he seemed to be bled I went over to the other shed, where there was a stream of water running off the lid, and washed him. I took the cup off my canteen and set it there to fill. Then I went back to the fire. I'd never cleaned a pig either but I figured it would work like a fish. I spread out a newspaper, split him down the belly, took out the gut, wrapped it up, all except the liver, and threw it on the other side of the track. Then I washed him some more. Then I took the knife and cut the skin, bristles and all, off the four legs. I went over to the other box, felt around, and found a fork, one they use to fork ballast with. I laid it over the fire, so the tines made a grill. I laid the meat on it. Brother, was it a smell, when that shoat began to broil! "Jack."

"Yeah, Hosey?"

"It'll cook better if we section those hams up, so we got smaller pieces."

"Right."

We turned all the pieces twice, and when they were nearly done, Hosey began to talk: "Buck, our supper's about ready now, but before you get any of it, I'm holding a kangaroo court on you right now, and this is what you've got to do: First, you've got to say you're sorry, to me and Jack both, for the bughouse way you've been carrying on here, that's beat anything I ever hear tell of, I think my whole life. Second, you're going to apologize special to Jack here, because he's the one that's done everything for you and that you've got to thank for being here where it's warm with something to eat on the fire, instead of being left in that ditch, to die. And third, you're going to say please."

"Go to hell!"

"Can't you smell that pork?"

"You heard me."

"Don't you want to live at all?"

"God damn it, have I got to—"

"Hosey."

"Yeah, Jack?"

"Feed him."

Hosey took the meat off the fire and I took Buck by the back of the neck and sat him up straight. It was the first I had any idea what he even looked like. Except he was so beat up, he was kind of a handsome kid, twenty four or five, with light hair and blue eyes and maybe three days' growth of beard. He blinked at the pork, smelled it, then turned to me: "You ever shake hands with a damn fool?"

"No, but I wouldn't mind."

His face lit up with a friendly smile, nothing like a hobo at all, and he held out his hand. "I been watching you, Jack, and I'll say please, but it's because I ought to and want to, not because I got to."

"O.K., Buck."

"You hear me, Hosey?"

"O.K., so you say it."

I remembered my cup and went over to it. It was nearly full but I thought it would be a good idea to have something else catching water while the rain was coming down, so I opened the other chest and felt around inside for a can or something. Then my hand touched glass and there was a clink. I caught it and held it up to the light and it was a bottle, maybe two thirds full, but with no label on it. I took the cork out and smelled it and it was white mule, good old Georgia moonshine. I slipped it in my pocket, went back, offered the cup, and they had a drink. There was still some water left and I hooked the cup on the inside of the bucket so it was resting on coals. "Even if we got no coffee some hot water would go pretty good."

"Say, that's a hunch."

"O.K., Jack."

When the water began to smoke I took it off, Then, after I pulled the cork with my teeth, I spiked it with the mountain dew. I stuck the bottle back in my pocket, put the cork in, and tasted what was in the cup. It was raw, but it hit the spot. "Boys, try this, see what you think."

"Hosey, Hosey, the guy ain't human!"

"What is it? . . . Holy smoke!"

So we sat there, and sipped and talked and laughed and felt good and weren't coffee grounds any more, but men.

* **14** *

YOU got three musketeers, and maybe it's a beautiful friendship, but it's a cinch to be a gabfest all the time, with one and two talking about three, two and three talking about one, and one and three talking about two. Through all the hunger and dirt and sickness and cold that we had the next few months, I'd say the part of us that could still think was trying as much to understand the other two as it was to do something about the spot we were in. But mainly it was Hosey trying to understand me and Buck, and me and Buck trying to understand Hosey. Hosey would talk and talk and talk to me about Buck, and how he'd never learn the ways of the road, and just kept lousing things up for right guys that were willing to live and let live and didn't want any trouble. Like the way Buck always acted with the bulls. He never could let them call it like they were paid to call it, and shut up and figure it was all in a day's ride. He had to cuss at them like he had at me that night, and a couple of times he landed in jail. It was pretty tough waiting for him till his five days were up, once in the Baptist mission there on the Esplanade in New Orleans, and another time at a lousy jungle on the riverbank at Alexandria, but I couldn't quite get sore at him for it, even so. He yelled what I felt, and I didn't ever mean to feel dif-

ferent, or come around to the idea there was justice in it, I
didn't care how often I had to wait. But to Hosey, it was a
stab in the back to two pals, and you'd think we had a date
with Clark Gable out there in Hollywood, at a certain time on
a certain day, the way he beefed and bawled and bellyached.
He said Buck would never be a real hobo, that was the long
and the short and the size of it, and the way he told it, you'd
think real hobos were some kind of an order, like Odd Fellows
or Masons or Elks, but exclusive.

And me and Buck, when it was Hosey's turn to scavenge
up something to eat, would talk about him, and this real hobo
idea, and Buck could hand you a laugh the way he'd take that
malarkey off: "The real hobo don't ever get in trouble with
the railroad bulls, because if he ever got his arm high enough
for a sock it would fly over the telegraph wires, on account
the mulligan don't have enough vitamins in it to keep the
bone from coming apart at the elbow." And: "The real hobo
never steals his grub, on account if he tried to sneak up on
anything he'd stink so bad there'd be a hurry call for the
department of health, and after the exterminator squad got
done he'd amaze hisself one day by waking up to find he was
a bedbug." And: "The real hobo always leaves the jungle like
he found it, in shipshape for the next fellow, same as a
tumblebug always leaves the manure like he found it, in shipshape for the next tumblebug, so he can show the world he
is a real tumblebug and not no goddam cockroach. . . . Jack."

"Yeah, Buck?"

"How that son of a bitch loves a jungle."

"To him it's home."

"But *why?* To a flea it couldn't be home!"

"He likes it."

You've probably never seen a jungle, but you may have read
about it. I had too, and somehow got the idea there was something to it, inside stuff that you had to know about, that once
you got the hang of, would give you the chance to cook your-

self something to eat, take a little rest, and have some sleep.
Well, that's a lot of hooey, because what's there is nothing
at all, covered with dirt. Picture to yourself a bank, a stretch
of grass, a bare spot under the trees, sometimes a slope. Here
and there, four or five or six feet apart, are gray spots that
would turn out if you kicked them to be the remains of old
fires. Off in the bushes are old cans, buckets, pans, or whatever
it would be, some of them with holes punched in them and
wires attached, to hang over a fire, but none of them clean
enough to cook a meal in for any self-respecting skunk. Not
so far off a ditch to use as a latrine. And that is the hobo's
dream of heaven, the free apartment house he's supposed to
flock to, and sing his own particular songs, and have sociability
and relax. That's what Hosey was always trying to sell us,
except he never quite did. Well, why this place and not some
other place? Why not any place, if that's all there is to it?
Buck figured that out one day: "Jack, you ever fish?"

"Me? In Chesapeake Bay? Sure."

"Me too, in Lake Erie. One time my three uncles all came
to spend the Fourth of July with us at once. My mother
bunked them down in the garage, and then they and my
father decided to go fishing and they went, and took me
along. They chartered a power boat and we ran out in Lake
Erie and baited up and put our lines down—hand lines, on
account there were too many in the boat for poles. And
boy, did we bring them in—whitefish and perch. I never saw
so many fish in my life. We came home with two baskets full
and my mother almost got reconciled to it, having three
brother-in-laws in the house at the same time. She fried the
perch and put the whitefish away, some in the icebox, some in
a basket with ice on top on account the icebox wasn't big
enough for them all. Next morning when she went to look,
the fish in the basket weren't there, and by night we knew
why. The rats had got them, and they were in between the
walls. Brother, they stunk. So that was a summer, tearing out

laths, getting the fish, and putting the poison around for the rats. At night, my father would check every tap and spigot and sink, screw everything down, and even wipe away drops. 'The thing is,' he'd say, 'to fix it so when they've got to have water they'll go outside for it and die there. With arsenic, the thirst is unbearable, and if you cut off everything in the house you're all right. But God help us if they find water inside and stay inside.' Jack, you see any connection between them rats and Hosey's jungle?"

"I'm beginning to."

"There's just one thing you'll find in them jungles, and that's water. Some goddam fool put it there and forgot about it, maybe a tap to water the grass, or fill up his steam boiler, or wet down his cabbages, or maybe it's a spring. Whatever it is, it's water, and it draws hobos, like rats. You hear me, Jack? Hosey's a rat."

"He's not far from it."

"When did you go on the road, Jack?"

"Oh—year or two ago."

"*Why* did you?"

"Little trouble at home."

"That's it, we all had a little trouble at home, you and me and a million others that are riding the cars. But do you know how long Hosey's been on the road?"

"I never asked him."

"Since before the war. The real hobo, you know, always has his papers in order, and he was showing me his registration card, for the draft or whatever it was. He got rejected, he says, on account of physical, but that card said 1917. *Nineteen seventeen, Jack*—he's been on the road all his life. Jack, don't he *ever* work?"

"I wouldn't know."

He leaned close to me. "Jack, will *we* get like that?"

One time, riding the U.P. out of St. Louis bound for Kansas City, or K.C. as the hobos call it, we got thrown off I guess eight or ten miles the other side of Independence. We'd spent the winter in New Orleans, Alexandria, Shreveport, Port Arthur, Beaumont, and God knows where else, and it was a little warmer down there than some other place, but how they treated hobos was a crime. So, soon as winter began to break, we hit north, in the early spring of 1934. Pretty soon we slid over to the highway and began hiking for Kansas City. But we hadn't gone very far when we came to a road-building camp, where they were doing a relocation job, with bunk shacks, and mess shacks and all the rest of it. So of course Hosey headed for the cook to see what he could mooch, and Buck and I sat down to wait for him. But then we noticed no work was being done. Mexicans were standing around talking, and off to one side three or four guys that looked like foremen were in a huddle, but no dirt was being moved, no concrete was being poured, no shoulder was being smoothed. Buck knew about road-building, and he kept saying something funny was going on. When Hosey came back he had nothing, and said everybody was sore, on account of the blacksmith quitting. "They've sent to town for somebody to take his place, but right now they're closed down."

"Blacksmith? What's he got to do with roads?"

"Jack, I only know what they told me."

We sat there a few minutes, then Buck said: "I got it figured out, I guess."

"Yeah, what is it?"

"You see that bunch of stuff over there?"

Off to one side in a field was a ledge of rock, an outcropping with a face on it, with big slabs and pieces lying under that, and in front some machinery, with yellow dust all over it. "Jack, that's their stone quarry. The thing out front is a crusher. And those boulders are stuff that's been shot down and that has to be blockholed and shot and sledged before it'll go into the crusher. That's what's holding things up. The blacksmith, he has to sharpen their bits for the blockholing teams, and he's gone off. Without fresh stone for the crusher, there's nothing for these mixers here by the road, and that's why they've shut down."

"So?"

"Let me think."

So he thought, trying to figure an angle, and I did, and I guess Hosey did. And then I remembered the smithing course I'd taken in college, something I hadn't paid much attention to because I hated hot metal and the stink of the forge made me sick. But if I hated the smell of coke it was nothing to how I hated an empty belly, so next off I was legging it over toward the Mexicans, asking for the super, and when they pointed to a little shack near the mixers I went in there. "Hear your blacksmith quit."

"My blacksmith got fired, for being drunk, him and his no-good helper both, and if you're some relation of his—"

"Me? I'm a blacksmith."

". . . Oh, yeah?"

He looked me over, from the hat I still had from Baltimore, that had dust, dirt, and sweat ground into it till you couldn't tell what color it was any more, to the jeans that had been boiled in every jungle from Macon, Georgia, to St. Louis, Missouri, and to the shoes, a pair of brogans I'd got in the Good Samaritan Inn at Columbus, Ohio, just before heading south. It was something, at least, that he couldn't see the suit, inside the overalls, with the snags and rips and tears in it. I kind of bowed in a very elegant way, and there wasn't much he could do but bow back, and then I went on to say if he'd put me and my two helpers to work, by lunchtime I could have stuff sharpened up for him so he could start his crusher that afternoon and put his whole crew to work. By that time Buck and Hosey were hanging around outside, and he thought a minute, but one thing on my side was he had a bunch of idle men on his hands, and every minute they didn't work was piling up trouble, and besides maybe he had some penalty clause in his contract with a bonus for speed, and I could see he wanted to get going. "Of course, chief, I don't kid you any—a bright hombre like you I wouldn't even try. Before we work, we've got to eat. On an empty stomach we're a little weak. And, while we're filling up, I could be having a look at the stuff you've been using."

"What stuff?"

"Why—your drills. Your bits."

"What for?"

By the way his eyes bored into me, I knew I'd pretty near overplayed it. But I acted surprised, and said: "To see the color, how they're tempered for the rock you're busting. That is, unless you want some broken shanks before I see what I'm up against."

"O.K., O.K."

Just the least thing that sounded like I *might* know my business was all he wanted to hear, and the next thing the three of us, Buck, Hosey, and me, were in the cook shack, putting away sow belly, beans, flapjacks, and coffee with plenty of sugar and condensed milk in it, something we hadn't tasted in months. I've heard that when you're starved for a while and then sit down to a full meal you can't eat anything. Well, if somebody tells you that, you can say I investigated the matter that morning and there's nothing to it. We ate so much that even the cook went bug-eyed, and he wasn't exactly used to delicate appetites. In the middle of it the super, whose name turned out to be Casey, came in with an armload of steel, ⅞″, 1″, and 1¼″ pieces, in lengths from a foot to eighteen inches, and dumped it on the table beside me. "O.K., chief, that's what I want. Thanks."

"Say when, Jack."

"How are you on tempering fluid?"

"Four cans, more on order."

"Coke?"

"Plenty."

"Tub?"

"Two or three or four of them."

"I'll be right over."

He went and I had a look at the smaller pieces, the bits I mean, and they were just straight cutting edges, crosswise of the length of the rod, like a little square block had been set in there, cocked 45°. The edge was longer than the steel was thick, as it would have to be, naturally, if the shank was to follow the bit down in the hole, and on the shorter pieces quite a lot longer. The big pieces, though, the 1¼″ stuff, really gave me a creepy feeling in the pit of the stomach. Because the end had been bulged out, then creased four ways so the face was like a four-leaf clover, then fixed up with four cutting edges, and how to smith any of it I had no more idea than the man in the moon. I studied a while, then leaned over to Buck. "How do these goddam things work?"

". . . You mean you don't *know?*"

"Come on, let me have it!"

"A guy sits on the rock. On the rock they're breaking up, the block, they call it. He holds the drill, with both hands, against the stone. Then two other guys, three if they're in a hurry, beat on it with striking hammers. Six-pound hammers, that look like croquet mallets, with handles about three feet long. The guy holding it, every time one of the hammers strikes, he turns the steel a little bit. They do it in time. Sometimes they sing. It sinks down, two inches, two feet, as deep as they want. Halfway through the block. As it goes down the guy holding it pours water in, to cool it, and wash the dust out. When it's down far enough the powder man sets his charge, and at quitting time they light fuses and duck. Next day it's ready for sledging."

"How about these big steels?"

"They're for the power drills. They're used on the face of

the rock. They drill holes sometimes ten feet deep, maybe deeper—"

"And they use steels that long?"

"Sure, they've got to be."

"They made here, on the job?"

"Of course."

"*How* are they made? Can you tell me that?"

"They got a dolly or something."

It began to come back to me, what I'd learned in college, and all of a sudden I could hear Dr. Buchhalter, the metallurgist, ding-donging at us, over and over: "Upset it, upset it, upset it, you must upset it first, before you can make anything from it at all." Upsetting it is to take a length of steel, an octagonal rod, an inch thick or whatever it may be, and heat the end for maybe six inches up the shank to a cherry red, then stand with it beside the anvil, hold it in both hands, raise it above your head, and bang it down, over and over and over again, until you've bulged the end of it out so it looks like the rubber cuff on one of those things a plumber uses to clean out stopped-up pipes. It's tough work, and if it slips or you don't hit the anvil or something you're liable to mark yourself up for life. But at last I understood what I was supposed to do, and when the super came in again I said: "O.K., Mr. Casey, why don't I get some of these small drills in shape first? Then you can bust up the stuff that's already shot down, set charges tonight, and in the morning send your sledgers in, so by lunchtime you have something for your crusher?"

"That makes sense. And be sure on anything less than two feet, to make those bits plenty wide, so when we switch to longer drills they slip down easy and we don't get jammed."

"I'll be watching it."

The fire had been started by the time I got to the forge, and I stuck four or five short pieces of steel in there, showed Hosey how to turn the blower, and stood around till they were cherry red. Then I picked one up, beat on it to shape it, then

began hammering it to spread the bit. When it widened a little
I'd shape some more. Then I gave it some licks to sharpen it,
and so far as I could see it looked all right. I held it up to
Casey: "O.K. for size?"

"Looks fine."

Now I had come to the one thing I remembered right, or
thought I did, from my college days, which was tempering. I
heated it up again until the shank was red for about two inches
above the bit. Then I waited until it came down from cherry
to crimson, then I dipped the bit in the fluid. It sizzled and I
took it out. The bit was a hot, bubbly gray, like it ought to be,
and the shank was just going from red to black. Then pretty
soon here it came, the straw color I wanted, creeping down
the shank, with the purple just behind. I waited till the straw
was all over the bit, then I plunged it in the tub of water. I
took it out and handed it over. "Try that."

They quit at four thirty, and set off their shots, so at last I
could rest. We took a shower, all three of us, before checking
in at the mess tent, and there was no hot water, but at least
we got clean. Then we ate. Then we headed for a bunk and
sat down for a little rest. For Buck and Hosey that meant a
smoke. They had drawn cigarettes at the commissary, and I
could see their eyes closing, as they lay back against the
blankets, like a couple of hopheads in a Chinese joint. I lay
back on the blankets. They smelled like disinfectant but they
didn't stink, like the beds in the missions. They stink like feet
and puke and sweat that's soured. Around sundown Casey
came in. "Jack?"

"Yeah, chief?"

"Feel like a little work?"

". . . So it's just a little. I'm shot."

"For overtime up to twelve it's time and a half. After that, if it runs that long, I can make it double. Double time. I need drills."

"I left you a dozen."

"I mean the big ones."

"I can't do them tonight. I'm too tired."

"Jack, I got to have them. If I can have some ready by morning I can start work on my face and have a batch of stuff shot down by tomorrow night and really get going again. If I've got to wait till tomorrow before I've got them all working my gang falls apart and I'm behind and it'll be a week before I get them together again, and—I'm in a spot."

"Plenty more men where they came from."

"These are Mexicans. That makes it all different."

"Let me rest."

"O.K."

So I rested, then told him he had to take on Buck and Hosey, and he said O.K., and around seven o'clock we went to work on the big stuff. I cut six of the pieces in half, so he'd have a dozen ten-foot lengths to start. I made Buck and Hosey do the upsetting, so I could save my strength. When they had a bulge on all the pieces big enough to suit me, I took a chisel and put four light creases on each bulge. Then I upset a little more myself. Like I thought, the splits deepened, and I had my four-leaf clover. Then I took the dolly, had Buck hold it in place while Hosey held the steel, and beat on it. I could feel it bite in. When it was in solid I pulled it away and looked. As well as I could tell the cutting edges were right. I heated and tempered, but let the straw almost flicker off before I plunged, as I figured on the big stuff, the shank could be a little softer. I made another, another, and another. Along about number eight Hosey cracked up. I thought Buck would kill him. "That goddam simple-looking jungle buzzard, even when a blower's all he's got to turn he can't do it! What the hell good is he? Why don't he—

"Leave him be!"

"But—"

"Stop it!"

We let Hosey sit, so he could run up his time, and I think he slept a little, there near the forge, in the heat. Wrestling the steels, dolly, and blower was more than a two-man job, and I almost cracked up too, but we got along somehow. By three o'clock we had stuff for the power crews next day.

What woke me up, some time around four o'clock that afternoon, was the anvil. There's no sound just like it, that clink-clink-clink, flop-it-over-on-the-other-side, clank-clank-clank. Somebody else was working that forge, but it had no business to be anybody but me. I got up, showered, and dressed. When I went outside, it seemed to me the cook was awful friendly. "*¿Sí, sí, señor?* Feel like some grub, yeah?"

"Who's the blacksmith?"

"Ah, some goddam fellow. Who cares?"

But coming over from his office was Casey. "Jack, I got bad news for you. . . . This morning, after you turned in, this yap showed up from Kansas City."

"And?"

"I had to hire him."

"Why?"

"He had a note from the home office, and—what the hell, Jack? I rang up and raised hell and told what you'd done for me and how it helped us out of a spot and all, but they got a waiting list too. Guys they laid off two, three, and four years ago they feel they got to make way for, if any making way can be done."

"Nice appreciation a guy gets."

"Boy, I hate it."

". . . What else you got around here?"

"Nothing."

When we hit for K.C., with a little money in our jeans at last, the driver wouldn't let us on the bus we were so dirty. Up the line were three boxcars we'd seen unloading, and it looked like sometime a train would come along to haul them out. We camped down there and Hosey found a crate and we built a fire and tried to keep warm. We saw something back of us, and pretty soon an express rolled up and stopped and we got ready, because that meant they were waiting for a freight to take the siding and let them by. Pretty soon, maybe a mile away, we heard it whistle. The express began to roll, and the diner came in sight, with people eating soup, steak, ice cream, everything we hadn't tasted in a month of Sundays. Hosey jumped up and shook his fist at them. "Damn you! Damn you all! Damn every son of a bitch in there, and your—"

"Hosey! Take it easy!"

"And all their goddam brother-in-laws and stepfathers that are keeping us out of a job."

"Tell 'em, bo."

"Damn 'em!"

That was one thing we did, unanimous, was damn the people in the dining cars. We used to talk how if it was us in there, and hungry guys were out on the road, we'd invite them in to have a bite and rest their feet. We used to talk how we'd give them jobs. We used to talk how guys had taken enough, and it was their turn now. It makes no sense, but you try it for a while, out there in the cold, with no food and no hope and no place to sleep, and see how much you like a guy that's unbuttoning his vest on account he's full from the meal he just finished.

* 15 *

I DON'T know how it is now, but at that time Kansas City was a wide-open town, the only one, outside of the Nevada places, that was left in the whole country, any way that I heard of. So the day after we got there Buck came up with his bright idea. We were in a little hotel on Walnut Street, though in single rooms. There were three things I meant to do: get clean, lock the door on the whole human race, and tell somebody to do something and hear him say: "Yes, sir." But he came in pretty often, and this time he camped on the edge of my bed, talked about how good it was to have a place to sleep, and pretty soon said: "Jack, I been hearing things about the town. She's free, wide, and careless."

"Meaning?"

"They got houses."

"With red lights on them?"

"So how about stepping out? Take ourselves around to one of those places and have ourself a time."

". . . That I would have to think about."

"You don't like it?"

"It's a new one on me. I—don't know if I like it or not. I'll have to let it cook a while, see how it hits me."

"Don't you ever think about the red lights, Jack?"

"I heard about them. That's all I can say."

"I always wanted to see them."

"We got all day. They don't open till night."

"Oh, there's no hurry."

He sat there and talked about spring being in the air, even

in a dump like this, and while he talked I thought. I guess the man never lived that didn't get a prickle up his back when he thought about a house, I don't know exactly why. Maybe it's like what a guy told me once, in England, about the bullfights in Mexico: "If it was my own country I'd be against them, and do everything I could to get them stopped. But when it's somebody else's country, and there's not one thing in the world I can do about it, I go. They get me. And as to why they get me, if you ask me, it's because they're so horribly, intentionally, and completely evil—evil all dressed up in purple satin, with lace sewed down the side." Something like that was running through my head, listening to Buck, but pretty soon I knew I wasn't going with him. To pay a woman for what had always been kind of a dream was something I couldn't do. Still, that was something locked inside me, that I wouldn't have wanted to tell anybody, and anyway it seemed a little over Buck's head. So after a while I said: "Well, count me out."

". . . I'd been hoping you'd come."

"Little old for that stuff."

"How old are you, Jack?"

"I was born in 1910."

"Twenty-four—old, say, that's a joke."

"How old are you, Buck?"

"Twenty-five."

"When did you go on the road?"

"Three years ago. Oh, I'd left home before, so far as that goes. I started out when I was eighteen, to get me a job so I could get married. She was fifteen. I started on road work, got promoted to power shovel, and then came 1929 and the shovel blew up and the road job blew up and all jobs blew up. I'd been home quite a few times, and gave her a ring one Christmas, but when I didn't have any job she started in teaching school, and then when I still didn't have any job she lost interest. Then at home one thing led to another and I blew."

"Change it around a little bit it's me."

"It's everybody."

"Getting back to the lights: No."

"Any special reason?"

"Might catch something."

"These places are inspected."

"They were, up to last night. This is tonight."

"Some things, Jack, you got to take a chance."

"Not me, I haven't."

He sat thinking, and seemed so down I felt half sorry for him, and remembered what I'd heard once or twice: that one reason a mug goes to a house is he's so lonesome he'd give anything for a half hour with a girl and the chance to forget who he is or what he is or why he is. But then he had another proposition: "Well, if you don't want to go how about keeping me company while I do some visiting? You know—buy some girl a drink, sit out the dance, but—be there?"

"Me? Buy some tart a drink with dough that will mean another night out of the weather if I can hold on to it that long? Besides, you can't buy a girl a drink in those places. It's drinks up for everybody every time you call the maid, and what do I care for a bunch of stockyard cowboys and their sweeties? They got money. Let them spend it."

"You mean—there's ropes you got to know?"

"They'll teach you. Take you, too."

"Jack, just as a favor to me—"

"Buck, no."

"But I never been to a house."

"Me neither."

"But you know your way around, and—"

"You'll find your way."

After a while there was a knock on the door and I opened and it was Hosey, with a bundle. Of course he hadn't come to the hotel with us, but hiked himself over to some mission back of Union Station, because if no real hobo would work he wouldn't pay either, or do anything but mooch. But it was all right, it turned out, for me to pay and him to wash up in the hot water I had, and that's what the bundle was for. If you think I said help himself, just out of the kindness of my heart, you don't know Jackie. I bawled him out for the filthy jungle buzzard that he was, told him I wasn't going to have my bathroom stunk up like a mission bed, and said if he wanted to wash he could march himself downstairs, plunk down his money, and get a room like decent guys did. But he just sat there with a little grin on his face, his eyes shifting around like a rat on a dump. Pretty soon Buck said: "Hosey, what you doing tonight?"

". . . Nothing, that I know of. Why?"

"How about going out among 'em?"

"Among who?"

"Why—the pretty dollies."

"You mean *women?*"

"Why not?"

"You don't *know* no women."

"Don't have to know them. Here they got women that's so sociable you don't even have to be introduced. They're broad-minded. They got whole houses full of them."

Hosey stood up and his eyes turned black and you wouldn't have thought he could dig up that much excitement, let alone care about anything enough to go on like he did: "Buck, I'm telling you something, for your own good, right now. The real hobo, he don't have nothing to do with women, of any age, shape, or kind—they're *out!* They're no part of his life. He just has to give up any thought of women. In the first place, he can't afford it. In the second place, if he keeps it up, the kind of women he meets, he going to get himself a disease, and if he does, God help him. For typhoid or diphtheria or pneumonia or whatever else he catches, or a broken bone if he falls off a train, or anything of that kind, he can go to a clinic and they'll take care of him, the public health will, wherever he is, some kind of way. But let him get something like that, and he's just out of luck and nobody'll do anything for him. In the third place, sooner or later some woman he's with is going to get caught by friend husband, and then God help him. There's plenty of guys doing time right now for rapes that was never committed, just because some two-timing dame had to say something quick, and hung it on them. Buck, I'm telling you, *leave women alone!*"

By then he was so hysterical he could hardly talk. Buck looked at me and I looked at him and then we begun talking about something else. Hosey picked up his bundle and went out. "Well, Jack, what the hell do you make of *that?*"

"It was real hobo talk, whatever it was."

"Is he a *preacher* or something?"

"In some ways, of course, it made sense, but—"

"Yeah, but he *looked* so funny."

The next night I was in bed, reading a magazine, when there came a rap on the door. I unlocked it and Buck came in. He looked pretty solemn. I waved him in, shut the door, and got back under the covers again. He sat down on the bed and lit a cigarette. "Well, Buck, was she nice?"

"—And pretty."

"Then if you had a good time, what the hell?"

"I didn't have any good time."

". . . I don't get it."

"I don't either. God, you wanted to think, now let me do a little of it. Jack, there must be something the matter with me."

"You mean—you've *got* something?"

"No, something else. Jack, I couldn't go in any of the houses, once I found one. That part was easy. I thought I'd pay a taxi driver fifty cents to take me to one, but hell, before I could even see a cab a cop showed me. But I was afraid to go in. I don't know why. There was guys ringing the bell of a dozen places and women letting them in, but—I couldn't get up the nerve."

"I'm not sure I could."

"I thought about you, and didn't feel so bad, somehow. So then I went over on Broadway, to see a picture maybe, before coming back here. And there I saw two girls. They were kind of cute and one of them looked at me and said something to the other one and I got excited, because she was a pretty little thing, maybe eighteen or nineteen, Mexican, but with color in her cheeks and not as dark as some of them. Another thing, she had on just a little cheap dress and coat so I didn't feel so bad about this suit I had on. I started to cross, but just then a bus stopped and the other girl got on. My girl, she waved goodbye, then went on up the street. But just once she looked back and I piled after her hell to split. When I got close I spoke and she laughed and then we were arm in arm and I said something about a drink and she said she knew a place and then we were in one of these new cocktail bars they got all over now, and she ordered a bottle of red wine and we drank part of it. Then she said she had a place we could go and we took our bottle and walked quite a way, to some kind of Jimtown across from the yards, and went past Mexican shacks and then she took me inside a place made out of old boards and dry-goods boxes, but not too dirty, and with a couple of chairs and a coal-oil stove with two burners. We drank the rest of our wine, me loving her up all the time. And—that's all."

"What do you mean, that's all?"

"Nothing happened."

"Why not?"

"I—couldn't."

"Did something *scare* you, or what?"

"Nothing scared me. Get how it was. She was pretty as a

picture. She was small, with as nice a shape as I ever hope to
see. And she wanted me. I guess maybe she could be bought,
I don't know. I gave her five dollars when I left, but it didn't
seem she could be bought. I don't think I *had* to buy her. I
think she *liked* me. But—that was all. I couldn't."

"How long did this go on?"

"I guess an hour."

"And what did you do then?"

"What would you do? After a while, from being friendly
and laughing and all that, she just sat there looking at me, then
just sat there. I got up and pitched the five dollars in her lap
and left. . . . What the hell does it mean, Jack?"

"I don't know."

"I wanted her, bad."

"You wanted the idea of a woman, bad."

"Yeah, but that's the main part of it."

He sat there a long time, looking at his feet. It seemed a
pity, much as it had been on his mind, that things should
have turned out like they did. His face began wrinkling up.
"What did Hosey mean?"

"If anything."

"Jack, he meant more than he said. Nobody could get that
hot under the collar for the reasons he said were his reasons.
There's something else."

After our money ran out in Kansas City we swung off
through Kansas and Colorado and then south, and everywhere
we went it got tougher. I mean, on the trains they didn't
bother you so much any more, because the big mob was gone,
but in the towns they treated you like a polecat with the itch,
and meant get out and stay out. That was on account of the
CCC. It drew guys off the road all right, but at the same time
it gave people the idea things were under control and there

was no need to mooch. It was under control, if you'd go home
and get certified by your family, or establish residence somehow, to prove you were entitled to help. But that was something Buck and I wouldn't do, and Hosey couldn't do, for
reasons that kind of seemed to be there, once you got thinking
about them. We applied of course, all three of us, in Denver.
But when we found out the terms, having to go back home I
mean, Buck and I backed off, and Hosey got almost hysterical:
"It's nothing but a stunt to get votes, that's what it is. A guy
ain't no hungrier home than he is any other place, and he
ain't no better. But he's on the books there, or can get put on
the books, and if he affiliates right, he's in. But how about
them that can't—"

If he hadn't stopped so quick I don't think Buck or I would
have paid much attention, but when he went out like some
radio that blew a tube, we looked at each other. Then we began
to wonder if Hosey had done time, and if that was why he
couldn't get put on any books. And then pretty soon he began
hinting around that if a man had made a mistake once and
learned his lesson, was that a reason to shove him out in the
cold for the rest of his life? Buck made a crack about work,
but Hosey had a comeback: "Work—what work? Sitting on
the onion bed, keeping them bullubs company while they
grow? That's all I see them CCC bastards doing. That and
wait in line for the privy. That's a sight for you. You want to
know if it's a government job you don't look for a flag no
more but only if it's got a goddam green-and-white privy.
What a country!" He got pretty bitter and talked so mysterious
we began to wonder if the Communists had got him. They
were in every mission by then, telling guys where to go to
hear the dope handed out. But then we began to tumble that
Hosey wasn't talking about Russia, he was talking about grub,
and was nothing like as hot for the law and keeping out of
trouble like a real hobo does, as he had been.

All that, though, was before Albuquerque and what hap-

pened to me there, or didn't happen, as it turned out. We were
in the Santa Fe yards, getting ready to catch out West, for
Arizona and maybe even California, if we could hang on that
long. The shacks had said our train would leave around nine,
so we parked on a flat while the yard engines slammed it together. When we saw three work cars pulled out, we got kind
of excited, because if one of them was open and had bunks
we might be able to have ourselves a trip. As I was the one
that had mooched the supper Buck and Hosey said keep still,
that they'd go see. So they went. It was quite a way, because
the head of the train was half a mile away, so I got as comfortable as I could and began looking how bright the stars are
on a New Mexico night. Then a passenger train pulled in. It
made the station, then pulled out slow, with diner and club
car going by, and me bitter as usual against people that were
eating and drinking and reading and doing things I couldn't
do. Then some sleepers went by, mostly dark, but you could see
porters in there making up berths. Then a sleeper began going
by that was all dark, and then the train stopped. I was paying
no attention until all of a sudden, not five feet from my face, a
light went on. It was in a compartment, and who had turned
it on was a girl. She was blonde, not too big, and with one of
those shapes you see on a magazine cover. She switched
around in front of the mirror, turned and twisted, and looked
at herself from every angle there was. Of course that gave me
an angle on every angle there was. Then she began to undress,
and everything she took off she'd flirt with herself in the
mirror again, and swing her hips from side to side like a
dancer does. Pretty soon she hadn't one stitch on, and I'd hate
to tell you what she did then. Then the train began to move,
and she was gone.

"What do you mean it did nothing to you?"
"What I say. Nothing, Buck."

"Well, what the hell—with a window in between—"

"With a window in between or a whole glass mountain in between, for a guy to see that girl, what she was doing, and not have any reaction to it, don't tell me it was just a little case of what-the-hell. There's something funny about it."

The work cars had been locked, but when the train began to move, Hosey stayed forward, in a sand gond that he liked, and Buck dropped off to join up with me. He kept calling my name so I wouldn't go by without his seeing me, but I was so numb from what I had seen that I almost didn't answer him. But I woke up in time to pull him aboard, and then when we got rolling I told him what had happened and what it didn't do to me. He figured on it a while, then said: "You've forgotten something, haven't you?"

"Like what, for instance?"

"Me and my Mex. And Hosey, how he carried on."

"And what's that got to do with it?"

"We just haven't got it any more, that's all. That's what he was holding back. That's what riled him like it did, and got him so excited he could hardly talk. That's why a real hobo don't have anything to do with women. It's because he can't. It's not only that he stinks and they won't have him and he wouldn't even have the price of a bunch of flowers if they would, it's because even if they would have him he can't have them. He's gone. Well, who the hell would expect any different if he thought about it awhile? That's a life we lead, isn't it? Sleep in some shed or tool chest or mission or boxcar or cattle chute, cold as hell, hard as hell, dirty as hell, and get the hell out before dawn for fear some bull will chase us. Shave out of that canteen cup of yours if we got any blades to shave with—shave every day with cold water, muddy water, any kind of water there is, till our face is raw or even got blood running out of it, because if we don't shave we can't mooch or even bum a ride or stay on a train without we get run in—because a guy without a shave, he's just a bum that any judge would send up after one look at him. Then mooch a breakfast, whatever we can find, a bowl of soup with grease all over it or a bowl of grease with a little soup under it or six boiled potatoes from last night's dinner or a cup of coffee and a piece of bread or whatever anybody'll give us. Then work the stem a while if we're clean enough to go on the stem, and if we're not, find some goddam jungle under a railroad bridge where we can bring a can and some water and boil up our lousy clothes and hang our stockings up to dry and knock the mud off our shoes and hope the cops haven't got orders to run us out while we're sitting there naked with our knees up under our chin. Then into our clothes again and out on the stem again, and if we split it up right and Hosey finds a crate and you work the butcher shops and me the kitchen stoops, maybe we come up with enough for some mulligan, and if none of our stuff was rotten, we don't get sick that night, but if some of it was, we spend half the night in some ditch before we start in town again trying to find another place to lie down and be warm and get some sleep. Next day we decide it's the fault of the town and hop a freight and start all over again. You think that life puts anything in your bones that would be any use to a woman, you're crazy. Glass, my eye. If there had been no glass there, nothing but a welcome sign, it wouldn't have done you any good to go in. Would it?"

"No."

In Phoenix we washed dishes in some restaurant for something to eat, and then Hosey went on back to a shed they had in the back yard, with gunny sacks piled up in it, where they said we could sleep. But Buck walked on over to a gully beyond the fence, and sat on a rock, and I could see him staring at the traffic that was going by on 80. Pretty soon I went out there with him. He was pretty glum: "Some life, Jack."

"Bad as it can get."

"Worse than I knew it could ever get."

"I'll go that far too."

"What the *hell* are we going to do?"

"If I knew, pal, I'd tell you quick enough."

We sat there a long time, and then my head began to pound. "Yeah, Jack, what is it?"

"Really, you're still talking about one thing. What I found out through the glass, and you with your Mex."

"If it wasn't for that, Jack—"

"I could put up with the rest of it."

"Come on, let's have it."

"Buck, the sleep part, we can manage, specially out here in the Southwest, where it's warm, and at this time of year, when almost anywhere is a place to sleep. The rest of it's grub. All right, get this: What we've lost, what we haven't got any more, I mean to get back. I don't mean to turn into just a thing, like Hosey is. I'm going to be a man, or else—"

"Yeah, Jack, that's what I want to hear. But *how?*"

"I'm going to take it."

"The grub?"

"You're goddam right."

"You think you're doing it alone?"

"Then we'll both do it."

"Jack, we got it coming to us."

"All right, then we got it coming to us. But I'm going to eat, whether we got it coming to us or not. Now if you want to come in—"

"Jack, shake just once and shut up."

We sat out there till the traffic didn't run any more, and you could hear birds warbling, and talked about how we were going to do it. By that time we knew where the grub was and how to get it and a whole lot of things nice people don't know, but guys on the road do. The only difference was, would we or wouldn't we? From now on we knew we would.

* 16 *

TO do it right, what we were figuring on, took three, because we'd be all day and all night getting a meal, if two guys had to spot a place, watch their chance, steal the grub, and then have to mooch a can to cook it in and wood to cook it with. We had to have two stealing and one mooching, and that meant on the jungle end of it we had to have Hosey, but we had one sweet time selling him. We argued for two days about it. But there we were, still washing dishes and stacking and shoving ice and barrels around this dump in Phoenix, and nowhere to go but out, soon as three guys showed up that they liked better. And there were those trucks going by all the time, full of CCC guys yelling at us, and I think that was what finally got Hosey. Anyway, out of a clear sky one afternoon, sitting by the side of the road, he said O.K., and then knocked us over by really getting in it, and telling us what we had to do if we were going to get away with it, and he had it down so pat you couldn't help wondering if he wasn't kind of a postgraduate recruit. The main thing, he said, was to keep it small, so to begin with the cops didn't take any interest in the job even if it was reported. The next thing was to confine it to food, because three guys filling their bellies was one thing, but three crooks really stealing would be something else. The next thing, he said, was to get the lay of every job before we pulled it, so we'd be in and out and gone before they even knew we'd been there. The last thing was: Don't be too proud to run.

All that was about the way Buck and I had figured it, but

we still thought Hosey ought to be in charge of the mooch department, and fires and cans. He thought so too. So around sundown he started for the Salt River, where we were going to do our cooking, and Buck and I slid out to the west end of town, where we were going to do our stealing. Under our shirts, when we said goodbye to the restaurant man and his wife, were a couple of gunny sacks we neglected to mention to them.

Out Van Buren Street is a bunch of motor courts and hotels, and not far from them two or three cafés for tourists, and not far from them some stores. As to whether we'd raid the restaurant pantries or the stores we hadn't quite made up our mind, and we were going to be guided mainly by how things looked when we got there. And we no sooner walked up the street than we knew what the answer would be: one of the stores. And why it suited us was that it had no second floor or bedrooms of any kind connected with it. It looked like when they closed it they left it, and we'd have it to ourselves if we could get in there. If there was a burglar alarm we meant to run, but at the same time it didn't scare us a whole lot. We'd heard plenty of burglar alarms, the time we'd been on the road, and if anything was ever done about any of them it wasn't while we were there. So that danger we disregarded and had a walk around the block and checked on the little dirt road in back, that ran past all the stores for the delivery of stuff, and marked our place by counting the back doors. In the back window were bars running across, and at the side of the back door what looked like an iron grill, folded up. That was O.K. We figured on stuff like that, and were ready for it. Then we went off to take it easy so we wouldn't be dead on our feet when the time came to go in there. We didn't at any time hang around, or stop and take long ganders, or attract attention in any way. We walked fast, with good long steps, like we were headed somewhere, and when we came to a corner we turned it sharp, like we knew where we were going and meant to get there. Just the same, by dark we had it all, and found a place we could stand and watch.

By eight o'clock lights began going out in the motor courts, by nine our place was dark, by ten the restaurants were closing, and all you could hear was radios in the bars. "O.K., Buck, it's time."

"It's now if we're going to."

"I'll take your spike." We had remembered those railroad spikes the first night, what we'd been able to do with them, and got ourselves one. We figured it was as good as a jimmy.

We slid down Van Buren and then into the cross street, to take a flash at the alley. We didn't see anything. Then I stood by the alley and he went back to Van Buren. He looked up and down, lifted his hat, smoothed his hair, began walking back and forth like he was waiting for a bus. The hat meant all clear. I went down the alley, turned in back of the store, got out my spike. By now the iron lattice was in place, with two padlocks holding it, top and bottom, and I meant to break them, if I could. But first I had a look at the bars on the window, and felt them with my thumb. You could hardly believe it, but all that was holding them was screws. I mean, the end of each bar had been flattened and an eye punched in it, and the screw driven in through that. On my jackknife was a screw driver, small but stubby and strong. I opened it up and shoved it against one of the screws. It turned. In about five minutes I had the three lower bars off. I tried the window. It was locked. I jammed the spike between the sashes and shoved. Something cracked inside. I raised the window and stepped in. My bowels were fluttering and I wondered if the lights would snap on and a face behind a gun tell me to put them up and keep them up. Then somewhere in the distance a bell began ringing. It stopped. I got myself under control and looked around.

It was just a little store, with canned stuff, open crates with vegetables and fruit, and packages of stuff like crackers. I could see well enough, by the light from the street, so I got out my sack, where it was folded against my stomach, and went to work. The first thing that was wanted, what Buck and Hosey talked so much about, was chicken. They wanted the boiled chicken that comes in a wedge-shape can, and I began hunting for it. I was in the place altogether, Buck told me later, exactly twenty-five minutes, by a clock on Van Buren Street. But if I tell it like I remember it, I was in there twenty-five years, with the lights going dim every so often where they were executing somebody back of the little green door, feet tramping over my head, where the trusties were marching in from the farm, and me there in my dark little cell with bars over the window, getting a little stir-happy by now on account of the time I'd served. After ten or fifteen years I thought to hell with chicken, drop something in the sack and get out. I grabbed cans of beans, mock turtle soup, even beets, on top of raw potatoes, oranges, bread, soap, anything. Then all of a sudden it was like a football game, with the first quarter nearly up, the flutters gone, and my mind clicking. My hands began reaching for exactly what I ought to have, I took three chickens in cans, then peas, carrots, and corn. I took pears, for dessert. I found the icebox and dropped butter in. I took a quart of milk and another of cream. There were special shelves with shoe polish, fly swatter, and stuff like that. I looked for razor blades, found a whole box, dropped that in. My thumb snagged a beer opener. I dropped that in, began looking for beer, found it, dropped a dozen cans in. I found instant coffee, condensed milk, and a sack of sugar, and dropped them in. I found a sack of salt and dropped that in, and a can of pepper.

All that I did so fast I'd breathe and then not breathe, but pretty soon I knew I was done and started for the window. Then I saw the cash register. All that stuff about taking only food ran through my head, and even while it was running I dumped the sack on the floor and reached for my spike. I jammed it in a crack and bore down and something popped. I yanked open the drawer. It was empty. I began growling curses like a wild man. I picked up the sack again and started out and then my eye caught the cash drawer, under the counter, that hardly anybody would see unless they'd worked around some business place like a garage. I tried it and it was locked. I jammed the spike in and nothing gave. I reached under for keys. You don't see them when the storekeeper makes change, but they're there just the same, four or five or six finger taps that work on springs and have to be pressed in combination before the lock releases. On this drawer there were six, and that meant probably a three-key combination. I tried 1–2–3, 1–3–4, 1–4–5, and 1–5–6, and inside of me something kept yelling to get out and get out quick, but my fingers kept working the combos and my head kept ticking them off, so I wouldn't waste time trying one twice. I started the two-series. The drawer pulled open and I saw steel. It was a metal box, and it was locked. I set it up on its edge, held the spike on the lock, and used a box opener that was under the counter as a hammer. There was a snap and the lid was off. Inside was money. I could see ones and fives and tens, but I didn't stop to count and didn't take the silver. I stuffed the bills into my pocket, picked up the sack, and stepped out the window. I closed it, then looked around. I didn't see anything, slipped into the alley, and down to the cross street. On Van Buren, Buck was still there, waiting for his bus. I waved and he ran toward me. "God, Jack, I thought you'd never come."

"Had to find stuff."

"Gee, you're loaded. We better split it, so we can make time."

"Not here. Let's hit for the river."

"O.K. Come on."

The river is one of those Western jobs, ten parts sand and rock and gravel to one part water, but it wasn't too rough, and we figured we could follow it easy enough, and we wouldn't meet anybody. We hit it in a half hour and began looking for Hosey. He was to light up a fire, so we'd have a torch to steer by. But we walked and walked and routed up about forty things that rustled and hissed and scrabbled, and still nothing but black ahead. "Jack."

"Yes, Buck?"

"Did he say *upriver?*"

"Not once but twenty-eight times."

"Does the bastard know upriver from down?"

"Well, feel the water! You can feel how it—"

"Yeah, Jack, I can and you can. But can *he?*"

I'd say we went two miles, feeling like twenty. And we saw a flicker of yellow, and then we could hear him: "Yay Jack, yay Buck!"

". . . Well, why didn't you pick Alaska?"

"It's perfect. It's a—jungle! Look over top of you!"

Overhead was a bridge that made shelter, where the railroad went over the river. That it was worth two miles of walking, by the dark of the moon, I couldn't see, but I didn't argue about it. He had cans, big ones, for boiling, and little ones, to eat out of, and plenty of wood. We fed up the fire, set water on to heat, and pretty soon put the chicken, soup, peas, and other stuff in, still in the cans. Then in one can I made coffee. When I put that instant stuff in, with sugar and cream, they began gulping it without even waiting for the other stuff. Then we opened the soup and drank a can apiece. Then we had the chicken, but one can was all we were able to get away with. Then we had peas, carrots, and corn, and canned peaches. Then I broke out what I hadn't said anything to them about. That was the beer, that I had stashed in the running water so it would get cold. They took one look at those cans and began mumbling those cusswords that are little prayers of thanks in tough guys' language. I cut into three, and we sat there with the foam sliding all over our mouths, and the cold beer sliding down our throats. Buck began to mumble how they both owed plenty to me. Hosey said they sure did. I said thanks, pals, thanks.

By then it was daylight, so when a train came along we slid out from under to have a look at her. She was a passenger train, westbound, all curtained in, but on the observation platform, smoking a cigar, in pajamas, dressing gown, and slippers, was a fat guy. We waved, and he stared, like he couldn't believe his eyes. Then he leaned forward, held on to the brass rail, and spit at us. ". . . That dirty son of a bitch."

"O.K., Buck, tell him some more."

"God, boys, would I get like that? First they throw you out, then they spit in your goddam eye. That fat slob! No, not one of the three of us would get like that. At least we'd give a guy a break. At least if he waved at us we'd wave back. But that fat bastard couldn't even give us a wave. Not even a kind look."

We went back to the fire and began talking what we'd do if we had it good and three guys off the road came in and asked for a break. We said we'd feed them and bed them down till they were ready to talk and then line it up for them to get a job. In the middle of that Buck took off his coat, crawled inside his gunny sack, stuck the coat under his head and went to sleep. Then Hoscy did. Then I did, or tried to. But all the time the beer and chicken and the rest of it were taking me down I kept thinking about the money and why I hadn't said anything about it. It seemed to me I was as close to them as brothers. And yet I was mortally afraid to open my trap about it.

Around noon we built up more fire, heated some beans, made some coffee, filled ourselves with all we could hold, and then began to boil up. I boiled everything, even my suit. What to do with the money I didn't know but I climbed the bank, stuck it in an angle of the abutment, put a stone over it, and came on back. We worked on ourselves, first in the cold water in the river, then in the hot that we kept boiling, until we were pretty clean. The soap came in as handy as anything, and we took turns with it, scrubbing and slopping and lathering with it, until it was just a sliver and then even that was gone. Around four maybe, our clothes were dry and we got dressed. But along toward sundown dogs began barking downriver, and if there's one thing a real hobo hates worse than work it's dogs. Hosey began to get nervous and it was easy to see if we were going to keep him we had to move. We talked about where we'd move to, and he was scared to death to go through Phoenix again on a train, as he said they'd "be laying for us, sure." And yet we all wanted to beat West, instead of going back East, on account of the weather. Finally we decided to break up, each one to hitchhike separately by road, and meet again in Shorty Lee's jungle in Yuma, that Hosey said was the best in the U. S., bar none. So that's what we did. We had to break up, because three guys together would scare any private driver to death, and on the trucks, on account of a new no-rider clause in the insurance, there was no chance at all. There had been trouble, hijacking and stuff like that, so the companies put it in the policies that if riders were aboard, all bets were off. Kind of rugged for Mr. Thumb, but it gives you an idea how things were.

Me, though, I caught a through bus. The driver looked at me funny, but I knew I didn't stink so I looked right back, and when I got out my roll that talked. It was a day coach, not very full, so there was plenty of room on the wide seat at the rear. I stretched out, got comfortable, and counted my money. There were two or three tens, some fives, and the rest ones, altogether around ninety dollars. I shoved it in my pocket again, then sat there, staring out at the road where it was rolling out behind, working on something that had been bothering me all day: Why had I hid that money? Why hadn't I said something about it to Buck and Hosey? Why hadn't I cut them in? Here they were, maybe not the buddies I would have picked some night when I was all dressed up in a dinner coat three years before, but some kind of buddies, and what was pretty important too, all the buddies I had. And yet, at my first stroke of luck, I had ratted on them one hundred per cent, like any real hobo. I began thinking about something else: Why had I passed up the silver? So nobody could hear it clink, seemed to be the answer. Yeah, but who? A cop, when I was toting that sack, if he ever got near enough to hear something clink, would already have nabbed me. Once more, it spelled Buck and Hosey. And at last I admitted to myself, what had been slewing around in the back of my head: I had kept quiet, I had even passed up the silver, because I was afraid of them. On food, as Hosey had said, there'd be nothing to tell. At most it would be thirty days in jail, or more likely ten, serve your time or vag out by sundown. But money was different. Buddies or no buddies, rat or no rat, I'd never put myself in their power by letting them in on it.

Or at least so it seemed at that time.

Shorty Lee, the hobo's friend, had fixed up a jungle that was a lulu, all right, and though I wouldn't exactly trade off my membership in the University Club to get into it, it did things to you that somebody had put up a couple of shacks that guys could sleep in, got them some clean pots to cook in, bricks for their fires, and connected up a shower so they could get clean and a water tap so they could drink. I didn't go there right away, though. I hit town around ten o'clock, checked in at a little hotel down by the river, then went to a café for dinner. It was just a cheap café, like a million of them all over the country that had opened up since Prohibition got repealed. It was the first time in my life I'd ever been in a bar. In Baltimore, they had served liquor, of course, but it had come in a cup and had no name and you drank it quick. I ordered a Martini, with steak, fried potatoes and coffee. Then I noticed two girls on stools, talking to each other and not with anybody that I could see. They were just Western barflies, in checked blouses, dungaree pants, and stitched boots, but not so bad either. One of them saw me, looked sharp, then looked again. I looked back. Then I began to wonder if she was having any effect on me. I mean, I was trying to figure if it was getting anywhere, this campaign Buck and I had started by stealing some grub. Next thing I knew the waiter was shaking me to wake up and eat. Looked like I had some little way to go. I felt my money. It was still there.

In the morning I found some other place, and had sliced orange, ham and three eggs, flapjacks, and coffee. They treated me O.K., but by now I was getting more and more self-conscious about my scrubbed-out jeans. I began looking for clothes. The good places I stayed out of, because I figured they'd be shy of the stuff I wanted. But on a side street, back of one of the hotels, I spotted a place that said "summer clearance sale," and walked over there. First I picked out a pair of heavy khaki work pants, the kind that go up under your chin in front and fasten with a pair of suspenders behind. Then I tried on shoes. I needed brogans, but got the best-looking pair I could see. Then I got two pair of woolen stockings. I think they felt best of all. On the road, if you've got any socks at all you're lucky, but if they're not all full of holes that cut your toes and blister your heels, then you're asleep, dreaming. To wobble my foot and feel clean wool all over it was wonderful. Then I picked out drawers, undershirt, and shirt. I wanted a check, like the girls had had, but I happened to think it might be the one thing somebody would remember me by, if they were pinned down in court. I said make it khaki, to go with the pants. Then I picked out flannel pants, to wear under the khaki, a dark coat, and a brown hat, one of the two-and-a-half-gallon jobs that practically everybody wears in that neck of the woods. I dressed in the backroom, and told them to throw my old stuff away. Was I glad to kick it all in a corner, and step out of there clean, whole, and with a decent smell!

Outside, on a bench, at a bus stop, I counted up again, and had nearly sixty dollars. I sat there, trying to think what I was going to do. Across from me girls kept going up and down, and I wondered if my sixty dollars, provided I ate three times a day, would get me in shape so they looked like girls, instead of just things in skirts. But I had to cut Buck and Hosey in, I knew that, and if I felt it had to be my own way, to be safe, I still had to do it. I walked on down to the store again, and bought them the same outfits. There was no trouble over sizes. I'd heard them call theirs, so many times, in the missions, I'd have known them in my sleep. I took the stuff up over to the hotel, taking care to keep all sales slips in my hip pocket, in case. I still had a little money left, so I went out and bought beans, bacon, eggs, and stuff. I still had my gunny sack, that I had washed out with the other things in the Salt River, so I opened all packages, dumped them in, and threw away the wrappings. I shook it up, like it had been filled in a hurry. I took it over to the S.P. tracks. From there, following Hosey's directions, I hit the jungle, and there, believe it or not, feeding a fire he'd made between two piles of bricks, was Buck. "Well, for God's sake look at Adolph Menjou!"

"Buck, how are you?"

"Sir, I'm fine."

"Hosey here?"

"Out mooching grub. He'll be along."

"I brought some grub."

"Well, will you *talk?*"

"Slight case of theft, that's all."

"You mean—?"

"Well, what do you do in a case like that? I was walking along, going about my business, when up the street a piece of fire apparatus went by. Well, I stopped and looked like everybody else. Then, in front of a store, a party came out, and went running up there, to see better. Or maybe it was his house that was burning down, I don't know. Well, could I help it if that was the place I'd decided to price a few small articles I needed? I went inside, stomped on the floor, hollered, and whistled three times, and nobody came. So I filled my sack. Every pile I saw, I took three of a kind, and then slid out the back way. But going past the kitchen I noticed some things to eat. Anyway, I dropped them in the sack on the principle we needed them most. Then I beat it."

The way he grabbed those socks, and smelled them, and hugged the shoes to him, made you want to turn your eyes away. Hosey came, with a sackful of the rotten potatoes and bread heels and the crab bait that we always had whenever he

went out to mooch. He acted the same as Buck, only worse.
When we finally got the grub cooked and they were outside
some of it and all dressed up in their clothes, I could hear little
giggles coming out of them and they'd keep passing their
hands over their mouths, to hide their grins, or maybe rub
them off. I kept thinking how funny it was, that I had to cook
up this yarn, because I couldn't trust them with the truth.
But then, sure enough, Hosey had the wind-up on it: "Boys,
we got to move."

"Why?"

Buck wasn't any too agreeable about it, full of food and all
dressed up like he was. "Can't we just set, for once in our
life?"

"They'll be looking for us. The cops."

"And how would they know who did it?"

"Ain't we wearing the evidence?"

I wanted to tell him for God's sake be his age, but I'd told
them this dilly, and if I went back on it I'd have to tell them
the truth, and that didn't suit me. So there was nothing to do
but listen to him line it out, how we'd pulled two jobs here in
Arizona, and had to get out of the state, quick. So that's how
we came to hit for the bridge and cross into California.

* 17 *

WE pulled jobs in Indio, Banning, Redlands, and San Bernar-
dino, then doubled over and pulled one in Mojave. That was
a little grocery on one of the streets off the highway, railroad
track, and rabbit run in the middle of town. But when I had

the stuff sacked, and was tiptoeing out, Buck called. There
were shots, and bullets went past my head. I ran so hard that
when the three of us met, in a jungle by the water tank, I
couldn't talk for an hour. We cooked our grub and ate it, but
figured the time had come for another change of states and
hopped the U.P. for Las Vegas. There, after making two
dollars parking cars in a lot on Fifth Street, I took a fifty-cent
room in a motel near by, washed, shaved, and looked myself
over. In the face, I looked what I was, a hard, sun-baked bum.
On clothes, I looked good enough, though not quite good
enough to sign in under my own name. Ever since Atlanta, in
all missions, flophouses, and joints, I had used some phony
monicker, like Dikes or Davis, and that's what I did now.

I went out and tried my luck on the wheels. I bought a
dollar's worth of ten-cent chips at a cut-rate place, and tried a
few passes, red against the black. I won. Then I moved over
to the numbers, and bet the first twelve against the second
and third. I won some more. I raised the ante, and began
making support bets, little gambles that didn't add up to much
if I lost, but meant a whole lot if I won. I mean, on the first
twelve I'd put fifty cents. Then on the first four I'd put twenty-
five cents. Then on number one I'd put ten cents. Then if the
ball fell in any number higher than twelve I was out eighty-
five cents clean on the whole spin. But if it fell in any number
below twelve I cashed a dollar for my fifty-cent bet, and made
fifteen cents. If it fell in the first four I made $2.25 more. If it
fell on number one I made $3.50 more. Since then I've seen
plenty of gambling, and done a little, and have nothing to say
against the system I figured out that night. Any betting's a
gamble, but I'll say this for support betting: It's offensive, and
if you win you take home something. Hedge betting's defensive, just a way of stringing it out longer. I didn't have too
much luck for a while, just a dribble now and then, but then
I landed with number one, and felt the tide come in. I quit
after three straight losses, and left with thirty dollars or so.

It felt good to be able to look up Buck and Hosey, where they were laying kindling, and tell them the truth, and invite them to a room in the motel. Hosey, he hated to cough up, but so long as it was my money he had to. We slept, and then in the morning Buck and I hopped a bus to Boulder Dam, or Hoover Dam they call it now, that was building then, to get a job. They weren't hiring, but said come back next week.

So we went back to our motel and cinched our belts, and tried to make our money last by laying on the bed, so as not to get hungry. Then Hosey wanted to move, on account of the guy in the next room to him, who he said had a gun, and kept shifting it around, from the bureau drawer to his trunk to his suitcase, so it got on his nerves. Buck and I didn't quite attach the importance to it that Hosey did, and fact of the matter we wouldn't have paid any attention to it at all, if I hadn't picked up another day on the parking lot, and when things were slack, slipped across to the filling station next door to use the toilet. The manager was fixing a flat, and part of the time he was outside the toilet window with it, beating on the tire with a hammer. Following him around was a kid that seemed to work there, who as well as I could figure out had been transferred to another station of the chain, and wanted tips on how to act. The place he was going seemed to be the "flagship" as the manager called it, the main station, and the kid was a little nervous about what to do. The manager told him how to get there, by following Highway 91 and watching for the sign, and some more stuff that I remembered later. Then I heard the kid say: "When do they open?"

"Seven a.m., same as here."

"And close nine?"

"No, ten."

"Gee, that's bad."

"No, you'll like it. They split it up so the week you're on early, you're off before dinner, and when you're on late, you don't come in till after lunch."

"Funny, though. There's no business after nine."

"The chief, he don't bank in Nevada. So every night, after they close, the station managers turn our cash in there, at the flagship. It's put away, and then in the morning it's sent over to Barstow, California. Which is why the place closes one hour later. All guys expecting their wife to bring suit for divorce have a strange enthusiasm for keeping their funds in some other state."

At the motel, I lay there in the dark and listened to people snore, and kept telling myself to forget what I'd heard. I kept telling myself to put it out of my mind I might ever try anything real with Buck, or Hosey, or anybody. I kept telling myself to get rid of any idea I could do it alone. And all the time I kept thinking of those station managers, driving in late with their little canvas sacks. I kept thinking about Mojave and the bullets, and wondering why, if I had to play shooting gallery, I didn't do it for dough. I guess that was what got me, more than anything else. I began going over it, Hosey's idea that stealing grub was O.K., something the judge would go easy on if we ever got caught. Who said he would? Who said he wouldn't send us up for ten years, to show the law was meant to be obeyed? It came to me, we weren't talking about any judge. We were talking about ourselves. What we really meant was: Everybody's entitled to eat, and if they have to steal to do it, then O.K., so long as there's no other way. But anything more than that, regular stealing, that we weren't equal to, to figure the right and the wrong of it. But the way my head kept pounding, I knew I didn't care.

In Buck's room, next to mine, the door opened and footsteps went down the hall. Then the screen door squeaked. Pretty soon I caught the smell of a cigarette. I got up, put on some clothes, and went outside. Buck was squatting on the ground, in pants, coat, undershirt, and shoes, smoking, and staring at the lights of the town. I sat down too. "Kind of restless, boy?"

"Jack, what do we do it for? Tramp. Steal. Rat."

"I don't know."

"Why, stead of catching the goddam freight, don't we let the freight catch us? You know any good reason we shoul roll away from those wheels?"

"Tell me something, Buck. This guy with the gun—?"

". . . Hosey's friend?"

"Where does he keep it? If you know?"

"In his room. Different places. Mostly places he lets Hose see, so Hosey don't get any idea he might go in and begi feeling around. Anyhow, that's how I dope it."

"Could you find it?"

"Couldn't you? What locks are there in this dump?"

"You sure he doesn't *carry* the gun, Buck?"

"I *think* not. Why?"

I told him what I'd heard in the filling station. "I figure for a while at least, we could take care of things by gettin ourselves a little dough."

"I'd call that a little risky."

"O.K., but I've noticed something."

"Which is?"

"It's a wide-open town, same like Kansas City, only mor so. On account of Boulder Dam the girls have flocked here.

"Listen, Jack, I'm listening, but—"

"Yeah, but how long?"

"Then O.K."

He stretched out and began to talk the gloomiest kind o way about women and how he's no good any more and neve will be, and I calmed him down a little by owning up I wa in exactly the same shape. But, I said, what we needed wa rest and grub and water on our skins once a day and mayb now and then a couple of jokes. He said to hell with this ide we were just going to steal a little bit, and I said: "Might a well be hung for a sheep as a lamb." That was it, Buck said. After a while we heard something, and when we looked there was Hosey. "Couldn't seem to sleep."

". . . Oh. Neither could we."

"Hot."

"Yeah, Hosey, sure is."

"I heard what you guys was saying. I couldn't help hearing. All I got to say is: You got the right idea."

"You mean—?"

"Count me in."

Next morning Buck slipped in, while I was shaving. "Well? Jack, what do we say on letting Hosey in?"

"I guess it's off."

". . . I'm not so sure."

"Him? I wouldn't trust him— Listen, Buck, it's not that I don't think he likes us, or that he wouldn't give all the right answers if we asked him how he felt about us, or whatever. It's just that I don't think he's got anything left any more. Hell, I think they could break him with the smell of coffee. You don't go to war with a bunch of goddam cripples."

"And we, we have got something left, hey?"

"More than he's got."

"Jack, we can use him."

"For what?"

"Watching, for one thing. He can smell a cop further than—"

"All right."

"If either one of us had anything left, we wouldn't be pulling something like this. We're trying to get it back. Maybe he is, too. Maybe—"

What he really meant was that Hosey had it on us whether we liked it or not, and if we were going to pull this job instead of waiting to pull some other job we had to take him. He was more use than we expected. He went over there to this flagship later that morning, dropped dead in front of the door, and when they brought him to with ice water he came up with stuff about not having eaten for three days, and they let him make a buck cleaning the place off with a squeegee. He came away with a pretty good idea of where everything was, and said as far as he could see there wasn't any safe, that the money was kept in a cash drawer out by the pumps, that they opened every time a customer paid. He drew up a plan of the station, with all streets marked, and distances in yards. He had the names of the station manager and the boss of the chain.

In the late afternoon I figured to get the gun. It's when most guys want a drink, and while we didn't have much money left, we did scrape together for some liquor and one or two things. I got a pint, with some fizz water, at a drugstore, and they gave me some ice in a container. There was a phone booth in there and I rang a picture theater and got the time of the feature, the newsreels, and all the rest of it, for Hosey. I checked on a bus he'd have to ride, to join up with us later. When I got back to the motel it was around five.

"Buck, you got a beer opener? . . . Oh, I beg your pardon. I thought this was my friend's room. I was thinking of throwing a drink together, but I've got nothing I can use to open my carbonated water. Well, have *you* got one?"

"No, I wish I could accommodate you, but—"

"I'll find something."

"Would—pliers do?"

"I bet they would work."

"You're welcome to try, if you think—"

"Well, say, why don't *you* try?"

"Is that an invitation?"

He was a shriveled little guy, maybe forty, with wrinkles around his eyes, a little red mustache, and a jut-out chin that slewed over sidewise from his jaw, just about what you'd expect somebody to look like that had a .38 in his bureau drawer. How quick he found the pliers was funny, and we went in my room. They didn't work, but by a funny coincidence, the screw driver on my jackknife did. I unscrewed the top of the whisky, that was so cheap it didn't even have a cork, got out the glasses, poured drinks, and said: "Here's how." Right away he got friendly and began asking me if I wasn't from Virginia. I said no, Tennessee, just outside Chattanooga, and he said he knew it was below the line somewhere. We talked along, I poured more drinks, said: "Here's how" again. But about that time somebody outside began whistling *Casey Jones* and I started out. "Excuse me just a second—be right back. Help yourself to the liquor."

"Thanks."

Outside, crossing the street, were Buck and Hosey. A block away, I caught up with them. We strolled along and I made Buck show me the gun, to make sure he had it. He spread his coat pocket and I looked in. It was an automatic. We went over it then with Hosey, what he was to do, and explained it to him once more, that it was all part of his alibi, in case he had to prove one. He was to buy a ticket at the theatre, and sit in a loge seat at the back. If no usher bothered him he was to stay there. If an usher did ask to see his ticket, he was to show it to her and put up an argument, but kind of a rube's argument, without much steam in it, enough that she'd remember him, not enough he'd get thrown out. Then he'd move and stay in his new seat till the newsreel started, which would be a few minutes after nine o'clock. Then he was to leave, by one of the fire doors marked "Exit," so nobody could say exactly when he left. Then he was to walk down to Highway 91 and take position about a half block away from the filling station. At anything that even looked like a cop he was to signal us. "O.K., now. Put your fingers in your mouth and try that screech whistle we've got to have if you're going to be any good out there."

"Listen, Jack, I've whistled that way ever since I was—"

"I said try it."

"Here goes."

". . . Good."

"How much is the theater ticket, boys?"

"Thirty-five cents. Here's a buck. Better have yourself some java and beans first, and don't go in much before eight o'clock. Take it easy. Act natural. Talk straight from the shoulder. Let both girls, or anybody you meet going in the theatre, see you. Smile, act friendly, so they really remember you."

Buck and I had some beans at a dump near the station, and when we got done it was eight, and time to get ourselves a car. We walked on toward a residential section, then found a street with some cars parked out on it. At that time cars still had running boards, so in the middle of the block we sat down on one, facing across the street, pretty much out of sight, and watched. We figured that incoming cars, full of people coming home, would be no good to us. Those cars would be driven into garages, and to follow them in would be just staking ourselves out. We aimed to catch somebody visiting, that had left their car at the curb and would be going home around eight thirty or a little after. From the time it would take them to leave some house, get to their car, climb in, and find the key, to the time we'd get there, would be just a convenient interval. I suppose we'd been there a half hour, getting pretty nervous, when three people, a man, a woman, and a boy, came out of a house up the street. Buck reached for the gun. "No."

"What's the matter, Jack, you getting cold feet?"

"We can't handle three."

"We better be handling somebody."

"Let them go."

They went, and two more parties went, a two and a four. And then came a girl, from a place three doors down. She had more comical jokes, saying goodbye, about not doing anything she wouldn't do, not taking any rubber nickels, and being good, than you could count. I could hear the cusswords rising in Buck, and chocked him hard, with my elbow, to keep him quiet. But at last she came skipping along, humming under her breath. She got in from the curb side, and we were at the left-hand window, watching her switch on the ignition, before she had any idea we were there. "Easy, easy, easy."

"*What?*"

"Not so loud."

"Who are—?"

Buck slipped his hand over her mouth in kind of a gentle, regretful way, opened the door, and pulled her out. I hopped in, found her bag, started the motor. Then I slid over, in the right-hand seat, so Buck could hop in from the left, where he was holding her. He let go of her and she started to scream. He got in, took the wheel, and started. I looked back. A couple of people were at their front doors, but nobody was running and nobody was shooting. "Look in her bag, Jack. We've got to have dough, to pay for the gas we order—"

". . . A five and a one. And change."

"O.K."

"And something *else.*"

"What?"

"A watch."

"Are you kidding?"

We'd spotted a drugstore with a clock on it, and we'd expected to check by it, so we'd come to the filling station exactly when we wanted. But the watch meant we could take a drive, relax, and get our nerve.

✳

Out of town a few miles, toward the California border, he began to talk: "Jack, how many guys went on the road, do you think, about the same time we did?"

"How many eggs in a shad?"

"Millions, you think?"

"I saw at least that many."

"What happened to their sisters?"

". . . How do you mean, Buck?"

"You ever see any girls on the road?"

"Well, I heard stories."

"Yeah, we know about those two bums in a boxcar, come one, come all, everybody welcome. But I'm talking about those other girls, in homes that were just as hard put to it to feed them as they were to feed their brothers. What happened to them?"

"Well, I'll bite. What?"

"How would I know? Except what I think."

"Which is?"

"They stayed home."

"Well?"

"I've cussed out the goddam country, tonight I stole a car, and I'm getting ready to do more. But a country that lets a million good-for-nothing tomatoes sit around home till things get better, just because they're girls—well, somebody thought something of them."

"You couldn't mean the country's O.K., could you?"

"Somebody took care of them."

Around nine forty we slipped back to town, and the radios and juke boxes and orchestras were beginning to hit it up, though not loud like they would later. We checked on Hosey, and there he was, exactly where he was supposed to be, by the sycamore tree, in the shadow of a little real-estate office near the sidewalk. We drove past and waved, so he'd know we were there. We turned the corner, went past the station, checked the manager was at his desk, inside, doing paper work. Nobody else was around. We went down the street two blocks, cut our lights, turned around. Then we rolled back toward the station and parked facing it, maybe a hundred feet away. He didn't look up. A car drove up and a guy got out, in the white pants and peaked cap all the managers wore, and a black sweater. The man inside went out and they seemed to be counting money. Then they opened the drawer Hosey had spotted, and put something inside. The guy in the black sweater drove off. The other one went back to his desk. "O.K., Buck, get out your matches."

"There's no matches in this."

"I said get them out. We draw for it."

"Every job we've pulled, you've done the dangerous part. This job, I'm doing it. I've got the gun, right here in my pocket, so we don't have to do any shifting, and—"

"Cut the argument!"

"Then cut it yourself."

He started the motor, snapped on the lights, and pulled out from the curb. In two seconds we were rolling into the station, beside a pump. The manager came out and spoke to Buck: "Yes sir? What can I do for you?"

"If I'm not too late for some gas—"

"We're open. Fill her up?"

"That'll be fine."

The car was almost empty, so he'd be some little time. Buck and I got out and went in the men's room, Buck leading the way. I kind of relaxed on one hip and walked with a limp, so I could fudge three or four inches on my height. Inside, I passed over the money he'd need when the time came to pay. He went out. A wild idea flashed through my head. From somewhere I could remember those descriptions of wanted persons, saying they were "light" or "dark" or whatever. I lit a match, charred it, and blacked my eyebrows. Then I took a piece of paper, wadded it up, and jammed it in my mouth, between the front teeth and the gum, the way Denny and I had done with cotton, for the pro football pictures. In the mirror I didn't know myself. Instead of being light I was dark, and I had a buck-tooth look that was somebody else, not me. I slouched out again and the manager barely looked at me. Buck had his back to me. I climbed in, took the wheel, and started the motor. Buck said: "O.K., what do I owe you?"

"Two fifty-five."

Buck passed over the five, the manager went to his cash drawer, and opened it. Inside, from where I sat, I could see thick piles of bills, in their compartments, bulged up high. He picked up two bills and some change, turned and was looking into the .38. "Step back. . . . Put your hands on your chest and keep them there. Not high, we don't want a gallery. That's it. Now take it easy, don't get excited, and—"

When it started I don't know, but it seemed I'd been hearing it for years in some kind of a dream, this whistle of Hosey's. Then, off in the night, a shot sounded. Buck twitched, went three feet in the air, then came down like he had turned into a sack of meal. I went out of there like a bat out of hell. Somewhere I saw Hosey, his face white, running toward me to jump in. I didn't even slow down. Next thing I knew I was out of town, whether two miles or ten I couldn't tell you, waiting at a grade crossing while a freight went by. All of a sudden I cut the motor, left the key in the ignition, and jumped out. That freight, brother, wasn't meant to be boarded by anything on two feet. I mean, it was going fast. But it was headed west, that was all I wanted to know. I raced beside it, grabbed a handhold, hit the side of the car. I waved my foot around, found a step, pulled myself up. I was on a boxcar. I felt something funny in my mouth. The paper was still there. I hooked it out with my finger. Then I rubbed my eyebrows off. All I could think of was the miles that were clicking by, between me and what was lying there in a Las Vegas filling station, that had once been my pal, and the other one, that was still my pal, or wanted to be, but that knew something to tell on me.

Up ahead, I could see the brakeman coming. I didn't move. When he got to me I waved. "Hiya, big boy."

"Hiya."

* 18 *

FOR three days I sat around the Midnight Mission in Los Angeles, washing dishes for my grub and sleeping in their main dormitory. But it kept worrying me, spending nights with other guys. I was afraid I might talk in my sleep. I picked up a buck or two on some parking lot and moved to a little hotel over on Sixth Street, fifty cents a night and no questions asked. For the first time since I'd been on the road I signed in under my own name, because I wanted it in black and white I was in California, not Nevada. I kept talking to the clerk like he must remember me, and saying how glad I was to be back in Los Angeles from up in Fresno. It turned out he was new there. But then something happened that helped quite a lot. A guy came downstairs, carrying a vacuum cleaner, and telling how well he'd cleaned the upper halls, and the clerk said fine, he'd mark him paid right now. So he did. It was just an old-fashioned register, where guys signed their names, or F. D. Roosevelt, or whatever, with their address, if they had one. On the right-hand side was the room number, and beside this was marked "pd." Soon as I handed over my fifty cents I was marked "pd." But if this guy was working for his bed, and all they did about it was mark him "pd." too, that meant there was no cross-check on cash, and *that* meant, if a name was there, a few days back, this clerk wouldn't know if the face behind the name had been there or not. I watched my chance, then went to the register and began turning pages. I found July 10, the day we held up the station. The page was full up, solid. I looked at July 9. It was full. But on July 8 there was a blank line. I picked up the pen and wrote "Jack Dillon, City." Then beside that I wrote a room number, and then with my thumb I smudged it. Then beside it I wrote "pd. pd. pd. pd." All that time I watched the clerk. He went right on with what he was doing. I went up to my room, lay down, and felt better. It wasn't much of an alibi, but it was some kind of alibi.

I felt better, but not much better. By day, I tramped around to every garage, shop, and filling station I could find, trying to land a job, and now and then picking up a buck fixing flats. If things had been bad before, they were as bad now as they could get. By night I worked on my clothes with spot remover, then pressed them under the mattress, trying to get myself in some kind of shape in case a chance would come. But it all spelled Skid Row, and sooner or later I knew Hosey would come along, or I'd bump into him in some soup kitchen, and what that would lead to I didn't know. Maybe he was harmless, but I was afraid of him. So pretty soon, when I got two parking jobs in a row, and had five dollars I could call my own, I made up my mind to blow. Where I didn't know, but I marched myself up to the bus depot at the corner and bought me a ticket for some town down the line.

We were slowing down in Whittier, I guess a little before eight in the morning, when I noticed a bunch of men standing around on the sidewalk. They were in jeans and looked like Mexicans, but I knew they were guys hoping for work. I still had thirty or forty cents' worth of ticket, but at the next stop I got out and went legging it back to the mob. I guess there were twenty or thirty of them, all talking Spanish, but I found out they'd come down from L.A. for lemon-picking, on a call from a state bureau. Pretty soon a door opened and we all went inside an office, where a tall guy with a hatchet face began talking in some kind of Spanish. I pushed up front but he kept passing me by, and the Mexicans had all been given cards with numbers, and were back outside, waiting for a truck to pick them up, before he turned to me. "What's your name?"

"Jack Dillon."

"You American?"

"Native."

"What do you want?"

"Work."

"This is lemons. You want that?"

"Yes."

"Why?"

"Got to eat."

"What else have you tried?"

"Fixing flats, washing cars, parking jalopies, sacking wheat, shoveling guano, blacksmithing drills, panhandling, and stealing. I've tried everything there is, from East to West and North to South and back again, and if there's a living in any one of them, I don't know which one it is. If lemons are what I've got to pick, then I mean to get at it, but what you've got to do with what I've tried, I don't exactly know."

"You tried the CCC?"

"Yes."

"So?"

"They wouldn't have me."

"Why not?"

"You've got to be certified. I won't go home."

"What other reason?"

"Commies."

"Then O.K. Let's talk. To me, an American's as good as a wetback, who is a Mexican that we don't know how he got here and we're much too polite to ask, but if he happened accidentally on purpose to do it by swimming the Rio Grande River, his hindside would be a little wet."

"One would think so."

"Just the same, I don't recommend this job to you."

"What's wrong with it?"

"You can't stand it."

"How do you know what I can stand?"

"All I know is what I found out from twenty years in the business and watching about eighteen hundred other Americans go down there and topple over in the heat and quit before lunchtime. A Mexican, he was born to heat, and before you or I or Columbo ever got here he was working in an Aztec chain gang with a tump line over his head and a whip over his back so a nice lemon grove 110 in the shade practically looks to him like a political job. If you want it, it's yours, and here's your identification. But don't say I didn't warn you."

"Thanks. Sorry I blew my top."

"That's O.K. God knows what you'll blow next."

We rode down in a truck, all of us jammed so close together standing on each other's feet I hated to think what would happen if we hit something. Two or three miles out of town we turned in between two concrete pillars and began running between miles and miles of orange groves and lemon groves and grapefruit groves, with concrete water pipes all around. Some of the fruit was in bloom, and some of it was ripe and some half ripe, there didn't seem to be any rule about it. Then we came to the ranch houses, the main office and store and mess hall and commissary and bunkhouse and garage and employees' houses, all painted white with green trim and looking like a dairy would look in the East, or maybe a horse farm in Kentucky. We piled out and went in the office and turned in our cards and got rings and nippers and chalk. The rings are made of heavy wire bent with a ring to measure lemons and a little one for a handle. The lemons are bigger than the ring, then O.K., cut them even if they're green. In the packing house they'll grade for storage and don't have to be sold right away, as happens with tree-ripened fruit. If they go through the ring, let them hang. The nippers were for cutting. The chalk was to mark your number on your boxes. That stuff they issue to you when you come in and take up when you go. On lunch boxes, you were supposed to bring your own, and Mr. Holtz, the super, seemed annoyed that I didn't have any, though it seemed to help that I had a canteen. He asked me some questions, and then, after he sent the others off to work in the truck, took me over to the company store, fixed me up with a box, and said I'd better take something to eat with me, or I might get a little weak before night. I took a can of beans, and he was surprised I could pay and he didn't have to write me an order. Then he took me to the bunkhouse, assigned me a bunk, and said I'd do better if I shed all my clothes except the khakis, undershirt, and hat. I changed, and while he wasn't looking smelled the blankets. They smelled like hay, and were clean. I made up my mind that short of falling dead I'd have that bunk. We went to the trees in his car, and on the way passed the jalopies of the fruit tramps, with tents put up beside them, that stunk so bad I was glad when we were by. Now they're called Okies and Arkies and Louies, as they've been written up and it has been discovered what wonderful characters they've got, but then they were just fruit tramps, whole families of men, women, and children that travel around, and pick fruit and fight and stink. "Just what is the system here, Mr. Holtz? I mean, where do I eat, where do I bathe, how does it work? I'm a little new, and I'd like to know."

So he explained about the mess hall and how I could cook my own stuff, with the pots there in the kitchen, and about the bathhouse and the rest of it. Now, a ranch has a cook and the pickers board with him, but at that time they were on their own, with three or four splitting it up in a cooking team. "And what do I get for all this?"

"The pay is ten cents a box, if you work by the box, or thirty cents an hour, if you want it that way, plus four cents a box."

"Which pays best?"

"By the box, if you can pick."

"Any great trick to it?"

"Well, it's pretty hard, for a beginner, and there's quite a few tricks to it. If I were you, to start, I'd try the hourly rate. We don't expect too much, the first day or two, and if you don't last, at least you have something in your pocket when you leave."

"Do many Americans last?"

"Except for the fruit tramps, practically none."

I've played football games till I thought I'd drop, I've hung on to freights till my hands were numb, I've taken my share on the chin. But for that kind of stuff, that day picking lemons, on the Green Hills Ranch, Whittier, California, topped anything I ever saw or hope to see. You stand on a stepladder that you move from tree to tree, with a pouch slung under one arm, your ring in one hand, your nippers in the other, and pick fruit. Where you first feel it is your back, from the reaching and being off balance all the time. Next you get it in your arms. In boxing, you have to shoot your punches straight instead of swinging them, or the other guy will lay all over your wrists with his elbows and make you arm-weary. That's how it is reaching for those lemons. They're off to one side, they're over your head, they're under your knees, they're any place but straight in front, easy to your hands, so you can size them and cut them and pouch them without any work. At last you get it in the legs, from the strain, heavy aching pains that start back of your thighs and creep down past your knees and into your heels. Long before lunch I was so far gone I thought I'd pass out, and wondered how the women pickers, the fruit tramps' wives, could stand it like they did. Then pretty soon a guy passed out, right on top of his ladder. First he was leaning over backwards, reaching for fruit, and then he was leaning too far. It crossed my mind, why didn't he throw out his leg, to catch himself? Then he hit, flat. A girl screamed and scrambled down her ladder. Then she fell. Then a dozen people were around them yelling for a truck. It backed up and took them aboard. Then it was lunchtime and I opened my beans, but by the time I got my back straightened up so I could eat somebody said: *Ole.* How the afternoon went I can't tell you, except now and then I'd get a box full, and carry it to the end of the row, and start back, and a Mexican would yell something at me in Spanish, and I'd go back and mark my number on it, in chalk. After a while, off in the trees, I kept hearing a motor, where somebody was trying to start it, and it would cough and die. Then there'd be an argument in Spanish and another whine from the starter and another cough. At last I couldn't stand it any more and went over there. I thought it was the fuel pump, and sure enough, wrapped around it was a wad of rag they'd used to wipe it off with, just frazzed threads but enough to foul it. I pulled them out, had them start it, and it went. I went back to my ladder. At least that was one less thing to go crazy about.

At last it came time to quit. I rode back with a couple dozen Mexicans, went in the store, bought some canned stuff and

Nescafé, and went to the mess-hall kitchen. I heated it up,
whatever it was, and ate it. Then I went to the bathhouse and
showered. Then I went to the bunkhouse, took off my clothes,
and at last stretched out on my bunk. I had it all to myself, as
I'd had the kitchen, because the Mexicans were all outside,
laughing and smoking and talking, and hadn't even thought
about eating yet, let alone sleeping. I had my mind on one
thing, and that was sleep. Inside me were twitches, jerks,
and hysteria, all trying to break loose, but I fought them back,
and was just getting quiet when three Mexicans came in with
Holtz and began jabbering in Spanish. Then they came over.
Holtz said: "What's this about that spray?"

"What spray?"

"That you fixed."

"I thought it was a fire boat."

"What ailed it?"

"Fuel pump. Tell them next time they wipe it off use something that won't fall apart in a bunch of ravelings like an old
flour bag."

"You understand machinery?"

"Little bit."

"You want a job? A regular job?"

"Yeah. What is it?"

"Tower man on that spray. Tower man is foreman of the
gang, three men and yourself. These boys, they kind of went
for the way you helped them out. If you want to try it, it's
sixty cents an hour, start tomorrow morning."

"If you've got water, oil, and gas, I'll make it go."

"Then O.K. And one other thing."

"Which is?"

"You stuck. That impressed me."

I slept for a month. On the food, it turned out I didn't have
to cook it, as tower man was a company job, and I could

board with Mrs. Emory, wife of the irrigation boss, who had one of the cottages beyond the ravine, two or three hundred yards from the fruit tramps' camp. She was expecting another addition to the family, so she was glad to make some extra cash, and fixed my lunch box and let me eat the other meals with the family. When I came in from work I'd shower, dress, and go to supper. Then I'd go back to the bunkhouse and go to bed. By that time the Mexicans would be hooking it up with phonograph, radio, guitar, or whatever they had. They're the noisiest breed of man on earth, but I slept through it like I was doped. Then after a while I didn't sleep so long. I'd wake up around four or five, with everything dark out there, or maybe the moon still shining, and the birds warbling in the trees, like they do all night in California, and begin to think. I'd think about my father, and try to remember what he'd done for me, and forget the other things, so I wouldn't feel so bitter. I'd think about my aunts, and how silly they were, and want to laugh and want to cry. I'd think about my mother, the one time I saw her, and about Miss Eleanor, and how proud she'd been of me for beating up the organist. It seemed funny anybody'd ever been proud of me. I thought about Easton, and she seemed a million miles away. I thought about Margaret, and the miserable way I'd treated her. I thought about Helen, and that was just a stab through my heart. And down under it all I kept thinking about this thing I'd lost, that Buck had given his life for, and kept wondering if I'd ever get it back.

✳ 19 ✳

THE Friday before Labor Day I got paid, quite a lot for a ranch hand, as I'd made extra by working three or four Sundays getting Holtz's trucks in shape, and that night I went in to Whittier and got stuff I needed, shirts and things like that. Next day they didn't work, and I lay around and read magazines. Then after lunch I thought if I didn't go somewhere I'd go nuts and around one o'clock I started out. I hitched a ride to 101, and a couple of hundred yards from our entrance was a bus stop. I walked down there and stood around watching people buy fruit from a little stand off to one side. Pretty soon here came a guy with a box of tomatoes, staggering toward a coupé that was standing there. He was a big guy, burned brown as terra-cotta pipe, with kind of a twinkle in his eye, like carrying tomatoes wasn't exactly in his line, but he'd do the best he could with it as long as he had them. He had trouble with the door, and I yanked it open and slipped inside and took his box and shoved it up on the ledge behind the seat so it wouldn't fall but at the same time he'd have plenty of room. "Well, thanks, that helps a lot."

"Kind of left-handed, loading stuff in a car."

"Give you a lift, maybe?"

"Well—depends on which way you're going." It depended on which way I was going too, but that was something I hadn't got around to yet. But I heard my mouth tell him: "I'm headed for the border."

"Oh—Tia Juana?"

"I believe they call it that."

"In that case, if you want to ride with me over to 101, I think you'd do better on the busses than here. I mean, over there, there are more of them. You got to get to San Diego first anyhow, and the through cars all go down the coast, or anyway most of them do. And in Long Beach you'll have more luck."

"Isn't this 101?"

"The other's alternate."

"You got two?"

"California. We do it big."

He grinned and I laughed and he climbed in and we started. As we rode he talked. He'd been over to Whittier, he said, to arrange with the photographer to be at his church the next night, to take pictures of the surprise party they were giving the rector in celebration of his tenth anniversary. He didn't hide it any he was annoyed with the rest of them for not postponing it a week on account of the Labor Day week end. "I have charge of the music, you see, and what they don't realize is that all summer I've been running with pick-up singers, kids and visiting firemen and whoever I could find, while our regular choir members are away to the mountains or some place and nobody due back till next week. The trouble I've had to round them up I'd hate to tell you."

"You a musician?"

"Hell, no. Oil's my business. Been at it thirty years, ever since I was twelve years old. Kind of a roving wildcat, I guess you'd call me, anyway till I put down a well for a lady that had a property and then married her. After that I settled down, if you can call it settling down to try and manage the little end of some of the worst made deals ever seen in the field. But it's all I know, so I do it. That and the choir. No, I'm no musician, but I found out something funny about them a long time ago. They know all there is to know about music, except music. I mean, they can yiddle their fiddle or tootle their tooter or bear on their beartone so long as somebody tells

them *what* they yiddle or tootle or bear down on. But to pick
out something themselves, and get it in the right key, and
learn it, and sing it, why, that would be a little too original for
them. So when I went in the choir I began doing some of
those things myself, and next thing I knew I was in charge of
it all. I just about know two flats from three sharps, but if
you sit down and learn it by heart you can teach it to them
well enough, and if I do say it myself, when we've got everybody present and our things rehearsed up, we've got as nice
a little choir as you're going to hear in some time."

I said I'd been a boy soprano when I was young, so of course
that made us buddies, and we talked along pretty sociable. I
kind of wished he'd talk more about oil and less about choir,
but at that I kind of liked him. We came in sight of the sea,
the first I'd seen of the Pacific Ocean, and he stopped to let
me take a gander at it. Then he went on and pretty soon
turned into a place that seemed to be his, and said he had to
make a couple of phone calls, but then we'd go. He parked in
front of the house, and I could hear him in there talking, but
there seemed to be quite a lot of it, so I got out and took a
stretch. It was a pretty place, a white frame house with a
garage out back, tall trees around it, and lawn clear out to the
road, maybe a hundred yards of it. Pretty soon he came out
and said a guy was going to call him back, but it wouldn't be
long. I said he should take his time. Pretty soon I could hear
him at the piano, going over some kind of church music that
sounded familiar, but he played so bad I couldn't place it.
But then pretty soon I had it: a Dudley Buck *Te Deum* I'd
sung a hundred times. I hummed it under my breath, and it
seemed funny that the whole melody part was too high for
me, though once I had stepped into it like it was nothing at
all. But when he came to a bass solo it was just right and I
rolled it out:

"The glorious company of the apostles praise Thee!"

Well, if I'd set off a pack of firecrackers out there I couldn't have got action sooner. He was at the door in a second, looking all around, and then, at last, at me. "Was that you?"

"Just helping out."

"Holy smoke, what a voice!"

"No, just a barroom buzzo."

"But it's great! Say, you said boy soprano, but you never said a word about what your voice changed to. Look, that sounded like the Metropolitan Opera."

I explained a little about singing to him, how easy it is for a fourflusher to sing a few notes so they sound like a million dollars and really not be any good at all. Nothing I could say made any impression on him. So far as he was concerned, somebody by the name of John Charles Chaliapin had fallen out of the sky and hit him over the head, and he wasn't going to have it any different. "Well, all right. If you think it's good, who am I to argue about it? Once I got five hundred dollars a week for it, and if you insist, we'll agree it's worth a thousand now."

"Well—"

"Yeah?"

"Never mind."

What he meant, I didn't need any mind reader to tell me, was that I should sing in his choir the next night, and why not? I had nothing to do, and it had been quite some time since anybody had admired me, unless it was Holtz, for the way I fixed flats. "However, if you really believe all this, and feel your choir could use me over the week end, we might waive the question of pay, and—"

"Would you? *Would you?*"

We shook hands and told names. His was Branch, it turned out, Jim Branch. He took me inside, and next thing I knew he'd shaken up a drink, a housekeeper was serving sandwiches in the big living room, he was playing me some new Pinza records he had, I was singing along with them, and he was as excited as a kid with a new puppy. Then pretty soon we seemed to have a party going on, with six or eight or a dozen of his friends, all sunburned like he was, all looking like they'd get more fun out of a nice pile driver than a grand-opera record, but all pretty good guys, willing to humor him along. He was about as bad on the piano as he could get and still hit a few notes, but we had some *Maine Stein Song* and *Vagabond King* and *Mandalay,* and I threw in plenty of winks with it, so nobody got the idea it was to be taken seriously. And then all of a sudden, off in a corner by itself, I see a gimlet eye drilling me through and I almost went through the floor. Because to me that spelled Las Vegas and trouble. I kept on yodeling, but began thinking fast. And the more I thought the less I knew what to do, because if I slipped outside and tried to beat it, he wouldn't have been human if he didn't pick up the telephone, and then there'd be a patrol car, pulling up beside me with cops. If I stayed, at least I'd know what was going on. So I bellowed some *Old Man River* and they clapped and yelled for more, but pretty soon he lurched over in front of me, took a sip of his drink, and said: "Y' call y'self Dillon?"

"That's right."

"Why?"

"Dillon's my name."

"Who y' think y' kidd'n?"

"Why, nobody, that I know of."

"*Me?* Y' try'n kid *me?* Why, goddam it, I seen y' play. I seen y' play football, play right halfback f' Fall River, seen y' play against Prov'nce, 'n y' name's *Healy!*"

I guess there was more, something about a touchdown I scored on some pass I intercepted in the last quarter, quite a play, the way he told it. But I didn't exactly hear it. All I got was a mumble, as they all began talking to each other, and then a silence, as they sat looking at me. I got my breath and said: "That's right, except it wasn't Providence. It was Green Bay."

"That's right. Goddam if I—"

"And I did call myself Healy. Under the rules, the eligibility rules, I mean, you can't play college football once you've played pro. But if you need the money, you've got to change things around. So—"

"You *Jack* Dillon?"

"That's me."

"Of—Mar'land?"

"I'm the guy."

"Holy jumping. . . ."

I told you, they were more bedrock than musical, and at the way he kowtowed in front of me, they all went into a different key. They were nothing but oil men, drillers and contractors and engineers, but most of them had been to college, and there's something about a guy who uses steel that goes for football more than he does opera. All of a sudden it was a different kind of afternoon, with the piano forgotten and the party going on around me, with drinks and jokes and friendly talk. Most of them were from the West and had never heard of me, but that made no difference. And changing my name made no difference either. That a guy could even stay on the same field with the Green Bay Packers and not get killed was wonderful to them. To me, it all felt great. I wished it could go on that way forever.

Somewhere along the line I took a trip to the powder room, and from there to the bar to sweeten my drink. At a table, reading a magazine, was a woman, and I remembered I'd seen a car drive up and heard some kind of whisper going on. I started to go, but she motioned to me, and then looked up. "*Oh!* I thought you were one of the oil gang, or petrol patrol, as I call them."

"No, just a visiting fireman."

"I've been told. Mr. Dillon, is that it?"

"To his friends, Jack."

"And quite a celebrity, I believe?"

"You're supposed to bow."

She got up and bowed. "I'm Mrs. Branch."

"I'm very pleased to know you."

"To her friends, Hannah."

"Now I'm not only pleased, but honored."

"I don't believe you are at all."

"Anyway, excited."

"Now *that's* more *like* it."

She fixed my glass and made a light one for herself, and we stood there looking at each other. She was maybe twenty-five, a little less than medium height, kind of thick in the chest and what went with it, slim in the waist and what was below. All that you could see fine, in the blue slacks and a peppermint-candy sweater with stripes running around. But what you noticed most was the eyes, and I still don't know if they really looked like they did, or were a production job, from what she did to bring them out. Her hair was light, with a brassy green in it, and fell on her shoulders in curls. But her skin was copper, like some vase in a Chinaman's window. I've seen plenty of sunburn in my time, but never anything like that, and it made the eyes look like something that came out of the sea. They were big, and light gray to start with, but with that dark color around them, they had a dangerous, slaty, sharky expression, and I think she knew it, and did everything to heighten it. But when we got to talking, it was about me, and what I did. She acted surprised when I said I squirted spray on a fruit ranch. "A celebrity, engaged in labor? I thought at the very *least,* you tasted tea, with sighing maidens bringing it to you, with a rose petal in every cup."

"Well, the dope's brought by Mexicans."

"The—what did you say?"

"Dope. Soup. To kill the bugs. They bring it in trucks, roll off the drums, and stack it up at one end of the row so we can put it in the tank and squirt it on the trees."

"Sounds fascinating."

"But—let's talk about you."

"Me?"

"That sunburn. Are you that way all over?"

". . . I wonder."

She stared at me so I couldn't look away. I went over to where she was perched on a stool by the bar, and I knew, and she knew, what I meant to do. I was going to give that sweater a wipe, from her waist to her neck, that would tell how she was all over. But from somewhere inside me came a warning, a gone, sick feeling that reminded me of what the liquor had made me forget: If that wipe did tell something, and we began to whisper date, I'd be no more use to her than a cigar-store Indian. So when I got to her I stopped, mumbled how good-looking she was, gave her a light kiss on the lips, and took a sip of my drink. Her eyes flickered, and she looked at the floor. Then: "Have I got something *on* me?"

"On you? How?"

"Like Flit. Or Larvex? Or Clorox?"

"No. Why?"

"Just wondered."

She drank out, put down her glass, and went in where the party was, while I sat there. But then she was back. "Why did you do that?"

"What?"

"You know what I mean."

"You got a husband?"

"Aren't you his guest?"

"Then ask *him* why."

"You mean it's honor? Man to man? That stuff?"

"It could be."

"I'll be damned if I believe it."

"There's some of it around still, whether you believe it or not. A guy gives me a lift, invites me in, treats me fine—that would be swell, wouldn't it, if I turned around then and made a pass at his wife."

"There's only one thing wrong with that."

"Which is?"

"You *did* make a pass at her."

"Says who?"

"You think a woman doesn't know? It could be a mile away, but if it goes click, it's a flash that goes from one to the other, and it's like nothing else on this earth. And it could be an inch away and mean nothing, like that rotten little kiss you dusted me off with."

"Maybe that's when I remembered."

"You mean, honor?"

"About time, I'd say."

She thought that over, then said: "No. A woman does that. Remembers her honor, or whatever she winds her clock by. But when she does, it isn't easy. It's a struggle, and costs her plenty, and she sighs and sobs and moans. But you, you didn't struggle. It went click, and then—nothing. *It was just as though the juice had suddenly been turned off.*"

"Somebody leaned on my disconnect switch, probably."

"Oh, God, *is* there such a thing? Can I buy one?"

The party went on the rest of the day and most of the night, there and in town and all around. Pretty soon I got so I knew one from the other, and they began to have faces and names I could tell apart. It turned out nobody had come for social purposes especially, but had dropped by on business, just regular Saturday-afternoon powwows. The guy that had spotted me was named Dasso. He was tall, thin, and red-haired, maybe around thirty, with glasses so thick they had circles in them, and gave his eyes that gimlet look. He worked for Branch, as super at the wells. He had brought over a driller named Butler and some geological dope that they were taking to Bakersfield Monday. Then there was Mr. White, that seemed to be connected with the bank, and a couple of engineers he had brought with him, that managed to get in quite a few looks at the blueprints. Mr. White I went for pretty heavy. He was tall, square-shouldered, and around fifty, but quiet, with a little grin when something made him laugh, and dressed in white duck, that advertised him for an old-timer, as not many wear it any more. It was at his house we had supper, and of course cocktails, and in his pool I won the bet with Dasso, five dollars I could touch all the ladders under water, one time around, without coming up. Around midnight I was back at the Branches, with a room all to myself, and fresh pajamas, shirt, and underwear waiting for me. Next morning, in church, we did the *Te Deum* and two anthems, and I sang *The Lord's Prayer*. That afternoon we fished off Mr. White's boat, but were back in time for more anthems and Handel's *Largo*. The singing I made pretty solemn, and maybe it wasn't so hot, by Victor-Red-Seal standards, but at Sts. David and Joseph, in Long Beach, California, it went over fine.

During all that time she'd been out there, on the edges somewhere, drinking long drinks at the pool, sitting in a back pew of the church, stretched out on a hatch cover while we fished, rubbing herself with oil so the sunlight would get in its effect, quite something to see. I wasn't talking to her, though, until Sunday midnight, after we'd all come back from the church, and she went out to the kitchen to fix lunch for Branch, Butler, and Dasso, on their trip next day, as the house-keeper'd been given the holiday off. I went out and helped, anyway to cut bread crusts off and spread butter while she sliced up ham and tongue and egg. She was in the same dark dress she'd worn to church, but when she put on a cellophane apron she looked more like herself. I mean, it was invented to display goods, and does. I strictly kept eyes front, but pretty soon she said: "Is there something I can get for you?"

"I'm not hungry, thanks."

"Drink?"

"If I put down any more booze, I'll fold."

"If there's anything you'd like, please ask for it. You did sing like an angel, as perhaps I should have mentioned sooner, and are certainly entitled to *something* in the way of special indulgence."

"Nothing I think of now."

"Can't you *look* at me?"

"I'm cutting bread."

". . . Jack, I can't figure you out."

"Any law you've got to?"

"Maybe not, but you can't blame me for thinking. Yesterday I washed you out, for reasons we needn't go into. But today, and especially tonight, you sang, and the reasons I had didn't make sense. I mean, what came out of your throat was something a woman could go for. And yet, you're cutting bread. What's the answer?"

"If I told you, you'd know, wouldn't you?"

"And I certainly want to."

"It's the same one: Your husband's a nice guy."

"And how would you know?"

"He's been pretty nice to me."

"But not to everybody, you might find."

"Pretty near everybody, from what went on yesterday and today. He's got an awful lot of friends, guys that seem to think the world of him. Guys in the oil business, with hard rock in their bones and something like it, anyway good solid stuff in their souls. And their wives. At the church, I noticed *they* like *him*. I didn't notice them falling all over themselves over you. You were left off by yourself, I'd say—far left, and rear."

"I don't go for old fogeys."

"Maybe they don't go for you."

"Maybe that's the trouble."

She got the tears going on that, and began a long song and dance about the lonely life she'd led, since she buried her father "beside my uncle and my mother, in the little cemetery on the hill." Then she said: "I had to have somebody to run the wells, and these awful filling stations I'm afflicted with, and he came along, and it seemed like the thing." But, she said, it "hadn't worked out," and she was beginning to wonder if it all wasn't a "terrible mistake." All it cut up to, to me, was a twenty-minute egg that had grabbed a good manager by marrying him, and then began shopping for a little excitement on the side. She let the cat out of the bag one time, I thought, while she was going to town on the way she was treated, when she said: "And what do I care what they think? What do I care if they *all* gang up on me? Maybe it's mutual."

"O.K., but why pick on me?"

"You really want to know?"

"Just for curiosity, I'd like to."

"Your curls, for one thing."

"Baby, I just need a haircut, that's all."

"You get them cut, and I'll murder you. Right there, the way they peep out, over your ear, I could eat them. Them and your dimples."

"My—? What the *hell* are you talking about?"

"You don't know about *them?*"

"I haven't got any."

"They're right under your shoulder blades, on each side. I didn't notice them till you made that crazy bet with Dasso, and I could see them, where you were swimming around down there. I thought at first it was water, the way it dapples in the sunlight, but today, when you were heaving that line, there they were again, the cutest things. Right—here—"

"Take your hands away."

"Why should I?"

"The circumstances."

"What do you mean, circumstances?"

"Hot pants, cold heart."

I tried to sleep, but couldn't, on account of what was running through my head—not about her, but the church, and the singing I'd done, and the crazy twenty-four hours I'd had, with jokes, and a little liquor, but mostly guys slapping me on the back, telling me I was swell. I guess that sounds silly, that a little of that kind of thing could take me so high, but not to somebody that spent two years on the road, and divided the world with the rats. It meant so much to me I kept going back over every little thing that had happened, and thinking what I might have said, swell gags that would have made everybody laugh. Around about daybreak I must have dropped off, because what woke me was the sound of voices downstairs, men's voices, pitched low, and the smell of coffee. Then, just after sunlight began to shine in the room, there were footsteps outside, the roll of a garage door, and the sound of a car. It was out on the road before the door slammed shut. I lay there, inhaling the cool air from outside, and feeling good, I could smell the morning in it, like I could when I was a kid. And then all of a sudden my heart began to pump, because I knew why that was: what a summer of food, drink, and sleep couldn't quite do, a little sociability had. It was back, what I'd worked for, hoped for, prayed for. I wasn't a thing any more, I was a man.

Then hammers began going in my head. There hadn't been any woman's voice down there, and that meant she was still in bed, on the other side of the partition from me, not ten feet away. I knew I had to get out of there. I jumped up, dived in the bathroom, and shaved. I stepped in the shower, turned on the warm water, and let it splash over me. The back of the shower was black marble, and I could see reflections in it. Then it seemed to me they moved. I turned and caught my breath. She had on red shoes, red cap, and red enamel on her fingernails, but the rest was pure copper. If that was all, I think I might still have thrown her out. But she closed her eyes, and her lashes lay out on her cheek, like an angel in some old painting. I folded her in my arms.

* 20 *

THE Mexicans were still playing cards that night when I went in the bunkhouse, and they didn't even look up when I walked by. I sat watching them, and pretty soon a boy came in, son of a driver, and said Holtz wanted to see me. I went over to his house and he wanted to know what I had on next day. I said spraying as usual, and he said let it go. That time of year it wasn't so important, and he'd put the Mexicans to leveling road for a while. I, he said, was to stand by a ditch-digging machine that was coming in, to put in a trench for pipe that was to be run over to a field where new trees would be put in whenever the nursery could deliver. "We've been digging our own ditches, but on a long one like this, I've decided to find out if it wouldn't be cheaper to hire this fellow and his machine. I've got him by the day, though, and that's where the catch comes in. If he's broke down half the time, he'll cost us more, time the job is done, than all the Mexicans I can hire. I want you there. The main trouble with those machines is they're just one jam of toggle plates, and spite of

hell they get fouled up with mud. Take a tank cart with a
hand pump, and the first sign of trouble, clean him off. Keep
him washed, and maybe we'll get the doddam thing dug some
time between now and Christmas."

"*Christmas?* Three days ought to do it."

"Then fine, take it away."

I went back to the bunk, found the *Saturday Evening Post*
under my pillow, opened it up to the story I'd started two days
before, began reading where I'd left off. It seemed funny, here
I'd had the most terrific week end of my life, anyway in the
things it had done to me, after what I'd been through, and
nobody even knew I'd been away. Everything was so much
like it had been that I think I'd have wondered if I'd been
away too, if it wasn't for this thing drilling in the back of my
head, this sense of shame over the fine way Branch had treated
me and the lousy way I'd paid him back. All during the next
three days, out there with Stelliger, the guy with the ditching
machine, listening to him brag about how well he's done with
this thing and his bulldozer and his tractor and his shovel and
his truck, I kept wishing I could have back the day that had
changed everything, and yet knowing I couldn't have resisted
it, once the chance came to me. And I kept dreading Thursday
night, when I knew Mr. Branch would be over, propositioning
me about rehearsal that night, so we could work up something
for Sunday that would be really good. And sure enough, right
after supper there he was, over by the store, waving at me with
a little grin on his face, and coming over. He apologized at
the way he'd run out on me Monday, but said he knew of
course his wife would get me home all right. Then he went
back over it the swell time we'd had. He said Mr. White had
been especially impressed with me, and not to be surprised
if something was arranged for me, maybe with the same
little independent refinery that backed up right behind Mrs.
Branch's property. I said swell, and wished he would go.
Little by little he got around to it, and I could hear myself

saying it in a shifty, two-bit way that I hated: that we were awfully busy that week, and I didn't see how I could possibly help him out with the choir—but some other time, sure, some other time. He swallowed two or three times, and looked away quick. He was like most other hard-rock men, shy on the inside as a young girl, and I stood there with my hat off to him for it, and yet not able to say so.

He was hardly out of sight than there came the pop of a horn from the trees near the shop, and lights blinking on and off at me. I went over and she was at the wheel of her car. "I was looking for you, and then *he* drove up, and I had to get out of sight, quick. What did he want?"

"Choir."

"And he came clear over *here?*"

"What do you want?"

"What do you think?"

"I've no place to take you."

"I have, Jack, as it happens. Nothing but a cottage by the sea, or in plain English a beach shack. But a place—I can take you."

I tried to tell her to go, that I was ashamed of what we had done, that I was through with her. No words came. Next thing I knew I was in the car with her and we were rolling through the trees. She kept on down 101 to a road that turned right, then ran over to the Long Beach traffic circle. From there she ran on down below Seal Beach. When she came to a concrete apron drifted over with sand, she turned in. We got out and she opened a garage door, got back in, ran the car inside, got out and closed the garage door. We climbed over the dune, that bulges up at that point in a way to make it look like the sea is higher than the road. On the other side of it were shacks. We turned into a little cement walk, she got a key out of her handbag, and opened a shack door. When we stepped inside it was stuffy, like it hadn't been opened for some time. But after the wind from the sea it felt warm, and we were in each other's arms, her mouth pressed hot against mine, almost before we shut the door. We stayed an hour. Then we had to leave, so she could take me to the ranch, drive home herself, and still be able to say she had been to a picture show. ". . . Which one? Do you happen to know?"

"I saw it this afternoon."

"On purpose? So you could be with me?"

"Yes, of course."

That went on all fall and through the winter. It was one of those southern California Januaries where it's spring right after New Year's, and when she began picking me up Sundays as well as Thursday nights, she'd put on a red bathing suit and go splashing out in the surf. That made me nervous, because it was one more thing to make people take notice of us, but at least, peeping at her through the window while she was out there, it did give me a chance to get some kind of an idea what she looked like. That may sound funny, but getting a glimpse now and a flash then, mostly at night when we were both so nervous we could hardly draw our breath, I still thought of her mostly as a whisper in the dark. Well, she looked like some college girl in her little red trunks, red shoes, red hat, and red halter, and now that the sunburn was wearing off, she didn't have so much of that coppery Aztec look. And her eyes, now they didn't show up so funny, were more human too, and sometimes, specially when she'd keep looking at me while I was doing something around the place, soft, and warm, and pretty. And yet, right in the middle of them, was a light that never quite left them, and that was hard, and meant to take whatever it wanted, no matter who got hurt. She made it plain, morning, noon, and night, that she was taking me. I made it plain she wasn't and we had a couple of fights about what a tramp she was. Once, when she came to the ranch, I refused to get in the car with her, and she stayed out there, by the shop, with her lights on and her elbow on the horn, till Holtz called an officer, and it wasn't till he got there that she drove off. The other time I beat it out of the beach shack before she was dressed, and took half the night thumbing my way to the ranch. Both those times I missed her bad, every way there was but the right way. When she showed up after those fights, each time on a Thursday night, I was so glad I was ashamed of myself. "Listen, you big lug, I lie awake thinking about you. I—yen for you. You're in my hair."

"O.K., then. I can say the same."

"You mean you love me, Jack?"

"I didn't say so. Don't get so excited. Yen."

"How'd you like to go to hell?"

"On my way."

"Jack—no!"

"Then watch how you talk."

"All right, yen. But a lot? Yen, yen, yen?"

"Yeah, and yen."

All that time, as I say, she kept looking at me, and I guess I liked it, anyway at first, but then I could see it wasn't all yen. I'd ask her what it was about, and she'd laugh. But then one afternoon, when we were making a Sunday of it at the beach, she said: "Jack, wouldn't that be funny if I'd been making the same mistake I made once in a poker game?"

"So you're a gambler too?"

"I've done a good many things."

"And what was this mistake?"

"I drew to a straight and filled a flush."

"That's impossible."

"You sure?"

"Unless, holy smoke, it was a *straight* flush."

"I found that out, when I was getting ready to throw up my

hand. A flush wouldn't have been one-two-three with what was against me. But then I looked again, and saw I had filled a flush *and* a straight."

"Did you clean up?"

"Twenty-seven bucks."

"And what's that got to do with me?"

"When I drew you, I fell for your beauty."

"My dimples. I remember."

"But these last few weeks I've been noticing a look in your eye. And I've been listening to you talk. Especially about those big dynamos and things you studied in college. And *I've* been wondering if perhaps I shouldn't have fallen for your brains. I decided, quite some time ago, that a smart dame would keep romance and business separate. I married business, and I guess it works—pretty well. I play around with romance, and I know that works—damned well. Do you hear me, Jack?"

"O.K., but what's the rest of it?"

"I said it works damned well. What do you say?"

"So does a stink bomb."

"That's not nice."

"Neither is it. Even if it *does* work."

It was an hour, I guess, before she decided to go on. Then: "I'm trying to say, if you'd stop insulting me every minute, I had a hunch. Some weeks ago. Like the one I woke up to in the poker game. That maybe you're a straight and also a flush—beauty and brains all in the same package. I mean, if you tried, you could make the *business* go damned well, too."

"Meaning, on husbands, you want to switch?"

"Well?"

"No."

"Jack, I'm sorry, but for me pretty well isn't well enough. It has to be damned well or I'm not interested. For three years now that jerk has been trying to sell me something just as good. Telling me I shouldn't get excited. That I should take it easy. That I should wait. That things are bound to get better.

And I've listened to him. Owning property that should make me rich, that could mean something if it was handled right, I've stood by and watched it go from bad to worse, until it's a *mess*. My wells are pumping less all the time, and in a few years they're going dry. And yet I have to keep this miserable shack, when with smart work I could have a real place at Pebble Beach, all because a damned jerk—"

"That jerk is a swell guy."

"A jerk is a jerk."

"If he says wait, I'd bet waiting does it."

"I want what I want when I want it!"

"Who sang that was a basso named—"

"Shut up. . . . You going to spray fruit all your life?"

"I didn't start my life spraying fruit, and I don't expect to end it that way. But just at the moment, until I see where I'm coming out, I'm doing it. I booted the beans into the fire just once too often, I'm sorry to say, and the way I paid for it I hope you never find out, because I'm not going to tell you. But at that, compared with the onion-hoeing I see most of them doing, and the lousy grand operas some of them are singing, and all the other stuff that's being done by guys too proud to spray fruit and too dumb to do anything else, my job suits me fine."

"Jack, I'm talking about big things."

"You're not talking about anything that I can hear."

Now I was myself again, quite a few things had come back, and one of them was the twist in me that made me blow my top when somebody was trying to make me do something I didn't want to do. And I was finding out things about cold heart. As long as it's a toy, it can be as childish as anybody, and roar, or kick slippers through the window, or whatever. But when it really sees something it wants, it can wheedle, wait, and watch you for the right time, the right night, and the right place. She let me run down, and when it got dark lit the grate, so we sat there in the blue light from the gas. Then she made coffee and opened some chili con carne. When I said it was time we got started back to the ranch, she got up meek as pie, handed me my tie, and helped me on with my coat. I'd got some new clothes, and she said they looked swell.

But when we got to the Long Beach traffic circle, instead of cutting inland she kept on through Long Beach, and pretty soon turned to the right, into a small narrow street. And then all of a sudden we were in oil, with the reek of it everywhere and derricks all around us, thick as trees. "You like that smell, Jack?"

"Would anybody?"

"You would. For one thing it speaks to your damned machinist's soul. And for another thing you've got brains enough to know it comes from the guts of the earth, and turns wheels and things, and is important."

"It's pretty terrific."

"Couldn't you say so?"

"I could, if it wasn't a build-up."

"For what?"

"The big switcheroo."

"You're damned right it is."

"You're wasting your time."

"I generally get what I go after."

There are no street lights in an oil field, and we rolled along pretty slow, through gray tanks, gray pipes, gray pumps, and gray steam. But then, ahead of us, was a string of lights going straight up, in the air, and when we got nearer I could see they were hanging from a derrick. "Now *I'm* excited, Jack. That's a new well going down."

"They work on Sunday?"

"Sunday, Monday, every day, three shifts twenty-four hours around the clock. They have to keep going. If they didn't, if they broke it off for any length of time, the cuttings would settle in the mud, they'd have to clean out their hole, and they'd lose hours and hours."

"Mud? What's that for?"

"It's pumped through the drill."

"Oh, to cool it."

"And carry away the cuttings from the formation. It's pumped out then."

"Didn't they ever try water?"

"I don't know."

"Well, if I could think of it they could think of it. Maybe water's too thin to carry all that sand and grit and shale away with it."

"Yes, I think that was the trouble."

When we got near she cut over, straight across lots, and then we could see the drill crew, five or six of them, in slickers and hard composition hats, all around the rotary table, that was turning in the middle of the derrick floor, a few feet above ground level. They waved her back, but she kept looking them over, and pretty soon spotted one she knew, and spoke to him. He recognized her and said something to the driller, who craned around at us from the levers he had hold of, that were connected with a big drum that had cable spooled on it, and regulated the feed to the bit. He nodded and waved us over and we got out and climbed up there. "We're putting on a new drill in a couple of minutes, if you want to see it done. I'd stand over by that rathole if I was you. We're setting pipe on the other side."

The rathole was an open pipe, sunk down in the ground, that they drop the Kelly in, as they call it, when they're changing bits. We stood over there, and sure enough, they began coming up with the pipe. A guy went up to what they call the fourble board, that platform you see, about two thirds the way up on all oil derricks, and the guys on the ground began pulling out pipe. The traveling blocks would go up with a stand of pipe, and grab it with a tongs. Then with what they call a cathead they'd break the joint, spin it out with the rotary table, and when it was free, lift it out with a spring hook. Then the derrick man, the one on the fourble board, would guide it behind the·fingerboard, as they call it, a rack that holds the pipe, one stand beside the other, as they take it out. Then another section of four would come up, and another and another. So fast I could hardly believe it, they had that pipe out, four thousand feet of it, by my figuring, a new bit on, and the pipe going down in the hole again. The bit was one I'd never seen, though I'd read about it. It had three pinions, with teeth in them, that rolled around and cut the rock, and in the middle of them was a hole that the mud circulated through, to pump out drill cuttings between drill pipe and casing. It made the bit I had smithed up, for the road quarry that time, look like something used by Indians ten thousand years B.C. She explained it all to me, as well as she could, and as soon as the rotary table was going again, so they were making hole, the driller came over and explained it, and in between, the roughnecks explained it. Everybody explained it, and I couldn't help eating it up. I could have stayed there all night.

When we left the well, she took a different road, that led up a hill, and pretty soon she stopped. We got out, and she led me up a rise, past a cemetery, to a plot that had half a dozen wells on it, with one or two pumps going, but with the derricks removed. She explained that a wooden derrick is generally left standing, as there's not much it can be used for anywhere else, but the steel ones get taken down and put up again. All the well needs, from then on, she said, is a Christmas tree, so there's no use wasting valuable steel. The Christmas tree is an attachment for the control of natural flowing oil wells. She showed me one, and from the number of gauges and valves on it, all of them round and most of them different colors, you could see how it got its name. When pressure eases off, so they have to install pumps, the Christmas tree is taken away. I got the flashlight from her car, and climbed down into concrete pits and over pipes and through shed doors, and she answered my questions, pretty well, I've got to say for her. Then, after a while: "You know what place this is, Jack?"

"Yours, I suppose."

"That's right."

"Where'd you get it, if I may ask?"

"From my father."

"I remember now, Mr. Branch mentioned it, that first day I met him, when he gave me a lift. But he said something about your uncle, too."

"My father and uncle came here from Ohio, all hot to go in the oil business, and my uncle persuaded my father that the future of oil was in the selling end of it, not the production. They'd had romantic dreams, you see, as the papers were full of the boom out here, and they had some money they got from selling the hardware store they had run, back in Toledo. But then my uncle got to reading about the gold boom, back in the fifties, and how Mark Hopkins had made so much money, not from sluicing gold, but from selling shovels and boots and bacon to those who were sluicing it. He sold my father on the idea of garages, to sell the oil, or filling stations, as they're called now, instead of wells, to produce it. So my father had to give up all his fine dreams, and try to get interested in these coal-oil sheds, as he called them, and presently he sent for my mother and me. And we had hardly got to Los Angeles when my mother caught cold in the miserable damp hotel my uncle had found, and it went into pneumonia, and she died. And my father arranged to bury her, as he thought in Tropico, as Glendale was called then, on the hill that's now Forest Lawn Cemetery. But where the procession came was this hill, Signal Hill, as it's now called. It was pretty forlorn, and my father hated to leave her here in the little cemetery we passed on the way up. He took it pretty hard, and after a while he decided that forlorn or not, he wanted to be near her, so he bought a lot, and almost every night we'd come to it, and stand looking over her grave and the ocean, and imagine what it would be like when we got the house built and began living in it, as at least he'd have his memories. My uncle was against it, but by that time nobody paid much attention to what he was against, as the filling stations weren't located right for the way the town was growing, or anyhow most of them weren't, and nothing that he touched had gone right. And then on Signal Hill they struck oil. So instead of building a home on it we drilled, right here on the land you're standing on. And my uncle couldn't get over it that in this way, almost as though God had taken a hand in it, my father had got what he wanted. My uncle messed things up, though, before he died, as usual. My father was for selling the stations and putting the money in this little refinery back of us, that had just been built then, and had cost too much, and could be had, cheap. He said when we knew what we were going to do with our oil, then would be time to go ahead on wells. But my uncle was frightened at something with any size to it, or anything except the peanut way he always wanted to do business. He insisted we get some wells down first, so we had money coming in, and then see about branching out. So that's what he did, and had to borrow even more money from the bank than we would have had to do to take over the refinery. And the more oil we pumped, the cheaper we had to sell it to the pipe-line companies, and to get gas for the stations, the dearer we had to buy it back. It was just a squeeze. At that time nobody knew what an integrated company was, but that's what they call it now, and that's what my father, just on instinct, wanted —a company that produces its own crude, manufactures its own gas, lube oil, fuel, and asphalt, and sells in its own outlets. But we bumbled along, and always it seemed if we could just get one more well we could break through. Then my uncle died, and a few months after him, my father, and they're buried there, beside my mother. Then the bank ran things awhile, and after I came of age I ran it, with a little assistance from the bank, or anyhow the bankers. That's where I got my ideas about men, in case it interests you, and maybe I'm wrong, but nothing's come up to prove I am, yet. We had some wild parties, but the squeeze went on, exactly the same. And then, on the last well that was drilled, with money from the bank, I began seeing quite a little of the contractor. And it seemed, from the way he talked, that *he* might know what should be done. So in a soft moment, I married him. And just for a little while, we were headed somewhere, or that's what he said. One more well, and we'd have that margin, that safe extra income, that would make it possible for us to talk deal to the refinery. So that's what we're doing now, getting ready for another new well—letting contracts for the derrick, for the cement, for everything except the drilling, because of course we do that ourselves because we used to be in the business and can do it cheaper, and in addition to that can give a lot of old pals jobs. So there's the bank, just where it always was except it's holding new paper for the old notes we paid off, and there are the wells, getting a little older each year, and here I am, not getting any younger that I notice."

"Does anybody?"

"It's a mess just the same. And if all that wasn't bad enough here, now there's the allocation."

"The—? Did you mention it?"

"I don't say it wouldn't have worked, the safe and sane policy, though it reminds me a lot of my uncle. But then came the price wars, after the depression got started, with everybody pumping oil like mad, and selling it for what they could get. So of course that would damage the field, by lowering gas pressure. So after the election, in connection with the blue eagle there was all kinds of talk, and they were allowed to do some regulating. It's all supposed to be voluntary, but they tell you what you can pump just the same. . . . Twelve hundred barrels a day! For my six wells! When they're capable of yielding three times that! Is that fair, now I ask you? What good is a new one going to do me if that's how it's got to run? And—he makes me perfectly furious with the *attitude* he's got toward it."

"What attitude?"

". . . Maybe that's where you come in."

"*If* I come in. What are you hinting at?"

"Suppose there was all kinds of undercover stuff going on. Suppose not everybody believed in this blue eagle. Suppose quite a few people said it was nothing but a blue buzzard? Would you pay too much attention to this allocation stuff? Just how much do you believe in ethics?"

"You mean, would I sell it bootleg?"

"Yeah, that's what I mean."

"No."

"I never noticed you so terribly honest."

"Oil and wives are different."

We started climbing down, and at the cemetery she turned in, walked over, and after a little way, stopped. I saw her drop something on a grave. It was chalk white, and I was pretty sure it was one of the geraniums that grew in a bed in front of the shack, something quite a few people have, as it's one of the few flowers that'll grow near the sea. It crossed me up, as usual, that mixed in with the hundred-per-cent bad was something good. She came back and I gave her arm a little pat. She took my hand in hers and we went back to the car. "Will you think it over, Jack? Because if you'd take it over now, before we get started on that new well—"

"I won't take it over."

For two or three weeks she kept it up, with a lot of talk about how she was just as fed up with two-timing as I was, and wanted to ring down on it, and get started in some kind of decent way, but couldn't, with that well about to start, because if that got under way before she had the showdown she'd have to let him go through with it anyway. After a while she quit talking about it, but one Monday night she was over, and it turned out the well had started, and as it took all of his time she could get out any night now. We went down to the shack, then on the way headed for Long Beach. I was nervous, and kept begging her to watch where she was going, for fear we'd run into somebody. She found a place on top of Signal Hill, not far from the refinery, and peeping around the bubble tower we could see Branch with two or three guys, poking around with a flashlight. "The rig-builder has just set the concrete for the four derrick corners, and Jim has to see how the work is done." After that, every night we'd have a look, and almost sooner than you could believe it they were putting up steel, and then it was in place, and the crown block was up. She tried again, to get me to take over, and said she had money, a lot of money, that was mine if I'd only say yes. I kept telling her I knew nothing about oil, but that just made her beg harder. One night, when we parked, we could hear the rotary table, and see the white helmets under the lights. They were drilling.

Two or three nights after that we went to the shack, and she cried, then lay in my arms without saying anything. After a while she went out in the kitchen and lit the gas and put on the kettle. In a minute I went out to keep her company, and we stood around a few minutes in the dark. Then, just as she was reaching for the coffee, a car door slammed on the other side of the dune. She looked out and then cut the gas. "Oh, my God, Jack. It's my husband—and Dasso!"

"Well—you asked for it."

"Why in the world didn't I think of it? It's about two miles closer to the well than the house is, and—*Jack, what are we going to do?*"

"I don't much care."

That wasn't, strictly speaking, true. I hated the whole

damned business, but not like I hated the idea of facing
Branch. Maybe I'd got to a certain point, but if there was still
any way to duck a showdown, I'd take it, so when she grabbed
me and pulled me in the living room and shoved me in a
closet that had been built in one corner to hold rods and
tackle, I went as fast as she did, and held my breath maybe
a little tighter. It seemed funny to be jammed in there with
her, half of me scared to death, the other half full of the same
creepy feeling she always gave me, of wanting her.

Outside, they were knocking the sand off their shoes on the
walk, then the key clicked in the lock and they were inside
and a light was shining through the crack. Branch said sit
down, he'd rustle something up in a minute, and went in the
bedroom, where the liquor cabinet was. In the living room,
there was scraping and bumping and moving around, and I
don't think Dasso was doing a thing but looking at the pictures of Branch catching fish, but he sounded like a whole
troupe of acrobats practicing the double front. Then Branch
was back, and they seemed to be pouring a drink, and for a
minute or two neither of them said anything. Then they began
talking about the well and Branch said he was quite satisfied
with the way it was going, and said Dasso ought to take quite
some credit to himself. Dasso said it was going all right and
they had another drink. Then all of a sudden Dasso said:
"Well, goddam it, who said it was going all right? It's going
the best of any well I've seen put down, and maybe it's something yours truly had a little to do with, but mainly it's the
big boss, a guy named Branch. A well's like everything else,
it goes in exact proportion to how you plan it. And this one's
been planned right, believe me. Everything's been taken care
of, from the right crew to the right geological report to the
right contracts to the right equipment. If we're drinking to me,
we better hoist one to you while we're about it, and make it a
good one."

"O.K., then. Drink out."

"Drink out yourself."

"I've still got a little."

They got around to number three in due course, but not until she almost choked on the dust in there, and had to squeeze on my hand till I thought the nails must be drawing blood to keep from coughing. Pretty soon I heard her breathe: "Thank God," and you could tell from the scraping and bumping that had started again that the drinking was over and Branch and Dasso were ready to go. And then I heard Dasso say: "Jim."

"Yeah, what is it?"

"What's the window doing open?"

"Well—you put it up. . . . Didn't you?"

"*Did* I?"

"Or—maybe I did."

"Did either of us?"

There was a long time when nothing was said, and then: "Jim, were you ever shadowed?"

"Not that I know of."

"I was once. On that forged title case, over at Santa Fe Springs. It had hardly started before I knew it, and I didn't know how. . . . Jim, I got a funny feeling we're not alone."

"Come on, have another drink."

"No, I mean it."

"Well, for God's sake, let's have a look."

"O.K., let's."

She felt like some violin string, tuned to the point it breaks, and all over the place were footsteps, and then they stopped. Then: "Dasso, you're seeing things. There's nobody here."

"O.K. If I can put a little water in it, I'll have that other drink."

"Help yourself."

The kitchen door squeaked, and in hardly a second it squeaked again. Then Dasso said: "Jim."

"Yeah?"

"That kettle's hot."

There was the longest silence I ever heard, then the front door opened, and footsteps sounded outside, going around the house, but of only one person. How long we stood it I don't know. We just stood there and stood there and stood there. After a while her hand tightened on mine, and then loosened. Then her breath began to come in gasps. I knew she'd pass out if I didn't do something. I opened the door.

He was facing us, in one of the beach chairs on the other side of the gas log. When she staggered out of there, he sat like a stone. But when he could see who I was, he jerked up on his elbows for maybe a second, like he could hardly believe his eyes. Then he leaned back. But he didn't only lean. He shriveled into his clothes, so that what had been a big man seemed small.

She sat on the table, and poured a spoonful of liquor into one of the glasses, drank it, and shivered. I sat down somewhere. It was a long time before anything was said, and then he said: "This is why you wouldn't sing for me?"

"I guess so, Mr. Branch."

"And it started then, that Sunday?"

"Yes."

He turned to her: "Hannah, why didn't you tell me?"

"How could I?"

"But—there's nothing you can't tell me."

"Would I stab a knife into you?"

"But I think you've forgotten, it was what we said. I told you if ever there came anything you were to tell me. There's nothing I couldn't forgive you, Hannah—except not being frank with me. That makes me feel—all alone—left out of your life. I don't know anything to do about it."

"I'm sorry, Jim."

It came to me they weren't acting like a man and his wife. They were acting like a father and his child. Instead of taking her by the throat, or me by the throat, or somebody by the throat, he was reasoning with her, being noble, or whatever it was. And she, instead of roaring around and asking what he was going to do about it, was acting meek and sorry and lowly, like some kid that played hooky from school. I said: "Can I say something to you two people?"

Neither one of them said anything, but I kept at it: "Never mind what I have to do with this. You know when you're a heel or you don't. But as to how things were before I got here, all I can say is that I think Hannah turned to you, Mr. Branch, at a time when she was pretty low about her father, and that what she reached for, even if she didn't know it, wasn't a husband, but somebody to take the place of her father, and that's why—"

He cut me off: "We've been all over that."

"Yes, Jack. Naturally.

"You mean you *knew* it?"

They didn't answer me, and then she began talking to him: "It all seemed so simple, Jim, and so wonderful, the way you said it. My father was gone, and you wanted to be a father to me, and take care of me, and see that no harm ever came—and you did. How could I try to tell you you didn't? You did everything you said you'd do, but you were a little late. I looked like a little girl to you, and some ways I was, but there were other ways you didn't know about. There were those years in college, and the years right after—and then I wasn't a little girl any more. I was a wild dame, looking for a good time, and plenty grown-up. Oh, I was honest enough. I wanted our life the way we said, and I felt saintly, the way a woman ought to feel. But when I was alone, I'd want to be wild again, and then—I popped off one day, that's all. It's not

Jack's fault. At least he wouldn't keep on wearing a surplice, and singing for you. You've got to say that for him."

"I haven't chided him . . . or you."

He poured himself some liquor, and I thought he drank it off pretty quick. Then he had some more. Then he asked her if her car was here, and when she said it was in the garage, he said he and she could take that and Dasso would drive me to the ranch, then gave her a little pat and said it was time they were getting home. She didn't move. He said it again, with all kinds of explanations about how of course he would forgive her, and more of the same, until my teeth began to go on edge, though I wanted her to make it up with him. She still didn't hear him, then started to cry. He started to cry. I wanted to cry. He poured himself another drink and drank it, then had another and another. Then Dasso was there, tapping him on the shoulder, saying come on, the new shift was coming on, they'd have to go. He got to his feet, picked up the bottle, drained the last of it, tried to set it down, and missed. I picked it up, put it on the table. He picked up the cork, put it back in the bottle. It took him five minutes. Then he went reeling to the door, Dasso's arm around him.

When I heard them drive off I lit the gas, went out in the kitchen and made coffee, and made her drink some. Then I put her to bed. I spread a blanket over her. I found a blanket for myself, wrapped it around me, and camped in a chair. When the sun came up, she was asleep, but I was still sitting there, trying to figure where I was at with my life, if any.

✳ 21 ✳

THE Sunday after that I slept late, as spring means work on a fruit ranch, and I'd had a hard week. Around ten o'clock, when I strolled over from breakfast, church bells were ringing somewhere, and I had a wild notion to sing in the choir because I felt like it, and at last have peace, even if it hadn't much glory attached to it, or much pay. It had been a week since I'd seen her, and it seemed that maybe I never would again, and that I could forget about her, and everything she'd mixed me up with, and especially Branch. It wasn't all hope, either. One night, on a trip to Whittier with the light truck, I had taken a sneak to have a peep at the well. It was just like it had been, with the rotary table going around in the middle, a driller camped at the drum, roughnecks standing around, and Dasso off to one side, giving orders. It looked like she didn't need me, and I might be out. That suited me fine. Because coming home that Monday morning, with her at the wheel saying nothing and the gray damp drifting in from the ocean, I'd had a bad time. It had hit me all in a lump as it hadn't before, that it was all very well to talk mean to her, and maybe she was cold and maybe she was wild and maybe she was bad, but it took two to cook up the kind of cross we had tried to get away with, and here at last I tumbled that one of them might be me. But a week had gone by, and I'd heard nothing from her, and there was no getting around it, I might be out.

This Sunday morning, though, I had hardly gone in the bunkhouse before there came a rap on a horn, fast, sharp, and nervous. I went out, and there she was, in the car. I walked over and said: "Well stranger, where you been keeping yourself?"

"Jack, I've been keeping myself a good many places, and I'm fine, and it's a beautiful day, but—will you please get in so we can talk as we go and not take the whole day about it?"

"We in a hurry or something?"

"All hell has broken loose."

". . . What kind of hell?"

"At the well! Will you get in, so we can go?"

I got in, and we whizzed to 101, and were leveled off for Long Beach before she went on: "It's the police, and what they're threatening to do to us if we don't take care of the mud. It's—all over the place and you'll have to do something about it."

"All over what place?"

"The street!"

"If I'm to help, say something."

"When they pump it the cuttings add to volume, and water is added too. So more comes out than goes in. The increase in volume makes an overflow. It has to be pumped somewhere. Generally a sump—a big sink banked up with dirt. But the man my husband made his arrangements with, on the next property, has changed his mind, or needs his sump himself, or something. He says it was on a personal basis with my husband, and now it's different, or—I don't know what he says, I haven't even seen him. But we're cut off from his land, and we can't stop drilling and the mud's running out into the street, and it's a violation, and the police are there, and—"

"Can't your husband do something?"

"He isn't there."

"Where is he?"

"At the Hilton."

"What's he doing there?"

"I don't know."

"The last I heard of it, he was going to carry on for you till this well was down. Now he's at the Hilton and he's not carrying on. Come on, what's happened?"

"He's been drinking."

"On account of us?"

"I guess so. Jack, you'll have to—"

"Why can't Dasso do something?"

"He's nothing but an employee."

I wanted to ask what I was, that I could do something, but as I've said, I'd got it through my head by then that it took two to make a mess like we had, and if I'd started it, I had to finish it, or try to. We drove on, and pretty soon we were in Long Beach, and I kept trying to picture what the mud was like. And when we turned into the little street that led up Signal Hill, there it was, trickling down the ditch, the same kind of gray, with a greasy shine to it, they have on the upper Eastern Shore of Maryland. And there at the corner, where it was slopping down a grating into a drain, was a cop, poking it with a stick to keep it from caking. And on the other side of him were two firemen with a hose, playing water on it a little further up the hill, to keep it liquid, so it wouldn't choke the whole ditch. We went up the hill and all up and down my back I could feel this sick feeling, because I had no idea at all what I was going to do about it. At the well, except for cops in a car and the mud running out of a pipe into the ditch, things looked as usual. The driller was at his brake, the rotary table was spinning around, roughnecks were there, and Dasso was off to one side, talking with a police sergeant, who kept looking at his watch.

When he saw us park, Dasso came over. "Well, Hannah, I guess this does it. I've told him we daren't stop that drill, but he says we've got ten minutes to get that mud under control, and if we don't, he's shutting us down."

Dasso was looking at her, but he was really talking to me. The officer came over and she pleaded with him and said to

close the well down now would practically mean they'd lose
hundreds of feet of hole, and he said he realized that. He said
he'd given two hours already, and wanted to accommodate
her every way he could. But, he said, the law was the law.
Strictly speaking, he was obliged to shut her down now, but
he didn't want to be any harder on her than he could help.
She asked what he wanted her to do, and he said he didn't
know, but that mud couldn't indefinitely discharge into the
street. Dasso began to whistle something, the cop looked me
over, and she was biting her lips, hoping I could do something.
I didn't know what I was going to do but I got out. Off to one
side were two tanks that had been brought in to take care of
production when the well started. I didn't know what they
were doing there at that time, but I could see they weren't
connected up with anything, and that they were empty. I
made a quick flash and flashback with my eye, and it seemed
to me if the mud pipe were turned at the elbow joint up near
the well, the end of it, where the mud was pouring out, would
just about swing over the nearest tank and would even reach
the other. I went over, grabbed it in both hands, and pulled.
It didn't move, so I called to the men for a little help. Then it
turned and the mud splattered all over me. We walked the end
around until it was over my head, where the ground fell
away to the tanks. I was in a shower of mud, but gave a last
push and then heard it drumming on metal, inside. I turned
to Dasso: "That ought to hold you for a while. Soon as one
fills, use the other."

Dasso's glasses clouded from the venom in his eyes. Then he
looked at her. "Yes, Daz, I think that'll do it."

". . . Is he in charge now?"

"As my representative."

I turned to the cop: "As I figure it, those tanks will do it
till tomorrow, when I'll have a proper sump put in."

"Well, not quite till tomorrow, I'd say."

"Violation's taken care of for the present, isn't it?"

"Well, yes sir, only—"

"Then O.K."

I said it like a grand duke dismissing the barber, and he called to the cop down the hill and to the firemen, then went to the car and drove off, with the other cops. "Jack! Get in! I *have* to kiss you—before you wash off that mud."

"Got no time."

I didn't need any cop to tell me I was talking much too optimistic about those tanks, that they couldn't hold us any more than a couple of hours. I'd be back where we started, if I didn't make a place to dump mud. For a minute I concentrated, trying to remember the name of the guy with the ditcher, but then I had it: Stelliger. I went in the shack they used for an office, looked him up, got him on the phone. I'd hate to tell you what a hundred-per-cent American mechanic takes for a little Sunday emergency job, but pretty soon here he came, riding his ditcher, with his truck and shovel right behind. I started him in right away, on the hillside just above the drilling rig where the tanks were filling. With the ditcher, I had him make four deep trenches, then start in at right angles and criss-cross them, so one was falling right in on the other. Then with the shovel, I had him begin loading loose dirt on the truck, dumping it at the other end of the property. If I looked around, I knew I could probably find some guy not so far away that was making land in a marsh somewhere, and get rid of my dirt there, but I didn't have time to look around. I dumped dirt where I could dump it, then the last few loads I piled it up around the hole I was making, and pretty soon it was a regular sump—not a very neat one, but a fair job for a rush order, and big enough to hold all the mud we'd pump for quite a few days. When they were done she drew the check. "I'm sorry, Hannah, at the cost, but—"

"I'm not. I'm glad."

"But it had to be done, and—"

"Will you get in now?"

"Can we eat?"

"Me, if you want to."

The night shift had come on by then, and everything seemed to be going fine, so she took me to a drive-in, where we had sandwiches and coffee, and then to a little hotel on Anaheim Boulevard, where I called up Holtz and told him I was leaving. He raised holy hell, as I expected, and offered me more dough, which made me feel proud and sorry at the same time, but there was no help for it, I'd taken over an oil well and had to see it through. As she was lending me her car, I took her home, had another look-in at the well, and finally went to the hotel and turned in. By sunup I was back on the job. Around noon Monday was when the trouble started.

We were running mud into my makeshift sump by then, but I wanted to get things lined up right, so I got ready to make a regular sump, over on the far end of the property next to where the first well had been drilled. So you'll get it straight, all that happened later, I better tell you how it was laid out. There were two streets, not any bigger than lanes, one going up the hill, the other across it, and her property lay right at the intersection. Over from her, next to the street that ran across the hill, was the cemetery. Up the tilted street, the one that ran over the top of the hill, and separated from her by nothing but a barbed-wire fence, was the little refinery, with its compressor unit in one corner. Out of every well comes oil and gas, and the gas is first trapped, then run into a compressor unit, or absorption plant as a big one is called, and the casing-head gasoline extracted. That's the high-octane stuff that's mixed with all good gas like Central American coffee is mixed with ordinary coffee, and for the same reason, to give it pep. The oil goes to a refinery to be cut up into something that will sell, or in the case of a big company with plenty of dough to spend, to a cracking plant, which is the same as a refinery, except they do it under a pressure a refinery doesn't have, and get all kinds of by-products the refineries miss. This refinery was a teapot, with three stills running gas fires, pipes leading to flash towers, bubble towers, storage tanks, and the rest of the stuff that goes with a job that stays on a half acre of ground. Her land was an acre, with six wells running along one side, by the barbed-wire fence, all with the derricks removed but pumps going, each with a gas trap, which is a little inverted tank about the size of a house hot-water tank, and two gauging tanks which are eight or ten feet high and maybe six feet across, the same kind I used for mud. They're always set up in pairs, so one is filling while the other is emptying into the pipe line. She had an annual contract with Luxor, or luXor, as they spelled it, and everywhere you looked was some kind of valve with their X on it, connecting with their lines that led to their plant, down the hill maybe a quarter of a mile. Near the refinery, on the other side of a wooden fence was another small independent like herself, named Mendel, the one that had let Branch use his sump, and then changed his mind.

The new well was near Mendel's fence, starting another row of six. The temporary sump I had made was right alongside of it, and the new sump, the bigger one I was going to build that would hold us a while, was at the lower end of her property. But on something of that size, I couldn't jackleg the way I had on the little sump, so I told Stelliger to come on Tuesday, and that Monday morning drove up to Long Beach and found a place that had a second-hand transit. Then I came back, borrowed a roughneck off the driller, and began setting stakes for the grading. I'd been at it maybe an hour when that sixth sense, or my ear maybe, told me something was wrong. I looked over. Dasso was nowhere around, but the guy on the mud pump was at the screen, looking down at the stuff that was flowing back over it, Then the driller noticed something and looked up. Then the pump gave two or three coughs, while the pump man dived for the throttle. He was too late. It blew out with a noise like a cannon. Steam roared all around, the driller reached for his throttle, and everything stopped.

By one o'clock, a trouble-shooter was out there, from a pump company I found in the classified phone book, that I *had* to find somehow or other, if anything was to be done, as Dasso didn't show for an hour, on account, he said, of slipping down to the Hilton to see Branch. He acted like that was all right, and while they were putting new parts on, I took a little walk around so I wouldn't blow my top and pretty soon that brought me to the refinery. On the other side of the fence a guy was standing, watching what was going on. I guess he was around fifty, tall, thin, and leathery-looking, the way they all seemed to be in this business, and he had on the same overalls, canvas cap, and open shirt the rest of them wore. He spoke, and I did, and he told his name, which was Rohrer, and there didn't seem to be much to do but tell mine, which I did. He said he figured I was the new super on Seven-Star, which was the first I knew we had a name, and I said I was. He kept looking at me, like he was trying to size me up, then said something that sounded like some kind of a feeler: "Always had a friendly place in my heart for Seven-Star. Great little company, not too well handled, if I may say so."

". . . How do you mean, Mr. Rohrer?"

"Well, they've made their deal, or I hear they have, with Luxor, and it's none of my business and year after year they pass me by. But between you and me and that gatepost over there, a little refinery can often switch things around, these days especially, in a way the big company can't. Or shall we say—won't?"

He winked and I asked him if he ran the refinery and he said he did: "All by myself most of the time. Hits people funny, on an oil plant, that you don't need a whole gang running around and eating lunch when the whistle blows at noon. They forget it all works on valves and gauges and shut-offs, and one man, if he knows what he's doing, can handle it just as good as twenty."

"*If* he knows what he's doing."

". . . I guess you're kind of new here."

"Well—just a little."

"As we all are—once."

He studied the gang for a while, then said: "Little trouble, I see, with your pump."

"Blew a cylinder head on me."

"Unusual, nowadays. . . . Used to be, a pump would blow out almost any time, but not now, the way they get corings whenever they want, and can tell what they've got. Mr. Dillon, just from what I know of the formation they're into down there, I'd say that mud needs conditioning. There's a lot of material over there, piled up over there in bags, but I haven't seen one pound of it dumped in all morning." Then, as I could feel my face get hot, on account of never having heard of weight material, he went on: "You're new here, as we've said, and you probably don't know it's up to the drilling foreman to watch what you're in, from the corings, and keep the mud at proper consistency, to control its viscosity and weight as required, and it *has* to be him that's responsible. And— speaking of matters of that kind, I'd say yesterday was a very funny time to get caught short of a mud sump, and still funnier time with nobody around to see *where* the stuff was running, for somebody accidentally on purpose to put in a call for an officer."

". . . What are you getting at, Mr. Rohrer?"

"I told you I felt friendly?"

"You sure did."

"Keep your eyes open, boy."

I went back to the pump, and they had it going again. The guy from the pump company checked two or three things, then said to me: "Mister, it's all the same to us, and fixing pumps is our business. Just the same, unless you want to have this trouble again and practically all the time, if I was you I'd keep an eye on the consistency of that mud."

I thanked him, watched how the roughnecks kind of looked at each other, and at Dasso, who stood there shaking his head. I let it jell on that basis, and then, kind of easy, without getting excited, I said to him: "Dasso, I think he means you."

"Means—*who* did you say?"

"Were you watching it?"

"Well—I wasn't here, Jack. I—"

"*Where* were you?"

"I told you. I was at the Hilton. Mr. Branch—"

"Nobody came to me for leave to go to the Hilton. Myself, I was putting down stakes. I can't build sumps, watch the condition of mud, and do eighteen other things you're supposed to do. Now if you want to stay on here, I got to know if you're where you're supposed to be, accepting your responsibility, or over to the Hilton cocktail bar, lolligagging all over the place on things I'm not even informed about. Now which is it going to be?"

"O.K., but if a goddam pump man can't—"

"He doesn't issue materials."

He stood blinking at me, and he wasn't kidded: he knew I didn't know. But when I'd stood up for my pump engineer, that put the men on my side, and for that round he had to go along. The trouble-shooters left, he pulled down two bags of Aquajel to dump in the tank. But we'd lost plenty of time.

"Hannah, it's just plain sabotage, and the guy is out to throw a monkey wrench into us every way there is, and as

often as he can get away with it. So far as I can see, and from
the little that Rohrer said, it's him alone and doesn't involve
the rest of them. I mean, it may have, as of yesterday. The
three drillers were on the Bakersfield jobs, and they were
friends of your husband's, or anyhow had worked for him.
The rest, the boiler man and the pump man, are local, and I
don't think they care, one way or the other. Whatever they
may think of me coming in, they take it like it comes. But
Dasso means trouble. And if you'll take a tip from me you'll
do one of three things. You'll fire me, and at least make some
kind of a play to get going again with your husband. With
me out of the way, Dasso can run it fine, and will, whether
Branch sobers up or not. Or, you'll fire Dasso and let me
muddle through, which I don't recommend, but I'll do my
best. Or, you'll fire us both and let a drilling company take
over, which considering everything, is what I think you should
do. But you're just piling up trouble for yourself if you let
things go on as they're going now."

"We're keeping him, and you're going on."

"But look what it's costing you."

"Nothing like what it'll cost to fire him."

"How do you figure that out?"

"There's the bank end of it, for one thing."

"You mean—on the loan?"

"If we have a little trouble now and then, over a sump or
a pump or something of the sort, that's nothing. They all
have trouble, and nobody thinks a thing of it. But when something human comes up, what they call a moral risk, God help
us! They'll call for immediate amortization, for more security,
maybe liens on the filling stations, I don't know what. Because
they know that once I make any major changes, everything
stops, and within twenty-four hours it's practically a new deal.
Whatever we do, we don't joggle it. So Dasso's a rat. He'll
pull stuff, and it'll set us crazy, and it'll cost. But at least the
hole is going down, we've got our crews, we're a going con-

cern. The other way, we're just an abandoned rig. And besides—"

"Yeah? What else?"

"I'd like to see you lick him."

"What is this, entertainment?"

I'd gone over to her house, and she was lying on the sofa in the living room, a red corduroy dressing gown folded around her and a magazine in her lap. She stretched now, like a cat, and beckoned me over to her. I said to hell with that, I had too much on my mind. She nodded, watched me a while, where I was walking around, and said: "I don't care what it costs. If it breaks me I don't care. I've been a piker long enough. You're going to lick him, and down to the last dime I'll back you up."

So we kept him, and I settled down to one damned thing after another that cost fifty dollars an hour to fix, shop charges extra. I learned the difference between a twist-off and a wobble-off, and maybe you don't think that's something. A twist-off is where they've got too much pressure on the bit, the table gives more twist than the pipe can stand, and she pops. A wobble-off is where they've got too little pressure on the bit, it gets to spinning faster than the pipe, and she pops. Either way it's a fishing job, and they lose an hour or more even with the special tools they've got, and by the time they've caught their fish and rearranged their drill pipe a lot of time is lost before they're in formation again. There's plenty of that grief on any well, but a lot depends on the drills they use, with some suited to one formation and others to another, and I could tell from the way the drillers were acting they didn't think much of Dasso's ideas on the subject. So that meant I had to have separate huddles with them, and they co-operated, but it all took time, especially as I hated to tip how little I

knew. And as soon as I'd licked him on that angle he crossed
me on the cement. On an oil well, you've got one continuous
visitor you don't hear so much about outside the business.
He's the inspector from the state department of oil and gas,
because you're regulated to the last inch, on account of the
way one loused-up job can ruin a lot of surrounding wells, as
happened in Mexico, where the richest field in the whole gulf
area was drowned in salt water so it'll never run more than
forty per cent of what might have been its capacity.

What they run you ragged about is cementing casing at
the right points, and in fact cement is to oil what the gin was
to cotton or wing camber to airplanes, something that took
them out from behind an eight ball that had had them completely stymied. Because in mountain fields, fresh water
flooded the wells long before they hit oil, and in coastal fields
salt water, and in coastal-tidal, which pretty well covers California, both. And not only could water flood any well that
was drilling, but a wide area as well, so it might easily involve
a whole lease, and bankrupt the operator. So in 1903, when
the industry had hardly begun, they figured a way to shut it
off. They pumped cement down through the casing, with
enough pressure back of it to force it up and around, between
the pipe and the formation. It worked. It shut off everything,
inside and outside, solid as a rock; inside the pipe they drilled
the cement out, and went on down to the oil with a nice
clean hole that wouldn't flow oil ruined by salt water when
they got to the surface with it. That was the beginning of oil
in a big way, and in a few years they made it law most
places that a man *had* to shut off his water with cement
whether he wanted to or not. Nowadays they pump through
a plug, as they call it, a block of concrete with valves in it
made of plastic, so when they're set with their cement they
just drill right through their plug and go on with their hole.

But when the corings began showing water sand, and Mr.
Beal, our state man, told me to set my cement, I'd never

heard of cement, and once more I had to get busy with the classified phone book and tell a cement outfit to be on deck in the morning. But when I saw Hannah that night she began to roar. "Cement? Why, that contract was let months ago!"

"You know who with, by any chance?"

"But of course! With Acme!"

"Then I'll ring them up, and tell them to stand by for a call. And call up this other outfit and say I'm sorry, but I don't know a cement contract from a left-handed monkey wrench, and they needn't come."

"Didn't Dasso tell you?"

"What do you think?"

"You mean he just sat there and let you talk?"

"He's your sitter, not mine."

When I finally did pop Dasso on the chin and tell him to get out of there it made no sense, as it was the one time he wasn't guilty of anything. We were getting deep by that time. Around four thousand, when gas began coming up through the mud, Beal said get connected up with the blowout preventer, so of course that meant nothing to me, but the driller swung his hook out for something that had been on the ground ever since I'd been there, and that looked like a cross between a bell buoy and a slide trombone. He and Dasso and the roughnecks swung it up in the air and over the casing, and for the better part of an hour they were bolting it in place. Then we got going again. Pretty soon we began getting oil, and that was a heartbreak, because Mr. Beal ordered continuous coring, so we'd have a record of all formation penetrated, else we'd have to set and cement more casing. The reason for that was the terms of our permit. From the first pool, our six other wells were taking all we were entitled to, and if we were to put another well down, it had to go further and find oil deeper down. Other wells in the field were tapping that second zone, but whether it extended under our property nobody could be sure, so it came under the head of new development. Everybody knew how it was, so nobody had much to say, and then the driller looked around and wanted to know where were the core heads. There weren't any. With that it seemed to me I'd had about all I could take. I didn't really swing on Dasso. My fist seemed to do it, and he hit the dirt and sat blinking at me. Then he took off his glasses and looked. Then I remembered you weren't supposed to hit a guy with glasses. Then I felt like a heel and helped him up and handed him his hat. Then I went over to the shack and wrote his time. Then I went back and rang up the service company that kept our stuff in shape, and they said Mr. Dasso had already phoned, and the truck was on its way over with the core heads. So of course that made me feel great. Instead of going over to the crew, who had heard me at the phone, I went over to the wire fence to get my face set again. Rohrer was there, and I knew he had seen it. "Well, kid, I think things'll be better now."

"That I wonder about."

"It was due, and overdue, and your gang'll respect you for it."

"They might, if it didn't so happen that when I rang the service shop it turned out Dasso had already done what I fired him for not doing, and I never knew any gang yet that bought it when somebody got the wrong end of the stick."

"Did he tell you what he'd done? Was he tongue-tied that he couldn't say it? Did he ever tell you what he was doing, or give you any report you didn't crowbar out of him? Don't you worry about that gang. They know if it wasn't this it had to be something else, and it didn't make much difference what, or if all the fine points were right or not. He had it coming. You'll get along better."

We got along so much better it was no comparison, and I began telling myself I'd learned more about oil than I'd realized. Stuff that we needed began coming on time, instead of three hours late like when Dasso had charge, the fishing was cut to half what it had been, and counting all cementing, setting of new casing, and everything else we had to do, we were making half again as good time. Hannah was dancing all over her living room whenever I saw her, and wanted to open champagne for me. I said let me do my work. At fifty five hundred feet we began to get gas, and I got so nervous I hardly left the place, but slept on the desk that was in the shack, and got up every hour or two, to keep track of what was going on. Pretty soon our corings came up with kind of a combined smell of coal tar, crackcase drainings, and low tide on a mud flat, a stink you could smell ten feet, that was prettier than anything Chanel ever put out. It meant oil, and this time we could keep it, with no need to go to a deeper level. Everything had that feeling in the air. The state man said take it easy, and we slowed to half speed. Scouts, supers, and engineers began dropping around from other wells, so at any time there'd be eight or a dozen of them standing around, waiting. The super from Luxor dropped over, and we picked out where the new gauging tanks would be put: right over from the head of our double row of six, the first of a new double row of six, as we hoped, with the foundations all in line. I got out my transit and set stakes for the concrete. I ordered a Christmas tree.

One night around eleven I went to the Golden Glow, a cocktail bar that caters to night shifts. Not many were in there at that hour, so I drank my coffee, dropped a nickel for a tune on the juke box, and rested. Then, in a booth, I noticed somebody, and when he turned his head I saw it was Dasso. It threw me out, because it still bothered me, the way I had clipped him. Jake served him something, and some time went

by, but still he sat there. After a while I went over. I said
hello and he said hello but kept looking out the window. I
said I was sorry I'd hit him, that I'd been under a strain. He
kept looking back and forth, first at me, then out the window,
and didn't seem to hear me. I lifted up a prayer I should be
kept from hitting him again, and went back to my table. I
paid and went out. I began to cuss and get hot under the collar
and took a walk down the hill. I came back.

Then it began creeping in on me there was something
funny about it. He hadn't sneered at me, or cracked mean, or
done anything. He just hadn't heard me. Then it came back to
me, the way he'd kept looking out the window, and the long
time he'd been there, talking with Jake, eating his sandwich,
doing all kinds of things he didn't generally do, because if
ever there was a wolf-it-down-and-get-out kind of guy, it was
he. Then something shot through me: He was waiting for
something, and that window faced right on our well. Next
thing I knew I was running. I'd shamble three or four steps
up the hill, then slow to a walk, then run again, and all the
time there was growing on me some hunch of something
about pop. I got in sight of our well, but already I was too late.
Dead ahead of me the string of lights began to shake. Then a
guy yelled. Then, far up on the rig, something began to move
down, on a slant. I saw it was the derrick man on the fourable
floor, sliding down the safety line. Then here it came. Brother,
if you ever saw six thousand feet of drill pipe go up in the air
and then come down and wrap itself around an acre of ground
like a plate of spaghetti, you won't forget it in a hurry. And
when on top of that, the friction of drill pipe against casing
sets what's coming out of the ground on fire, you'll hardly
know which scared you worst, the roar of that flame, the
thunder of stuff coming down all around you, the screams of
your crew, or the way their white hats looked like some kind
of horrible bugs, getting out of the way before the world came
to an end.

I slammed face first in the mud, and screamed and prayed like the rest, and then all of a sudden I didn't even do that, because something banged on my head, and that was the last I knew for a while.

* 22 *

I DIDN'T come to all at once, as it was part of the crown block that hit me, a pulley shackle I found a couple of days later, and I took the count from loss of blood as much as concussion. But the whole time I was under, the roar of the fire was in my ears and its glare in my eyes, and I think they'd have reached me in hell. After a while there was yelling, and I was being rolled, then carried on a stretcher. Next thing I knew, I was waked up by water in my face, but the yelling was still going on, and the roar and glare were still there. I began to look around, and saw I was in the Golden Glow, stretched out on the bar. The water I couldn't figure out. Then I saw they'd jammed a garden hose on the spigot over the sink, and run it out of the window to keep spraying the building, so it wouldn't catch fire from the heat. But it was just a jam-on connection, and there was a leak that spouted over me. I moved, and was clear. Then I heard the flap of canvas outside, and footsteps on the roof, where they were pulling a tarpaulin over one whole side of the building, so they could wet that and be safe. That cut off the glare, but nothing cut off the roar.

I was out for a while after that, and then a fellow with a

white coat was shining a light in my eyes and looking at my head, and I heard him cluck, like what he saw was bad. Then he shot something in my arm and went. I wanted to crawl outside and run, but I couldn't move. I don't remember anything of the ambulance backing up or the orderlies carrying me out or the trip to the hospital or going up to the operating room, where they put the stitches in. When I did come to it was all at once, in what I could see was a hospital room, with the roar fainter, like it was some distance away, but the glare still bright enough to read by. My head hurt, my face twitched, and my belly fluttered. When I turned my head I could see somebody at the window. It was Hannah. She came over and patted my face, but all the time she was looking outside, and in a minute she went back to the window. "Can you see it, Jack?"

"No, thank God."

"It's just horrible. And it frightens me to the inside of my bones. It—ruins me, I've no illusions about that. And yet—it fascinates me. . . . What happened?"

"I don't know."

"Something must have gone wrong."

"Ask Dasso."

". . . What's he got to do with it?"

"He was up there, waiting for it. In the Golden Glow, parked at the window, all but holding a stop watch."

It seemed to me I had to get over by the well and do something, I didn't know what, but terribly important. Pretty soon I jumped out of bed, and went staggering to the closet for my clothes. "Jack! You can't go out! You're in no condition to! And besides your clothes were sent out to be washed—they were filthy, from blood! There's nothing there but your suit."

Off in the hall I heard a buzzer, where she was calling a nurse, and in a minute one came. All I had on was a hospital shirt, but fat chance that stopped me. If coat, pants and shoes were what I had to wear, I might as well be getting them on.

Come hell or high water, I was due on the hill, and meant to get there.

The taxi man couldn't get within two blocks of it on account of the crowd, or at least he said it was the crowd. If you ask me he was plain scared, and I didn't blame him. What was coming out of that hill was the most frightening thing I'd ever seen in my life. It was shooting straight up in the air, a red plume in the night, just like one of those torches you see at the end of a pipe, burning gas off the wells in Texas, except instead of being three or four feet high, this was three or four hundred. It swung this way and that, sometimes licking down to the ground, when there'd be yells and screams, and all the time sending off thick clouds of smoke that were black one second, blood red the next. To one side, leaning at an angle, was what was left of the derrick, with girders curling up like bacon on the griddle, and dropping off with a clatter. On the other side, by what would have been Mendel's fence if it hadn't burned to a row of charred string pieces, was the pile of drill pipe, all twisted up like a mile-long snake, and part of it showing red hot. Later in the day the firemen dragged it off with a falls they rigged, and cut it up with a torch. Now, though, they were letting it lie, and concentrating on the oil that was plopping in gushes out of the well, where the pressure would force it to the top, but didn't quite carry it up in the air. It was running down the hill with flames all over it, where it was burning, and from that, and the heat, came the danger to people standing around, and other property, that it would catch fire. So the firemen on the three foam generators were smothering it with foam. The guys on the engines were drenching everything with water within two hundred yards: Mendel's stuff, the refinery, the Golden Glow, the grocery store next to it, the garage next to that, the filling station on the corner, and even the trees in the cemetery and derricks on beyond. Oher firemen had pushed up the road, within maybe fifty feet of the well, and were racing back and forth with cans full of dirt. I couldn't tell what the idea was, at first, but then I saw they were making a trough, kind of a ditch on our land, that they could divert the burning oil into, and run it into the big sump I had made, below the refinery. In a few minutes they had their bank of dirt ready, and then the oil flames began sliding toward the sump, which was billowing with foam before even the oil slid into it. The foam put the flames out.

I'd been crouched with about forty other people, two or three hundred yards away, down the hill. I heard somebody call. When I turned, she was there, at the wheel of her car, and then I remembered seeing some car following the taxi. She said the hospital doctor had given strict orders I was to come back, but I paid no attention. I still had this idea there was something I had to do, and looking back at it now, I can understand how Caruso, when he got caught in the San Francisco fire in 1906, came running out of his hotel with a signed picture of Theodore Roosevelt clutched to his chest. It maybe didn't look like much, but probably hit Enrico as the most important thing in the world, something he had to give his life for, if necessary. If from now on I acted like a bit of a fool, you might remember there's something about fire that affects you that way. All of a sudden it came to me what this was that I had to do. Sliding around on my belly, trying to work my way closer, I'd come to three of my roughnecks who were fried up pretty good by the look of their faces, but weren't paying any attention to themselves, on account of trying to do something for Funk, the driller that was on duty when she went up, who was under a blanket and weeping and bawling like some kid. And up close there, through the smoke I could see our shack, and every piece of paper we owned, our payroll cash, every contract, every permit, as well as our safe, was in it. It was on fire. The firemen would douse it with a hose, it would steam, the flames would go out, and then here they were again, just like somebody had lit them with a match. And it seemed to me I had to save it. I stood up in front of Funk and the three roughnecks. "O.K., men, let's get our shack."

"God, Mr. Dillon, do we *have* to do that?"

That was Funk. He sounded like some hysterical girl. "You want your money, Funk? You want to get paid?"

"Yeah, but can't them firemen—"

"What's the matter, you afraid? You want your money, that's where the money is, and I don't know how to pay it to you without first we go get it."

They looked at me, the shack, and each other, and how much they wanted of it was nothing at all. But when I led on they followed. We slid downhill, where it was cooler, and at least that made them feel a little better. Then, up the road beside the cemetery, we began moving toward the fire again, and they began to whimper. I kept leading on. Every few steps we'd hit the dirt, face first, and crawl.

Then at our feet, running along the side of the road, I saw a length of hose. Pointing toward the shack, not ten feet away from me, was the nozzle. And then I knew if I could only get up there with it, get the door open and knock a hole in the floor, I could shove that nozzle through somehow and wrap it around the joist that ran under the doorsill. Then we could use the hose as a hawser, to pull the shack out on the road. It didn't make sense, but nothing did, that night.

I yelled to Funk and the roughnecks to hold everything, grabbed the hose and began dragging it toward the shack. It was awful heavy that way, and the best I could do was two or three feet at a time, jerk, rest, then jerk again. But then once the fire licked close and I yelled from the pain of the heat, even while I was diving for the ground. It veered off, but after that it was too hot for anybody. I had to have something to shield me, and a few feet away, at the upper end of the Luxor property, I saw one of those signs that read "Keep Right" on one side and "Closed, Please Use Other Entrance" on the other. It was nothing but a board, maybe two feet wide and three feet high, but it had feet, so I could shove it ahead of me and hide behind it. I went and got it, put it between me and the fire, then under cover of it I pulled my hose two or three more feet, then pushed the board three or four feet, then pulled up my hose, and so on. Once, from up the hill, there was a yell, and I'd just squeezed myself behind it when here came the flame, licking all around me, and so hot I thought I'd go crazy. But water came too, where the firemen up the street had seen me and given me protection with their hose, even though they didn't know what in the name of God I was up to. At last I got near the shack, so it was between me and the fire, and had a little real protection. The door was locked, but I threw my weight on it and it broke. I reached my hand inside, and sure enough there was the hatchet I had used to sharpen stakes. I came down with it on the floor, and pretty soon I had one board loose, then another. I pulled up the nozzle, pulled it through and jammed it, so it was caught. I went racing back to Funk and the men. "O.K., boys, come on with it—heave!"

We heaved, and it was nothing but an eight-by-six shack any wind could have blown over, but it could have been the Woolworth Building for all we were able to move it. I began to scream, but Funk put his hand on my arm and I looked. A car was backing up. It stopped, and Funk bent the hose over the rear bumper and said something. It ran ahead two or three feet, then stopped as the hose tightened. Then the rear wheels spun and you could smell rubber. Then it got traction and the shack began to move. It came slow at first, but once it was over the ditch it came sliding almost as fast as a man could run, right down the middle of the road after the car, with me and Funk and the gang running with it and yelling, and people cheering from behind the ropes in the block below. Then the joist pulled out and what had been a little building with door and windows and a roof just collapsed into a pile of kindling. A woman got out of the car and opened the luggage carrier. The gang got the safe aboard, then the filing cases, transit, hatchet, and junk. Next thing I knew I was in the car, and then I saw Hannah was driving. "Well, Jack, are you satisfied?"

"Yeah, I guess so."

"Pretty silly, you know."

"Couldn't let the stuff burn though."

"What stuff? It would have been replaceable, except for the cash, and even that's in the safe—a guaranteed fireproof model, and it ought to be, as it cost enough. But *you're* not replaceable."

"Gee, that's tough."

"Will you go to the hospital now?"

"I won't go anywhere."

"Look at yourself in that mirror."

"What for?"

"You're burned. Badly."

"O.K."

But it was daylight and I caught sight of the car. It looked like smallpox had hit it, with the paint raised up in blisters all over, and the foundation red bleeding through in big ugly blotches. I began to get sick thinking what I must look like, and all the time she was unloading the stuff in a filling station my stomach kept fluttering and clutching. All around were star clusters, and the trademark "Seven-Star," which was the name of the gas she sold, the first I'd seen of it. But I wasn't paying any attention. My face and hands had started to feel hot, and all of a sudden I was begging her to get me to a hospital, quick, for fear I'd claw all the skin off before they could fix it.

❋

I stayed in the hospital that week and the next. In addition
to the bandage on my head, that they kept changing, there
were bandages on my hands and neck, and all over my face,
except for three slits over my eyes, nose, and mouth. In spite
of all they had smeared on, I itched like I'd been put down in
quicklime, and about every hour a new doctor was there,
saying the head wasn't so bad, in spite of a pretty deep cut,
but the burns, which I had inflicted on myself, were critical.
Between doctors were Chief Wolfson, of the fire department,
Mr. Bland, the city attorney, and Mr. Slemp, head of the
department of oil and gas. They asked me plenty, but they
all came back to the blowout preventer, and I thought I'd go
nuts tracing it back and forth, when I came on the job,
whether I'd inspected the thing before I had it attached, how
many wells it had been used on before, and so on. About the
second day Chief Wolfson let the cat out of the bag. They'd
got a hook on it after they dragged the pipe out of the way,
pulled it out, taken it over to fire station No. 1 and gone
into it, taking pictures, and making a record of every nut,
bolt, screw, and part. And the rubber gasket inside, that
forms part of the packing that takes care of pressure, was
rotten. I'd been expecting something like that, so what I said
was I hadn't known about it, but would rather put off talking
until the hypos had worn off, and my mind was clearer. But
Wolfson was no sooner out of the door than she jumped up,
where she'd been sitting there listening, and blew off. "So
that's what Dasso was waiting for!"

"Nice guy, Dasso."

"Then at last, Jack, we've got him."

"What for?"

"Putting on a faulty blowout preventer."

"I thought I did that."

"But if you didn't know about it—"

"If not, why not?"

"You mean you're just going to do *nothing*?"

"What would you do, for instance?"

"Why—*report* him!"

"Who to?"

"The city. Of course."

"O.K. But when he sues for that million-dollar slander, million-dollar defamation of character, and million-dollar personal injuries, caused by your super having the bad judgment to bust him in the kisser, don't say I didn't warn you."

"When he—"

"Unfortunately, it's what you can prove."

In addition to the visits, there were the newspapers, with pictures. I never saw so many columns given over to smoke and water and flames in my life, or so many pictures of a guy in charge of a job. They ran four or five they took in the hospital, when the reporters showed up for interviews, and then the A.P. must have picked it up, so the East got busy. Then there were pictures of me passing, kicking, tackling, and everything there was. But it really got good when they dug up Little Lord Fauntleroy, with the blond curls over my collar and the angel-of-sweetness look in my eye. In between that they had editorials that practically said I ought to be run out of town. And every night, as soon as the street noises died off, would come the roar, like they'd brought Niagara Falls in to spend the summer. And once it got dark, the glare never stopped. After a while it began to give me the hibby-jibbies. I mean, when a fire started they were supposed to get it out, weren't they? But nothing that was said, by the state man or the fire people or the city attorney, sounded like they had it out or nearly out. They kept getting tighter in the lips and rougher in the talk.

Around the end of the second week, on a Tuesday, I still had the bandage on my head, but it was gone from my face and hands, and though I couldn't shave and looked like something in the Monday line-up, at least I had on clothes she had brought me from the hotel, and was sitting up. Then sometime before lunch the phone rang and she took the call and from the quick way she said I'd been taken up on the roof, I knew it was bad. Then little by little as she talked I got it that it was Mr. White, of the bank, talking for other operators in the field, and that he wanted to bring them over to talk to me. When she said no, he waned her to bring me to a meeting in the Luxor offices at two o'clock, but she said the doctors wouldn't permit it. There was more talk, something about his seeing her that evening. She still said no, and after a while hung up. Then: "I don't know what it is, Jack, but he's got that or-else sound in his voice, and you mustn't under any circumstances talk to him until I can find out what it's about. He holds paper from them all. They're in a spot. The fire department has closed a lot of them down, wells and all, Luxor's main cracking plant hasn't run a barrel in two weeks, everything's at a standstill, and something has to be done—or so he says. The worst of it is the field. Every bit of that gas that's burning is saleable, eventually, to the gas company, if it stays underground, but when it blows off that way, it's a dead waste. To say nothing of the oil."

"What's to be done?"

". . . Could you take a ride?"

So she lent me the keys to her car and I went off for a ride, so as not to be there in case he came. I headed south, and there it was, still doing business at the same old stand, pouring flame and smoke right into the sky and spreading a pall over the city that made the sun look like some kind of a thin red dime. I passed the hill, and off to my left could see firemen and ropes, where they had it blocked off. When I got to the traffic circle I couldn't hear it, and when I leveled off toward Seal Beach I couldn't even see it, or the smoke. It was a beautiful sunshiny day and for a few minutes it was like being let out of jail to be able to leave it behind, feel like myself once more, and just roll, even if it was in a car that looked like it had smallpox from what the heat had done to it. But then, around Huntington Beach I began to think about it again, and I guess if you left a tiger in the front parlor, you'd run away if you could, but there'd be a limit to how far you could go, or how much you could drop him out of your mind. Pretty soon I turned around, and in almost no time I could see it, a red torch shining against the blue.

I parked at the ropes, got out, and went through. A fireman stopped me, but when I said who I was he let me pass. I walked to the bottom of the hill and circled around, and all the time I stared at it, and listened to it, and inhaled it, where the heavy greasy smoke would lick down. And once more, I could feel myself get a little wild, as I beat against the question: Why did this thing, this crazy, roaring thing out of a nightmare worse than any nightmare I ever had, have to happen to me? Then I began getting a little weak, and edged around, hoping to get to the Golden Glow and get something to eat. That brought me to the top of the hill, and below me was spread a deserted forest of silver derricks and towers and tanks, with not a wheel, not a walking beam, not a rotary table moving, with no fire showing under a still, and no human being in sight, except for kids staring through the ropes and a few firemen running a water pumper and a foam generator, just in case. Everywhere, on the refinery, on Mendel's property, on the upper end of Luxor, on the stores and cafés and filling stations, were sheets of asbestos, held on by wires, or nailed to roofs with little tabs to keep it from tearing. The firemen kept one hose going, so everything, once every ten minutes maybe, got a good wetting.

I tried the door of the Golden Glow and it opened and Jake

stared at me ten seconds before he knew me. He asked how I was, and I told him, and he said they'd had a time around there, yes, sir, quite a time. But he wasn't too friendly, and when he had my order, for beer and coffee and sandwiches, he went off. Over near the bar were three firemen having lunch and talking about baseball, which had just started again. My stuff came and I ate and felt a little better, then felt somebody looking at me. I looked up and it was Rohrer, in another booth. He finished his coffee and came over and looked, like he couldn't believe his eyes. "Is that you, Mr. Dillon?"

"Yeah. Little worse for wear, but it's me."

"They sure fixed you up."

"Fire out there. I went too near it."

"I saw you. They gave you a hand, as I recall."

"They should have waited. In the hospital I was better."

"That I can believe."

He caught me up on what had happened, but so far as real stuff went, there wasn't much to tell. Soon as they got first things under control, like the oil and near-by property, the firemen had gone to work on the fire itself from the well. "Getting apparatus near it was the tough part, but working behind shields and throwing up barricades of one kind or another, they got a concentration of water lines in there, four or five on each side, with fog nozzles on them. That took them a couple of days, but then they let go with them, driving right into the flame, and got wonderful results. Right away, sprayed fine like that, the water turned to fog, and then in a few minutes to steam, or pure vapor, all around that fire, cutting it off from oxygen, choking it. It was a beautiful thing to see, as the fog crept up and up, and above that they began hitting it with regular streams, and *they* began turning to fog, so for a minute or two, except away up in the air, there was hardly any flame, nothing but black smoke billowing all around, which was the real sign, because of course flame is nothing but incandescent smoke anyway, where the carbon particles are heated white hot, and when it goes black, it's cooling. A big crowd was out there, and you could hear the mutter go around, and yells as boys hollered to other boys to come look, so you had that feeling, it's been licked, they've got it. Then I heard one of the firemen begin to yell cusswords at the top of his lungs, and here it came, just a little puff of wind that didn't last five minutes. But it tore a hole in the fog, and the fire leaped back to the hole, with a roar like nothing you ever heard, just like when you light a gas log in the parlor, you know how it does? Just leaps around, purring like a cat purrs, but this was more like a herd of elephants purring. Then they had to start all over again, and I guess they tried it a dozen times. But they never got a real fog again, and I guess you can't blame them, when they kept it up for three days with no luck, just to quit. A dozen of them were in the hospital with burns and all kind of injuries by that time, and they're human too."

He told about how he'd had to drain his own tanks and whatever he had, but the battalion chief had been decent to him, letting him run his stuff into my sump, so he could burn the gasoline a little bit at a time, while they foamed everything but one corner. "But—we're standing still. Not doing a thing. Does that mean anything to you, Mr. Dillon?"

"No more than the rest of it. Fact of the matter, I've reached the point where one more thing closed down is one more thing, that's all."

"A wonderful time to buy a refinery."

"A—? For *who* to buy?"

"You, maybe."

"How would *I* buy?"

"You could get the money."

"Off those trees that got burned up?"

"Off something else that's burned up."

"I don't get you."

"That dame would let you have it, Mr. Dillon."

". . . Has she got it?"

"She could have."

"I doubt if she's got enough."

"What you got to go on? To doubt on?"

"She's hard hit too, you know."

"Kid, I said *it's a wonderful time to buy a refinery*. Have I got to say more? Listen, my owners are up against it. They're doing no business and they got to do business or they're sunk. I mean they owe money. I mean there's a certain community builder of this locality, that might answer to the name of White if somebody happened to look him up, that's accommodated them to the tune of quite a few thousand bucks, and he's been reasonable, I'll say that for him. Him and his bank. But the more reasonable they were, the worse it is now. I mean, the result of all that reasonableness has been that nothing has really been paid off since 1929. We got notes, they all got notes, that have just dangled, with a little chopped off them now and then. But at least we were working. But now that goddam thing is running wild, it's burning and nobody knows when it's going to stop. These gassers, they go on for months sometimes before they shoot 'em or tap 'em or they cave in or whatever makes 'em quit. I mean, they're really little volcanoes all by themselves, and nobody knows what's going to happen, or when. Boy, they're scared, and White's no help. He's scared too, and he's putting on the heat. They need dough, and any reasonable amount—! How do *you* know she can't afford it? I'm telling you, *it's a wonderful time to buy a refinery!*"

It was the first it had entered my mind, the idea that if you had a hole in the ground that was running wild and on fire at the same time, there might be a way to make something out of it. Later on, I polished that idea up, and as I've told you, hit the jackpot. But not that day, even to rise one inch to the bait. He shook his head and said: "Kid, I like you, I see things in you only an old-timer would have eyes for, and I've felt it, it's in the cards you should get this teapot I work for. With that property of yours—assuming those wells are not injured and I don't think they are—and this little pop-goes-the-weasel I've got, we could have the snuggest little business around here. And you don't even hear me, you don't even know what I mean."

After a while he looked up and I swear he turned green. He put his hand on my arm, then was standing beside me laying a buck on his check. He said: "You don't mind, kid, if I duck? If I beat it the back way? It's better they not find me here! I mean, it's better you and I not be seen talking together!"

With that he was gone. Outside, there were voices, and then, through the window, coming into the place I saw White, Branch, Dasso, and four or five of the guys who had been at the house that first Saturday afternoon, when I was a gentleman and a scholar and a good judge of liquor, besides being an all-American back and a bass singer.

✳ 23 ✳

THEY jammed a couple of tables together, out in the middle, and I leaned back where I wouldn't be seen, but couldn't help hear, though God knows I didn't want to be there, and would have ducked out with Rohrer, if I could. They ordered sandwiches, and talked along, and it turned out Branch was working for Luxor now, and had cut out the booze, and had Dasso under him. They all made quite a lot over him, but anybody could tell this mob was really being steered by White. Then pretty soon one of them, a guy named Perrin that sang bass in the choir, but had a property next to Mendel's with four or five wells on it, opened up, and who he was talking about was Mr. Jack Dillon, and what he had to say about the gent was slightly hot. He talked like he was just hashing it over once more, what had already been said somewhere else, maybe in the Luxor offices, if that was where they met before they came here, and was toning it down a bit so as not to string it out too long. I'd hate to hear him when he was really putting in the fine points. He kept wanting to know why I wasn't indicted and sent to Folsom prison, because, he said, "if ever a son of a bitch was guilty as hell that guy is, just as much as any arsonist they've got in there now, and in some ways as much as any murderer."

For some reason, White, the one he was talking to, put it up to Branch: "Have you explained to him, Jim, how that is?"

"I've tried to, Mr. White."

"Perrin, it can't be done."

"Why not?"

"Matter of law."

"Isn't ruining our oil field against the law?"

"The law says 'willful negligence,' 'willful destruction of property,' 'willful failure to use caution and care'—and that stops us. If he'd been on speaking terms with Dasso, if he'd given him a chance to have that blowout preventer opened up and put in order, if he'd once rung Jim Branch about it, then we'd have him, because if he was informed, and failed to act, he'd be nailed for the whole trip. As it is, no court would sustain an indictment. What's more, even if we could get an indictment, sustain it, and convict in court, I'd be against it."

"But my God, Mr. White—"

"What good would it do you?"

"Isn't that some good, to put him behind bars?"

"And your fire going on all the time?"

On that, there was a long time when nobody spoke, and I could hear lunch being served, and some of them, at least, eating. Then White went on: "The law governing oil development is lax, it certainly is. If you ask me, nobody ought to be allowed to touch a spoonful of mud around a well without a license, and I'd make it as hard for a man to get a super's ticket as a license to skipper a ship—and for the same reason: lives and property are at stake, and he's responsible. But they didn't ask me, and we've never gone after that much law for fear we'd get ten times that much, and the fact is, no license is required. That puts it on the criminal side, and unfortunately being a goddam fool is not a crime, not when this supreme court we've got gets through with it. And furthermore, once you indict him, maybe he skips. And if he's not here to do something about her, she'll still be aburning come New Year's Day. That's what we got to remember. It may be your pool but it's his fire, and he's the one that's got to put it out."

"Yeah, but *when?*"

"If I can get to him, I'll try to find out."

Two or three more guys came in, that I'd never seen before, and Jake took their order. Then he came over with my check. All of a sudden a chair scraped, and Perrin was standing there looking at me. "Oh hello, Dillon, so it's you. Well you been sitting here. What you got to say?"

"Who wants to know?"

"Come on, you—"

I got up and he squared off, but Dasso jumped up and grabbed him and I could see Dasso hadn't forgotten the punch I'd given him there by the well. White kept looking at me with a little smile. Then, after Perrin sat down, he said: "Well, Dillon, as they say, you asked for it. If I'd known you were there I suppose I'd have laid off a little, just as a matter of

manners—but I didn't know it, and said what I really thought
—and I suppose you heard it. Yes?"

"Sure."

"Well—what about it?"

"The fire you mean, or what you think of me?"

"Why—the fire."

"I thought that's what you meant."

"Listen, Dillon, if it's a question of what I—"

I stepped over, and he stopped, but I didn't take any satisfaction in it, even if I had shut him up. ". . . O.K., the fire.
My fire, I think you said. What about it?"

"What are you doing about putting it out?"

"Well—am I? If it's my fire, what the hell have you got to
do with what I'm doing? Maybe I like a fire. Maybe it'll come
in handy to light my cigarette with—of course I don't smoke,
but for a lighter like that I could learn. Maybe I think it's
pretty."

"Listen, Dillon, cut the comedy and get down to bedrock.
That fire's on your property, that's true—or Mrs. Branch's
property, but we understand you're rather high in her counsels
now, as they say. Just the same, it's a community affair, and
a damned serious one, so don't think it's just a private show
of your own, to crack jokes about."

"O.K., let the community put it out."

"Hasn't the community responsibility, with regard to the fire
department and all, been explained to you?"

"Why don't they put the fire out?"

"They've tried. They've tried everything they have the legal
right to try. They've tried foam, and they've tried fog. They've
done what they can. The rest is up to you."

"You mean, where fifty firemen flopped, I can go out there
and tell it to stop and it'll stop? Say, I'm good, ain't I?"

"Dillon, you've got to shoot that hole!"

"Why don't *you* shoot it?"

"I've told you, stop trifling! You—"

"Wait a minute, *wait a minute,* WAIT A MINUTE!"

It was one of the guys that had just come in, and he got up and stared at White, who called him Mr. Mace and asked him what was on his mind. "Listen, Mr. White, I've been sitting here, paying attention to what's been said, and I'd like to ask that question too: Why *don't* you shoot it?"

"What are you trying to insinuate, Mr. Mace?"

"I'm not insinuating, I just want to know."

". . . Mr. Mace, my bank is not in the oil business, or in the business of putting out fires. We're in the business of discounting paper on proper security, and whether you believe it or not, our only interest in this is getting our security, which is the property that has been pledged for these various loans, back on its feet again, so it's good instead of bad!"

"Yeah, but just the same, the longer this goes on, the more operators get foreclosed out and the more property the bank acquires. And by New Year's Day—"

"I resent that!"

White was like some lion as he got up and walked around the table. And sore as I was, and sick as I was, I believed him. I didn't believe the bank wanted a bunch of properties that had been ruined, or was up to any tricks, but all of a sudden four or five of them, the small operators, were on Mace's side, pretty excited. Pretty soon Mace turned to me. "Did you mean that, Dillon? That you'd let somebody else shoot it?"

"You want me to cross my heart?"

"You understand what this is? If that well is shot, that could wreck it. That could be the end of it, and that's why the fire department can go just so far and no farther. You know about that?"

"What good's the well doing me now?"

"And you'll let *us* shoot it?"

"Brother, I'll kiss you for it!"

She was pretty sulky about it, specially at the idea of how much she owed, what the well had cost her, and all the rest of it, as it lined up from the point of view of the future. But she didn't argue about it, or act like there was anything else to do, until I happened to remember Rohrer, and his line of chatter about it being a wonderful time to buy a refinery. I told her about it as something funny, but she began staring at me, where I was back in my hospital bed again, and hardly said anything when the nurse came in with my dinner. She closed the window, to shut out the roar, and put the screen up, to cut off the glare, then went back to the chair that had been put facing the bed, and watched me eat. Then she poured my coffee and when I was done, took the tray out in the hall. Then she came back and sat there some more and stared at me some more. Somewhere around seven she said: "We are in the pig's eye going to let them shoot it."

"*What?*"

"Something funny goes on here."

"Like what, for instance?"

"White, and what Mace was talking about."

"There's a well blowing off, if that's funny."

"And money's being made out of it."

"Listen, White's a banker."

"He's a banker, and he's not in the oil business, and he likes to flirt with me in a quiet way, and he's a swell guy, and I like him. Just the same, without his wanting it that way, or trying to work things around that way, money's about to be made out of that gasser of ours. Big money. Right on the dot, as soon as the notes say he's got to, he's foreclosing, and that means if that well keeps burning long enough, he'll own the whole hill, and—oh no, Mr. Dillon, we're not letting them shoot *that* well. Not till we're cut in. Not till—"

"I'm sorry, I've given my word."

"And who are you?"

"I'm sorry, just an employee. A former employee as of now.

You want to block them off, you get somebody else to do it.
So far as I'm concerned—"

"Jack."

". . . What?"

"Quit kidding me."

"You think I love you too much to walk out?"

"No. You don't love me at all, though maybe I can make
you if we ever get out of the woods with this. But that damned
machinist's soul won't walk out, no matter what I do about
it. Jack, listen. If they shoot it we're sunk. We've got no well,
all we've got is the six old ones, and what we owe will swallow
up what they pump for the next hundred years. Except it'll
more than swallow them up, and that means we're just like
the rest, we're foreclosed. Can't you see how it works? If the
well goes on, White gets those other places all around, and
probably the refinery. If it's shot, he gets us, really the best
property of all, because while I've only got six good wells,
I've got a whole acre of land, and can get permits for more
wells, which are the main thing. But—if White wants us, he's
got to make a deal. Rohrer was right, to that extent. It's a
wonderful time to buy a refinery—or steal one.

"Think White'll buy you one?"

"He might, when I get through with him."

"Doing what, for instance?"

"You'll see."

If my face hadn't been red from the fire, and what White
had to say to me, it would have been the color of steamed
lobster after listening to that judge. He gave her the temporary
injunction that she asked, of twenty-four hours, sight unseen.
Then next day he heard the case, with Mace on deck as de-
fendant, and ten other operators that were going to chip in
and pay the cost of what they were going to do, and about

a hundred newspaper reporters, photographers, townspeople, and God knows who-all. I hated it with everything there was in me. I hated it I had promised Mace, and had to renege, I hated it the fire was still going on, I hated it that we had caused a community catastrophe, and were trying to use it for our own gain. But I couldn't turn against her, and I had to go on the stand and say that while I had given Mace a tentative promise, I'd gone into the matter further and come to the conclusion that our interest was seriously involved if we destroyed the well; that experience had shown that as soon as the pressure eased, with the escape of gas, the fire could easily be controlled; that a little time was the main factor, and that we were entitled to it; that all danger to surrounding property had been abated by the fire department; that no emergency any longer existed. I stepped down, and there were arguments by lawyers, especially by this young guy Horlacher that she had called up that night, and had a huddle with at her house, without me being present at all. After a while the judge took off his glasses, polished them with his handkerchief, then began swinging them back and forth by one earpiece, while he thought. Every so often he'd look outside, in the direction of the hill, where you could see the thing, burning brighter than ever. Then he began to talk. He talked mainly at me. He said it was common knowledge I had accepted a job, a job of grave responsibilities, which I had no capacity to hold, either in the matter of training, or by temperamental fitness. He said it had been alleged repeatedly in the newspapers, and not denied so far as he knew, that the catastrophe had been brought on by my negligence, a negligence all the more egregious in that science had relegated such things to the past, or had so relegated it if the most elementary appliances were properly utilized, which they were not. He said the fire involved the whole town, and especially every participant in the Signal Hill field. He said for me then to resist, on the basis of specious, trifling, and as he suspected, insincere arguments, the relief which public-spirited citizens were willing to provide, at their own expense, was an exhibition of contumacity unparalleled in his knowledge. He said my real motives, whatever they might be, were a subject on which he was not informed, but he could only wish it lay within the power of the court to punish me, and severely. He said in view of all these considerations, and the emergency, he was denying the application with the harshest rebuke he knew how to administer—costs to the plaintiff.

In the corridor, Mr. Slemp, the state oil and gas man, grabbed me by both lapels and all but shook me: "What are you trying to get away with, Dillon? Do you know what this is I've got in my hand? It's an order, requiring you to abate that nuisance, that threat to this whole oil field, by shooting that well or whatever means there are available to you! By doing, at your own expense, exactly what they're now getting ready to do, free—at least to you. That's it, I sat there, listening to that judge, letting him sock it to you in words, and not doing what I had a perfectly good legal right to, sock it to you in dollars, grief, and sweat. You hear me, Dillon?"

"I hear you."

"You're in luck and you don't know it."

"O.K., you said it."

"Don't expect me to say it twice."

He turned and went off. She had been trying to get a word in edgewise, and tell him it was her, not me, that had cooked the thing up. That didn't take care of me feeling more and more like one of those untouchables they've got in India, or maybe a leper with a couple of hands and a foot missing. I must have looked glum, because she said: "I'm sorry, Jack."

"Thanks."

"Well, you don't have to snap at me."

"I don't have to be here, so far as that goes. I'd just like to say, though, that so far as I'm concerned at this time in this company and at this particular place, a nice chummy boxcar, with a floor board busted loose to let the fresh air in, a hot journal under one end and a flat wheel under the other, would come under the head of something to throw nip-ups about."

"Now you're being just plain nasty."

"But not like our well is nasty, sweetie pie."

So that was how come we all gathered the next morning to see the grand exhibition of fireworks that was put on by Mace & Co., not incorporated. They had wired two guys in Texas that make a business of putting out oil-well fires, but found they were tied up and went ahead on their own. Before we even got there, from court that afternoon, they were putting in concrete anchors for their poles, one in the road beyond the cemetery, the other in a vacant lot between the well and the Golden Glow. In the wet concrete they sat big steel eyes, and it was hardly set before they were bolting their masts to the eyes, big hundred-foot steel poles, that they rented from a company that made stuff for broadcasting towers. They worked all night, and by daybreak they had their guy cables rigged, and were pretty near ready with their main cable, a half-inch line between masts that was to carry their traveling blocks, so when they had everything ready they could lower their charge on a falls, explode it and put an end to the show. The masts weren't in line with the well, as there was a danger that if the main cable tightened right over it, it would melt in the heat and come apart. They were set so it would run maybe twenty feet to one side, but the idea was that a light guide cable, worked by two crews maybe two hundred feet apart so it didn't run over the well either, could pull the charge over in position. So that's how it was done. When the concrete was set, the poles were raised and guyed. The main cable was pulled up, and the traveling block, with the falls under it, attached. The charge, one hundred and fifty pounds of blasting powder, was in a big can that rode on a steel seat, with the detonator wire rigged in through the top. By ten o'clock everything was ready. Mace gave all signals with a police whistle, and when he sounded four sharp ones the can began going up in the air. Then he sounded three, and it began to move on the main cable, swinging and spinning like something going aboard ship. When it got to the middle, he whistled once and it stopped. Then the gangs on the guide cable began to tighten up, and it began swinging toward the hole. But to my eye it was low. By now, with derrick gone and rotary platform gone and everything wooden gone, there was just this casing sticking up out of the concrete cellar floor, that was flush with the ground. There were four or five feet of it, and why, instead of bringing his can up level with the top of it, or above it, Mace kept bumping it along hardly clear of the ground, I couldn't quite see, though Rohrer was to explain it to me later. But here it came and here it came, and hit the pipe like a croquet ball hits the stake, and hit it again and bounced off again, and still no signal from Mace, and still it didn't rise higher. Then came a flash and a shock that sent poles, cable, blocks, and everything crashing to the ground. She and I were standing by her car, near the Luxor place, at least three hundred yards away, and even though we dived we weren't any too soon, as stuff began falling all around us. But when we took our fingers out of our ears the fire was roaring just the same, and when we looked it was brighter than ever. Up near it men were running. Two of our gauging tanks were tilted over at a crazy angle, one of the masts was lying across the hind end of the Golden Glow, asbestos had torn loose, and was scattered around everywhere.

She kept straining to see. "But look, Jack, it's still burning!"

Uptown, newsboys were yelling my name. When we bought a paper it said the grand jury was going to investigate the blast, and see if criminal charges could be brought against me. What I had to do with it they didn't explain, but when we pulled up in front of the hospital, three guys that seemed to be waiting jumped out at me. She gunned the car and shook them off, then started for her house without going back to the hospital. When we got inside she sat me down in the living room, and made me a drink and had the housekeeper, Irene, get something to eat. Irene treated me as though I wasn't there. Hannah paid no attention, but rang the hospital, and said I was in a somewhat rung-up state on account of something that had happened, and she was keeping me with her till next day. I had another drink, then began to feel sleepy, and must have corked off, because when I woke up it was late afternoon and the phone was ringing. She answered, and somebody seemed to be coming. She was pretty glum.

When the bell rang, a little after seven, it was Rohrer. He was in one of those hard-rock suits they all seemed to have, and was shaved and shined and had a haircut, but his face was long, and he sipped on the drink she poured for him without saying anything. Then after a while he mentioned how he'd known her father, and talked along on quite a lot of stuff that didn't mean anything. Then he got started on White, and how bitter the little independents were against him. It seemed the foreclosures were starting. "They feel it's not right. They feel it's an act of God that they had nothing to do with, and there ought to be a moratorium. You may be surprised to know I'm on his side. The refinery's in hock to him, we've got our foreclosure notice too, we're hit just as bad as anybody. Still and all, White's up against more than they realize. It's not a question of being a good guy and giving other good guys a break. He's got government examiners and the federal grand jury and all kind of things to think about. I mean, if the paper and law say foreclose, and he don't foreclose, then he's liable, and if the stockholders should lose, or if the bank shook, then all the independents from here to Texas and back couldn't save him. He's got to take those properties, whether he wants to or not. And yet in spite of that and of how they feel about him, I believe what he says when he tells them he's not in the oil business, he's in the banking business, that he'd rather have good paper than bad land, and will do his best to save them—if he can."

He asked what about her foreclosure notice, and she said it wasn't due for ninety days, as all payments had been kept up to the time of the fire, and no more were due right away. He said he wished he was fixed like that, that his foreclosure was set for next week. Now at last he took a paper from his pocket, some thin typewritten sheets with a blue cover that looked legal. "Mrs. Branch, as I often told your father and I've told Mr. Dillon here, I've thought for a long time if we could only marry your wells to our refinery, well, we could go places. There's a lot of angles to it I don't go into here, but not to get too mysterious about it, we have one son of a gun of a time getting oil to run on, and from the beginning we've just done a trucking business and we're running stuff that moves by the dark of the moon, both in and out. And you're under contract, for the next couple of months anyhow, to a company that don't care if you go well or not, that's got all the oil it can handle, that leans over backwards to observe all this red tape they've sewed us in, that won't take but a limited amount of what your wells can pump, and that's got no more in the way of a future for you than a snowball has in you know where. Well, I'm a stubborn fellow. I hate to give up. So this is what I've done. I got an option out of them, my owners I mean, that says you can buy that place for ten thousand dollars. The refinery, that is, with lease on the land and everything that's on it, and they'd be glad to get it. Cost me fifty dollars of my own money, twenty-five dollars for the option, twenty-five to a lawyer for drawing it up. They're hooked up all wrong for the oil business, but they're straight people and you needn't be afraid they'll play you any tricks."

"Who are they, Mr. Rohrer?"

"Just fellows Mr. Dillon has seen a dozen times around,

that chipped in for Mace and his dynamite job, and never even bothered to tell him their name. Little fellows in the oil business, that have to be crooked in order to be straight. I mean, maybe their oil is hot but their word is good."

We sat talking about it, pretty gloomy. He made no bones about it, it was a pretty poor deal, an option to buy for ten thousand dollars, something that would be foreclosed in a week, and so useless, from what was roaring next door, that nobody would lend a dime on it, or anything. "But, Mrs. Branch, I only say, where there's a thousand-to-one chance, let's take it. You got the ten thousand dollars, or can get it on this residence property here, or somehow, and I've got the thirty-day option. We admit it's a poor outlook. Mace has got going again, and got authority from the state man, and money enough, to tunnel into the well, under the cemetery, and tap that casing. That'll be plenty of time for most of them, as the foreclosures aren't all due as soon as ours, but it'll take ten days to two weeks, and it won't do us any good. However— we don't know. Maybe it rains hard and the fire stops. Maybe the pressure eases, and the well stops. Maybe—it's a thousand to one but at least it's a chance."

"Can they do that? Go under the cemetery?"

"Probably."

"My family are buried there, it so happens."

"If it was a question of blocking them off, like you tried to do once, maybe those graves would do it, though it's my impression that whole cemetery question was settled long ago, as there's hardly a company, including yours, that hasn't whip-stocked under there for whatever they could pump out. But as it's a question of hurrying them up, or would be if it was possible to hurry them, why I'd say your family's no great help."

She went out, came back with her handbag, and laid down some money. I could see it was ten-dollar bills, and she counted out ten. He handed five back. "I don't ask anything for myself in this, Mrs. Branch—though of course, if we get a deal, I wouldn't be offended at an offer to take over the whole production end, from wells to gas, oil, and asphalt. But I'm not interested in corings from the option. The fifty dollars I paid out, O.K. on that. This other fifty dollars I can't accept."

She picked up the tens and he began reading her some kind of assignment, in her favor, he'd had typed on the bottom of the option. Then he signed it and handed it over to her. "It's yours now any time you want to exercise it."

"Just a matter of ten thousand bucks."

"You never can tell."

We sat there, all pretty gloomy, and she put out another drink and we drank it. After a long time he turned to me and said: "You know why Mace has got to go in the side of that hill with a tunnel and timbers and big gang of men—or thinks he has?"

"I bite. Why?"

"He wrecked that casing, with his shot—or thinks he did."

"Well—wasn't that the idea?"

"You think so?"

I said what else would it be, and he looked at her, and she didn't know any different, and he kind of grinned into his drink, then said: "I talked to quite a few people. I talked to a dozen people today—two dozen. All in the oil business, and they all thought, same as you, that the purpose and object of the shot was to wreck that casing, to stop up the hole and shut off the fire and leave them all sitting pretty—to say nothing of ruining a well that cost Mrs. Branch two hundred thousand dollars."

He began to giggle into his glass, and she freshened it. Then: "Isn't that the most amusing thing you ever heard in your life? Don't that show how little people know about their own business? Imagine that! There's casing there, five lines of it, one inside the other, from the eleven-inch pipe you started with down to the five-inch line that's carrying the gas. It runs up through a cellar floor made of solid concrete, and yet with a charge of dynamite Mace thought he could wreck the top of the well, so dirt and rock and stuff would cave in on it and stop it up—*if* that's what he thought, though I'm beginning to wonder if he really thought *anything*. I mean, there's such a thing as bringing up stuff to go *boom,* closing your eyes, and trusting to luck. You ask me, Mace heard all his life about shooting a burning well, got it in his mind a certain way, and had no idea why you really do shoot it, and neither did any of his friends. And mark what I say: He shot it. He's going around saying the heat set it off prematurely, and as he was using a push-button switch, that just snapped off after he pressed it, it didn't know any stories to tell on him. But listen: I was with him, and I know. I was right in the next room there in our little refinery office, where he had his wires, not looking outside, but looking at *him,* because I was wondering why he didn't give them one on his whistle, to hike his powder up higher—"

"I remember—it was dragging the sump."

"And I *saw* him press that switch!"

"But *how* should he have done it?"

It was she that said it, but I was opening my mouth to, because by then I was plenty crossed up. He said: "He should have exploded it *over* the well. Over the open end of the casing, where the gas is pouring out. That would have made a tremendous concussion, enough to drive the gas down in the pipe—we don't know how far, because nobody was ever down there to measure. But far enough. A real jolt, to interrupt the flow for one, two, or maybe three seconds. Then it roars out again, but the fire is out. It's just like your gas stove. You cut it off one fifth of a second, the shortest time it takes you

to close the valve and turn it on again, and it's out, isn't it?
It's the same way with a burning well. Stop it that long and
it's still roaring, so far as the gas goes. But the fire's out. You
can get in there, and look at it, and work on it. You can stand
next to your pipe. There's no more heat."

"Yeah, and then what?"

"You shut off that gas. With a gate."

"A—? Something we swing on?"

"A valve. You close it."

"You got one with you?"

"What you need, you get it made. Any good oil-tool works
can do it. And it's no great job to put on. If the flange is still
there, the attachment with bolt holes around the edge that
goes on all casing, to hold the Christmas tree when the flow
starts, you just slip the edge of your gate over it and drop
one bolt through. Then you turn it till all holes are in position
and the gate is square on the pipe. Of course the gas whistles
and hisses and scares you to death, but it'll go through without
any trouble. Then when all your bolts are tight you just close
your valve and you've got it. It's got handle bars on it, so a
couple of men can turn it—or if you're getting fancy with it,
you have it made hydraulic. Me, I'd take handle bars. In
emergency, make it simple. . . . And if the flange is gone,
you shove in an inside pack. It's the simplest thing in the
world. You take a length of pipe small enough to go inside the
inner casing with some room to spare, and around it put three
wide bands of rubber. Around it, above the rubber bands,
threaded on it to turn, and sized to slip easy inside the casing,
you fit a collar. On the end of the smaller pipe you fit your
gate, handlebars and all. You slip the whole thing down into
the casing, with everything open, so the gas flows right on.
Then you screw down the collar till it bulges out the rubber
and makes a tight seal against the casing. Then you screw
down your gate, and you've got it. To put the thing on, once
it's made, ought not to take more than two hours."

"Why doesn't Mace do that?"

"Maybe he don't know about it. But if you ask me, he's gun shy. He made a mess of one shot, and now he's dogging it. He's doing what they do when the casing *is* wrecked—when it's all gone, from sand and pebbles cutting it out, ten or twenty feet down in the ground, with the pressure throwing dirt up and cratering it all around. Then there's nothing to do but go down and get it. They work in by tunnel, peel off outer casing, throw a split sleeve around the inner pipe, cut through that, put a plug in, then come out through the tunnel with a new line of pipe and with that save the well. That is, if it all goes well. If not, in the end they have to get the East-man survey outfit in, let them line up a new well, whip-stock down with it, intersect the burning well at maybe five thousand feet, pump it full of mud, close it and lose it. Or drive into the oil sand just beside the burning well and take the pressure off. And all that is six-figure stuff—and it's on her. Under the law, she's booked with it. Nice."

"You mean, it would be just a two-hour job if that god-dam fool hadn't wrecked our casing?"

"Jack . . . *did* he wreck it?"

"Well—ask me another."

His mouth twisted over on one side, he hitched his chair closer, and said: "*He* thinks he did. So all right. He thinks he wrecked it, and that wrecking it didn't work. And as black smoke is bellying down, and nobody can see, why maybe he's right. Maybe he did wreck it. He sure wrecked everything else, so it's reasonable he'd be discouraged. But me, I've been looking at it. From my refinery office I've been looking at it, whenever the smoke clears a little, which it does every couple of minutes, when a puff of wind hits it. *That casing's just like it was! It's sticking straight up!*"

"After *that* blast?"

"You know anything about explosions?"

"Not much."

"They're tricky. They're governed by a little principle called the cone of burst, which is the direction the discharge of energy takes, so something right in the path of it is blown to shreds, and something three feet away is hardly jarred. If you ask me, it was just this crazy idea he had, of wrecking the pipe, that saved it. That can of powder was yawing around, there on its falls, like a boat coming about in the wind, and if it was four or five feet from the pipe at the time he touched his button, the cone of burst would run slightly over the end of it. Of course, *you* might have been shaken up plenty, if *you* had been standing there, but then you're not made of high-grade steel."

"Rohrer, what are you getting at?"

"Jack, why don't *we* shoot it?"

"You and me?"

"And her."

"O.K."

Her eyes had that shark look as she said it, and his face lit up as he raised his glass to her and had another sip of his drink. "That's it. All three of us, you, Jack, Mrs. Branch, and myself. The masts are still out there, lying around—they haven't got around to gathering them up yet. The cable's there, the firemen're there, and Mace is there. I'd just love to steal his men off him, so he has to stand around and watch us. Me, I'll line it all up. I mean, I'll get an outfit started on that inside pack and what has to be done. Her I want right by me, to run errands and phone and O.K. bills and handle finance. You. . . ."

"Yeah, me?"

". . . Jack, I'm not sure I'd have rigged those masts the way Mace rigged them. I think I'd have guyed one big mast to a step, and from that run a swinging boom—but those are the masts we've got, and we'll have to make them do. But the way I want to do it, I don't have any sap blowing whistles. I'll be in the refinery office, and I'll throw the switch. But the can of dynamite itself, I want to swing on that cable. Swing, like rockaby baby. And somebody's got to swing it."

"Meaning me?"

"Meaning you."

He looked at me, pretty sharp, and went on: "You'll have to be close. That can has to be swung a few times, short, controlled swings, so I can check how high it's going to go, and everything else. Whoever swings it has to do it with a wire. We can't use rope—it would burn in twenty seconds, once it got close to that heat. We use wire, plain baling wire. I'll need three, four, five, six, or a dozen trial swings, and then she's got to rock—one, two, and a heave. When she's right over the hole, at the one moment when anything swinging stops stock still, I'll touch my button. By that time you should be flat on your face, and with luck—and the cone of burst as I think it'll develop—you'll be all right. But get this, Jack: maybe. . . ."

"Maybe I don't have any luck—is that it?"

"Yeah. That's it."

It was all ready, the inside pack made, the masts rigged, and the dynamite wired up, around sundown of the third day after that. I was there, with Rohrer inside the refinery office, looking like Superman dressed up for goalie on the interplanetary hockey team, in asbestos from helmet to shoes. The firemen had seen to that, and fact of the matter, it seemed to me they used as much juice on me as they did on the fire, which was pretty hard to get sore about. I had a helmet, mask, flyer's suit, and gloves, everything either made of asbestos or quilted with it or stuffed with it, so if something went wrong at least I wouldn't get fried like a bug in a light. And it seemed idiotic, the little I had to do, in relation to what it might cost me to do it. My job, as Rohrer said, was get out there, close to the fire, and give signals, whether the can was to go up, down, or sidewise, and how much. Then, when it was hanging right, I was to swing it, a little bit, a little bit, then more, then wham. It would all take, as well as I could figure out, five minutes, no more, and hardly any work.

Rohrer had arranged the cable stuff a little different from the way Mace did it. Instead of having the main cable between masts, strung tight, and a hoisting job done on the can with the falls and traveling block, he had the can set and all adjusted so when the main cable tightened, everything would be in place with a minimum of swinging. It had been in place, as a matter of fact, for two days, pending arrival of the pack, which was what we were waiting for. Around five o'clock here it came, in the yellow truck of Fuller & Co., who made it. I reached for my mask, but Rohrer stopped me. Then he went in the next room and put in a phone call. Then he came back, and sat watching down the road. In about five minutes a siren sounded, and an ambulance came through. It parked by the Golden Glow. "All right, Jack."

I went out, stepped over what was left of the fence, and went on our property. I knew it must be hot but through my suit, and the asbestos soles on my shoes, I didn't feel it. I heard something and looked around. Two blocks away, back of the ropes, was a crowd. They were giving me a cheer. I grabbed hands and shook them. I found my baling wire, pulled it tight, and waited. In a minute I heard Rohrer yell and the main cable began tightening. The pulley on the falls began nodding and jerking, wanting to roll to the sag in the middle, but the firemen on the guide cable held it. Then little by little the firemen let the falls pulley have its way and the dynamite left the ground. As it eased toward the middle it began spinning around. I tightened on my wire, which was fastened through a hole in the bottom rim of the can, to steady it. When it was near center it stopped. I sighted and wig-wagged, and it moved to exact position. Rohrer called at me to start some trial swings. With the total height, which included the dip on the main cable plus the drop of the falls, it had quite a radius, and I was surprised how slow the swings were. It seemed to me the can was riding a little high and I signaled. They let her down. I tried again and it seemed O.K. Rohrer called me over. "Jack, she's not *quite* swinging true. Take position three or four feet to your right."

"O.K."

"When you hook her up, holler."

I went back, picked up my wire, and moved over to the point he said. I started her swinging again, and this time he called it was right. I pulled a little harder on the wire and the arc lengthened. I didn't take up slack, on my wire I mean, for each swing. I'd let it slip through my fingers, then, on the far swing, when it would tighten, I'd pull. It must have taken five seconds for that can to swing over and swing back again, and I'd hate to tell you how much will power it took each time to increase that pull. But then, pretty soon, she was due. I heaved, yelled, and hit the dirt.

It seemed to me I was in some horrible surf, made of wool, that was trying to tear me apart, and yet through it all I could hear the roar, and had a horrible feeling I had done something, I didn't exactly know what, all for nothing, and eternity would go by, and I'd never have peace again. Then I could hear her voice, calling my name, and some other voice, a woman's, talking to her, and a man's. They were a nurse and a doctor, it turned out afterward. Then would come this pain in my head, with balls of fire shooting around. That was from their pressing on my eyeballs, a little trick they've got, to bring you to. I must have answered, then, so they quit it, because everything stopped. I was trying to say something and she was talking to me. "Forget the fire. The fire's out. You put

it out. Don't you remember, Jack? You shot it out, then they
brought you here—"

"In how many pieces?"

"One—and a little concussion."

"Yeah, but the goddam roar—"

"Is gas. They're working on it. Open your eyes, you'll see.
There's no fire any more. You already put it out, and there
are pieces in the paper about it, and everybody thinks you're
wonderful, and—"

I opened my eyes, and it was the same old hospital room,
but the glare was gone, and even the roar didn't seem quite
what it had been. And then it stopped. She looked at me, and
we waited, and it seemed too good to believe that it wouldn't
start up again. But then the phone rang, and she grabbed it.
As soon as she answered she handed it to me. "Jack!"

"Yeah?"

"Rohrer."

"Oh, hello."

"She's out and she's in! Boy, oh boy, we've got her. We've
got her, and she's still good, the best well that's come in on the
goddam hill in a year, and Mrs. Branch gets her refinery, and
hells bells, boy, can't you say something?"

"Pal, I love you."

* **24** *

IT was a year, I guess, before I began sobering up, not from
the champagne we drank celebrating, but from the business,
and what I did for it, and from her. From the minute she

took up the option, things began to break, and everything I touched turned to gold. First off, when we started our pumps on the other wells, they worked fine, and no particular damage had been done, so right way we got stuff to sell. When we brought in the new well, it was a heavy producer. The tanks were a five-hundred-dollar repair job. Our Luxor contract was nearly up, so we could put in pipe to the refinery right away, and a few weeks later make the switchover. Next, Mendel asked for pipe, and a week later, Perrin, so instead of Rohrer having to beat all the bushes on the hill for enough crude to keep himself busy, he had all he could handle, and could run to capacity. They didn't have anything against Luxor, except that Luxor had done nothing while they were facing ruin, where I had risked my life and put out the fire. Then we had luck with still another well, that went down to the zone the previous permit had covered, and came in big. Next, we were offered a string of small filling stations, on lease, for so little we couldn't turn them down, even if I hadn't had a tip that the Sepulveda road, where three or four of them were located, was to be improved. So when pretty soon business began to grow, we had a deal that let us make money and put our Seven-Star sign all over Los Angeles, in fifteen or twenty different places. We were nothing but a little independent out-fit, but at last, as they say, we were integrated. We had wells, we had a plant, we had outlets. When our business was good, we got our price, retail. When it was off, we got rid of our surplus to other independents, but still made something. I made connections that took our lube, fuel, and asphalt, so wherever you looked, stuff was flowing. And wherever you listened, there was a pump. It's a wonderful thing, a pump. It's automatic: you sleep and it still goes. It's like a heart, putting life into you.

And if ever a woman could make a man drunk, from how she looked and thought and did, Hannah would be the one. Her eyes kept that shiny look, and she never got enough of me, which of course didn't antagonize me. On looks, she was a knockout, a lot more than I had had any idea of when I first met her. After things began to break for us she began to dress, and made me do it. We took in shows in Los Angeles, she in gold gowns, with gold shoes and gold things in her hair, so she looked like something from Egypt, and me in white tie and silk hat. Wherever you went you could hear them ask who she was, and you could see she was made for drawing rooms and boulevards and opera houses. She said I was too, so we got along all right. And yet, that first Christmas we had, when she worked three days on the snow garden at one end of the living room, I looked at it when she cut the juice into it, and wondered if I really cared whether the train jumped its switches or not, or the dancing doll was flush with the plexiglass pool, so she was really skating. I tried to tell myself to snap out of it, that I had everything I had ever wanted, a dream job, big dough, the respect of the business I was in. I had a car, a Packard that just floated. I had an apartment, looking right over the ocean, in the Castile Arms, one of the swank places on the water front. I had a woman with every kind of looks there was, and a husband, just to make it really good, because Branch wasn't making any motions toward divorce yet, and she couldn't marry if she wanted to.

And yet, if it was what I had been thirsty for, it never came clear, really to quench thirst, but had bubbles in it, like the damned champagne she was always drinking, and that I got so sick of I felt like life was nothing but one long string of Christmas afternoons. After a while I had it, or thought I did, what some of the trouble was. What stuck to my ribs was the job, and the stink of oil, and all the things I was able to do with it, so it really did things to me. But to her, for all her talk about my "machinist's soul," none of it meant anything but the money it brought in, and the things she could buy with it. Even that, I think, I could have stood, if she had stuck to cloth of gold and mink and opera tickets. But after a while she took the place in Beverly. It's about twenty miles up the line, where all the movie stars live and Eastern millionaires. Her house cost four hundred dollars a month, furnished, with swimming pool out back and badminton at one side, and it was just right for the parties she began to give. They got bigger and bigger, until pretty soon everybody came, columnists, stars, directors, and writers, and after a while even the gangsters, which in that part of the world is really showing class.

Little by little it began to get on my nerves. I'd get in around five, all full of some deal I'd made, and find some fish-faced dame sitting around with two guys, talking about what Lubitsch could do if he'd only try musicals. Hannah'd fix my old-fashioned, and I'd sit there grinning without saying anything, which was the tip-off, because a guy with a drink *and* a deal, if he's not saying anything, he just doesn't like it there. Then one day I came home and a party was going on out there at the pool, and when they went home it was getting dark. I sat finishing my drink when she started batting at something. Then a shadow began flitting around from the patio lamp. I looked up as she was swinging a newspaper, and grabbed her arm. Then I snapped out the light. Fluttering over the wall by the magnolia tree, went the biggest, blue-green luna I had ever seen. When I turned around her eyes were blazing at me. "What's the idea of the Londos grip?"

"Just a superstition of mine. About moths."

"Do you have to twist my arm off?"

Next day she showed me her forearm, that had a big blue mark on it from my thumb. "Jack, what got into you? I was killing a bug, and you jerked me around—look at that! It looks like Hogan's Alley on Saturday night."

"I told you—I'm superstitious about them."

"Yeah but—*look* at that bruise!"

When I couldn't tell her what the real reason was, when I knew that all she would see in it was a bug, I didn't kid myself any longer. This wasn't it, no matter how much I had yenned for it there in the rain, on the outside looking in, while fat guys ate rare meat and their women watched them do it. And yet, from the way I tried to smooth her down, and the quick nervous way my spine prickled at her look, for fear she would tumble to what I really thought of her, I knew I'd hang on, to the bitter end, if I had to. I didn't want her, but I did want the job, and I'd go pretty far to keep it.

One day, driving up Cherry Avenue, I got held by a light, and I heard somebody yell: "Hey, Jack!" There could be no mistake about that croaky voice. It was Hosey, and when I looked in the mirror there he was, not twenty feet away. As the light turned I started but here came a truck, and I had to stop or be hit. I looked again, and he was running after me. I got going at last and went zooming up the hill, but back of me I could see him, waving and running and yelling. And then I did one of the stupidest things I ever did in my life. If I'd gone on, just disappeared as I went over the hill, the chances are it was the last I'd ever have seen of him, because he never knew me by my right name, and he probably didn't take the number of the car. But I had it in mind to shake him, so when I came to the refinery I turned in. Then it came over me, how stupid it was, and I knew I had to get away quick. They thought I was crazy, I guess, when I asked if there had been any calls, then ducked out again. But just as I jumped in the car, he reached the main gate and began arguing with the watchman. I zipped out the back way and drove on down to the Jergins Trust Building, where I'd opened a headquarters to handle sales. I went through the main room and on back to my private office and told Lida, my girl, if any calls came through to take the message, but I didn't want to be disturbed.

Then I sat and cursed the day I'd ever seen Hosey, or called him a friend, or pulled anything with him, or had anything to do with him. Then I tried to think what I was going to do about him. I couldn't think. Somehow, the idea of having to take that scavenger's hand, and let him call me by my first name, and call him by his, and act like I was friendly with him, in front of everybody in the whole works, just turned me to jelly, and the thought of what he might tell on me turned me to soup. I've been scared in my life, but never worse than that morning, and never more ashamed of it. But after a while something began going through my head, and I grabbed it, and made myself turn into a man again, or something that at least could think. I said to myself: Dog it. You never saw Hosey. You never heard of him. You don't know what he's talking about, and while you've got all due sympathy for guys out of luck, your private opinion is, he's crazy. And just on his looks, that will sound like a highly probable idea. I checked it over and over and over, for something that would louse it. Unless they took me back to Las Vegas, and somebody in the motel remembered me, I couldn't think of anything.

In an hour or so, around noon I would say, Lida came back and asked me if we had anybody working for us by the name of Dixon. That was the name I'd signed on the registers of some of the hotels and flophouses and missions we had stayed at. But all I gave it was a dead pan, like I didn't want to be bothered. "Not that I know of, unless Rohrer has put somebody on he hasn't told me about."

"There's some bum over there asking."

"Tell Rohrer to watch it. Maybe it's a bum and maybe it's our friend Uncle Sam trailing hot oil. Not that we're buying any, but—"

I went over to the Hilton and had lunch, then went to the apartment. About two I rang Rohrer and asked could he drop over. He came around three and I started in on a road-tar deal, which was mostly imaginary, but I took an hour over it. I said nothing about Hosey, and he was almost out the door before he said anything, and I was getting nervous, as I had to know, but I dared not take any interest in it. Then he said: "Oh, by the way, Jack, what do I do about this bum that showed up this morning? Says we've got somebody working for us named Dixon, and won't go away till he sees him."

"I don't know any Dixon."

"Says he drove up in a black Packard car."

"I've got the only Packard around the place."

"So I told him. But he's still there. On the curb outside."

"Is he pulling anything?"

"No, but he's sitting."

"Then do nothing."

"Just leave him sit?"

"Isn't it a free country?"

"Why sure. And if the cops don't like it—?"

"Then he's their bum."

That night, when I got to Rodeo Drive in Beverly, believe me, I listened to the jokes and laughed at them. Next morning, instead of going to the Jergins Trust Building, I went direct to the refinery, and sure enough, there he was, still sitting and still waiting. He yelled at me as I went in the back way and I paid no attention but went and parked. But as I started for my office, Mulligan, the watchman, caught me, looking pretty uncomfortable. "Would you come talk to this guy, Mr. Dillon? I've just got the idea that in some kind of a cockeyed way he means you, and if you could just convince him he's got his signals mixed, maybe we can get rid of him. To tell you the truth, he's getting on everybody's nerves."

I went over to the gate, and when Hosey saw me he began to yell like some kind of a movie. "Jack! Don't you know me? It's Hosey! That hoboed all over Louisiana and Texas and Nevada with you and Buck? Jack! I'm ready to go to work. Remember that job we was going to give each other, whichever one hit the jackpot first?"

He meant it so hard he sounded phony. Even Mulligan turned his back. I blinked and said: "Well, Mulligan, he thinks he knows me, that's a cinch."

"Why, sir, that's ridiculous."

"No, he thinks I'm a pal."

"Pal my eye. It's just a racket—"

He went roaring on, while Hosey stared and listened. Then I said: "Anyway, get rid of him."

"You bet I'll get rid of him."

He started for the gate with his shoulders up, but I stopped the rough stuff. "Look, he's human too."

"I wouldn't be too sure about that, sir. But O.K. I let the cops do it."

But I took out ten dollars, shoved it through the wire at Hosey, and said: "My friend, I don't know who you think I am, but the times are bad, so buy yourself a meal and a bath and a flop, and keep the change. And if I ever run into somebody named Dixon, I'll give him your—"

"But—*Jack!*"

"Listen, goddam it, you want this ten or not?"

"Why sure, but—"

"Then take it and stop calling me Jack."

". . . And what would I call you, then?"

"Try mister, for a change."

"Mister what?"

"Just mister, pal."

He took the ten, turned away, and walked off. I started inside. Then something hit me on the head. It was a stone. We turned, and Hosey was standing there, in the middle of the street. "You dirty son of a bitch! I mean you, Jack. You heel! You yellow-bellied rat, that would do this to a friend! But I'll get you for it. I'll—"

Mulligan started for him, but I caught his arm. A drawstring was tightening around my belly, but I knew nothing could be done about it today, and the better I acted now, when the tote was made later, the better it would be for me. We stood there, and he threw more stones, and screamed and cussed and raved, and then when some kids gathered around, he went away.

It was a long twenty-four hours, a longer forty-eight, and a still longer seventy-two, but there was nothing I could do, so I did it. I shifted between the refinery, the Jergins Trust Building, and the apartment. Each night I'd stay in Beverly, and put on a black tie, and take her some place in the Strip. Because getting indicted for murder would be bad, and being claimed by some bum as a pal and college chum, that would be still worse. I meant, if I could possibly stack it up that way, that she'd never know anything about it. I drank champagne and called for more, but not enough more to get oiled and talk. Just enough more to have nothing on my mind at all, except what a swell party and what a swell girl. Everything swell, except by belly, which was getting slightly shriveled.

The third day, at the Jergins Trust Building, Lida came back around eleven and said there was a police officer out there that wanted to see me. I had her send him in. He was a young guy, and I saw him take a flash at my old football pictures, that Hannah had blown up and framed and hung there. He said nothing about them, though, but sat down and got out a blue paper. "Mr. Dillon, you got somebody here, working for you, by the name of Dixon?"

"No. Why?"

"You ever use that name? Yourself?"

"State your business."

I made it quiet, courteous, and cold. He looked at me some

seconds, which is something all cops make a specialty of doing, and I dialed a call. It was to Rohrer, and I told him to stand by for something important later, that under no circumstances should he leave. As he never did leave, except when quitting time came, he was all crossed up, but that didn't bother me, and I hung up. I had given an order and somebody had taken it, that was the main thing, and Mr. Cop had to wait, and speak when I was ready to be spoken to. It wasn't much, but it was something. ". . . I'm serving a warrant, Mr. Dillon. For the arrest of a party known as Jack Dixon. However, as our information is that he's a pretty big shot in the Seven-Star organization, and in fact is believed to be the general manager of it, it looks like he might be you. It's up to you whether you accept service or not, though I may as well tell you I have the power to take you in custody on this warrant, whatever you do about it."

"Well—could I read it?"

"If you would, that might help."

It was on complaint of the Las Vegas, Nevada, police, which meant that Hosey had spilled what he knew and some tele-graphing had been going on. Beyond "suspected of felony" it told me nothing, but reading it gave me time to think. I knew dogging it with this guy wouldn't do. His job was to bring me in, and if I got tough and he rode over me, I had lost the advantage I'd had, from the football pictures, and maybe his wanting to be friendly without my knowing it. And yet the last thing I should do was get myself booked, because that made it a public record, and led straight to the news-papers, Beverly, and her. I said: "Well—I guess I know about this. A bum showed up, called me by this name, and promoted a few bucks off me. Then he said we were buddies, and when I didn't ask him in, he got sore and went off, calling me names and throwing rocks at me. . . . Well, you've got nothing to do with that. I always say, if a guy says he's the victim of a mistake, O.K., but he should do what he can to straighten things out. I'm not accepting service of this warrant in any way, shape, or form. I don't know what the Las Vegas police want with me, I've never been to Las Vegas, and can't imagine why they've filed this complaint. But, just in a friendly way, why don't I go back with you, talk with whoever is in charge, and see if we can't straighten it out?"

"I would suggest that."

"Wait till I make a call."

I dialed the refinery again, got Mulligan on the line, and told him to hop in a cab and get over to the police station, as the bum was making trouble. Getting Mulligan in it wasn't from some angles the best judgment in the world, because my best play would be to go down there alone, with no lawyers, watchmen, or anybody else to help me. But Mulligan had been a cop and spoke their language, he thought Hosey was a phony, and he worked for me.

At the police station, which is in the city hall, we went in a room back of the main desk, and Mulligan was there ahead of us, sitting with Chief Lucas, that I'd met at the fire, a clerk, a heavy-set man in a blue suit, that looked like a detective, and a man in a blue blouse, that looked like a turnkey. Mulligan was roaring, pretty sore, and kept it up after I was brought in. There were two or three office chairs with hard seats, though Mulligan, the Chief, and the man in the blue suit were sitting on soft ones, upholstered in leather. I didn't sit down until the Chief motioned me to. Then I took a hard chair. I took care not to be sore, indignant, or funny. I was just a guy the cops wanted to talk to, and that took it pretty serious. The cop who brought me explained that I hadn't accepted service on the warrant, but had come on a voluntary basis, to give any help that I could. That seemed O.K. with the Chief, because he spoke to me then, by name. "You understand, though, Mr.

Dillon, that if any evidence comes to light of a criminal kind, we may still have to put you under arrest while the Las Vegas police start extradition proceedings to send you back to Nevada?"

"*Back* there? I haven't left there yet."

That got a laugh, but I played it straight and said: "Where this goddam fool got the idea I'm named Dixon or have been to Nevada I don't know, but wherever it is I'll face it, and I've got no fear how it'll come out. I never robbed any banks that I know of, but if I did walk in my sleep and they can prove it on me—then O.K."

That seemed all right, so far, though cops are a twenty-minute lot, and you can't always tell how you're doing with them. However, he nodded, and said: "I think the simplest way would be to get this guy in and let him chirp."

"What's your name?"

"Hosey Brown."

"Where you from?"

"Chillicothe, Ohio."

"What you do?"

"Structural iron."

"When you work last?"

"That was in Spokane, sir. In Spokane, Washington, before the depression hit. I haven't been able to get work since. I applied, but couldn't hit no jobs."

"You done time?"

". . . I don't just recollect."

"What you mean, you don't just recollect?"

"Chief, I was in an accident when I was twenty-two years old. I got hit when a I-beam fell on me. I don't know what I done for two years after that, or where I was."

"You don't remember Lewisburg?"

"No, sir, not good."

"But a little bit?"

"I hear tell of it, yes."

"You know this man here."

"Yes, sir, I do."

"Who is he?"

"His name is Jack Dixon."

"Where was this you knew him?"

"I met him first just outside of Chattanooga. Him and me, we got a fellow up that was fixing to die, name of Buck Mitchell. Then him and me and Buck, we traveled together for must of been nigh on to a year maybe, maybe two years. We was buddies, and we went all over the South and Southwest together."

"You pull any jobs? You and him?"

"Him and Buck, not me."

"What was you doing while they was pulling jobs?"

"Just waiting, sir."

"Where?"

"Up the street, generally."

"Not looking?"

"Of course I could see what was going on. But I never helped on no jobs, no, sir. I was up the street."

"Anybody bother them?"

"I don't just recollect. Some time, maybe."

"And what did you do, then?"

"Well, sir, what could I do?"

"You could holler, couldn't you?"

"Well, I guess I could, yes, I could holler."

"Did you?"

". . . I don't just recollect."

"Then you were lookout man?"

"No, sir, not me."

"And where was it you pulled these jobs?"

"*He* pulled them. Him and Buck."

"Where was this?"

"That was Phoenix, Yuma, Indio, Banning, I don't know where-all. The last place, where Buck got killed, was Las Vegas."

"You see that?"

"I was up the street waiting."

"And hollering?"

"I tell you I never done nothing."

"What happened on this hold-up?"

"Well, I was up the street, waiting, and Buck and Jack, they were to steal a car, first. Then here they come, in a little green coupé, and blowed the horn at me, and turned around and went up the street near this here filling station where they hoped to get the money. Then here they come back to the filling station in the car and went in to get gas. Then Buck and Jack got out and went in the men's room. Then they come out. Then Jack got in. Then Buck reached for the gun. Then a fellow stepped out from behind a car that was parked on the other side of the grease jack, leveled a gun, and then there was a shot. And Buck dropped. And then Jack come by in the car hell to split. I run out and yelled at him, but he drove off."

"That car—was it a Chevvie, 1933 coupé?"

"I don't know. It was green."

"You didn't see it later?"

"Not after that."

"You're sure you're not the one that ripped the seat cushions where it was abandoned out there by the grade crossing?"

"Not me, no, sir."

"When was all this?"

"Couple of years ago."

"Two years ago, in Las Vegas?"

"Could a been two, three years ago."

"Well listen, make up your mind."

"Maybe four year."

"Which is it?"

"Two, three, four year."

The Chief thought while the clerk wound up some notes on what was said, then motioned to the turnkey, who went out. Two or three guys came in that were cops, by their brick color, but they were in plain clothes. They sat down near me. The turnkey came back with two or three guys that, by their looks, were from the cells, then went out again. One had no coat on, the others had shabby clothes, and none had a shave. And then it came to me what this was: It was an identification. Through that door in a minute somebody would come to pick me out of the line. I don't know if ever in my life my head worked faster than it did then. I went over it in a flash, what I had looked like in Las Vegas four years ago, when I was hard, weatherbeaten, and thin, and what I looked like now, with soft, hundred-fifty-dollar tweeds on, a dark coat of tan, thirty pounds more weight, and a little Hollywood mustache I had sprouted. And I caught it with my eye, what a bum looked like, from the set of these faces the turnkey had brought in, that hadn't smiled in a month of Sundays, that had a dull heavy film on their eyes, and were covered with fuzz and grease and dirt. I knew I still had a chance, but something kept telling me—smile, smile, *smile!* Don't look like these bums! Don't be part of the line-up at all! Keep your head up, give out with it so anybody can see you, don't turn away like these guys are going to do, and SMILE! Smile so it COULDN'T BE YOU!

The door was still open, where the turnkey had gone out again, and through it came the station-house cat, a big black thing with yellow eyes and a red ribbon around his neck. I didn't overplay it. I didn't make a corny dive for him and grab him up in a hurry. I made motions at him with my fingers, and grinned at him, and whispered at him, and picked him up. Then I rolled him out on my knee and began scratching his chin.

"I couldn't be sure. It's been some time ago. But I'd say it was him. This one here, with no coat on."

I looked up, kind of like I didn't know what was going on, then went back to the cat. The turnkey had come back again, and with him was a little guy, around fifty maybe, that I'd never even known by name, but that had taken care of night calls at the motel where Hosey and Buck and I had stayed before pulling our job, and robbed the fellow of his gun. I didn't pay the least attention. I kept my head up while I was whispering to the cat. My heart skipped a beat when they brought in the guy in the filling station, the one that had sold us gas. But he didn't point to anybody at all. The Chief said O.K., the detectives went, all but the one in the blue suit, and the turnkey motioned Hosey and the prisoners and the two guys from Las Vegas, and took them out and closed the door. The Chief turned to me. "Mr. Dillon, what do you know about this?"

"Nothing."

"Just nothing at all?"

"Just nothing, period, new paragraph."

"You never been to Las Vegas?"

"No."

"O.K."

The guy in the blue suit got up, and it turned out he was a Las Vegas detective. He said: "Well, Chief, it looked to me like a phony, but you got to do something about it, even if you think it's a bum trying to promote a free ride. He saw the job, I'm sure of that, and probably traveled with a pair of yeggs a week or two, though not regular. One or two of those jobs, like the one he talked about in Yuma, were never pulled. But he never once mentioned that the one who got away in Las Vegas was a dark gimpy guy, and he never had the right name of the man that was killed. Of course, he could have called himself Buck, and maybe he used the name Mitchell. But the papers we took off him said Horace Burns, and if he doesn't know that, then we're chasing our tail to listen to him. Release this gentleman, I'd say."

"I'm going to. Sorry, Mr. Dillon."

"It's O.K. Cute cat."

"I found that gentleman in an alley when he was two days old and didn't have his eyes open yet. I raised him with an eye dropper and milk warmed on that electric heater beside your chair, and he's never known any home but this one. To him a cell is a front parlor."

"Pretty eyes."

"And fight his weight in wild ones."

"Nice seeing you again."

Outside, Mulligan went off to scare up a cab and I stood there waiting for him to come back. Then back of me I heard something, and turned. Hosey came running, and ducked across the street, to the park. After him came the guy from the motel and the guy from the filling station. When they caught up with him, the guy from the motel hit him and he staggered and then the guy from the filling station hit him and he went down. I turned my back, and when a cab came with Mulligan alongside, I got in quick and closed my eyes. "What's the matter, Mr. Dillon?"

"Not a thing."

"You sick?"

"Just tired."

He gave my apartment address and we started up. Ahead

of us, walking along, were the two guys from Las Vegas, the one from the filling station and the one from the motel. In the park was something lying on the grass. I felt big and cruel and cold, a thick, heavy-shouldered bunch of whatever it takes to be a success. As we turned into the ocean front it flashed through my mind I was going to do the one last thing, or try to, that I would have to do to hold what I had, so I could never be pried loose. Branch, at last, had decided to give her a divorce, and I meant, as soon as she was free, at the end of this interlocutory year they've got in California, to marry her and stay married to her. At least, even if I was a little shy on love, I could breathe easy, and if any more Hoseys came along, they might dent me but they couldn't break me.

$$* \quad 25 \quad *$$

ALL that time, that is since I consolidated the company and began getting my picture in the paper now and then, I'd been hearing from Denny. Every six months or so he'd write me, catching me up on the news back in Baltimore, and winding up with a gag P.S. that propositioned me for a job in the big oil empire, as he called Seven-Star. It was from him I found out my father was failing, that the Leggs were living on University Parkway, "snug enough on what they got when they sold the hotel"; that Sheila and Nancy were in mourning for my mother, "though just exactly why, considering the status quo ante, deponent saith not, not knowing." He acted like most of the things, like my father's health and the sale of the hotel and the death of my mother, I already knew about, and he was just putting in his two bits' worth. But I'd heard nothing, or next to nothing, in seven years, and most of what he told me, except now and then something like Byrd getting made president of the university, depressed the hell out of me. The death of my mother, and specially hearing it on top of a gag, knocked me for a loop. It was one more break with what I might have been. Denny seemed to think I knew about his marriage too, and had quite a lot to say about the heat being on from his better, "oh distinctly better half if we may rely on her view of it," to get out and get busy, to earn baby some shoes, now that his father had left him nothing but a lot of worthless stock in the way of an inheritance. But who he was married to, and when it had happened, were things I knew nothing about.

I never thought of him, though, when this question of astrology first came up, and in fact I had puzzled over it a week before it occurred to me he was the one guy on earth to take it over and do something with it. I had dropped in, on a routine visit, to one of our Seven-Star filling stations, the one on 101, just above Long Beach, where she and I had parked the stuff the morning I saved the shack. And out back of the pumps, over near the tire shop, I noticed a transit, the same one, as I could see from marks on the tripod, as I had parked there three years before. When Ed Moore, the manager, got through gassing a car, I apologized to him for leaving it, but said I'd forgotten it and would send for it the next day. "Well, fact of the matter, Mr. Dillon, I'd forgotten it too. It was put with the rest of the stuff you left here, but then when the files were taken out it was shoved in a corner with a stack of exhaust pipes in front of it, and I didn't even know it was there until one day, when I was moving things around and happened to notice it. And then I got to wondering if that glass was a telescope, and whether it would work on the moon. So I got it out and set it up, and come to find out it worked fine. Always been interested in the moon. Read a lot about it. Always wanted to study it with a nice glass, but till now never had the chance."

"O.K., but if it's in your way—"

"Not at all, not at all."

He looked a little funny, then went on: "And fact of the matter, I've been intending to call you up about it, because *I* think it's helping business."

". . . In what way?"

"People come in, just to look through it."

"At the moon?"

"At the moon, and then they buy gas. And at the North Star and Evening Star and whatever else we've got, too. And some of them fool around telling fortunes. That's what I was going to call up about. Somehow, I can't shake out of my mind there's a merchandising angle there. I don't know how much telescopes cost, but I know this much: Once you got 'em, they don't eat, and they don't burn any gas."

I thought about it, or went through the motions of thinking about it, for two or three weeks. At the end of that time, I knew I wasn't doing well. Putting telescopes in each of our stations, mounting them on tripods, and hanging a sign on them, "See the Moon," was about all I could think of in the way of promotion, and that didn't seem very good. Pretty soon I laid it down in front of her, and we took a ride to Ed's station, watched kids peeping through the glass and listened to couples arguing about the zodiac. She asked me what I thought we ought to do, but when I told her what I'd been thinking up she shook her head. "If you don't mind my saying so, it's not your racket. Putting down wells, pumping oil, cutting it up to sell—on that you're fine. But this is retail. This is one-hundred-per-cent bunk, but it has to make sense, like Jack Benny. It takes a special kind of intellect. It takes somebody that can make a scientific study of bunk."

That's when I thought of Denny.

"But of course, Jack! I may have laughed at your stories about him, but I may as well tell you *I* always thought there was something in him—that his 'initiative' was something a business could use. Bring him out on a tentative basis, and if it doesn't work out you're not hooked, but at the same time you haven't got yourself involved with one of these Los Angeles high-pressure boys who wants a mortgage on everything I've got."

He got off the plane at Burbank with an Eastern suit, an Eastern topcoat, an Eastern hat, and an Eastern color. But, except for some gray over the ears and a little more weight, he was the same old Denny, with that country-club good looks, and the quick, warm smile that really did things to you. I had reserved an apartment for him next to mine, and while we were running down he caught me up a little bit on himself, how he'd been driven, since the death of his father, trying to settle an estate that wasn't worth settling, how his aunt was taking care of his mother, how he'd had three jobs in the last five years, each of them in businesses that folded before he'd been with them a month. Then he asked me what it was I had waiting for him and when I told him he lit up. By that time we were within a mile of Ed's station and I asked him how he'd like to stop by and look things over. He wanted to, so I pulled in there and Ed gave him the works, everything he'd noticed, since the glass had been set up there. He asked how many of the customers were daytimers that switched to night on account of the glass, how many were people that had been buying some opposition gas, then switched, how many had a real interest in astronomy, how many were astrology bugs, how many were just peepers, on their way to the rest room, trying to get something free. He saw angles I hadn't thought of, and what he didn't see, Ed did. When we left he had a big stack of sales sheets Ed gave him, so he could tot day sales separate from night sales, and maybe get more angles. When we finally got to the apartment it was time to go out to lunch, so we did, and from lunch to the Jergins Trust Building and from there to the hill. I introduced him to everybody, and they all fell for him, which you would expect, anyway the secretaries. But when Rohrer fell for him, that was different. Rohrer knew a little of what he'd been brought out for, and between the looking around and explaining, he said to me: "He's going to be a wonderful help, that young fellow is. He *asks! He's not ashamed to let on he don't know!*"

So when we changed into black ties, and I drove him up to Beverly and he made a hit there, I wasn't surprised, but I was relieved. With her, he made his hit when she was stirring Martinis before dinner, with a couple of fast gags he kind of shook off the end of his cigarette. She knew he was her kind then, and played him up big when the picture people began dropping in around ten. They fell for the gags too, but one of the girls fell for something else, and began propositioning him to play tennis on her court. He sideslipped it, and Hannah liked how he did it. "He's done plenty of chasing, that one has. But when a guy knows all the answers and then keeps still, just because he's married and decent and in love with his wife, what do you do then?"

"Well, what do you do?"

"You hand it to him."

Considering Denny's broad-minded ideas on what he owed himself in the way of leisure when we were kids, it was surprising the way he bore down on this little problem of the telescope. He was at it morning, noon, and night, going over Ed's sheets, taking a job in the filling station, putting on coveralls, and studying every man, woman, and child that went near the damned transit. He moved it to this place and that place, to check which was transit trade and which was rest-room trade. He tried it with a sign and without a sign. He took it away and checked how many people asked about it. At the end of a week, one Sunday morning when he, she, and I had just finished breakfast in Beverly, he said: "Well, chilluns, I guess you're getting a little impatient, but I'm on the trail of something, and I want time. For just a pretty good job, I could begin now. The main point about this, as I suppose you know, is that it prolongs your period of activity from daytime into the night. It can add—it doesn't now, but we're talking about the future and promotion possibilities—it *could* add at least ten per cent to your sales, which is terrific. On top of that, for a daytime bulge and general sales angle that has a potential I haven't been able to calculate, there's the astrology. That lets in a radio show, a cheap one, that we can put on with just an astrologer and some records—fifteen minutes a day, on the coast network, or better still, one of the local stations that'll cost next to nothing but give us city coverage. So far, fine, it's cheap and it's good, and the telescopes don't, as you say, eat anything. But—it lacks something. I know what I'm doing here. After all, we're talking about stars, and I want something with some reach to it. Something good."

She said: "What do you think, Jack?"

"Let him meditate."

"Think, pretty creature, think."

I found a note under my door, at the apartment, one Thursday afternoon, two or three weeks after that, that said he was going off by himself a few days, and to count him out over the week end. I didn't pay much attention, except that by then I kind of looked forward to him, and she did. But I'd turned the utility car over to him, and if he wanted to drive off somewhere it was O.K. by me. But Sunday morning, around eight, when I was taking a few turns up and down her pool, I felt somebody around and when I looked, there he was, on the other side of the wall. When I waved he came over on a vault, in a sweat shirt, Western slacks he'd got for himself, and no shave. Then he began walking up and down. "Well, you big ape, I've got it, *I've got it!*"

"Swell, but it's early yet, so take it easy."

"O.K., but I'VE GOT IT!"

"Sh!"

But before I could shut him up, she said something from upstairs, and from the sound of her voice she wasn't even out of bed yet. In a couple of minutes, she was down, in shorts, without make-up, her hair twisted up in a knot. No servants were up, so she got breakfast herself, and served it on the table at the corner of the pool. But as soon as she had brought the eggs she told him to get going. "Laws, Hannah—you heard of them?"

"You mean like against arson, murder, mayhem—"

"I mean like gravity, forces, light—"

"Oh, physical laws!"

"That's it. Who found them?"

"Why—didn't Sir Isaac Newton? That apple hitting him on the—oh no, that can't be right."

"It is, though, you had it, first guess. And that reminds me to look up that guy's public-relations stuff. Did it ever occur to you that's the *only* scientific man an American has ever heard of, really to know who he was? They couldn't tell Archimedes from Hippocrates on a bet, and yet—"

"I said get going."

"I will, don't worry. So we show him. We put out a regular, special picture of him, all over the billboards, on every piece of advertising we run, there on the grass, with his apple. Dreaming up his law. But our scientists—get a load of this, Hannah—they study the stars!"

"We got scientists?"

"Jack's a B.S."

"Why does Jack study the stars?"

"To find new elements, or whatever they've got up there. Because that's our twist. The new way, they don't work with apples, they do it with a telescope, or spectroscope, or some kind of goddam scope, don't pin me down which, because I don't know what it is yet but I'll get it. The main point is, when you got some law like gravity, some element like neon, before they put it in a test tube, some slug with a glass found it in a star. Then they started looking for it here, in the middle of the Gobi Desert or some place. They—"

"Are you kidding me?"

"Then ask Jack."

"Scientist, is he kidding me?"

"No."

"O.K., smart guy. They—"

"They had to know it existed before they could go looking for it and put it in quantity production. You can't find gold in them thar hills till you heard of gold."

"So?"

"We're putting out a new gas."

"Are we, Jack?"

"Gas is gas. Why not?"

"Observatory gas, Hannah."

"Yeah, but *why?*"

"I'm telling you—*our scientists study the stars,* and we've got to put out a new gas to put that point over. For all that special *ethyl* that our gas has got, for that high-octane *pick-up,* for that good old *power,* for those extra *miles per gallon,* our scientists, the ones with smocks on their backs and slide rules in their hand and telescopes to their eyes, study the stars! And if you don't believe it, stop at the nearest Seven-Star observatory and look at a star yourself!"

"We got observatories?"

"We will have."

"Yeah, telescopes, but—what do you mean, observatories?"

"I mean the works."

"But—with domes on them?"

"And telescopes pointing up in the air—ten feet."

"Who's paying for this?"

"You are."

"I like that."

He'd been half gagging up to then, but all of a sudden he got serious and began popping it off the end of his cigarette, like he did when he was trying to put something over. He said it actually wouldn't cost a lot, as that was what he'd been looking into, these last two days since he took his powder. The telescopes, he said, you got from the Amateur Astronomers' Association, and there were at least a dozen members of it that he had already talked to, who were just praying for the chance to get a job together for us, and so cheap you could hardly believe it. The domes would be plastic, and he'd already got a price from two or three companies that would be almost within the estimates that had been turned in for new rest rooms on several of the stations, which had to be built anyway, and could be designed to let a dome in as well as not. That was the thing to remember, he said: the observatory, the rest room, the soft-drink vendor, the water bubbler, and all the rest of it should be one unit, a feature with some individuality. He kept talking about clean, nice rest rooms, and spoke about Standard and how many people go there just because of lavatory facilities. This, he said, would be the same idea, with the observatory an extra attraction. It would be in front of the rest rooms, and revolve with a mechanism he had already got a price on, from a junk dealer, who had a dozen circular tracks, seven feet across, with cogs on them, and pinions to fit, all for some cockeyed low price. The control wheels, so each customer could turn the dome, or turret, whatever way it suited him, he said had to be shiny brass, and he'd got quotations from another junkyard. But the big surprise for me and Hannah came when he told about the big tube of brass that sticks out of the top of a dome, and works in a slot that cuts it in half. "That thing isn't for any purpose at all but to shut out light, so you can see the moon in the daytime of you want to look, and so at night light from the Milky Way doesn't get in. The works of a telescope, what you see with, goes in a grip you can carry in your hand. The rest is just window dressing. Those tubes we get at a sheet brass works, and I've got quotations on them right here. They roll up a piece of brass to our order, catch it with rivets, deliver when we're ready to install—and there's our observatory. It shines like a fireman's hat, sticks away up in the air so you can see it a mile, it's cheap, and it's scientific! And on top of that we've got the astrology. But why the hell I've got to argue so much about it, I don't—"

"Sold, Denny. That is, if Jack—"

"Sounds O.K."

"I just love it!"

He organized it, I'll say that for him, right down to the last picture, copy, and release date, a regular southern California production job. We'd been making more money than I had really told her, so we could afford what he was doing easy enough, even if I did put the brakes on him here and there, just from habit, or sense of duty, or whatever it was. But it cost even less than I figured on, mainly because all that stuff, the domes, telescopes, brass wheels, and so on, looked a lot more expensive than they were. And whatever it cost, I think I would have O.K.'d it, because it was opening up something that until then I'd paid no attention to at all. I mean, it dealt with people. Up to then, my life had been things. Music, my voice, had been things, and a football was a thing, as a boxcar was, and a fruit spray, and a well. But this started with stars, the domes, and the glasses, and went on to how people felt about them. Denny tried his slogans, copy, and pictures, on everybody, from Rohrer and Lida and me and Hannah to Joe Doaks. Every reaction he'd get, he'd rethink and rewrite and redraw. After he'd tried the stuff on two hundred different people Sir Isaac was out. "It's O.K., Jack, it's simple and they can understand it, but in the first place it's comedy and in the second place it's crumby. I mean, we want everything streamlined, and then we show a fat old bastard in a Quaker Oats suit, sitting under a tree, rubbing his head with one hand and holding an apple with the other—and it's wrong. We'll take care of that stuff about the elements that were discovered on Mars before they were discovered on earth, or wherever they were discovered, but we'll do it in copy. We'll have a nice, re-fined column, no more than ten picas wide, running down one side of the page explaining about it, but the rest of it's got to soar. It's got to go sailing right off the page—out into the wide blue yonder so we lift 'em. You get it, Jack? It isn't only that we got telescopes. It's got to be a symbol of a whole world, of the world they live in—of infinity with a supercharger."

I guess it sounds corny, more like Eddie Guest than Walt Whitman, but it was poetry, just the same, to him, and I've got to admit it, to me. It opened up things, not quite the world he was talking about, but another world I never heard of just the same, the world that you scored in by controlling people's minds, and I don't mind saying I bought it all, and hard. We made our first announcement with a page ad in Westways, which is a magazine put out by the Automobile Club of Southern California, and he knocked me over with it, because he caught me completely by surprise. For the picture, he ran a photo of her, Hannah, I mean. But it was a special kind of photo, and caught her at night, all smeared up with some kind of glycerine so she shone like a glowworm, with a white silk jersey swimming outfit that showed every curve she had, but somehow looked scientific at the same time. I mean, she had on big, wide glasses with white rims and white pieces running back over her ears, and she was standing under one of our telescopes, with her hand on it like she was just about to peep through it, but looking up at the sky like she was going to make sure, first, what she was going to peep at. And those thick, solid shoulders somehow meant business, more than a hundred slim cuties could have meant, and caught the spirit of this new world he was trying to put across, and gave it that thing he was talking about, lift, the spring that carried it right off the page. On the left, where you didn't notice it till about the dozenth time you turned to the page, was the column of small type about the elements, and underneath a wide picture of one of our stations, showing the dome and glass sticking up. Up above were the stars, and Seven-Star had been changed from a circle cluster to the Big Dipper. But the main thing was that girl, with something classical about her pose that made it seem all right about the curves, and the way she was looking up, and the expression on her face. I went for it all, and I didn't miss it that other people would too. He was hardly out with the ad, and some newspaper stuff that released a little later, and hadn't even got started on the radio program yet, when he was invited up to L.A., to address the biweekly luncheon the Advertising Club holds on Tuesdays at the Biltmore. I didn't go, but she did, and sat out in the lobby and listened, and when she came back she dropped in my office to give me a special report. Then she said: "He's big time, your friend Mr. Deets. I hope we can hold him."

"We'll do our best."

"I think he rates a bonus."

"Just that—a bonus?"

"Well?"

"He does—but say it bigger."

"You mean real money?"

"We'd better."

"Jack, I'd say the main thing is: To keep building Seven-Star, so as it grows, his prospects grow and he has an incentive!"

"Yeah, but money talks."

I guess it was two or three months after that, when Denny had been with us nearly a year, that she came up to me at the refinery, where I'd gone to talk with Rohrer about putting a new unit in. I was standing at one of the stills when she came down the concrete stairs, said she wanted to see me, and went off in the direction of the office. I went over there. I was no sooner in the room than she piled in: "Jack, why didn't you tell me Mrs. Deets was here."

"Denny's wife?"

"She's been here a week."

"I didn't know it."

"He didn't mention it to you?"

"Not a word."

"You didn't notice he'd moved from the Castile?"

"He hasn't. When I stopped by the desk this morning the girl was still taking his messages. She'd never be doing that if he'd left there. She'd say he'd checked out. I was in the hotel business once. I know."

"He's paid up till the end of the month."

"Then he hasn't moved."

"Doesn't this all strike you as very peculiar?"

"It's his business. And his wife."

"Couldn't you have made it your business? A little?"

"I like to be friendly, I like to do things for people, I like to help a guy get settled, I like to welcome a girl to a strange place, and maybe have some flowers waiting for her when she sees her new living room for the first time. But I'm no goddam mind reader."

"You can hardly blame him, though."

"For what?"

"For keeping it quiet. After the queer way you've acted."

"*I?* About what?"

"His wife, Jack. Stop cracking dumb!"

"I've never said one word to him about his wife."

"Well, good God! Isn't that acting just about as queer as they come—or am I crazy? After all, you knew he was married, he's mentioned a hundred times he was married, he talks about writing his wife, and you've never said a word to him about her. Is that how things are done? Is that so nice and friendly?"

"His wife is from Baltimore. Or so I suppose."

"So what?"

"I don't want to hear about Baltimore."

"Jack, I'm not crazy."

"O.K., so I am."

She lit a cigarette, snapped the ashes at the ash tray four or five times, and began charging up and down like some kind of a leopard. I tried to talk. "Yeah, he mentioned about his wife, or tried to. He's tried to mention about a good many things, including my family. I've cut him off. I've tried to make it plain to him I don't want any news from home, and I've got my reasons. I never hid anything from you, particularly, and if you want to know what my reasons are, I guess I can tell you, but I'd prefer not to. I had a row. With my father. So I blew. I beat it out of there, but what I want to hear about him, or Baltimore, or any of it, is nothing. I've encouraged him strictly to keep his mouth shut about anything personal, and he's done it."

"But Jack—I was never so embarrassed in my life as when I blew into his office just now, over there at the Jergins Trust Building, just to say hello and ask how things were going, and he was standing there talking with this girl, and come to find out it was his wife, and she'd been here a week, and they've gone and taken a place on Willow Avenue, and I hadn't even been around to see if there was something I could do. Good God, Jack—is that making him like us? Is that saying bonus in a big loud tone of voice?"

"I tell you I couldn't guess it."

"Yes, but that's the whole point. When I actually did get him off by himself for a minute, and put it up to him what was the big idea, I couldn't even get him to talk then. He said you've acted so queer about the whole thing he supposed you'd prefer he said nothing about it, and so they did it this way. Jack, what are you hiding?"

"Nothing."

"There must be something."

"There is absolutely nothing, except what I've told you."

"Look at me, Jack."

"Listen, if you've got a shut-off valve, close it."

"O.K., but they're coming to dinner."

"So all right, count me out."

"No!"

"Then count me in."

"Jack, they're due at seven. I want you there at a quarter of, shined up and pretty, and I want you to take over the champagne, and see that she—"

"Suppose she likes gin?"

"Champagne!"

"All right, but stop yelling."

✳ 26 ✳

THE house in Beverly had a big entrance hall, with stairs rising out of the far end, a living room the size of Grand Central off on the left, and a little sitting room, with a table I used for a bar, off to the right. I didn't see the dinner rated all the whoopdedo that Hannah gave it, but I checked everything I needed, the whisky, brandy, and gin, for whatever cocktails they might want, with the cherries, olives, lemon peel, and orange on little saucers, and the champagne she doted on, well chilled. Irene, who had been brought up from Long Beach, came in with a tray of canapés, and right on the dot of seven the bell rang and she went out to answer. But Hannah was coming down the stairs, and said she'd go. I took out the champagne and began twisting off the wire. Denny came in, and I said the nicest welcome for anybody was champagne with the cork popping out of the bottle just as they came in the door. He seemed to like the idea, and I said why the hell hadn't he let somebody know he had a new arrival coming. He said getting settled first seemed the simplest way, so that was how they did it. I noticed how well he looked in his dinner coat. Like everybody else that comes to California he'd gone in for the salad-and-citrus diet, and it had slimmed him down, and for the sunshine, so he'd picked up color. Then I heard voices, and nudged the cork with my thumb and shook the bottle a little, so I could pop it when ready. Then I turned to the door so I could see the grand effect. Well, it popped all right, and it must have been a grand effect too, because I stood there with the champagne slopping

328

all over the rug and up my sleeve, till Denny grabbed it and turned it into the ice bucket to get it still enough to pour—and still I stood there, with my mouth hanging open and my feet rooted to the floor.

Who came through the door was Margaret.

After a while, when I got so I could speak and had the champagne wiped off my fingers, I shook hands and reached for whatever I had in the way of gags, while Hannah looked at me in a queer sort of way from the door. Then at last I got a glass in everybody's hand and we said here's how, and I looked Margaret over. She had on a dark-green velvet dress, gold shoes, and a gold fillet around her hair, and looked better than I had ever seen her. She was a little older than I, but I think anybody would have said she was ten years younger. Hannah had on her usual gold lamé, but she seemed to like Margaret all right, specially as Margaret smelled like money, and if there was one thing Hannah went for it was that. So after five or ten minutes we settled down and things eased. So then I said: "Well, for God's sake, when did *this* happen?"

"Oh—couple of years ago."

She looked at Denny, but he was looking at me. "Jack, goddam it, what are you trying to hand me? Do you mean to say you didn't know it?"

"Until now, I hadn't the least idea of it."

"But the papers carried yards about it."

"I haven't seen a Baltimore paper in eight years."

"And from all I had to say about the Leggs, and Margaret, and everything you never guessed it? You didn't tumble at *all?*"

I wanted to say if I'd had the slightest suspicion of it he'd never have been sent for, but all I said was no.

Hannah said: "Well, I do wish you'd catch me up on things.

Mrs. Deets, you and Jack seem to have known each other—was it something, shall we say, serious?"

"Oh, heavens no. We all grew up together, that's all."

At least it cleared the air, so we could talk. But there was none of that remember-the-time-when that people generally have if they're holding a reunion, which told me Denny knew everything, and didn't want to talk about it any more than I did. But that easy feeling, once we had it, began to get a little too easy, anyway on Margaret's end. I mean, Hannah began asking about her family, and Margaret told about her father and mother and "little sister," and said she was doing everything she could to get them to come out here, as she knew the California climate would do wonders for them, especially her father, who hadn't been well, and pretty soon her family, and how comfortable they would be in Santa Monica, and stuff like that, seemed to be all she knew to talk about. After dinner I saw Hannah hide a yawn, and fact of the matter it was getting pretty dull. It was dull because you could see that Margaret and Denny were nuts about each other, and I guess that's about the dullest thing in the world to be around, a happy couple.

Pretty soon Margaret said: "Jack, do you ever sing any more?"

"Not to people I like."

"He was a boy soprano, Mrs. Branch."

"Oh, and you *heard* him?"

"Heard him? I used to *play* for him."

"What's this?"

"Oh, we were in vaudeville together, me with a white dress with a blue sash, Jack in a Buster Brown collar and flowing black tie. Remember, Jack? Or have you forgotten?"

"I've been trying to forget it, don't worry."

Then Margaret began telling stuff about our tour together. She even remembered the woman that got to bawling over my singing out there in Loew's State on Broadway, and how we had folded up in the wings from laughing about it, and even remembered the name of the song. It was *The Trumpeter,* and pretty soon she remembered how it went, and sat down to the piano and transposed it to a low key and I sang it. Hannah sat there listening, then got up and switched off the overhead light, then camped off in a corner with the firelight shooting through her eyes. When I got through she said: "Well, goddam it, you don't have to make *me* cry."

We all laughed and had another drink.

"What was between you, Jack?"

"Me and Margaret?"

"Yes. There was something—more than music."

"Kid romance was all. I took her to dances, or at least a few dances, when I'd be home from college. On vacation. Stuff like that."

"Denny knows about it?"

"I imagine so."

"And still he said nothing? About marrying her?"

"Not a word. And I had no idea of it."

"Then it *was* queer."

"I don't get it at all."

"Unless. . . ."

"Yeah?"

"She's still torching for you?"

"I saw no sign of it."

"Me neither. What's your idea of it, Jack?"

"I haven't got one."

"I didn't feel any strain, though."

"You can't tell what she told him that made him feel self-conscious all this time he's been out here. About me, I mean. Maybe she blew it up big, when he was courting her. Maybe she gave him the idea she'd heard from me, and he better propose, and that's why he thought I was in touch with Baltimore. However, it seemed to me that whatever it was, it's all over now, and they'd like to forget it and start over."

"I felt that too."

"So—?"

"Sure, let's let 'em. I rather liked her."

"She's all right."

"And he's a duck, Jack."

"He's developed into something."

"And he's crazy about her."

"He's that all right."

"And she is about him. They're sweet."

"Nothing like it."

"You really mean that, Jack?"

"Of course. Why not?"

"Well—'why not?' That's a poem, isn't it?"

"Yeah, sure, I *really* mean it."

I had stayed after they left, and sat with her by the fire, and talked a while, and left, yawning, like I was dead for sleep, and had to get back to Long Beach, on account of heavy work next day. Then I was driving, and then I was forty, fifty, or sixty miles down the line, at some damned place, maybe Oceanside, sitting by the sea, trying to shake it out of my head, what was hammering in there, that felt the same as it had felt that day in the park when I was three years old, and saw the moth fly away through the trees. Once I was in the car, it was no trouble for me to put together what the mystery was all about. My letter to Denny had crossed them up bad, him and Margaret both. It might mean what it said, and it might mean nothing but a feeler, a lead, a trick, that pretended to be interested in him, and actually be pointed at Helen. But, if he wasn't doing anything at the time, except sit around

University Place and listen to Mr. Legg talk, they had to know. And the only way to find out was for him to come out here, take a look around, and report. But after he'd been here a while, and told me nothing, he probably felt too self-conscious about it to mention it. Either that or he had brought Margaret out here, long before they said she had come, used the Castile apartment as a front, and then got nervous I'd find it out, or see her by accident, and decided it was time to spill it. All that, though, I had figured out long before dinner was over, and what was racing through my head now was Helen. Just the thought that I might see her again was enough to send me out into the night to this pile of sand by the sea, shivering at the color of the moon on the waves, face to face with what I had run away from that awful night eight years before. I stayed there till dawn, and then I came back to my apartment at the Castile, went to bed, and tried to think. After a while I knew what I was going to do. I had done everything, turned my back on what I said I believed in when I had it tough, ratted on a friend, hung on with this cold bitch who could give me what I wanted out of life—to be kingpin in this terrific business, to have money, to be a shot. And I didn't mean to lose it all now, just for the sake of something I had given up years and years before. I was going to kill the moth. And I was going to do it when I saw her that night, by putting my cards in front of her—or some of my cards, enough to make her do what I wanted, as I thought.

"Hannah, Denny's got to go."

"You mean—we fire him, just like that?"

"We can make an adjustment. Give him a credit. Whatever seems right. But—get rid of him."

"In spite of his—success with our retail sales? They've doubled, by the way, did you know that? The telescopes are a hit, and the advertising is getting terrific results."

"I know about it."

"And in spite of your friendship?"

"I hate that part, but—he's out."

". . . May I ask why?"

"There's more to it than I told you."

"Involving her? Margaret?"

"I didn't mean to deceive you. I was kidding myself."

"You mean there was an affair?"

"No, but we were engaged. We were to be married."

"And—?"

"I don't want her around."

"You mean *you're* torching for *her?*"

"I mean it's messy."

"Not if it's over."

"It would make me uncomfortable every time I saw her, as it did last night. And what's more, the funny way he acted tells me he's just as uncomfortable about it as I am. It's just something he ought not to have allowed to happen. If they got married, so O.K. But he could have told me. He could have told me, and bowed out, because God knows I'd not have wanted him, in any way, shape, or form, if I had known it."

"Just a question of taste?"

"Something like that, yes."

She leaned back and puffed on her cigarette through the long holder she used and sipped her champagne. Around nine thirty she said she had a headache. I left, glad I didn't have to talk about it any more. I drove down to the Castile and went to bed and I guess I dropped off to sleep. Then there was a banging on my door. I got up and opened and she was there, in sweater, slacks, and polo coat. "Hannah! What are you doing here?"

"Just saying hello."

"What time is it?"

"About three, I'd say."

She came in, snapped on some lights and heat. "You better

put on something warm, Jack. We've got some talking to do. I'll make coffee."

I went back to my bedroom, put on stockings, slippers, sweater, and a flannel dressing gown. When I went in the living room she had the Silex on the table, with cups and some kind of crackers she'd found. "Sugar, Jack? There doesn't seem to be any cream."

"Just plain."

"Think I'll sweeten mine."

"At this hour, you could need it."

"Oh, a very good hour—for our business."

"I asked you once, what is our business?"

"Goodbye, I think. Of course I'm not sure."

"Well—take your time."

"Tell me about Helen."

". . . I know quite a few Helens."

"The sister. The one you fell for."

"When did you hear all this?"

"Just now. Tonight."

"Margaret told you?"

"She mostly. Denny, a little. I dropped in. Sweetest little place they have. A little bungalow on Willow Avenue. One of the new ones, you know with the car port, a long portico, mission tile, and thin pillars. All in yellow and blue. Their living-room furniture was saved out from the hotel and put in storage, after the sale. Does it strike you they got fixed up awful quick? I wonder if she's been lurking in the background some little time, without our knowing."

"Hannah."

"Yes, Jack."

"I was to marry Margaret. I told you."

"Yes, with affecting particulars."

"I broke it off."

"Yes, but why?"

"I didn't love her. I woke up to the fact I was a lot more

interested in a job at the hotel—or at least it had been decided
by certain members of my family that I should be interested—
than I was in her."

"How fascinating!"

"Meaning what?"

"Is that a habit of yours? Being more interested in the job
than the girl? It's one way to get on in the world, and I've
suspected for some time you know quite a lot about it. But to
find out you've been through it before, and made your singu-
lar decision—that puts a different face on it."

"Whose face, for instance?"

"Helen's."

"I tell you that's all hokey-pokey."

"Jack, there's only one thing wrong with it."

"Which is?"

"You're lying."

Why couldn't I keep on lying, lying, and lying some more?
I don't know. A lie's got no legs. Once around the track and
it's done, and all I could do was sit there and blink. She went
on: "Jack, if that was all I think, I'd let it go. I'm quite insane
about you. For your audacity. For that machinist's soul you've
got, that can see the stars reflected in a pool of oil and not smell
the oil—or smell it and make incense out of it. For your
beauty. You're a damned blond tower of sin that I love to
touch, that I'd give my eye teeth to cuddle right now. But I'll
not play second fiddle to—"

"Second fiddle! This was eight years ago."

"It was not. It's *now*."

"How could it be? Am I still in college?"

"If it wasn't now you'd have told me about her."

"Why would I? That would be nice, wouldn't it? To—"

"You told me about Margaret."

"Why sure. She didn't—"

I broke off and bit it back but the heartbeats pounded on

and all she did was sit and sip coffee and stare out to sea. After a long time, she said: "Go on, Jack, I'm listening. 'She didn't—?' I'm hoping and praying it's some kind of lie I can swallow down, and relax with, so I can come over, and sit in your lap, and pull your foolish-looking ears, that always make me want to cry. *She didn't*—WHAT?"

"Oh, to hell with her. Come here!"

"Let me alone! Margaret didn't *mean* anything to you, did she? Not a thing in the world. So we can get rid of her. And of Denny, your best friend. Who loves you, and has been stood on his head by the way you've acted about everything. We can get rid of them, *so that family won't come out here, and bring Helen, and bust up this mess of duck soup you've got, with me, and Seven-Star, and the banquets you speak at, and the pictures of yourself in the paper, and the mahogany office*—CAN'T WE?"

"Listen, Hannah, we're both dog-tired, and—"

"No! Not I!"

"Well, I am, if you don't mind."

"Jack, there's nothing I'd love better than to put my pride in my pocket, to come over to you, and to marry you, as you've asked me to do, and as I want to do. But I know what it would bring me. You're not that guy that you think you are, who'll take the cash and let the credit go, who'll put material things ahead of love. You're a damned romantic, who kicked the beans into the fire once, and will do it again. You really want love. And you despise me, as you've told me often, not because I gave up my husband for you, as you say, but because I'm not that kind of romantic sap. But whatever kind of sap I am, I'll not play second fiddle. When you didn't tell me about her, that's all I wanted to know. When it cost you something to choose me, when we have to fire Denny to be safe, so you can be sure of yourself and not have that ninny around the corner all the time—that's the tip-off. Oh, Mr.

Jack Dillon, I wasn't quite sure when I came in here. I was hoping. I can be a fool too. But now I know. This is goodbye."

"And—Seven-Star? Who's going to run it?"

"Denny."

She sat there crying a long time. After a while she got up, pulled on the coat she had taken off, then leaned against the wall while a perfect storm of tears came out of her. I tried to take her in my arms, but she shook me off. Then she whispered; "Goodbye, Jack," and went.

I sat down again, poured myself more coffee. How long I sat I don't know, if it was a day, a week, or a month.

* **27** *

1945 NOV 8 PM 8 19

MAJ. JOHN DILLON,
HOTEL TIMROD,
CHARLESTON, SC

YOUR FATHER'S CONDITION TOOK CRITICAL TURN TODAY IF YOU WISH TO SEE HIM PLEASE WIRE AND WE SHALL USE OUR BEST ENDEAVOR TO WIN HIM OVER AFTER WHICH YOU SHOULD START AT ONCE AS IT IS NOT GIVEN US TO KNOW HOW LONG HE MAY BE SPARED

                                                        SHEILA

To which, writing on one side of the paper and getting all words properly spelled, I wired back: WELL ISN'T THAT TOO UTTERLY NICE OF YOU BUT WIRING HIM AND USING BEST ENDEAVORS

ON ME MIGHT WORK BETTER. Then I sat around the hotel to sulk. Deep in me, of course, providing they wired me anything that made sense, I knew I was going. But I wanted to think about it, and I meant to take my time, as all and sundry, in that household at least, had certainly taken theirs. For three years, more than three years as a matter of fact, I'd been in the Army, but little they did about it, and they could have. I had got my greetings early in 1942, while I was still sitting around Long Beach. But, in accordance with the military genius of our War Department, which built all the camps in the wrong place and sent all the guys to the wrong camps, I was enrolled in California and ordered to Fort Meade, Maryland, which is south of Baltimore and east of Washington. Naturally, when I bumped into reporters from the *Sun,* there were pieces about me in the papers, with pictures. It seemed to me, if they were worried about somebody being "spared," either Sheila or Nancy or both of them might have come down there, maybe with a bag of cookies under one arm, and we could have had a little reunion. But nobody showed, so instead of taking my leaves in Baltimore, I slipped over to Washington, which I knew almost at well, from my student days. And when I went to boot camp and came out a lieutenant, it seemed to me they might have sent me a picture postcard or something, as that was in the papers too. But it drew a blank. And when I was ordered overseas, it seemed to me that might have stirred them up, as it had been hinted at in the paper too. But they slumbered on, my little gypsy sweethearts. So when I got to England, I quit worrying about them, my father, or anything that reminded me of Baltimore, the first time I ever really did. I can't say I was exactly happy in the Army. It was one long fever dream, with mud, fog, and rifle range mixed up with a stupor they call sleep. I got upped to first lieutenant, to captain, to major, and I didn't notice much difference, except the higher I got, the more hell I caught.

Then came June 1944. My division, the 79th, went ashore,

most of it, on the fourteenth, but it wasn't until the nineteenth that we were due to shoot krauts. Along about six o'clock the evening of the eighteenth, I began to worry about four trucks that were supposed to have come up, and that hadn't. They were bringing nothing but a load of K, just rations for my battalion, but by that time I'd got a little hipped on the subject of grub. In Washington, in the Library of Congress, I had done a little reading on the military thing. And the more I read, whether it was about Grant, and how nuts he was about water transportation, or Napoleon, and what he said about an army fighting on its belly, the more I saw that your outfit was as good as its supply. With K in their pockets, they could keep on going. With nothing in their pockets, they'd poop. So when the trucks didn't come, I called 313th regimental headquarters to find out why. There was no why. They were on their way. All couriers were at their posts to guide them in, it was all under control, be sure to report any movement of my CP—command post. In the last war it had been PC— post of command. Some bright brass, no doubt, got decorated with palm for figuring that change, but you've got to admit it was constructive.

2100, no K.

At 2200, or ten o'clock, after three more calls to regimental, I ordered my jeep and started back. At first we just crawled, on account of new stone the engineers had cracked up and put on the road, but I had Hayden, my driver, take the shoulder, and it was a little slippery but we made better time. About a mile from a place called Golleville I picked up the first courier. He said he'd talked to the next man about ten minutes before, and the trucks were stuck, on account of engine trouble. A few hundred yards further on, the next courier said the same thing. In a half hour, maybe, fighting our way back through three lines of trucks, guns, tanks, half tracks, and what had been coming ashore for ten or twelve days, we found my K. All four trucks were jammed in a little side road, where they'd been trying to bull their way into the main parade, but couldn't as the lead truck was stalled. When I got there the driver had eight GI's, the whole detail aboard all four trucks, swinging on a crank, trying to get it going by hand. I asked him what the trouble was. "Starter, sir."

"How do you know?"

"Got to be."

"Why?"

". . . I checked everything else."

It seemed like a funny answer, but I told the GI's to rest, raised the hood, and went in there myself—in the dark, of course, as nothing like a flashlight was allowed. I felt at the head of the cylinders, the fuel pump, the carburetor, things like that, and the more I felt the funnier it got. Then I got to the distributor. Right away I found a loose wire. I lifted the top of the box that holds it and a screw was missing, the one that made the connection with the dangling wire. I ran my little finger around, and not only was it gone from the connection, but it wasn't rolling around in the box. That didn't make sense. It's something that never happens, and if it had happened, the screw had to be in the box. I figured on it a minute or two before I said anything. I thought I knew the answer: that screw had been removed. But had it been thrown away? The more I thought the less like it seemed that a driver who had cooked up a trick to duck a trip to the front would leave himself on a limb so he couldn't take a powder back. And nobody knew, at that time, what was waiting for us. Maybe it was a rear guard, and maybe it was the whole German army. "Driver, where's that screw?"

". . . What screw?"

"From the distributor."

"Sir, I don't know nothing about any screw. I—never saw no screw. I—"

It wasn't a driver that was all crossed up because his truck wouldn't go. It was a guardhouse cadet at his own court-martial who knew perfectly well what I was talking about, but thought I couldn't prove it. Then it came to me what had hit me so funny before. It wasn't *cuss-hungry*. Think of that, it had to be the starter, the night before a drive, and yet he hadn't one goddam for it, or a kick, or even spit! I turned to the GI's. *"Men!"*

"Yes, sir."

"This driver has a setscrew in his pocket, a thing no bigger than a potato bug, that I need to make this truck go. Get it, before he throws it away, or swallows it, or—"

I turned my back. What they did to him I don't know, but from the way he whimpered it wasn't pretty. "Here it is, sir."

"O.K. Any of you men drive?"

"I do, sir."

"Take that wheel. I'll be in the jeep. Follow me."

When we got to the first courier, I turned the driver over to him, with orders to take him back and have him held for a court. The next courier, that we reached after another twenty minutes of bulling our way along, said: "Sir, my buddy and I have been out, looking things over in these fields. They're rough, but they're solid, with no heavy mud, or walls of any kind. We think they'd be better going, and get you there quicker than the road, with all this traffic."

"Fine, thanks."

I led the way into the field, and it was pretty bumpy, but we could move, with the four trucks jamming along behind. Each courier picked us up and passed us on to the next guy, and it wasn't long before we came to a side road, and the last courier stood at attention. "Straight into your CP, sir, a little more than one kilometer."

"O.K.—good work."

We bore left, and in about two minutes, when I figured

we'd gone about a kilometer, I stopped Hayden and got out. The sentry's orders were to have all challenges answered on foot, and by one person only, so it looked like it would save time if I reached him that way. I walked about a hundred yards. Then I went maybe fifty more. Then it came to me it ought not to be that far. I stopped and tried to see. It was so still I could hear my heartbeat. That's something they don't tell you about in the books, though sometimes they get it in a song: the death hush of a battlefield, around two o'clock in the morning. I couldn't hear a thing. I was about to start up again when I happened to look down, and my guts dropped through the seat of my pants. We had trouble coming out, as I've said, from loose stone. There was no loose stone here, nothing but Normandy mud. It flashed through my mind what had happened; the couriers, trying to help me out, in the dark picked the wrong road. Then, even while I was thinking, came something like an awful whisper from hell: ". . . *Nocht nicht . . . noch nicht. . . .*"

I did a belly slide into the ditch, behind some kind of a hay wagon that had been overturned there, and looked through a crack. I could see a little stone house, maybe to cool cream in, that had been built over a little stream that crossed the road, in a culvert, a few steps further on. In a second I saw something above it that was round and dark like a kraut helmet. I kept staring and it went down. Then here it came back up. Then beside it was another, and then another. But how many more there were, whether this was just some outpost or a battalion, I couldn't tell.

I had two grenades with me, and unhooked them and laid them on the bank. Then I slid down into the ditch. Then I let the first one go on a high lob, then heaved the other. In a second or two I heard them hit the mud. Then a kraut wailed: "*Jesus Christus—zurück!*"

But before they could hop *zurück* the grenades went off and Irish confetti began falling all around. I came out shooting and they did. Something hit my leg. Then I heard shots from behind me. Then came a yell, "*Kamerad,*" and then my ration detail was backing six krauts onto the road. One of them didn't back fast enough and a GI snapped up his gun butt against his chin. He went down almost on top of me and his eyeballs rolled on the road. They helped me up, anyway to stand on one leg, and through a GI that could speak a little German I found it was an outfit that had been sent out to booby-trap sheep, and had been cut off. I sent them back to headquarters under guard of two GI's, and counted up. There were three krauts lying there, besides the one with his face bashed in, and the boys said I had got them. There were two of my own men. That left me four. I had Hayden put me in the jeep and led on. We picked up the right road, a little way across country, but by the time we got to my CP, I knew I wasn't leading any advance that day. My leg was soaked in blood, and when one of my captains had me carried in a stable, and cut my pants away, he took command and ordered me back. It was a bad ride, and not only on account of the truck bumping me. My two GI's lay heavy on my heart. They kept on setting heavy, through the grand tour I made of the hospitals in France, England, and all over, and even after I hit Stark Hospital in Charleston. I think they would have stayed with me, if it hadn't been for Captain Barnham, one of the doctors there. He took a shine to me and headed off my transfer, so he could talk to me and put a little common sense, as he called it, to work. Pretty soon he had me buy a little car and take trips around, to Savannah and Atlanta and Miami and around, to get my mind off myself. Savannah I liked. It had been built right, by old Oglethorpe nearly two hundred years ago, so the parking problem was all taken care of, by "neutral ground," as they called it then and call it now, and the traffic problem, by a lot of little two-block parks, that scatter the bottlenecks, and the street-name problem by vertical posts, that you can see in your headlights, so you never have to stop and stare and wonder like you do in other places. The hotels had real food and real drinks and real service, and pretty soon I was slipping over there a lot.

All that time, in the Army, in the hospital, and driving around, I didn't think about my life, but at the same time it was there. I don't know if I was bitter about it, but I wasn't any too sold on it either, because I felt it wasn't all my fault. I had been a heel, but I hadn't wanted to be a heel, and I thought if things had broken different, I might not have been. Somewhere along the line, though, in the late summer of 1945, when the weather was getting a little cooler and Dixie was a place to be, I began to feel differently. I don't know what it was that woke me up, maybe seeing colored people in all the jobs that had once been held by whites, in the hotels, garages, and other places I'd be, even Cremo College, as they call it, where they make the cigars. Understand, if they could get away with it, I was all for it. It certainly showed they were as good mechanics as the next if they were allowed to be, and proved if they could get that kind of work they could do it. But it tipped me off it wasn't the same world as the one I had left. Ever since I'd been a man, in the 1930's, there'd been no work to do, and what had been human beings were let sink until they were worse than slaves, they were rats. And down under everything else, that was what had made me bitter, made me feel that being a heel was something I couldn't help. But if even colored field hands in the Carolinas could get jobs grinding valves and fixing starter teeth, that made me wonder if things might not, from now on, be different.

Then I began to hear about the new cars, and planes with pressurized cabins, and trains with vestibules you couldn't see, except on curves, and boats with Diesel-electric stuff that hadn't even been dreamed of before. It was my kind of world, something that spoke to what Hannah had called my mechanic's soul. Then I got a load of the frozen food, and for ten minutes I saw things, and couldn't fight them back. I mean, I saw something that made sense, and would fit in with my life, and let me get it back on the track, so it meant something. It seemed to me, if you could freeze stuff this new way, and have it taste good and be fresh, you could deliver dinner for a whole family with no home cooking necessary, except boiling of vegetables, and no washing up afterwards. A picture of the whole thing popped in front of my mind: central kitchens, to be located in each city I went into, where stuff would be cooking all day long, but not for any rush-hour trade, as everything would go in to freeze as soon as it was done; classified storage rooms, where everything would pack in portion units; assemblers, to work like department-store shoppers, and put each meal together in its container, with the dishes required, according to the order on the customers' lists; trucks, with freeze compartments in them, to deliver each container to the house where it was due; other trucks, to call later, maybe late at night, to collect the containers, with dirty dishes in them, where they'd been put out like milk bottles; dish-washing rooms, that would take all dishes as the collectors brought them back, and wash them up with machines that would fit the dishes and cut breakage to a minimum. I meant to make dishes of plastic, so they could stand some slamming around, and still not get smashed.

I went into it pretty thoroughly. I talked to manufacturing plumbers on the washer stuff, and plastic people about the dishes. I took trips all around, and learned how stuff is frozen in central plants, with the ice company furnishing refrigeration by the ton of product. I got it through my head what a terrific amount of food, like the muskrat carcasses they throw away in Louisiana, goes to waste in this country, stuff I figured I could use, and show a profit on. I began to think in terms of colored help, for the handy way they had, on mechanics, and the little trouble they'd give, on organization. I was out every day, and cruised from deep bayou country up to Tennessee, all around the TVA Valley, the greatest thing in the way of farm development I ever saw. It seemed funny to be zipping around, in my little Ford car, through country I'd hoboed over, but I tried not to think of that. I knew, of course, that Mrs. America wasn't going to do any standing broad jump into my lap for all the trouble I was taking over her, or do anything except act like the hundred-per-cent nitwit that in my opinion she was. From the beginning, I knew that this once more was a problem in public relations, or in other words that it involved people, instead of things. So, for one day I put in on freeze units, washing machinery, and fish, I put in two trying to figure the advertising, and wasn't too proud to remember Denny, and thank him in my mind, for what he had taught me. I went into publications, art, type, and ideas. I worked out a bunch of ads, to run in three national magazines, that would eat up a hundred thousand dollars before we ever served a meal. They were all about two women, one a pretty, slick, sexy blonde, named Dora Dumb. The other was a gray-haired, quiet, refined wife, named Bessie Bright. Dora was to be the queen of all the department stores in her town, the markets, the shops, garages, beauty shops, and massage parlors. She broke appointments, charged things on the account, had five dollars put on the gasoline bill for cash because she'd forgotten to go to the bank, sent things back after she'd ordered them, and everybody was just as nice to her as they could possibly be. She had a husband named John Q. Dumb, that never had any money, that was always in hock to the furniture store, the finance company, and the loan sharks, and would try, with pencil and paper, to explain to her that all that nonsense of hers was costing them two prices on what anything ought to cost, that the interest on all that installment buying was charged just like the lamb chops were charged, that there was no need for them to be broke all the time, if she'd just pay cash, use her head, and keep things, once she bought them.

Bessie Bright had a husband named Louis, who always had money, never was in hock, lived twice as well as the Dumbs, and all because she paid cash, kept things, gave the stores no trouble, and got the breaks. I made it clear that Dora Dumb could not trade at Dillon, Inc. That was to be an exclusive place, reserved to Bessie Bright and her friends. And the point I was trying to put over was, that if you took the Dillon Variety Budget Dinner, you got a different meal every night in the month, but with no daily order to fool with, no mind-changing at the last minute, no Dora Dumb nonsense, we could put it on the table cheaper than Bessie could cook it, so cheap as a matter of fact, and with so little work, that Bessie needn't keep a maid, and Louis, Jr. could have that car. I got pretty well along with it, at least in my mind. Then I went over to New Orleans and lined up my dough. I picked the biggest bank on Canal Street, went in, sat down with the cashier, and told him I wanted the name of a million dollars, "available for investment purposes." That hit him funny, as I expected it would, and we took it easy a few minutes, he being respectful to the uniform, but plenty shy of the idea. After a few minutes he said: "Major Dillon, I'm sure the investment you have in mind is a sound one, at least to your satisfaction, and well, you know, O.K. But I can't be sending you to anybody to—"

"Nobody's asking you to."

"That's what you said."

"I asked you for a name. I didn't ask you for a reference, anything of the kind. Naturally I'll leave you out of it."

"Yes, but even so—"

"Tell you what we'll do." I took a quarter out of my pocket, laid it down on his blotter. "There's a two-bit piece, with the eagle on one side and George Washington on the other. Now you get yourself called outside, to have a drink at that far water cooler. Before you go, you write a name on a slip of paper, this scratch pad here. When you come back it's gone, and I am. If I don't land the million dollars, you keep the two bits, and it's a comical little story for you when you've had a couple of these Sazerac cocktails they make down here. But if you land him, *you pay me*. Of course, I may use your bank to handle my money—that depends on how the million dollars feels. But it could turn out that way. Just a long shot, but worth two bits, I'd say, as a gamble."

He laughed again, wrote something on the scratch pad, went out. It was just one word, when I got on the street with it, a French name I'll call Douvain. Twenty minutes later I'd found out who Douvain was, and that afternoon I was in his office. I didn't talk much, or try to close a deal, or anything crazy, or big. I spoke my piece in five or six minutes, told my idea, said I hoped to interest him if he'd reserve time for me whenever convenient. I made it clear I wanted a great deal of money, "at least a million dollars—if you don't think in figures that big, say so and I'll blow." When I had it said, I shut up and sat there, letting him look me over. I guess it helped, what I'd learned standing reveille in the Army, to hold it an hour if I had to, without twitching my nose or coughing or scratching my leg, but I didn't make any vaudeville show out of it, giving an imitation of a statue of Lincoln, anything like that. I just let him study me, and looked out at the street, up on the wall at the signed pictures of four or five presidents, and at his bookcases. In about five minutes he picked up the telephone, told his operator to get his home. He spoke in French, to his wife, and it seemed to me, from the basic I'd studied in camp, he was talking about me, and about dinner. When he hung up he said: "Major, you take me by surprise. I hadn't expected to go into the restaurant business—or the polar storage business—or the farm business—or the advertising business—I'm a little confused which business you have in mind for me. But I have a feeling—some peculiar feeling of confidence you communicate to me. So I have spoken with my wife, and we shall be very glad if you can come to our home tonight, for dinner. Yes? At seven thirty?"

He spoke with a slight Creole accent, and didn't say seven thirty but "seven sirty." I didn't know it then, but I'd caught him on his weakness when I began talking food. I said yes, went on back to the Roosevelt and had myself pressed and shaved and shined and powdered till I didn't know myself, and showed up at his mansion on St. Charles Avenue at seven thirty sharp, for one of those dinner-coat things, with cocktails and lobsters and wine. By ten o'clock, I knew I was in, even if it was all in the France language. A girl played, and I sang the only French song I knew—*"Bonjour, Suzon,"* a thing Miss Eleanor had taught me for an encore. I went out of there with my future set.

As I walked to my car, it was one of those autumn nights they have no place in the world but Louisiana, soft, balmy, and clear, so the air has something in it that sets you nuts. I inhaled it, and as I looked up, there in a magnolia tree was the moth.

All that night it kept sweeping over me, the memory of what Hannah had said, that what had tripped me wasn't only the breaks I'd got. It was something else, the romantic in me, that had kicked the beans into the fire twice, once in Baltimore when I'd thrown up the hotel and everything else for a girl that hadn't even taken the ribbons off her hair yet, and again in California for the memory of her. And I faced it out with myself then, once more, lying awake in the Roosevelt Hotel: What was I going to do, leave that ghost to haunt me, and maybe louse me once more, or what? It was no trouble to remember what she looked like. I had dreamed about her, every few months, from the night I had left her, and always she looked the same, sunburned and blue-eyed and light-haired, and always twelve years old. I began to ask myself if I should go back to Maryland, or wherever she was, and get it over with. Either I'd still be in love with her, and maybe we could begin where we left off, or I'd be cured with one look, and that would be that. I asked myself if it was all imagination, if I was just being a fool, if I should go to sleep and forget her. But that night in the car, more than twelve years before, driving to hell and gone all over the face of the map, wasn't my imagination, and being thrown out of Seven-Star wasn't, either. I slept, of course, after a while, and saw Douvain the next day, and checked over my finances with him, as to whether I was in any personal need, as he wouldn't be able to take up anything in detail until after the first of the year, which was two or three months away. It pleased him I was well enough heeled, at least for a major in the Army, as I still had quite a lot of the California money, several thousand as a matter of fact. He asked me questions about that and I told him the truth, anyhow that I'd been kicked out on "a difference of opinion about matrimony." He laughed, as a Frenchman would. I had him solid, but somewhere in my belly I was uneasy. I left New Orleans after lunch, and for the night holed up at the Cherokee in Tallahassee. I got going early, and made the De Soto, in Savannah, in time for late lunch.

* 28 *

WHEN they came in, I don't know, but I'd got to my coffee, and the place was almost empty, when the younger one, the blonde, went out, maybe to powder, and came back again, and I felt my heart skip a beat at the graceful way she walked. Both of them were in the uniform of Navy nurses, but on her it looked like something by Adrian in Beverly, while on the other one, who was around forty, it looked like the shine on a blue serge suit. I tried to keep my eyes off their table, and did, I guess, but could see them there, talking to each other, and laughing. I poured myself another cup of coffee, and wondered if I wanted it, or was making an excuse to sit there. I wondered if I shouldn't have a third, and watch that walk some more, and try to forget the moth. Pretty soon the older one went out. Then the younger one, the one I'd been watching, came over. ". . . Major, don't you think we should speak?"

I jumped up, shook hands, and pulled out a chair. "We *most* certainly should, Lieutenant. Can I entice you to join me? Perhaps for a liqueur?"

"Well—could we have apricot?"

"Waiter! . . . Two apricot brandies. Be sure they're Apri."

"Apri. Did you learn that in France?"

"I was in France eight days."

"Off agin, on agin, gone agin—"

"—Finnigan!"

We both laughed, and the waiter brought the drinks. When he had gone she said: "I bet you don't even know it."

"Know what?"

"Finnigan to Flannagan."

I'd never even heard of it, except the off-agin-on-agin part. She recited it, pretty funny, a whole lot about a section boss named Finnigan "a-boilin' down his report" about a wreck, for a superintendent named Flannagan. We sipped our drink and I kept peeping at her hair. It was the color of honey, and I wanted to touch it with my hand, like it was a powder puff. She said she'd just come from France, that she'd been in Cherbourg three months. I'd never even got to Cherbourg, and we talked about what it was like, and the gray color of the sea, with the gulls white against it. I said on the Pacific the gulls looked black, as the sun blazed away in the south, and the shadows were on the near side. She thought that was interesting. We drank out, and she pushed her glass away. I paid and we went out in the lobby. "Well, what do you feel like doing, Lieutenant?"

"Oh, my. Have we got to be doing?"

"They've got shows."

"I saw a show."

"Would you like to ride?"

"I think I would."

We went out, got in my car, and started off. She said something about the Isle of Hope, to see the terrapin farm, and we headed for it. Next thing we knew, we were rolling up the coast, and there didn't seem to be any terrapin farm. I started into a filling station to ask, but she said: "Oh, let's forget the turtles. Can't we just ride?"

"All right. You could sit closer."

". . . Oh, could I?"

"If you care to."

She measured, with her hand, the distance between us. It was about one span. It was also about the prettiest hand I'd seen in a long while, and I took it. ". . . Well?"

"Let me think a little bit."

If she had laughed, that would have been one thing. If she had said: "Want to think about it," that would have been something else, meaning something but not much. When she said: "Let me think a little bit," it meant she was really thinking, and I felt a prickle go over me. I let go her hand, and we drove quite a while. Once she said something about not going too far, and I asked her if she was stationed in Savannah. She said no, in Miami, but she was visiting the other nurse, at her home. I said I'd have her back in plenty of time. I nearly hit a cow, which is a feature they've got all over Dixie. We rolled through some more scrub woods, the same scrub woods, as I've said, that starts in Anne Arundel County, Maryland, and ends at Sabine, Texas. After a while it began getting dark, and we were twenty or thirty miles from Charleston. ". . . How about having dinner with me?"

"In Charleston?"

"It's not good, like Savannah, but it'll do."

"I'd like to. I've never been there."

"I'm living there, and I'll do my best."

"Thanks."

With that she moved over. I put my hand down and she put hers in it.

We ate in a place near the old market, pretty gruesome after New Orleans and Savannah, but we managed to get a meal. She talked about the Civil War, and I told her about the *Star of the West* and Sumter and the rest of it, anyway a little bit. Then she said she had it in her mind that Poe had been here, and said he'd always been a favorite of hers. I said he'd been a soldier at Moultrie, and as a matter of fact laid *The Gold Bug* on Sullivan's Island. She got pretty excited and talked about the cryptogram and how wonderful she had thought it was, when she was young, the solution of it. I said we could drive over there. She asked if we had time, and I said we could still get to Savannah before it got too late, as we'd make better time at night. "Unless we hit cows."

"Oh, they go to bed."

"A black cow just *looks* like she goes to bed."

We thought that was pretty funny, and laughed, and then were in the car, driving over the Cooper River and on past the flats. I'd stop now and then and show her Moultrie and Sumter and Folly Beach, where Gershwin is supposed to have written *Porgy and Bess,* no great chapter in history, I would say. They were nothing but bunches of lights, but I kept on talking. We went on, to the island at last, which is nothing but a stretch of sand, with a flock of cottages on the south end. But we drove along, and the ocean was out there, and pretty soon there weren't any houses, and I pulled off the road, and stopped. We got out, walked around, and watched the surf, where it was coming in, but not rough. We came to kind of a dune we could sit on. My hand went down in the sand and it was warm. I had a bright idea and slid down, so the dune was at my back and the warm sand spilling over my pants. Then I grabbed her by the feet, and pulled her down. Then we were in each other's arms, and she was whispering: "At last, at last, it's been so long."

I don't know if it was an hour later, or how long, that I looked out to sea, and into the silver path to the moon, and knew if the moth would fly across it, I could watch it, and love it, and not have things happen inside. I knew it was the most beautiful moment of my life. She was lying close to me, her cheek under mine, her nose against my neck, when I raised up and spoke to her. "Lieutenant—"

"Yes?"

"Isn't it time we told names?"

She raised up and stared at me, a look of horror in her eyes. Then she jumped up and went off. I lay there a minute, wondering what the trouble was. Then I got up, felt around for my barracks cap and started after her. By then she'd put on her shoes, and was on the road, running back, toward town. I tried to run, but kept slipping back in the sand. Then I remembered the car. I ran back to it, got in, and started the motor. But when I shot power to the wheels they spun in the sand. By then I could barely see her. I jumped out and cut beach grass, with my knife. When I had a little pile I jammed it under one wheel and tried again. The car gave a jerk and I rolled on to the road. I raced along, trying to spot her, and couldn't. Two or three hundred yards away, I saw a bus stop, take somebody on, and go off. I overtook it. Every time it would stop, I'd be right behind, watching who got off. Pretty soon I could see inside of it, ahead of me, on the bridge. It was empty.

I went back to the island and drove all around. Next day I went down to Savannah and asked, and the day after that called Miami, anything to find her. So that's what I was doing when I got this wire from Sheila. And that, once I'd answered, was what I kept right on doing.

1945 NOV 9 AM 11 51

MAJ JOHN DILLON
HOTEL TIMROD
CHARLESTON SC
SHEILA HAS JUST SHOWN ME YOUR TELEGRAM WHICH WAS FIRST I KNEW SHE HAD COMMUNICATED WITH YOU MY HEART IS ACTING BADLY SO WOULD BE GRATEFUL IF YOU WOULD AC-CEPT MY INVITATION TO VISIT ME WHICH AM NOW IN POSITION TO EXTEND IF IT WOULD NOT BE TOO UTTERLY UTTERLY TIRE-SOME TO YOU

                                        PATRICK DILLON

IT was one of those yellow November days that they have in
Maryland, when I got there, with red and brown and spotty
green leaves still hanging to the trees, and the air clear but
everything damp. I had spent the night in Richmond, then
got going early, so I rolled up the terrace a little after noon.
I had a look at the new statue to Martin Luther they'd put up
in the park since I left, took a turn up the street, so as to park
in front of the house, got out and went up there. I had my
thumb on the bell, then figured a minute, my heart beating
fast, and decided it would be friendlier to use my key, which
I still had. Then Sheila opened the door. I caught her in my
arms, and held her tight, while she cried. Then Nancy was
there, and I hugged her too. I kissed and patted them both,
and noticed how gray they'd got. Then they took me back to
the den, and I was shaking hands with my father, who was
in a wheel chair. His color was a little queer, pink in the
cheeks but white around the eyes, but outside of that he looked
all right. He asked about my trip and I told about the stopover
in Richmond at the John Marshall Hotel, and my aunts said
I was lucky to get in there at all, the way things were now.
Then he and I were alone. We were alone, that is, except for
the silence that came in, parked its hat, and sat down with us.
After a long time he asked: "Well Jack, how have you been?"

"Oh, can't complain. And you?"

"I could complain, but—"

"Then hell, complain!"

"At any rate it's a disease that's enjoyed sitting up, not lying

357

down, which is something. And what have you been doing with yourself?"

"Oh, this and that."

That wound it up for a while. Then he said: "And them and those?" I didn't connect, and he looked away quick. "Just injecting a little lubricant into a conversation otherwise a little creaky. Perhaps the quip limped, but the intention was amiable."

Sometimes, when he went into his Derry brogue and used grammar in the grand style that only an Irishman seems capable of, it brought a lump to my throat, and one came there now. I began to talk about Charleston, the Timrod, the poet it was named after, the Civil War, anything, so it made words. It was chatter, but seemed to please him. "Are those major's leaves on your shoulder, Jack?"

"Yeah, dime a dozen."

"However, Anderson was a major."

". . . Who?"

"The commander you were talking about."

"Oh, at Sumter."

"He presided at one of the epic moments of history, and every detail of his conduct shows he knew it for such, and yet he was a major—a dime a dozen, as you say. In those days they had different ideas about rank. Where did you serve?"

"France."

"Yes, but how?"

"Target."

"You were in action?"

"These rifles on my collar mean infantry."

"I don't see well any more."

But he was looking at my chest, where there wasn't any fruit salad, as I didn't wear it. I opened my brief case and got out the little leather box and handed over my ribbons. They were just routine, as I'd never been cited. The Purple Heart he looked at quite a while. "What was the wound, Jack?"

"Slug in the leg."

"Where was this acquired?"

"Normandy."

"You were with Patton?"

"No, Wyche was our guy. That made it easy for the guard-house poets. Cross of Lorraine Division, we called ourselves." I showed him our shoulder patch, the gray Lorraine Cross on a blue field. He asked if it wasn't the same as de Gaulle's emblem, and I said it was. Then I got out a brochure some-body had lent me in Charleston, that had been printed in 1919, to explain to the boys about the insignia, so they'd under-stand what it meant. "Though, the way I heard it, the cross wasn't picked on account of the ideals it represented, but because General Kuhn happened to see it on a beer-bottle top in Bar-le-Duc one night, and decided it was what the outfit needed. Until then they had been the Joan of Arc Division, and Miss Geraldine Farrar had agreed to break a bottle over their heads. But all that was while the General was away in France, observing how things were done before the division was sent over, and it so happened that Miss Farrar was to do her stuff the night he got home. He raised hell, and stopped it. Nobody had told the division yet that to the French Miss Arc was a saint, and he figured they might not like it to see her picture on every doughboy's shoulder. So they went across without having any insignia, until he had this inspiration, which to my mind hit the spot in a very noble way."

"I'd have given five dollars, cash of the realm, to have heard the remarks of Miss Geraldine Farrar on this highly interest-ing occasion. In fact, had I been the General, I'd have taken my chances with the French."

"Little temperamental, hey?"

"Some girl."

He glanced through the brochure, then wanted to know

more about my wound. I told him it was above the knee, on the outside, and had required plenty of surgery, massage, and heat. "Are you all right now?"

"Yeah, sure."

I wanted to say more, but nothing would come out of my mouth. He closed his eyes for a while, then said: "Jack, I'm going to die."

"Hey, quit talking like that!"

"I have angina pectoris, which in Latin means agony of the chest, the most painful way in nature that a man can go. That I can face, or hope I can. But—I ruined my life."

"I wouldn't say so."

"There were those who could have said it."

"Did they?"

"If they didn't, they forebore."

"Are you talking about my mother?"

"I'm talking about a good many things, some of them hard to talk about, some of them hidden and obscure and shameful, almost impossible to talk about. I'm trying to say, what I've done to my life I don't want you to do to yours."

"Oh well, I probably have."

"What are you talking about? It's hardly begun."

"It's half lived. I'm thirty-five."

"It's a matter of youth, and it's in your eye. Your face is battered and seamed and hurt, but the look of a boy is still on it."

"I interrupted you."

"There are things I want to tell you."

"O.K., shoot."

". . . Jack, I can't talk to the man who says: 'O.K., shoot,' and he doesn't want to talk to me. Why deceive ourselves? Your tongue is as paralyzed as mine. We live under the curse of the inarticulate, some horrible murky screen that's always been between us. Think of it, it's thirteen years this fall, since you left this house, and yet, when I ask what you've been doing, you tell me 'this and that.'"

"I've been doing a lot of things."

"I know, lots and lots."

"Some things I'm not proud of."

"I know of them."

". . . What do you mean, you know of them?"

"Rumors reached me."

"Rumors?"

"Let us say, inquiries."

I don't know how long I sat there, blinking at him, but after a while I said: "All right, I had some trouble with the police. Just once, on mistaken identification. You bat around like I did, you can have. What did they ask you about me?"

"When you went into the Army, telegrams were sent me, and I answered them. I'm not interested in your police record. I've one of my own, it may surprise you to learn. I got into a brawl on O'Connell Street one night, and before I was done with it they had me in Dublin Castle and some filthy jail, and it was days before I was done with it, and was out. It's not important, and it's been years since I thought of it. But the frilled shirt on the statue of George III, but a few blocks up the street, in the old Grattan's Parliament Room of the Bank of Ireland, that's important, and it's of such things I'd like to talk to you about. Think of it, every thread, every knot, every flower, is hewn from the virgin marble, with the light showing through every tiny opening, and one mislick with a tool could have ruined it. John Bacon spent years on it, and even then died before it was done, and his son, John Bacon, Jr., had to finish it. It's a trivial conception, like engraving the Lord's Prayer on the head of a pin, and yet it represents one man's consecration, and a second man's acceptance of it, to an ideal, and has sustained me at times when I thought about it. I'm not talking of jails, or police, or incidental things. I'm talking of fundamentals, of what men believe in, and dedicate their lives to, of what your heart dreams of, and may yet have, and what mine wanted, and lost."

"Threw away, I've heard said."

"Aye."

That had slipped out on me, but the quick way he agreed to it set me back on my heels, and for some time nothing was said. Then: "You did big things, Jack—or so I was told."

"Anyhow, I was proud of them."

"Are you still?"

"I don't know. They're a closed chapter."

"But they were big?"

"The blues were a million dollars. I call that big."

"And I. If for no other reason, I can understand that you were proud. The man doesn't live, though he damn it and denounce it, who doesn't think a million dollars is a matter for pride, and I agree with Julius Caesar, who once boasted he lacked fifteen million sesterces of having nothing at all, that even such a debt is something in the nature of an accomplishment. I now make you an overture. I should like to hear more about it."

"That I can't tell you."

"Why not, if the ice is broken?"

"I've no gift for words, Dad. I'd tell the brawl on O'Connell Street and leave out the statue of George III. I'd tell the what, and leave out the why."

"I've had similar trouble, trying to piece together what happened to me. Because on the face of it I was a fool, as were Brutus, Columbus, Burr, Davis, Bryan, and all the misfits of history. And yet when somebody takes one of these, an Othello, a Macbeth, a Hamlet, a George III if you like, and carves a little deeper than the world's eye sees, he achieves something not possible with heroes. I believe it to be no accident, Jack, that the world's great literature is peopled by a swarm and rabble and motley of a hundred-per-cent heels."

"I should fascinate."

"And I."

The flicker of a smile passed between us, one of the few we'd ever had. He said: "And Jack, these medals didn't come by cultivating the colonel's good regards. You've been places only a brave man would venture into."

"Who's brave? If you're really brave you're a fool. If you're not you're a fake. I've saluted brave men, but they were dead."

"There was a battle once, Jack, in what this country calls the Revolutionary War, fought in the South, at a place called the Pens, or Cowpens, as the town is now named. It's lovingly studied by the military men, as General Daniel Morgan, the American, defeated General Banastre Tarleton, the Englishman, in a battle of decisive consequence. The point of interest is that Morgan disposed his green men, with reference to the terrain, so they couldn't run and had to fight. 'Twas the last word in cynicism, the disbelief in heroism and glory and the colors of a parade, but I've often wondered if it didn't summarize most what's known of courage and war."

"I've run. Or as we say now, ducked."

"And lived to fight another day, I see."

"Anyway, I'm here."

"Jack, it's melted a bit. Our barrier."

"Then fine."

"But not completely. I don't think it will. And yet, I've hit on a plan that may help. That will help us both, if you like it."

"Which is?"

"Write it."

"Who—me?"

"Well, in my condition, hardly I."

"I'm sorry, I'll never learn grammar."

"The American distrusts it, for its exactitude, which he associates with theology and metaphysics and logic, and identifies with superficiality. I don't say he's not right, but I'm a

Trinity College man myself, and had as lief drop egg on my
waistcoat as split an infinitive. I don't wholly accept the American canon. Yet it's wholly distinctive and I hope you don't
hesitate on that account. Never forget, the foreign colony,
during the Civil War, looked down on Mr. Lincoln because
of his uncouthness of speech. The greatest literary genius who
ever sat in the White House, which is indeed a title—and the
precisionists voted him down. Can you quote one phrase ever
uttered by the minister from the Court of St. James during
this memorable administration? Do you even know who he
was?"

"If I ever knew, I've forgotten."

"He bitterly criticized the gorilla Lincoln for his syntax."

"Getting back to me, I can't write."

"The art of writing consists of having something to say."

"And wanting to say it."

We dropped it for two or three days. I found a place for my
car, took my stuff to my room, settled down. It was all pretty
much as I'd left it, and it touched me, the way they had kept
it for me. I'd get a little thick, when I'd remember how he was
leaving out the one thing that had to be told, which was what
had happened about Helen, and where she was now, and all
the rest of it, things Denny hadn't gone into, or Margaret.
Then I'd ask myself if I wanted to know about Helen, after
what had happened in Charleston. Something had gone wrong
between me and that girl which I didn't understand, but given
a little time, I'd catch up with her, and maybe get going
again. Then something happened that made me want to please
my father, whether it pleased me or not. I don't know if you've
seen a man in one of those spells they have with angina, but
if you have I don't think you'll forget it in a hurry. First of
all the color left his face until it was gray. Then his eyes took
on a set, terrible stare. Then he began to labor. He didn't
move, and yet you could see he was doing everything God
would let him do, just to get his breath. I jumped up, began

calling for my aunts, and held him up straight in his chair. He began banging on the arm of it, with a handkerchief he had crumpled in his fist. Something went clink, and he held the handkerchief over his nose. A funny smell filled the room, he relaxed, and I could feel he was getting relief. What got me was that when he was himself again, maybe in five minutes, he never said a word, but picked up his paper and went on reading. If that wasn't enough to start me off writing, the cable from Douvain was. I'd written him where I was, and why, and now came this wire saying he was tied up until the end of winter, but to count him in, definitely, and get things in shape for him when he was free. It didn't worry me, I mean I wasn't afraid he was backing out. But it would be three or four months. Between him and this girl I couldn't find, I suddenly thought about writing—anything, to keep from going nuts. And so, one morning I cleared out a room over the garage, had a typewriter sent up, and got going.

So I've been at it all winter. As I'd finish it I'd show it to him, one hunk at a time. He cut it up into chapters, and put some curlicues in to break it up, and cut out a lot of stuff where I'd repeated myself. I let him. I caught it before very long that at last, in his death chair, he was doing something literary, something that hooked up with what he had studied when he was young, and that didn't have to do with cam shafts or differentials or fan belts or grease. He wasn't easy to please. About some things he told me stuff I hadn't known. For instance, about my mother. That morning in church was the one time I saw her, but she saw me, he said, many times. About some of it he got bitter, not so much at me as at himself, and specially the way he had thrown away my money, after insisting on keeping it for me. I tried to get over to him I didn't hold it against him. On my GI's he convinced me it was not my fault. On Buck, he took the better part of two days, talking to me, explaining it to me, getting it through my head it was only partly my fault. He didn't try to say it wasn't at all my fault, but he kept pressing on "partly." "You were caught in a web of circumstances unsurpassed for cruelty, for I hold the depression that began in 1929 was one of the most tragic eras ever seen. It broke up homes, it cut the heart out of the nation, it dismayed young people as nothing ever did. If, in consequence, you were planning a hold-up, God help you there were plenty more, and they had their reasons! If the boy got killed, you didn't kill him, and if the other limither, the one you call Hosey, was unable to implicate you, so much the better for justice and the good sense of the police. They're a peculiar breed. In some ways, the stupidest of men, but on a moral matter, strangely profound. They know, as 'tis said, the difference between a crook and a crook. As they released you, I think you may trust them, and no longer concern yourself."

But when he got to my fine scheme, my frozen food, he almost had a spell with his breath, he hated it so. "If there's one side of the Americans that arouses only my contempt, it's their genius for standardization, their acceptance of it, their pride in it, as though there were merit in their damned assembly line. Glory be to God, is this what you've arrived at, with your conquest of oil, your bravery in France, all the other things you've done, that you'll put Detroit on a trailer, and haul it to Carolina, Tennessee, Louisiana, and places that have been fit, until now, for a man to live in! Ford going to Dixie—there's a project for you! I hate every part of it, from the way it sounds to the way it looks to the way it tastes to the way it smells!"

"Well, thanks."

"You're wholly welcome."

"I wasn't asking you, however."

"You're still welcome, and many of them."

We must have come closer though, because it didn't upset me much. Then, some days later, just like he'd never blown his top at all, he said: "I've thought of your scheme, the central kitchens, the distribution, the advertising, Miss Dumb and Miss Bright, and I feel they're an inspiration, that you're on the right track. As I say, the whole thing revolts me, but it's your life we're planning, not mine. As your friend, your very amusing friend, Mrs. Branch, so cogently observed, you're a romantic."

"This is business."

"This is *penance.*"

"This is—what did you say?"

"This is the act of contrition you feel you must make to all these women you seduced, or think you did. In my own opinion, it was a plain case of abduction, with you in their arms, the victim of their wiles. I don't subscribe to your notions of women—they're quite as prehensile as man, as physical, as grasping, and as ruthless. I feel you were taken, as they say. But in yourself, there's some sense of guilt. Perhaps it's my fault, for letting you sing as a child, and acquire a special picture of yourself, in a blue velvet suit, with flowing tie and rolled-down collar, and women figuring maternally, as though you were too holy to defile. Whatever the reason for this macula, you've been touched. Now, you want to make up for it. You want to strike the shackles from women, to free the sex from the labors it's heir to, redeem man, by this sacrifice, for the wrongs he has done them, at least in your imagination, forever and ever, *in sæcula sæculorum, amen.* But at the same time you want to give them a piece of your mind, lecture them on the waywardness of their characters, tell them what you think, get them down on their knees. You seek to feed them and emancipate them and raise them to the heights with one hand, and give them a good spank on their delicious little bottoms, with the other. 'Tis a strange conceit, but yours, and it'll work. I loathe it, and wish it well. It's yours, and will bring you health, happiness, and success."

And so far he's been right. As I correct the last of this, there has been a price break, with things, stocks, and bonds tumbling all down the line, and plenty of people are nervous. I guess I am. But I'm not afraid, bitter, or helpless any more. Whatever you think of this idea I've got started on, *I* like it, which is what my father couldn't say for the idea he got started on. I like it, I know how to pull it off, and I believe in it. If I can haul a bunch of American women out of kitchens and put them somewhere else, I don't care if it's only picture shows, I'll settle for that, because I think picture shows are a better place for them to be. And whether it's worth doing or not worth doing, the country I'm doing it in seems mine, which it didn't before. I did some work for it and I helped fight for it —one night, no more, but also one bullet, no less. It's not, from where I sit at least, a mess I didn't make but have to take the rap for. There'll be tough times, I don't kid myself about that, if not this year then another year. But, unless I louse myself some way I don't foresee now, I'll have the heart to face them.

All that time, free as he talked about women, my father never once brought up Helen, the girl in Charleston, or anything in connection with them, which I thought was funny, as they were the key to everything else. But then one day he said: "I've located your little friend Helen."

". . . Did I ask you to?"

"I took it upon myself."

"Taking things upon yourself, you might have found out by now, isn't always indicated. I appreciate your interest, but something has intervened."

"The little lady in Charleston?"

"Finding *her* would have been a help."

"I still bet on Helen."

"Why, may I ask?"

"The context of your narrative. Over all that you've written she presides like some little divinity. She's in your blood, she's part of you. It's the fool who doesn't know when a woman is part of him, that lets specious things, small, meaningless things, come between."

"It's over. Try minding your business."

"I won't."

I wrote on, and patched, and rewrote, as he corrected. And then one day I heard his bell. I came down from my work-room, crossed the back yard, and found him on the sun porch. He had me sit down, looked shifty, and fidgeted for several minutes. Then: "She's in there waiting for you. You'd better see her."

"Who?"

"The little one. Helen. In my study."

"There it goes! *Goddam* it, why did you do this to me?"

I blew my top, but good. I wanted to know if he'd ever let my life alone, so I could live it, and not have it loused. "And especially as I've told you repeatedly, that's over. If it wasn't over, the Charleston thing would have killed it. Why did you do this?"

"I did what I thought best. She was away all winter, but at last she came home, and I got her on the phone. She holds things against you, most grievously. But, when I told her she was the only woman in your life, it seemed to me I'd made an impression. Then when I made a personal matter of it, explaining I was too feeble to visit her, she consented to visit me. And discuss it with me. Sheila and Nancy are out on an errand I arranged, and you, so far as she knows, are still in the Army, somewhere in the South. But, before I left her just now and wheeled myself out here, I made progress with her on a number of matters, and cleared up some things. I think, when you learn how I pieced them together, you'll have some admiration for me."

"My admiration could be sufficiently expressed with a poke in the jaw, and anything short of that comes under the head of a gentle caress."

"Jack, I'm going to die, and I—"

"Shall I start *Rock of Ages?*"

"And I ask that you see her."

"I heard of these cowards, that die a thousand times, the brave man only once, but they ought to see one of these Irish busybodies, that dies every hour and a half by the clock, with music—but unfortunately won't stay dead."

"That, as de Koven said to Gilbert, is something that time will cure."

"I'm sorry."

"There's an element of truth in it, but there are other reasons, too. Because what, after all, has loused you, as you put it? Me? Yourself? Circumstances? All three, to some extent. But mostly the time in which you've lived—a calendar. Now, thank God, it's shed its leaves, to kiss me out, to kiss you in—and her in if you'll let it. As you observed, she was guilty of a crime, that she was twelve years old. Now she's twenty-five, and a luscious twenty-five, at that."

"I told you, there's somebody else."

"She may be in there, too."

"She—? What are you talking about?"

"I'm not sure, I dared not ask something that might have straightened it out, but it could be—this is pure conjecture— that I *have* found that one for you, too. Ah, that makes it different, doesn't it?"

✳ 30 ✳

I KNOCKED, got no answer, opened the door, and went in. My heart skipped three beats when I saw her, as he said, the girl from Charleston, sitting behind his desk, in a dark dress, mink coat, and big floppy hat that made her hair look like it had been lit. I looked around for Helen, but nobody else was there. When I saw the glitter of tears I knew she still held her grievance, whatever it was, from the night she left me on the beach. So I picked it up where we'd left off. I closed the door, then marched over in front of her in the rough shoes, flannel pants, and sweat shirt I wore when I was working. I said: "I asked you if you didn't think we should tell names. I thought that was a good idea then and I think it's a good idea now. My name is Jack Dillon. Who the hell are you?"

"You don't know?"

"No, but I'd like to."

"Then I was just a girl you picked up?"

"I didn't pick you up. You came to my table and asked if we shouldn't speak, and as I'd been peeping at you a half hour I said yes, and asked you to sit down, and you did. Then we went driving, and I don't know what you did, but I fell in love."

"I was already in love."

"So was I."

She burst out crying and I pitched a handkerchief at her. She pressed it to her eyes. "Jack, I'm Helen Legg."

I had to sit down quick, and did, and stared at her. Of the girl I had known before, when she was twelve and I was twenty-two, I couldn't see a trace. But then I remembered the graceful walk, in Savannah, that had caught my eye first, and what my father had told me. After a long time I said: "Then if I was already in love with you, and fell in love all over again, all I can say is, it seems like something pretty terrific, that had to take over, no matter where we found it."

"I don't. It makes me just sick. I could hardly breathe, when I saw you there in Savannah, and supposed you didn't quite know what to expect, so sent Drusilla on her way and came on over. I thought it was amusing to call you Major, and laughed when you called me Lieutenant. I didn't talk about what had happened—it seemed better to make a fresh start, somehow. And then, when I found out you didn't know me, that to you I was just a pick-up—"

"How did you find that out?"

"You said—"

"I said let's put it on the line. And now—"

"I'm going home."

"No, you're not."

She had got up, but I blocked the way. "We're not talking about something, we're talking about nothing, and I won't have it. I found you and you're mine. And at last we *both* found out how dumb you are. We—"

That did it, and she was in my arms, laughing, and her tears and mine were getting mixed and at last it was over, my long voyage home.

The Leggs, when I took her back that evening, were pretty meek, and didn't put up much argument about our getting married. We saw each other morning, noon, and night then, while Mrs. Legg began getting ready in a big way, for the wedding, there at their new home, or what to me was their new home, on University Parkway, near Charles. Then Margaret was there, putting the fine touches on, specially the artistic points, like which orchestra. Then one night, in my father's study, I began going over it, and said: "Listen, Helen, why the big show? Can't we just get married?"

"But they want a wedding, like Margaret had, and—"

"Well, who's getting married?"

". . . What's your idea?"

"My idea is, it's one o'clock now, we get in the car, point her south, and head for this job, this pretty big job, I've picked out for myself. That we get married on the way, in whatever place we happen to be in around breakfast time, and—"

"But what about clothes?"

"Stores sell clothes."

"And your father?"

"Will make it, where he's going, without any help from us. And if you ask me, he will like it, when we ring him today —after we've gone and done it, to have that special call, all for himself—better than a super-duper production he won't be able to attend."

"Now that, *that* makes sense."

"At last, I'm glad I thought of something that—"

But she slammed me down on the couch, the way she had when she was little, and began beating me up, and laughing, and at last I saw the little rowdy I had fallen for, when she was a kid, and I was. Then I hollered uncle and we didn't wait, but went outside, without even a toothbrush, and got in my car, and started off on our life.

✳ *ACKNOWLEDGMENTS* ✳

THIS story was some years growing and required help from more people than I can mention here, though I hereby tender them my very best thanks. I should like, however, to express my special debt to these: Frank F. Hill, formerly of the Union Oil Company, who conceived, tried, and developed the cement process for sealing water out of wells, a milestone as important to the oil business as the Whitney gin was to cotton, and who patiently instructed me in matters petrolic, both before and after completion of a script; Louis J. Brunel, of the Bishop company, who made valuable suggestions and opened doors for me that usually stay tightly closed; H. L. Eggleston and Wilton Shellshear, of the former Gilmore company, now part of General Petroleum, for the rationale of petroleum manufacture; Samuel E. Furman, of the Ohio company, who has wrestled out-of-control wells, and gave me the benefit of these grim experiences; David M. Anderson, C. M. Cotton, C. P. Cotton, and J. H. Abramson of the Jergins company, for geological fundamentals; J. C. Chuck, Bert Harrison, and Margery Proctor, of the Jerkins realty organization, for introductions, appointments, and field contacts of great value; A. L. Schmidt, of the Long Beach fire department, for methods of controlling burning wells; scores of superintendents, foremen, drillers, and roughnecks not known

Acknowledgments

to me by name, for elucidation of drilling, cracking, and selling, as well as various shoves and seizures which prevented me, on more than one occasion, from getting killed; William Moran, George Seitz, Ike Person, as well as many boes, known to me only as Joe, Luke, or Don, for initiation, sometimes painful, into the life of jungles, box cars, missions, and flop joints; F. F. Phillips, of the Santa Fe Railroad, and Earle W. Smith, of the California Employment Service, for data on the floating population of the '30s; Ernest Ballard, of St. James's P. E. Church, Los Angeles, for checking musical episodes; John A. Wood, of Honor Brands, for methods of freezing foods; Evaristo Diaz, of the Murphy Friendly Fields, for information about fruit ranches; Maj. Lewis Simons, of The Citadel, for suggestions as to episodes centering in Charleston, S. C.; Helen and Morris Markey, for checking Southern backgrounds; Thelma Jackman, of the Los Angeles Public Library, for her usual invaluable help on research; the late Vincent Lawrence, for story suggestions; my sister, Rosalie McComas, for checking episodes occurring in Maryland; my mother, Rose Mallahan Cain, for the musical background, acquired in childhood, that underlies a large part of the story.

J. M. C.

A NOTE ON THE TYPE
IN WHICH THIS BOOK IS SET

This book is set on the Linotype in Granjon, a type named in compliment to Robert Granjon, but neither a copy of a classic face nor an entirely original creation. George W. Jones based his designs upon the type used by Claude Garamond (1510–61) in his beautiful French books. Granjon more closely resembles Garamond's own type than do any of the various modern types that bear his name.

Robert Granjon began his career as type-cutter in 1523. The boldest and most original designer of his time, he was one of the first to practice the trade of type-founder apart from that of printer. Between 1557 and 1562 Granjon printed about twenty books in types designed by himself, following, after the fashion of the day, the cursive handwriting of the time. These types, usually known as "caractères de civilité," he himself called "lettres françaises," as especially appropriate to his own country.

This book was composed, printed, and bound by Kingsport Press, Inc., Kingsport, Tenn.